PRAISE FOR HAN SONG

"A work of unbelievable creativity and imagination. Han Song has taken Kafka's institutionalized horror and endlessly reproduced it with trillions of 3D printers, enough to fill the entire universe. Taking the image of an AI machine gone haywire or a cancerous growth spreading out of control; expansive yet utterly devoid of hope, it 'clogs every possible escape portal and blocks any possibility of running away, leaving behind nothing but a devastating and overpowering feeling of grief."

—Lo Yi-Chin, author of *Faraway*

"Han Song stands out among Chinese science fiction writers. His exuberant imagination engages history in total earnest, speaking to the darkness and perversity of the human condition. *Hospital* is his masterpiece and should be a landmark in the terrain of contemporary science fiction."

—Ha Jin, author of *Waiting, A Song Everlasting,* and *A Free Life*

"China's premier science fiction writer."

—*Los Angeles Times*

"The kind of science fiction I write is two dimensional; but Han Song writes three-dimensional science fiction. If we look at Chinese science fiction as a pyramid, two-dimensional science fiction would be the foundation, but the kind of three-dimensional science fiction that Han Song writes would be the pinnacle."

—Liu Cixin, author of *The Three Body Problem*

"Han Song's fiction has a uniquely 'dark consciousness' that offers deep reflections about history and keen observations about our contemporary world, all of which comes from an otherworldly perspective. *Hospital* is part of a stupendous trilogy, which is filled with a seemingly inexhaustible series of ghoulish episodes, grotesque figures, and sublime scenes of the wildest kind."

—David Der-wei Wang, professor (Harvard University) and author of *Why Fiction Matters in Contemporary China*

"Han Song's Hospital Trilogy is the second most important Chinese science fiction trilogy after Liu Cixin's *Three Body Problem*. Han Song is the Philip K. Dick of China. *Hospital* reveals strange visions from a fantastical universe, yet the true secret remains hidden under the skin of contemporary China. His twisted surreal vision seems removed from the everyday world of reason, and yet it is able to reveal a truth impervious to traditional realist narratives."

—Mingwei Song, professor (Wellesley College) and coeditor of *The Reincarnated Giant*

"Han Song is an important part of the legacy of critical humanism, from Lu Xun to the Chinese avant-garde writers of the 1980s."

—Yan Feng, literary critic

"The darkness contained within *Hospital* expresses the author's desperation with mankind's attempts at self-treatment and salvation. The novel's completely unbridled narrative path sets out in the direction of science fiction but ultimately arrives at the spiritual abyss lurking in the reality of today's China . . . and the rest of the world."

—Yan Lianke, author of *The Day the Sun Died* and *Hard Like Water*

"Demented, delirious, and one of a kind . . . *Kafkaesque* doesn't begin to describe this cunning labyrinth of a novel. Nothing I have read has captured so incisively (and searingly) the unrelenting institutional brutality of our contemporary world."

—Junot Díaz, author of *The Brief Wondrous Life of Oscar Wao*

HOSPITAL

HOSPITAL

HAN SONG

TRANSLATED BY MICHAEL BERRY

AMAZON **CROSSING**

Text copyright © 2016, 2023 by Han Song
Translation copyright © 2023 by Michael Berry
All rights reserved.

Previously published as Yiyuan (医院) by Shanghai wenyi chubanshe in China in 2016. Translated from Chinese by Michael Berry. First published in English by Amazon Crossing in 2023.

Published by Amazon Crossing, Seattle
www.apub.com

Amazon, the Amazon logo, and Amazon Crossing are trademarks of Amazon.com, Inc., or its affiliates.

ISBN-13: 9781542039475 (hardcover)
ISBN-13: 9781542039468 (paperback)
ISBN-13: 9781542039482 (digital)

Cover design by Will Staehle
Cover image: ©Smit / Shutterstock;
©EMILY19 / Shutterstock; ©BBBever / Shutterstock

Printed in the United States of America
First edition

Table of Contents

Prologue

RED CROSS ON MARS

The meaning of travel lies not in the journey but in the destination.

The destination of the SS *Mahamayuri* was Mars.

Leaving from Earth and traveling for 324 days, the SS *Mahamayuri* traversed 225 million kilometers before reaching the orbit of Mars. As its dual-mode nuclear fission engine decelerated, the planet's gravitational field captured the spacecraft.

Commander Lonewalker was checking the rodent-like humanoid cyborgs floating in the cabin. They had long necks and short-horned heads, and they looked like a cross between humans and monkeys, but the overall appearance was closer to that of a rodent. They were cyborg organisms with bacterial brains, special genetically modified flora having been implanted into their alloy skulls, working in concert with electronic nerves that not only determined the speed and direction of these rat-man cyborgs but also allowed them to enter into a perfect imitative trance through biochemical programming. The host could thus achieve a quantum state of transcendental meditation during flight, generating a consciousness able to connect with "the other world."

Although these rat-man cyborgs were referred to as humanoid systems (some people actually believed them to be the future of humanity), they also served as advanced probes, tasked with the mission of searching for the Buddha on Mars.

At fifty years old, Commander Lonewalker was a long-practicing monk. He was also an organic human.

With daily advances in science, a series of miraculous new discoveries had been made, chief among them the revelation that there are Buddhas all over the universe.

Only after the end of the world war had the SS *Mahamayuri* finally been dispatched into space. It was one of the first spacecraft to venture out once space exploration resumed after the war. All the empires of the old world order collapsed, while nations like India and Nepal rose up like a newly formed mountain range and exercised control over the world. Buddhism saw a global revival that originated in the Himalayas and went on to become the dominating belief system for a new era of humankind. With this change had come a reshuffling of people's belief systems and their relationship with materialism.

In addition to Commander Lonewalker, two younger pilots were aboard the ship: twenty-two-year-old Zhifan and twenty-eight-year-old Runian, both disciples of Commander Lonewalker.

Commander Lonewalker was able to reach a deep meditative state without the help of any auxiliary devices, but Zhifan and Runian still needed external help. Over the course of the past year, their brains and bodies had frequently required that they be hooked up to various machines in order to experience the unique sensation brought about by transcendental meditation, paving the way for their eventual communion with the Buddha.

Ever since the time of the Apollo landing in the year 2513 of the Buddhist calendar, no Buddhas had been discovered during any of humankind's space expeditions. That's because none of those missions had been specifically aimed at finding the enlightened one.

Mars, the planet bearing the most similarities with Earth, had languished in silence for billions of years.

The Buddha had appeared only once on Earth, 2,500 years before, and he had not appeared since. After the living hell of the most recent world war, all of humanity had been longing for the Buddha's return, but it seemed unlikely that he would appear again on Earth.

The deep space quantum entanglement detector, jointly developed by the Indian Space Research Organisation and the Indian Institute of Technology Kanpur, had discovered "species suspected of having god-like qualities actively spreading an information flow consistent with an advanced living being" in the high-dimensional space beyond Earth. This may have provided a hint at the Buddha's existence.

As a terrestrial planet that had given birth to life, Mars had been identified as one of the most promising targets for exploration.

In addition to Mars, manned spacecraft and unmanned probes had also been dispatched to other planets, into the asteroid belt, and even to the edge of the solar system. This wave of great exploration had become the theme of countless songs by religious artists all over the world.

On board the ship, the young astronauts were especially excited. Filled with curiosity, Zhifan asked, "Why did the Buddha first decide to take the vows of a monk?"

Although this was a question that he had answered countless times before, Commander Lonewalker was all too happy to respond patiently to his disciple's inquiry, a convenient way to lead his disciples to the gates of enlightenment.

"When Prince Siddhartha Gautama was seventeen years old," Commander Lonewalker explained, "Śuddhodana Gautama chose for him a young woman who was both physically stunning and of high moral character. Her name was Yasodharā, and they were to be married. However, the prince had long been practicing the 'threefold training' of triśikṣā in order to purge himself of the three poisons of greed, anger, and ignorance. This meant that while he toiled amid the dust and dirt, his heart remained pure, like the lotus that is born of mud yet remains unsullied. At the age of nineteen, after having lived deep in the palace for so long, Prince Siddhartha longed to taste the joys of the outside world. He asked King Śuddhodana Gautama for permission to venture out. His father, the king, sent many ministers and palace women to take him around the palace garden. The king also ordered one of his wisest ministers to personally tend to the prince's needs and answer any questions he might have.

"The prince first went to the garden near the eastern gate, where he happened upon a skinny, hunchbacked old man with pale skin, wrinkles, and a cane, whose every step was slow and painful. It was a difficult sight for the prince to see.

"The prince asked, 'Who is this man?'

"The minister replied, 'My prince, this is an old man.'

"The prince's heart grew heavy, and he became very emotional. *Everyone in the world faces the despair of aging. How can we be relieved of this?* After pondering this problem, the prince could not come up with an answer. He lost interest in the garden and returned to the palace.

"A few days later, the prince asked if he could go out again. This time he went to the southern gate, where he encountered a sick man lying on the ground beside the street. The man moaned incessantly, as if suffering from some terrible pain. It was a pitiful sight.

"Again, the prince asked, 'Who is this man?'

"The minister replied, 'He is a sick man.'

"The prince was deeply disturbed by the suffering he saw. The body is composed of the four elements—earth, water, fire, and wind. If they are not properly balanced, a myriad of illnesses springs forth. Besides the pain of major illness and disease, even small ailments like headaches and toothaches can lead to terrible suffering. Who in this world can escape from the curse of disease? The prince pondered this dilemma but was unable to come up with a means to relieve this type of physical suffering. In his frustration, he again lost interest in leisure and returned to the palace. The ancients had a saying: *It is only with the onset of illness that one becomes aware of the body's suffering. In times of health one is blinded by the joys of the five desires.* Those words contain much wisdom.

"The third time the prince asked his father if he could go out, the ministers and palace women accompanied him to the western gate, where they saw a group of people carrying a dead body. The corpse was oozing a bloody pus and emitted an atrocious stench. The family members of the deceased who accompanied the procession were wailing through tears. It was indeed a difficult sight to bear. Upon death, the four elements that compose the body disperse, and one part simmers in the hundred sufferings while what is left crosses from life to the other side, but such scenes of pain and suffering are not unique to the human world. Even an ox being skinned alive or a turtle being pried from its shell experiences similar suffering.

"The prince asked, 'Who is this person?'

"The minister responded, 'This is a dead person.'

"The prince realized that as long as humans live in this world, with birth must come death. *In the end, no matter who you may be, no one shall be spared the fate of death.*

"On the fourth occasion, the prince went out through the northern gate, where he suddenly came upon a dignified shaman. The robed shaman carried a walking stick in one hand and an alms bowl in the other, and he approached peacefully. Prince Siddhartha was immediately drawn to him and felt a great happiness in his presence.

"The prince greeted the shaman with a gesture of respect and asked him, 'Who are you?'

"The shaman answered, 'I am Bhiksu.'

"The prince then asked, 'And what does Bhiksu do?'

"The shaman responded, 'Bhiksu has taken vows to practice self-cultivation and pursue the path of the monk. Those who have taken the vows devote themselves to self-cultivation in order to free themselves and all other living beings of the four forms of suffering: birth, aging, sickness, and death.'

"Upon hearing that, the prince decided that he, too, wanted to free all living beings of the root causes of suffering. But just as the prince was about to ask for more detailed instructions on how to pursue this path, the shaman suddenly disappeared. The prince was left with a mix of happiness and sadness: sadness because he still had more questions to ask the shaman but did not know where to find Bhiksu, and happiness because he now had a model to follow in alleviating the four forms of suffering. The prince happily returned to the palace.

"According to the scriptures, during his trips through the four gates, the prince witnessed aging, sickness, death, and suffering. He also saw the model of self-cultivation practiced by Bhiksu, who was actually a manifestation of the Śuddhāvāsa, or the 'pure abodes,' who had appeared to help Siddhartha find his path."

Commander Lonewalker finished retelling this old story, which he knew like the back of his hand, and he flashed Zhifan and Runian a mysterious smile.

"So he finally left home," Runian said, "and began his journey of self-cultivation in order to solve the problem of aging, sickness, death, and suffering?" Runian often exaggerated her responses to rather routine things.

"How many times have you told that story already?" groaned Zhifan.

"But today we have already employed advanced medical methods to alleviate aging, sickness, death, and suffering," Runian said, visibly perturbed. "So why do we still need to find the Buddha?"

"Hey, Runian's got a point!" said Zhifan. "All of those sick people the Buddha encountered on his journey would be easily cured today! Modern hospitals are supplied with the most sophisticated medical equipment to treat ailments. The elderly can enjoy prolonged lives. And don't we now have advanced techniques that can resurrect the dead?"

That was indeed the case. The application of genome research had allowed the vast majority of diseases to be controlled. Through organ repair and replacement, the goal of longevity for all had been more or less achieved. The next step was to integrate artificial intelligence into the fold and move toward immortality. Scanning the consciousness of the deceased into a computer and uploading it into a robotic body would effectively resolve life and death and free all living beings from the cycle of infinite reincarnation.

Commander Lonewalker did not respond. He instead gazed out the porthole toward Mars, which looked like a red lotus blooming in a void of emptiness.

Humans' perspective on the planet had developed. Early on, they had paid attention only to whether there was a man-made "canal," but later they investigated more scientifically and explored its potential as a possible space colony. And then Mars had become one of the primary sites in the extraterrestrial search for the Buddha.

But something still bothered Runian. As long as one maintained a regiment of self-cultivation and lived long enough, one would eventually be able to see the Revered Buddha at any time or any place, because truth exists in all of our hearts. All living beings are Buddhas that have simply not yet been awakened, temporarily lost amid a cloud of deception. *So why*, Runian wondered, *do we need to travel to outer space to find something already inside us?*

As far as she was concerned, this trip was like a work of performance art. Naturally, religion and art are inextricably intertwined, but she sensed something strange and unsettling about the whole enterprise.

Showing very little tact, Zhifan jumped in with a rhetorical question: Why didn't Prince Siddhartha just stay inside his palace and practice self-cultivation there? Why did the Tang dynasty monk Xuanzang risk death to travel all the way to India to retrieve the Buddhist scriptures?

Runian's eyes filled with tears.

That was when the humanoid systems awoke, their bacterial brains interconnected through supersensation. They immediately began to exchange enthusiastic insights from their meditative slumber. Various disputes broke out between them, and the spaceship, which had been a place of dead quiet, erupted with chatter as if someone had lit a keg of gunpowder.

Runian wondered whether artificial life could achieve Buddhahood. Meanwhile, the portrait of the female Peacock Wisdom King Mahamayuri hung silently in the cabin, watching over everything.

Mahamayuri had four arms and rode a golden peacock. Her hands held one item each: a lotus flower, an expression of respect and love; a citron, expressing moderation; a bael, an expression of prosperity; and the peacock's tail feather, which symbolized an end to all disasters.

Mahamayuri is an incarnation of the Vairocana Buddha, also referred to as Shakubuku, who represents the two virtues of assimilation and subjugation. Owing to these two virtues, the Vairocana Buddha has two kinds of throne. The white lotus throne is an expression that one has assimilated the fundamental vow to show mercy to all beings, and the green lotus throne is a sign of Shakubuku.

Runian wondered if Mahamayuri might be the true commander of their ship.

After fifteen orbits of Mars, Zhifan maneuvered the spacecraft to a point 450 kilometers from their landing site and began to descend into the planet's thin atmosphere.

They had selected a landing site on the Tharsis plateau, near the equator in Mars's western hemisphere. Zhifan stopped the humanoid systems' bickering and released them into the atmosphere. The semi-mechanical life-forms immediately got to work: some surveyed the air, others landed and began searching the surface—all were programmed to look for any sign of the Buddha.

The being known as Shakyamuni could be inside any martian rock.

Neither the naked human eye nor any machine could "see" signs of the Buddha, which could only be detected by the artificial "alaya consciousness" formed by the union of these humanoid devices and bacterial brains.

The barren and solitary scene unfolding before them was like a vision of the other shore: crimson sand covered with rocks and gravel, volcanoes and craters scarred by signs of past devastation, the pink sky overhead like a massive umbrella. Many years had passed since the first group of human probes arrived on Mars, though it remained as it had always been . . . but not entirely.

Standing on a bed of stationary rocks of different sizes, Commander Lonewalker smelled something . . . it seemed to him the breath of the Buddha. He thought about a Chinese monk named Daosheng from the Eastern Jin dynasty. After he'd practiced self-cultivation for many years, Daosheng's understanding of Buddhist principles had reached a profound level. Based on the principle that "all living beings can attain Buddhahood," he proposed that with "one lecture to a prisoner, he can attain Buddhahood." That was unheard of at the time, and those who adhered to more traditional and conservative beliefs accused Daosheng of heresy and deceiving the public, casting him out from the order of the monks. But Daosheng stood firm by his beliefs. With no students to preach to, he erected a field of stones and preached to the stones. When he got to the part of his lecture when he claimed that "even the deluded one has Buddha nature within," he asked his stones, "Are my words not one with the Buddha's mind?" The stones nodded in affirmation, hence the famous saying, *As Master Daosheng preaches the scriptures, even the stones nod their approval.* Later, when the Nirvana Sutra spread to the south, the section about how "even the deluded ones have Buddha nature within" allowed Daosheng to win over all the monks with his profound vision.

The stones on Mars appeared as if they, too, had listened intently to the teachings of the Buddha.

A group of humanoid systems arrived at a gully-like geological structure that was thought to be a dried-up riverbed. The surface of Mars had once seen running rivers and suffered from massive floods. There are patches of frozen soil beneath the river sediment, and in certain locations, water still flows. Another set of probes headed for the snow-capped mountains and craters. That life once existed on Mars is an indisputable fact. Living bacteria may still be found beneath the rocks and snow.

In contemporary Buddhism, it is believed that the Buddha evolved from a very ordinary life-form. In the beginning, there were only chemical, inorganic, autotrophic microorganisms with primitive cells living in the ocean. But over the slow, unending course of hundreds of millions of reincarnations, they gradually ascended in their evolutionary journey. When the time was finally ripe, they surpassed their own limitations, and like actors onstage who suddenly change their appearance, they magically evolved into enlightened beings.

This process of transformation is the most magnificent spectacle in the universe.

When they realized that all life-forms, regardless of how lowly or lofty they may be, and irrespective of their beauty or ugliness, will all one day evolve into Buddhas, Zhifan and Runian each felt like someone had pricked them in the heart with a needle.

Yet according to credible sources, in all of human history, only a single enlightened one had appeared. That's a pretty low percentage.

According to the theory of causation in religious evolution, the birth of the Buddha conforms to the laws of natural selection and survival of the fittest, so even after thousands of years of assiduous self-cultivation, if the proper conditions are not met, that potential Buddha will be eliminated.

The difficulties of life are the same difficulties faced when trying to attain Buddhahood. If there were any traces of life on Mars, they were surely scarce and hard to identify. Could such minuscule traces of life be enough to give birth to the Buddha?

The Earth is very different, brimming with complex life-forms. There are 330,000 species of beetles alone, many of which depend on the consumption of flowering plants, which in turn places a lot of pressure on plant life, forcing the evolution of even more species. This dynamic has created a diversity of strange species, but in the end, only one has successfully evolved into what we consider humankind. And among the billions of humans that have existed over time, only a single Buddha had appeared.

During the recent world war, the very souls of all the living creatures on Earth came just a hair's breadth away from self-annihilation, brushing shoulders with the end of the world.

One might say that it was precisely owing to the scarcity of life, especially those precious intelligent life-forms, that we have the saying *Difficult to attain a human body, but now I have one. Difficult to hear the Buddha's dharma, but now it is clear. If I do not free my body in this lifetime, in which lifetime will I do so?*

Although it is extremely difficult, if people are able to pull their perspective back from the Earth to observe the full continuum of time and space, they will see things in a new light. The grand cosmos can accommodate all of the Buddhas, bodhisattvas, and sentient beings from the six realms. In theory, other spaces exist beyond the four-dimensional world that humans inhabit, higher-dimensional worlds. With the existence of parallel universes, the scope grows even broader, each world full of danger but also rich and colorful, a massive number of universes containing myriad possibilities for Buddhahood to arise.

This is also consistent with Buddhist law, which states, "When Buddha gazes into a pot of water, he sees forty-eight thousand insects."

If only one enlightened being appears on each planet with life-forms, an infinite number of Buddhas will inhabit the universe.

Humankind's definitions of conceptual ideas like life and wisdom were still quite narrow, but the breadth of the Buddha's existence in a realm of infinite time and space goes further than anyone could ever have imagined.

Back before the war, scientists had simulated the evolutionary process using oil droplets in a laboratory, demonstrating that even nonliving systems could evolve, a breakthrough challenge to the idea that only biological organisms could evolve. It can then be inferred that certain energy flows in the universe are also capable of producing consciousness. In fact, some stars are actually unique living beings. Galaxies themselves are organized in a manner similar to neural networks. Isn't it possible that such autonomous things also evolve to a state in which they reach Buddhahood? Therefore space exploration is not limited to planets where there is a possibility of life, such as Mars. The concept of the Buddha pervades everything.

The enlightened ones indeed exist, sometimes referred to as "the miraculous existence." Once they attain Buddhahood, they transcend all tangible, living phenomena, even the very state of material form. The nature of Buddhahood is "emptiness" and "nothingness."

However, as far as ordinary practitioners are concerned, life is essential. Take, for example, the flesh and blood bodily forms of human beings. No matter how short their existence, they still try to live to the fullest. This is what is meant by two sayings: *The human body is precious as a night-blooming cereus flower* and *Once you lose your body, you shall never escape from the cycle of eternal damnation*. And this is precisely why humans welcomed the Age of Longevity, the importance of which should never be overlooked and which gave new meaning to the value of medicine.

Commander Lonewalker felt extremely thankful that he'd had the good fortune to be born human. He also held modern medical science in very high regard. He had still been a young man when the great world war first broke out. He had lost both his parents during the germ warfare that ensued, though he himself was saved in the nick of time by a medical team. He was lucky to have survived. Had he died, he might have been sent to the realm of hungry ghosts, or perhaps reborn as an animal, and since his parents' deaths, he had come to embrace the religious life.

In contemporary Buddhist discourse, a special theory details how "the art of medicine is also the art of benevolence." According to Commander Lonewalker, medicine had led to the eradication of disease and helped humans to live longer lives, which were very different outcomes than the attainment of Buddhahood. However, to attain Buddhahood, maintaining one's health is an essential foundation. It has been said that in the past, practitioners entered a cave in the Himalayas on their holy path, but after several months they not only failed to attain enlightenment but caught colds due to the inclement weather and, tragically, died.

But isn't the practice of medicine imbued with boundless compassion and thus completely aligned with the spirit and precepts of Buddhism?

Humankind had continually searched for signs of alien life, Commander Lonewalker was thinking, despite realizing just how difficult it was for life to arise and survive. Could more innovative medical practices employed by advanced extraterrestrial civilizations have led to more enlightened individuals?

That was when the piercing shriek of the ship's alarm sounded throughout the cabin.

Images transmitted by the humanoid drones appeared in the microchip-controlled visual cortex area. The cyborgs had converged near Pavonis Mons, the large shield volcano in the Tharsis region, and begun to ascend the mountain. The peak was enshrouded in a thick cloud of red mist, allowing zero visibility.

"Have you found the Buddha?" Zhifan shouted excitedly.

But all they heard back was a set of terrified screams, and then all communication was lost.

"Did something go wrong?" Runian asked worriedly.

Commander Lonewalker understood that even if the Buddha were to be nestled somewhere on this planet, outer space still remained extremely dangerous. It had been a very long time since any humans had ventured here.

When it all comes down to it, the universe's many permutations are nothing more than reflections of the habits and frustrations that haunt the human heart.

A massive floating shadow appeared in the crew's visual feed, flying through the mist before rapidly disappearing. Advanced visual processing clarified the image, and they realized that what they had seen had resembled a bird, more precisely a flying creature that bore an uncanny resemblance to a peacock.

Runian's face looked like a piece of tinfoil under a shadowless lamp. "It is impossible for such a thing to exist on Mars." She had initially harbored reservations about visiting a planet so similar to Earth and thought it would have been better to visit Neptune.

"This must be the Buddha?" Zhifan's face reflected his excitement. "I never thought we would run into him so quickly!"

The portrait of Mahamayuri hung silently, watching over them.

Commander Lonewalker was struck with a deep feeling of grief. The most important reason to find the Buddha was to purge the desire to find the Buddha from their hearts. The humanoid devices with the bacterial brains were designed precisely *not* to have the human ego, but this was a paradox because, from the very beginning, the SS *Mahamayuri*'s mission had been driven by an excessively powerful directive.

When a journey fails, it is always due to the destination. A journey guided by a sense of direction and a detailed itinerary is inherently absurd. The moment that attaining Buddhahood becomes a goal, the goal has already failed.

As commander of the ship, Lonewalker knew that there was nothing he could do, and yet he was unable to explain this to his disciples. He ordered Zhifan and Runian to engage the engines and head toward where the humanoid devices had disappeared.

The ship arrived fourteen thousand meters above Pavonis Mons. As it passed through the thick mist, the crew caught sight of a large architectural structure built into the side of one of the volcano's cliffs. It was actually a series of massive, ashen, castle-like structures, with walls like ancient ruins, sharp and broken like the jagged teeth of an animal. Zhifan wondered if this was the ruins of a defensive martian city, and had they also established a Buddhist meditation garden like Jetavana?

Something unusual had been erected on the top of one of the buildings, a platform that resembled a fire-beacon tower, with a massive red cross on a metal frame. The cross jarringly pierced the crimson martian sky, like a simplified version of the Buddhist swastika—卍—with its four heads removed.

There was not a trace of anyone anywhere near the ruins.

Runian frowned. "It's a hospital . . ." Her voice trembled quietly. "These are the ruins of a hospital." The image of the six realms of reincarnation left her mind like the sun setting over the horizon.

"Wow," Zhifan uttered. "The distinguishing characteristics of a hospital are all there. It's not a temple for self-cultivation or a special holy site for propagating the Buddhist teachings. It's a hospital, exactly like the ones on Earth."

The spacecraft hovered closer to the site, its cameras zooming in on the debris spread among the rubble. The crew could see a bell jar containing something that looked like a peacock embryo. The embryo had clearly been dead a long time, and its internal organs oozed out in a disgusting thick black paste.

Commander Lonewalker put his hands together and offered a Buddhist prayer: "Amitabha."

At the foot of the cliff were the destroyed remnants of the humanoid devices, their artificial organs torn apart and strewn over the ground, reminding Commander Lonewalker of a gruesome battle.

Runian imagined the scene of carnage as a bloody operating room, as if an invisible knife had reached out from the void and performed surgery on the drones.

"Would the Buddha ever do something like this?" Zhifan muttered in shock. He started to vomit uncontrollably.

Runian gazed out to the red horizon with a look of sorrow. A dust storm was coming.

As they passed over the peak of the volcano, a flock of birdlike figures flew past, blocking out the sun. They descended toward the ship and, one after another, began attacking it, as if they wanted to knock the crew's own hearts and organs right out of their bodies. The cabin shook violently.

All of the birdlike creatures bore the mark of the red cross on their bodies.

Before and after this incident, spacecraft traveling the solar system discovered the ruins of similar hospital-like structures, including red crosses, on Mercury, Venus, Jupiter, Saturn, Uranus, Neptune, all of the planets' moons, and even some asteroids.

Someone or something had traveled to these worlds and built hospitals. But when? And why?

Commander Lonewalker speculated that the hospitals must have been part of an effort to save many lives, surely a holy mission.

Could a Buddha have appeared among the patients these hospitals cured?

Or were the hospitals built by intelligent life-forms from another galaxy? Could humankind have descended from these aliens, the result of their effort to create new Buddhas? Could aliens have secretly stepped in to stop this most recent world war, to prevent the great extinction we were heading for?

Were they sent by the Buddha to protect us? Or perhaps they themselves were Buddhas?

Beyond the solar system, in the Milky Way and other galaxies, were there hospital ruins like the ones on Mars?

Or had the Buddha returned to the material world, incarnate in the form of the hospital? Could the hospital represent the new gateway to dharma?

Or was this all merely an illusion triggered by space travel?

As space probes piloted by AI beings prepared to exit the solar system and undertake long voyages, venturing into new vistas of outer space, could these robotic astronauts, less susceptible to illness and disease than humans, have evolved into Buddhas themselves?

Trying to answer these questions would be more time consuming than searching for the Buddha himself. But then again, perhaps all would be revealed in a single instant of illumination.

In this world, when it all comes down to it, there are no questions, and there are no answers.

As the SS *Mahamayuri* began to break apart and collapse, Commander Lonewalker calmly sat in the lotus position and entered a state of deep meditation. The image of the red cross burned through Zhifan's and Runian's hearts, searing them from the inside out, transforming them into nothingness.

ILLNESS

1

NO MATTER WHAT YOU DO,
DON'T GET SICK

Whenever I went on business trips, I always tried to stay in the nicest hotels that my per diem allowed. I did it for comfort, to save face, and for all the bells and whistles those high-class hotels have to offer.

The hotel I booked in C City was part of an international chain. Inside, everything was bright and clean, with a postmodern style that appeared to be well up to standards.

After I checked in and went up to my room, I started to feel a bit thirsty, so I drank a bottle of the complimentary mineral water that was provided in the room.

Shortly after that I began to experience a terrible stomach pain. I didn't know what was causing it. Later the pain got even worse, and I collapsed on the bed and passed out. Who could have imagined that I would be out for three days and nights?

I awoke to discover two female hotel workers in gray suits standing beside my bed. I had no idea when they had arrived or how they had gotten into the room. Both women were around thirty-five years old; one had sharp features and a perm, the other had a round face and wore her hair in a ponytail.

When they noticed me waking, they explained, one word at a time, that they had received instructions from the manager at the reception desk to take me to the hospital. That sounded strange; how had they known that I was experiencing stomach pain? Remembering that I was here on business and still had official duties to take care of, I told them I didn't want to go.

"That's not an option," the women responded in unison. "You are sick."

As they reached to pull me out of bed, I explained, "I'm not sick. I just have a little stomachache. It's nothing, really."

They did not relent. "You are sick. You've been out for three full days."

"How could you know that?"

"We work for the hotel. How could we *not* know that?"

"Is it really that serious?"

"It is a matter of grave consequence. No matter what, you must never get sick."

Then I realized that something was really wrong. I might indeed be sick after all. "Okay, if I must go to the hospital, let's go to one that will accept my insurance," I suggested. "Otherwise I won't be able to get reimbursed for my medical expenses!"

"Oh, come on, don't worry about that!" the women responded. "We've already taken all of those details into consideration! It is our job to make sure that our customers are perfectly satisfied!"

They jumped into action and pulled me off the bed, then quickly dressed me and put on my shoes, their nimble hands suggesting that they had provided this type of service for hotel guests many times before. I felt like I had no choice but to follow their instructions. My main concern was making sure that I went to a hospital that would take my insurance. As long as I could get my hospital bill reimbursed, I was okay with the rest.

The hotel had already called an ambulance. Speeding through C City with its lights blazing and sirens screaming, the ambulance took the three of us to the hospital.

2

A PERSONAL SIDE GIG BECAME AN OFFICIAL BUSINESS TRIP

The mountain city was surrounded by rivers, a business hub with a robust population that supported a bustling tourist industry. The city was filled with tall ginkgo trees, and the architecture jutted out at steep angles, soaring into the sky like crescent blades defying gravity. And yet the city was always enveloped in a thick cloud of haze and smog, always cold and overcast, with a never-ending rain that left the air forever feeling sticky and humid.

I was in so much pain that I wasn't in the mood to admire the scenery. I had come to C City on business, and all of my expenses were covered by Corporation B, which had hired me to compose a corporate theme song for them.

My day job was to serve as a government functionary in the capital, where I spent my days writing up reports and preparing speeches for my superiors. It was a good thing that I had a side job as a songwriter, a hobby that helped keep me distracted from my tedious nine-to-five job. My songwriting had earned me a bit of a name for myself. Occasionally I was invited to write songs for various companies, allowing me to earn some extra money and improve my living situation. That is why Corporation B had hired me.

My supervisors at my day job had a habit of monitoring my communications, so they had confiscated the letter that Corporation B sent me. After reviewing its contents, they decided to send me on a business trip to the same city on behalf of our department. Suddenly, what would have been a personal side gig became an official business trip. This wasn't exactly a welcome change, but who cares? This kind of thing had been going on for so many years that I'd long grown accustomed to it. I just never imagined that as soon as I arrived in C City, I would fall ill.

Since we are on the subject of hospitals, I should mention that I was actually quite familiar with them. Just like the government agency that employed me, hospitals, too, are massive organizations. Moreover, they control the most fundamental facets of our lives: illness, aging, birth, and death. Here in my country, knowing your way around the hospital is the most fundamental quality for all citizens.

Stuck with a weak constitution and multiple ailments, I usually went to the hospital once every few days to pick up medicine. Ever since I was young, I had suffered from chronic insomnia, frequent headaches, endocrine imbalance, strange allergies, and constant exhaustion, and for some reason, I develop fevers and colds all the time. Like most everyone else, I hated going to the hospital, and yet I found myself strangely attracted to them. They pulled me in like a magnet. I couldn't stop myself. However, this was the first time I'd had the pleasure of paying a visit to a hospital in C City. I figured that might not be bad. At least I would have the opportunity to familiarize myself with the place. I would be doing some songwriting here in C, so it would be a huge complication if any of my old ailments flared up while I was in town. So not a bad idea to acclimate myself to the hospital here. I'm certainly not the kind of person that likes to stir up unnecessary trouble.

The ambulance went up and down the hilly terrain, winding back and forth through the city. I couldn't tell how long it finally took before we arrived at our destination. The hospital was built into the foot of a mountain overlooking the river, and like the rest of the city, it was a monumental site, a series of linked towers and pavilions and winding corridors with elaborate ornamental tiles projecting from the rooftops.

Parts of the hospital, dark and imposing, seemed to curl up amid the rain and fog like a wild supernatural monster.

As if they were finally relieving themselves of a heavy burden, the women from the hotel who had accompanied me in the ambulance finally announced, "This is our city's Central Hospital. If you are going to go to the hospital, you may as well go to the best! After all, Little Yang, you are one of our most esteemed guests!"

The women walked briskly, leading me straight to the emergency room entrance.

3

HOW CAN PEOPLE GO ON LIVING IF THEY CAN'T PROVE THAT THEY ARE SICK

Based on my previous experience at various hospitals, it took only one look to realize that this hospital's construction was really first rate. The main area for outpatient services featured high ceilings and a broad open-air hall, adorned with carved balustrades and marble tiles, like a universe unto itself with the overall layout mirroring the yin-yang meridian points. Hanging in the center of the hall was a horizontal sign, and in red characters against a green background, it read, **Good Service, High Quality, and Top Medical Ethics Make the Masses Happy.** The other side of the sign read, **Life Is Interdependent, We Entrust Others with Our Life, Together We Conquer Disease and Serve the People.**

Then, from out of nowhere, a massive wave of metallic white light shone into the room, reflecting in all directions and raining down on several dozen lines of people that seemed to have no beginning and no end. When I realized that these must be the registration lines, I couldn't help but express my admiration for how well organized they were.

The air inside the hall was thick and turbid. Almost immediately I began to get a prickly feeling in my throat. The faces of those lined-up patients looked blurry as they gradually moved like the flow of a great dark river. Some of them dragged suitcases; others carried small stools with them. Other groups of patients and family members continually linked up and merged with the primary stream of people, which occasionally led to some small disturbances. Meanwhile, every few steps on the shore was a guard post or a sentinel keeping watch. Security guards in raven-black uniforms with crimson armbands stood at attention, gazing at the crowds of people with piercing, fiery gazes, ensuring that a high degree of order and harmony was maintained.

Oh my, this was a scene I was only all too familiar with. When I saw this, my heart was immediately put at ease. It was at that moment that the women took my wallet from my pocket and rushed over to get in the registration line for me. My stomach pain started to worsen, and I curled up on a bench. The bench was littered with a dense mass of patients huddled together like flies, their moans converging into a constant buzz-like drone as if they were all trying to tell me, *Thank goodness you made it here to the hospital in time. You could have died in that hotel, and no one would have ever even known.*

It was only then that I was struck by a belated sense of fear. Our lives are, after all, of the utmost importance, and yet when I had first fallen ill, all I could think about was making sure I would get reimbursed for my hospital bills. But I suppose that is quite normal. Many people die not due to their illnesses but because they don't have money to pay their medical bills.

The patients clustered around like they were late for a train. The reception hall had the appearance of a grand spiritual temple, and upon closer inspection it resembled the waiting room at a train station. The air was humid, fishy, stale with the smell of instant noodles, and the marble floors were littered with layer upon layer of what appeared to be a mixture of mud, rainwater, sweat, piss, phlegm, and vomit. Advertisements displayed taglines like WHY STAND IN LINE? WE'LL TAKE CARE OF REGISTRATION FOR YOU! EXPEDITED HOSPITAL ADMISSION; GET ALL YOUR TESTS EARLY! and REPLACEMENT RECEIPTS: WE TURN YOUR OUT-OF-NETWORK RECEIPTS INTO IN-NETWORK RECEIPTS! The ads seemed at odds with the glorious exterior appearance of the hospital, but these days quite a few hospitals in this country are like this. I tried not to let any of that bother me. The meaning of a hospital does not rest upon those little details—what is important is keeping people alive.

Then, suddenly, a flatbed cart drove into the crowd. Two young men in dirty white jackets who looked like country bumpkins stood on top, waving a blackened soup spoon in the air and beating it on a large iron pot. They announced the sale of hot meals, including steamed stuffed buns, steamed bread, porridge, and pickled vegetables. The patients' eyes lit up, and they immediately descended upon the cart from all directions, so anxious that they beat their chests and howled like a band of wild orangutans. The men selling the food yelled, "What are you screaming about? There's plenty to go around!"

I started to drool and realized that it had been a full three days and nights since I had eaten anything. The fact that I wanted to eat something must have been a sign that I still had a good appetite, no? And didn't having a good appetite prove that I wasn't sick? And if I wasn't sick, then what was I doing in the hospital? But if I hadn't come to the hospital, how could I prove that I was not sick? And how can people go on living if they can't prove that they are sick?

At this point I couldn't help but laugh; humans are indeed greedy animals. But I would rather deal with the pain than deal with not eating. This wasn't a hotel, it was a hospital. Based on my own experience, I knew that besides curing the sick, hospitals are also a place to suppress one's desires.

After I had waited around for about an hour, the two women finally came skipping back to me, triumphantly waving my registration form like a signal flag. By then I didn't even have the strength to get up. All I could do was greet them with a look of surprise.

4

HAND YOUR LIFE OVER TO
THE HOSPITAL

The women pulled me up and helped me over to the triage area. As it was my first time visiting a hospital in C City, I was quite bashful, like someone out on a first date who doesn't know what move to make next. The women reacted with a combination of anger and humor, urging me, "Don't be like that! We've all been patients before!"

I felt embarrassed. "Don't worry, I'll be okay."

They started arguing about which of them would help me fetch my medical records. I hadn't realized it, but they had a full copy of my records in the hospital's underground storage facility. Something didn't feel right about that. I had never been to this city, and this was the first time I had visited this hospital. How could they possibly have a copy of my medical records?

Then again, you can't say that any of this was really out of the ordinary. The nation's development had been moving ahead with startling speed, and things were changing every day. For a moment I thought that maybe every hospital under heaven had been successfully linked online, and they were all part of a massive franchise that would allow patients to use their insurance anywhere. This would have been great news to patients. Modern medicine may have had its origins in the West, but our country had made glorious strides in its development.

The women went off together to get my records, leaving me to settle down and continue observing the situation around me. The main hall in the waiting area was filled with people selling wreaths, fresh flowers,

fruit, sewing supplies, exercise equipment, wheelchairs, cleaning materials, bedpans, bootleg books, clothing originally marked for export but
later approved for domestic sale, expired cosmetics, urns, coffins, wigs,
firecrackers, blankets, binoculars, compasses, flashlights, notebooks,
New Year cards, fruit knives, kitchen knives, Buddhist prayer beads,
statues of the Avalokiteśvara Bodhisattva, nail clippers, used television
sets, used radios . . . everything you could ever possibly need. An assort-
ment of salespeople tried to recruit guests for local motels or tenants
for their rental properties, and there were even fortune-tellers setting
up shop right there in the waiting room. The outpatient area was like a
big open-air market, filled with the rising and falling sounds of people
shouting, haggling over prices, crying, crashing into things, spitting,
coughing, wheezing, dragging their feet, utensils clanging, metal clink-
ing and clattering, clicking, voices babbling.

It was quite a moving scene, all the people waiting to be treated.
The number of elderly patients really grabbed my attention. I supposed the news reports were right: our country had truly become an
aging society. I have no doubt that this stressed the hospital system,
but it had also provided a robust flow of new patients. The look on the
elderly patients' faces told of an abyss of deep loneliness; facing the ear-
shattering noise in the hall, they looked calm and composed, as if they
didn't even hear the chaos around them. Many sat on benches wrapped
in old army coats with their heads erect. Their bodies emitted the smell
of muscle-pain relief gel, kidney stone elixir, and dust, creating an interesting aesthetic contrast with the lively merchants and salespeople in
the hall. Some of these patients already had cobwebs forming in their
underarms and crotches, and yet they still sat there, firm and still like
unmoving mountains, their bloated hands tightly clenching their tattered and rotting medical records.

After observing those elderly patients for a while, I had a much
better idea of what was going on. Reflecting on the fact that this was
my first visit to C City's hospital, I decided I should commemorate the

moment, so I pulled out my cell phone and took a photo, thinking that it might turn out to be a useful source of inspiration for a future songwriting project.

Several security guards immediately rushed over to me. Grabbing my collar, they screamed at me, demanding to know my intention in taking the photo. I'd been in many situations like this, and I tried to explain, but they raised their fists, threatening to hit me, and instead demanded that I delete the photo immediately. I wanted to ask them, *What right do you have to force me to delete it? What law have I broken? Did you post a No Photography Allowed sign somewhere?* But then I realized that since I was here as a patient, I had basically handed my life over to the hospital. I decided it was best not to act rashly, so I deleted the photo like a good boy. It didn't matter much anyway; this is just another thing you get used to when you go to the hospital.

The security guards walked away, cursing under their breath. But this little interlude made my stomach hurt even more, and the women still hadn't returned yet. I couldn't take it anymore. The other patients were staring at me. Ashamed, I struggled to my feet and made my way forward through the crowd.

The hospital corridors extended in all directions, winding around like serpents that had no end. Only occasionally did I catch a glimpse of what looked like a completely different world. A lot of patients were lost, collapsed from exhaustion, or simply passed out on the floor. I staggered down the corridors for what felt like forever before finally coming to a doctor's examination room. A series of vivid red-and-purple photographs hung on the wall, adding brightness to the dull gray and white that dominated the rest of the hospital. The first photo was of a stomach. It was mostly black but had a series of red ulcers growing on it. Another photo depicted a pale white esophagus, but on the outer membranes were a series of meaty, pearl-like growths and something that was bluish green and shaped like a cauliflower. Explanatory text declared this cancer of the duodenum. I felt like I was back in the capital, at one of those fancy avant-garde art galleries.

I realized I must be in the gastroenterology department in the internal medicine ward. Outside the door of the examination room, a huge crowd of patients waited anxiously to get in. Some even got into fights about who would go in next. I took a few seconds to observe the situation before shoving the patients aside and forcing my way to the front of the line, where I pushed the door open and entered. The crowd was angry, staring at me with hateful eyes, yet they remained silent, probably wondering what kind of special relationship I might have with the doctor. My many years of experience as a patient had paid off, and I finally had my chance to be seen first.

5

LIKE A THIEF CAUGHT
IN THE ACT

In the examination room sat an iron exam table, eaten away by red rust. Planted behind the table like a bonsai tree was a male doctor, around sixty years old, surrounded by a tightly packed crowd of patients. Saliva flew through the air, and they waved their arms wildly as they all vied to explain their symptoms to the doctor. It was quite hot inside the examination room, and some of the patients rolled up their shirts, exposing their bare stomachs. One patient, immediately after pushing his way in, unfurled a two-meter landscape painting that he insisted on giving to the doctor as a gift. Several other patients competed to place bags of peanuts, Chinese yams, eggs, and other local delicacies on the doctor's table. The doctor was probably accustomed to this and didn't seem to mind. His face's deep jagged lines accentuated his bone structure; he looked like one of those ornamental rocks you see in traditional Chinese gardens. He wore a long white doctor's jacket with a crisply starched collar, its pure white truly eye catching; it had the same effect on me as those magic bottles that Taoist priests use to suppress demons. I couldn't help but gasp out loud. In his front jacket pocket was a row of red, blue, and black pens, pencils, and ballpoint pens, and peeking out from under his perfect snow-white jacket was a dark tie at the top and a pair of shiny leather shoes beneath. He didn't speak much, just occasional follow-up questions to patients: "Have you given birth?" "When was your last period?" "How many times a week do you have intercourse?" I couldn't quite figure out what any of this had to do with

gastrointestinal disorders. For a while I even suspected that I had gone
to the wrong department, yet there was something uniquely beautiful
about just being there, so I lingered. After a long time, the doctor leisurely turned to me and said, "What's wrong with you?"

"I drank some water!" I tried to recount the main points of what
had happened as I had rehearsed it to myself, trying not to make myself
sound like a victim.

"The mineral water at the hotel?"

How could he have possibly known that? The doctors at the C City
hospital were amazing! I realized I might be in trouble if he was expecting me to hand him a red envelope filled with cash. What should I do?
My wallet was still with those two women from the hospital. I have
rich hospital experience, but at that moment I felt like a thief caught in
the act. My face turned red, and the patients around me suddenly fell
silent, staring at me.

"You're from out of town?" the doctor asked nonchalantly. His cold
look reminded me of a courtroom judge.

"That's right, sir." All of the pride I once had about being a government functionary from the capital vanished into thin air.

"What brought you to our city?"

"It was . . . it was . . ."

"Are you sure what you drank was actually mineral water?"

"I think so . . . probably . . ."

"Mineral water! Mineral water! You *really* think you can drink that?
My dear patient, this is not some foreign country!"

The doctor seemed dissatisfied with every one of my answers. He
took out a pencil and started to drum out a little rhythm on the table.
His entire being seemed to be enveloped in an aura of all knowing and
all seeing; in his presence, I was in a state of silent awe. Had this doctor
studied abroad? He barely even looked at me, didn't take the time to
hear what my symptoms were . . . hell, he didn't even test my reflexes!
And yet with one look, he could tell exactly what was wrong with me.

From his tone of voice, I inferred that the local mineral water must have a problem. Cheap, unsafe knockoffs? I supposed that C City wasn't like many countries abroad, where you can just turn on the faucet and drink directly from the tap. There must have been some fatal germs or bacteria in the water? Or perhaps the water was too advanced, too special, so that when people from out of town drank it, they got sick because their stomachs were not used to such fine-quality water? Was this the reason I had gotten sick? I had never imagined that the doctor would be able to diagnose me with such precision. But I started to get anxious when the patients around me began to stare at me, clearly taking pleasure in my misfortune.

It was precisely at this awkward moment that a steel storage cabinet in the room started to rumble. And then it exploded open.

6

NEVER GO TO THE HOSPITAL ALONE

I was scared out of my wits, but then out of that cabinet came the two women from the hotel, their faces lit up with a triumphant look of happiness as they squeezed out and, like two heavenly maids scattering flowers, waved my medical records in the air. It turns out that behind the cabinet was a secret tunnel leading directly to an underground storage facility. The layout and design of the hospital was truly unique and the triage procedure not what you normally see at other institutions, truly unlike anything I had ever seen or heard of. I started to get the sense that something was deeply wrong, and for a moment, I felt like I wanted to run away, but the doctor and the two women formed a human triangle and blocked me in.

The doctor winked at the women and flashed them a knowing smile as he leisurely took the records out of their hands. His fingers nimbly hammered out something on his keyboard, a list of the tests he wanted me to take: blood panel, x-rays, electrocardiogram, and a B-mode ultrasound. The doctor handed the form to the women, and without a single word, they propped me up and led me out of the office. A crowd of patients tightly blocked the door, eyeing us with looks of jealousy and anger, but on my way out, I didn't forget to turn and yell "thank you" to the doctor.

By the time we got back to the main hall, the shrieks of those vendors had grown even louder, their voices like sirens blaring on a national holiday. And the number of patients in the waiting room

seemed to swell and recede like the tide. An adult peed in his pants, fell
to the floor, and started twitching and convulsing. Someone from his
family kneeled to apply pressure to his "human center" acupoint. The
security guards just stood by with their arms folded, watching coldly.
Supporting me, the two women bravely passed through the sea of filth
spreading over the floor as patients stood in a long line to get the bill
from accounting, another to pay for the tests at the cashier window,
another for the registration window, and another for the examination
window. Along the way they flashed me signals with their eyes, as if
to tell me to calm down and not to make a big deal out of what was
happening around us. And so I waited. But deep down I felt at peace.

I'm not sure how much time passed before I could finally make an
appointment. Once that was done, yet another round of waiting. The
woman with the sharp features and perm said to me, "You see, had you
come to the hospital alone, you would have never made it!"

I hurriedly nodded my head in agreement. Never go to the hospital
alone; you should *always* have someone to accompany you. A visit to
the hospital is a marathon that tests your strength and will. I looked
around. Almost all of the patients had someone with them.

I waited for more than an hour before a voice called, "Number
658, Yang Wei."

The woman with the sharp features immediately chimed in, "It's
your turn. They were pretty quick this time." She pulled me to my feet
and led me to the window where they draw blood. She greeted the nurse
as if they knew each other.

The round-faced woman with a ponytail asked me, "Are you sensitive to pain? If so, they can take my blood instead!" As she spoke she
rolled up her sleeve, exposing her red, muscular arm, which looked as
firm as a Chinese yam stick. This was my first time in a situation like
this, and it made me uncomfortable. I rushed over to her. "Please don't.
Let me do it myself."

She pushed back. "It's all the same anyway! Nothing to be embarrassed about!"

But I insisted. "I can't let you do that. It's just not right!"

But the nurse adeptly drew a vial of blood from her own forearm. It would take two hours for the results. While we were waiting, the women wanted to take the opportunity to get my x-rays done. I dared not resist.

The radiology department was also filled with patients waiting in line, staring at each other with guarded, suspicious looks. At first I didn't know what to do, but this time the women helped me cut the line, leading me through a back door into a dark room.

7

THE PRINCIPLES OF RIGHT AND WRONG GO OUT THE WINDOW WHEN YOU ARE IN PAIN

The doctor in charge of x-rays was a skinny young woman whose hair was dyed golden blonde. She gave the women who brought me a quick hug, as if they were all old friends. The three of them warmly chatted for a while, discussing fashion and makeup, until the doctor suddenly turned to me and ordered, "Take your pants off!"

The two women who had brought me to the hospital playfully patted me on the head. "Don't worry, we won't peek!" They warned me to follow the doctor's orders; then they walked out of the room hand in hand.

I followed the doctor's instructions and took off my pants, but I left my underwear on. My legs looked like two naked Popsicle sticks left under the sun on a hot day. "Remove *all* your clothes!" the doctor yelled.

I complied. But at that moment, I was struck by another wave of stomach pain that made me double over.

"Stand up straight!" she ordered.

I clenched my teeth and forced myself to straighten up, my back pressed tightly against an ice-cold plate of steel. I couldn't see the doctor, but I could hear her sharp voice.

"Raise your head! Straighten your back! Look to the left!"

I immediately got hard. Oh my, it had been a long time since that happened. It was a good thing that it was dark in the room, so nobody noticed . . . I just had to bear it until the test was complete.

By the time it was over, my back was covered in sweat, and, before I even had time to put my pants back on, the doctor called out, "Next!" A female patient entered.

Utterly exhausted, I left the room, and when the two women saw me, they flashed me a thumbs-up. Again, I felt embarrassed; as a veteran patient, I had really come within a hair of making an utter fool of myself.

It was then that my stomach pain combined with some other indescribable pain, a strange kind of general pain that triggered a hallucinatory sensation that made me feel as if I had fallen into a snake pit. I was gripped by a feeling of uneasiness, but I figured, since I had come to the hospital, I should follow the course of nature—after all, it was just my life. I needed to let go and simply leave everything in the doctors' hands.

It would be another two hours before the results of the x-ray would be ready, so in the meantime, I was taken for the electrocardiogram and B-mode ultrasound. But the doctor refused to administer the tests, admonishing me for waiting too long and for drinking too much water.

"Make another appointment," the doctor said.

"When?" one of the women asked.

"Next week."

"That won't do. Don't you have anything sooner? He is about to go in for an operation." Her face revealed a hint of self-blame, which actually moved me. As the women negotiated, one of them took out my wallet and handed the doctor a hundred-yuan note.

The doctor took the money and said, "As it so happens, another patient just canceled. I can fit you in tomorrow."

I realized that this doctor was going out of his way to extend me kindness and flexibility, but what was this about someone having just canceled? Anyone else would probably be struck with guilt for cutting the line and delaying the treatment of other patients. Who knows, this delay might even result in some patients taking a turn for the worse, or even in their deaths. Was it really okay to prioritize my life over theirs?

Seeing me standing there lost in thought, one of the women gave it to me straight. "Thinking too much will have a negative impact on your treatment. The hospital may be a world of technology, but it is also a society of human relations. If you don't understand this basic principle, there really is no hope in saving you."

"That isn't what I was thinking," I responded. "Didn't I just cut all the lines and bust into the examination room earlier? The principles of right and wrong go out the window when you are in pain. I understand that." I expressed my gratitude to the doctor.

With that, the two women carted my sweaty body out like a piece of luggage. We found a place to sit down in the main hall to wait for the results of my blood test and x-rays. Not long after that, the woman with the round face and ponytail got angry with me and stormed out. I suspected that her anger stemmed from denying her the pleasure of taking the blood test on my behalf earlier. That left me with only the woman with the sharp features and perm. So there we were, a man and a woman, left alone in the hospital.

8

TREATMENT PRIMARILY COMES DOWN TO A QUESTION OF FAITH

Time crept by one minute, one second, at a time, as drawn out as a death by hanging. Meanwhile, my pain and anxiety, mixed with the sense of guilt I felt for the woman helping me, spread like morning glory vines, wrapping themselves around me. I told the woman with the sharp features and the perm that she could leave, I would be fine by myself.

"How could I ever agree to *that*?" she responded, without even taking a second to think it over.

"I've been to plenty of hospitals. There isn't any great danger to worry about."

"Danger is an entirely different matter. Didn't we just say that no one should ever go to the hospital alone?"

"You and your friend already spent so much of your time with me. I really feel terrible about putting you out. What's more, I've figured out how things work around here."

Big Sister wore a look of grave concern. "The problem is, if I were to leave, what would happen if you tried to escape from the hospital?"

"Escape?" I could feel my cheeks burning, as if she had suddenly seen through my secret.

"That's right. I'm sure this is something that, deep down, you have been considering. You're planning on escaping during your treatment. A lot of patients try to do that. They look at the hospital with a mixture of love and hate; they like it here, but they are also terrified. I've seen many cases like this."

"Huh? That's impossible. How could that be?" I quickly tried to defend myself. "Didn't I just voluntarily go to the examination room? Didn't I just give my blood and do the x-rays? I love hospitals! They're my favorite place! Whenever I go to a hospital, I feel like I'm coming home."

"Well, we can't entirely blame the patients. It has been less than a century since modern hospitals first appeared." She seemed to think I was being hypocritical and grabbed hold of my hand.

"That's not it . . ." I wanted to tell her that before all of this, for the past several thousand years in this land, there had lived so many people—how did she think all of them had survived? But I was silenced by her imposing manner and didn't dare speak another word. And the way she held my hand made it start to sweat.

"I can tell that you have been having certain questions. These days, everyone has all kinds of questions about their lives. There is nothing abnormal about that. I know you must be wanting to ask how that doctor knew you drank the mineral water, am I right?"

"That's right." I nodded my head in embarrassment as I realized just how incredible this woman was.

"That's because our hotel surveillance feed is directly connected to the hospital's computer network."

"So that's it . . . so the hotel and the hospital are jointly run?"

"I wouldn't say that. It is simply something that C City law requires for the sake of our guests' health."

"And why is the file cabinet in the examination room connected to the underground storage facility with all the patients' records?"

"Didn't you see how many patients are at the hospital? We do this to improve efficiency when it comes to providing patients a prompt diagnosis. Have you ever heard of big data medicine?"

"Oh, so the hospital uses big data analysis, I got it. But is this hospital really considered in-network by my insurance company? I can't be expected to pay out of pocket for all these expenses? I only brought enough money for . . ."

As she heard me speak, she whipped out my wallet, held it up over her head, and waved it before my eyes. "Little Yang, you're still worried about this?" With a consoling tone, she said, "What are you thinking? I told you before, this hospital has been approved by your insurance. That's precisely why the hospital is treating you with the same care and attention they would use to treat a rare panda. So why would you have any doubts? Of course I know you can't be treated without any money. There are a lot of people who think that the most important thing you need to get good treatment is money. They think that as long as you have money, you will survive, but if you don't have money, you are as good as dead. But in reality that is not how things work. Treatment primarily comes down to a question of faith. Do you have faith in this hospital? Do you have faith in your doctor?" The way she spoke revealed something that went far beyond what a typical hotel employee would ever say. Just who was this woman?

"I have faith," I said, wanting to make my stance clear. "Of course I have faith. Over the course of my entire life, I have never once strayed from the hospital."

"Humph, I can tell you still don't truly believe." She adopted a tone of blame and added, "Tons of patients superficially nod their heads and agree, swearing that they have faith, but deep down they don't trust their doctors. Instead, they look at them as competitors, even enemies. They believe that going to the hospital is one of the great risks we take in life. They are, of course, quite hypocritical and would never say these things in public. But this kind of negative attitude has a tremendously destructive impact on one's diagnosis and treatment. Moreover, if you want to have faith in the hospital and in the doctors there, you also need to have faith in our hotel. Money doesn't guarantee good treatment. Didn't we go through the trouble of waiting in all those lines for you? Didn't we help you get in to see the doctor? Otherwise how could you have gotten an examination so quickly?" Without really revealing anything, her words got right to the crucial point. Everything she said was true.

"C'mon, please don't be upset," I pleaded. "Please try to look at things from the patient's perspective." After her scolding I was left feeling so very ashamed, my gaze shifting as I tried to keep my eyes locked in on my wallet, which she swung back and forth like the pendulum of a clock. I felt as if that wallet contained my very soul. I used to always believe that: *Isn't faith in money basically the same thing as faith in doctors and hospitals?*

"How could I be upset?" she challenged me. "I'm happy as can be!" Then she changed her tone of voice. "You're from out of town. C is a city known for its hospitality toward visitors. We always want to ensure that esteemed guests who come to C to visit, invest, vacation, work, settle down, beg, gamble, prostitute themselves, or go whoring will live good lives, fall in love with C City, and help support its economic development. That is the only reason why we built so many top-rate hospitals here. The hospital is the basis for all else; you can't do anything if you don't have a healthy body. Since you are new here, there are a lot of things you still don't quite understand, but you need to hurry up and get all of those suspicions out of your head. Start adopting a more local mindset. Little Yang, you have got to pull through and go on living. You've still got a lot to contribute to society."

Her frank speech left me speechless. I just thought to myself, *That was beautiful.*

"So this is your job?" I asked meekly.

"That's right. Our job is to accompany guests to the hospital, a recent position that C City has instituted in order to protect the well-being of the people and encourage development," she announced proudly. "It has not only greatly bolstered our employment numbers but has also helped to focus and manifest a new level of interpersonal compassion and care. And most importantly, it has gone a long way in

improving patients' faith in our doctors and hospitals, which is something we especially need right now."

"But your colleague just left . . ."

"That was Ah Bi. It's not that she got sick of you; something unexpected came up at home that she had to take care of. She, too, is doing
her best to keep pace with this era of rapid development, but sometimes
we encounter unforeseeable challenges, and something unfortunate
recently occurred. Her only son, who is now a sophomore in college,
must have something miswired in his brain, because he started spreading rumors online that damaged the image of C City. He is now in
custody. And she just got news that her husband drank himself to death.
Her husband was the section chief at the High-Tech Development
District. One of his main duties was to take various government leaders out drinking, and that's how he ended up drinking himself to death!
Ah Bi stepped out to take care of the funeral arrangements for her husband. She's quite busy. C City is in the midst of a great development
campaign. It is a crucial era of monumental change, and in order to
acclimate ourselves to this new environment, each individual has been
working hard around the clock. As she was rushing back and forth
to the hospital every day to take care of our guests, her own husband
died! I'm in a similar situation. I left my kids alone to take care of you.
Actually, no, what I'm doing is *saving* you. So there is no need for you
to blame yourself. All you need to do is reflect for a moment about why
you didn't let Ah Bi do the blood test for you. She was relying on that
to earn some extra money that she could use toward her son's bail. Oh
my, I see that you still have a lot of questions. You are confused—please
don't be like that! When it comes down to it, it has nothing to do with
money. No matter how much money you have, you can't buy a human
life. It all comes back to a question of faith. Why don't you have faith in
Ah Bi? Do you even have faith in me? Do you have faith in the hospital
and doctors? When it comes down to it, the real question is whether
you believe that C is a friendly city. Ah Bi's husband died from drinking

alcohol—all you drank was some mineral water! I think C City has already been quite generous with you."

"Why didn't you tell me all of this earlier? I'm so terribly sorry!" I was filled with embarrassment and regret. I could almost see Ah Bi's blue veins pulsating under the skin of her round, muscular arms, extending out right before my very eyes, like in a dream. I began to feel as if her husband's death was now directly tied to me. I made a silent promise that I would one day write a song for the women of this special profession, extolling their hard work, bravery, and acts of selfless sacrifice. I may be a veteran patient, but as I stood before these women of C City, it was clear that there was so much I have yet to learn.

"It's okay. Ah Bi will pull through. If you can't pull through in C City, you're done for! We just grit our teeth and push forward. Little Yang, you, too, must push forward. Don't let a little pain knock you down!"

She gazed hard at me with a knowing look, but somehow I felt as if her eyes revealed a disdainful mockery. I felt like an amateur in the presence of a true master. I had recently turned forty and was a bit older than she was, and yet here she was speaking to me like a mother admonishing a child. I suppose that, too, is one of her professional skills. I wish everyone in the country could have as much faith and professionalism as she did.

I respectfully asked, "How should I address you?"

"Just call me Sister Jiang."

At that moment a sharp announcement suddenly came over the loudspeaker in the main hall: "Number 1020, Yang Wei!" The voice repeated my name several times, reminding me of airport announcements of the names of passengers late for their flights. I figured the doctor must want to see me.

But Sister Jiang exclaimed, "The blood samples and x-rays have already been processed by the automated transmission system and relayed to the doctor's office. We must hurry!" She grabbed my hand, and we rushed off.

9

A PROTRACTED BATTLE

It felt like we didn't have enough time. We waded through a sea of people to make our way to an examination room. Hidden behind patients huddled together like a horde of noisy birds was a middle-aged female doctor wearing a face mask. She had a pale complexion and thin frame, her head lowered as she calmly reviewed the results of my blood panel and x-ray as if trying to solve some esoteric math problem, but the impression she left on me was closer to that of a ballerina getting ready to take the stage.

She eventually addressed Sister Jiang—but not me—in a thin calm voice. "I don't think there are any big problems, but I can't rule out an intestinal obstruction. I can't rule out kidney stones. I can't rule out duodenal ulcers. I also can't rule out a stomach perforation. Take him to the surgery department, what do you say?"

"The surgery department? How will they handle this case?" Sister Jiang moved closer to the doctor. By now she really looked like she was a member of my family.

Her question made sense to me. I also wondered why I needed to go to the surgery department. Did they really think that the internal medicine department couldn't handle a simple stomachache from drinking some water? But I supposed they sometimes liked to handle certain cases like this.

The doctor appeared slightly annoyed as she started to sign the referral form. "This is definitely a case for surgery."

I figured that modern medicine indeed works in mysterious ways and the authority of the doctor is unassailable. I looked at Sister Jiang pleadingly, secretly hoping she might intervene.

"Okay then," she said, "let's let every department have a crack at you. It's hard for these doctors. They don't earn much salary, and yet every day their job requires them to pull people from the clutches of the god of death. It is a protracted battle, and patients will never understand all the challenges that doctors must face." She led me out.

After such a long and laborious journey at the hospital, this somehow felt like the true beginning. I staggered down the corridor with Sister Jiang, but after yet another round of drama, my stomach pain was getting much worse. It felt as if there were a wrench twisting and turning my intestines and everything before my eyes. The faces of those patients, the winding corridors, the rainwater, the vomit, the phlegm and piss, the vendor's cart and those products for sale, and that filthy, muddy floor—all began to spin and dance in the air like a fireworks show. I felt like I had fallen into the silken cave of the spider demon. I was concerned that the doctor in the surgery department might demand some exorbitant amount for his service. I had heard rumors that some doctors stop surgery halfway through and demand more money from the patient, and if the patient doesn't pay up, the surgeon just leaves them there, opened up on the operating table with their stomach and intestines exposed to the cold air. Sister Jiang kept walking faster, but I intentionally slowed down. I really blamed myself for all of this. How could I dispel the deep lack of faith lurking within me? Sister Jiang was right.

The surgery department was on floor thirty-three. As the saying goes, "It's lonely at the top." The corridor was filled with screaming patients. One of them was suffering from heart failure, another had a broken bone, and another had a brain injury. I was immediately assaulted by the foul stench of blood and guts. The gusts of air coming in from over the river blew sheets of cold rainwater through the open windows, and it fell on the dense forest of brown mushrooms growing all over the walls. More than a dozen small white mice with translucent bodies scurried around beneath the canopy of mushrooms. I tried to acclimate myself to this radical change of scenery, wondering if the mice had escaped from an experimental lab. But this only increased my impression of the office as mysterious and professional. Like a good Hollywood blockbuster, C City's Central Hospital created its own unusual visual effect.

After I'd waited in line for a long time, it was finally my turn. The surgeon took a cursory look at me before telling Sister Jiang, "Take another number and bring him to the emergency room."

"Understood!" Sister Jiang responded.

I started to grow increasingly anxious. "What exactly is wrong with me?"

"What's wrong with you?" the surgeon asked. "That's not something the patient needs to know. Your illness is the hospital's business." He couldn't have been more to the point.

Sister Jiang flashed me a look. "In some cases, the doctor only discloses the illness to close family members but doesn't tell the patient." With that she led me off again. Just before leaving, I thanked the doctor.

The emergency room was located underground, on sublevel B13.

10

IF THIS CONTINUES, I'M AFRAID I MIGHT JUST DIE

As we went down in the elevator, it felt like we were in a movie that kept fading in and out. I felt like I was an actor with a sprained ankle, a camera following me from behind. We finally arrived at a place that looked like a bomb shelter, dark and humid, overgrown with moss. Green beetles were crawling around, and on either side of the corridor was a massive fish tank, each containing a goldfish without eyes cruising around inside. I assumed this was another experimental creature from a lab. A bulletin board was filled with all kinds of notices and announcements.

The patients were like a wall of goblins crammed up against one another in more than a dozen long crowded lines. The whole scene was strange and fantastic, and yet everything seemed completely normal. Perhaps, like Sister Jiang said, this was simply the new normal. The patients bore this difficult situation with perfect equanimity, looking calm and comfortable. I supposed I really didn't understand C City like I had thought I did, and I also needed to learn from experience when it came to the hospital system.

"I'll go register," Sister Jiang offered. She had adjusted quickly to Ah Bi's departure and really stepped up to take charge. I waited for a long time, and when she finally came back, she delivered news. "This is the wrong place. They moved the registration window somewhere else." I stared anxiously at her as she rampaged down a different corridor; she really looked like a professional manager. She returned about an hour later with a new registration number. "Little Yang," she said, "my apologies. It is simply too crowded. This is simply the reality we have to deal with in C City. Everyone wants to get a spot here at Central Hospital. Even people struck down with the common cold would rather come here than their local hospital or clinic. And then there are people who come in from the suburbs seeking treatment, not to mention out-of-towners like you! This is what happens when you have a large population that wants to live a good life but has a relatively low average income. Everyone here tries to pull strings or go through the back door, but that doesn't work so well when everybody knows somebody. I hope you can understand the situation and forgive us."

She continued dragging me all over in search of a doctor. Groups of patients looked like extras from a movie, curled up on the floor making love, their faces all looking the same as they moved up and down amid the thick shadows. The oxygen underground was very thin, and a few people had already suffocated. The goldfish in the tank would occasionally leap out of the water. And yet there were no physicians.

"The doctor is administering treatment to another patient right now," a nurse casually informed us as she rushed past. "You can go to the main office and have the people there page him."

"That sounds like a plan," said Sister Jiang. "Little Yang, why don't you wait for me here while I go find the doctor?"

She left immediately, but after what felt like forever, she still hadn't returned. I wondered if she had started up a conversation with the women in the office or perhaps run into an old friend. One of the requirements of her job was to establish strong interpersonal relationships with all kinds of people. But eventually it got to the point where I could no longer wait. I'd been in the hospital a long time, yet I still hadn't received any real treatment or help. My pain was no longer a mild sensation. It had grown to a horrific pain, ripping apart my insides and leaving me with a feeling of undeniable terror. Both my faith and my morale suffered a terrible blow. *If this continues*, I thought, *I'm afraid*

I might just die. I've actually always been afraid of dying. If a public servant from the capital and veteran patient like me were to die in this faraway hospital, from some undiagnosed stomach disorder, that would just be too embarrassing.

I thought things over for a while before deciding not to wait for Sister Jiang. Instead, as difficult as it might be, I would strike out on my own in search of a doctor. In the end, we are all alone anyway.

The arrangement of things underground was much more confusing than the other parts of the building. I walked for a very long time before coming to a structure surrounded by a granite wall. A heavy iron door read **Treatment Room** in both Chinese and English. I had to push hard even to crack open the door, but through the crack I saw five or six pale figures crowded together, each one holding something that looked like a saw as they hacked away at some soft object on the ground. The floor was covered in a dark-red liquid that beetles seemed to be drinking. Was this some form of treatment? I thought I must be seeing things and immediately recoiled from the sight and started running back the way I had come, deciding never again to go off alone in search of a doctor.

It was another hour before Sister Jiang returned with a tall male doctor who had a certain presence. He wore a long white hospital jacket that fluttered as he walked, black glasses with wide rims and black frames, a faint mustache, and shoulder-length hair. He was handsome and seemed to be untainted by the world, with a slight look of childish innocence in his eyes. He looked like an installation artist or perhaps a mountain eagle. Clinging to his face was a look that seemed to betray a contempt for the world, but his hair was already completely white, like a blanket of snow. Finally, I saw hope.

The three of us walked to the examination room.

11

ALL EXAMINATIONS MUST BE ADMINISTERED BY MACHINE

That doctor who had just appeared so healthy and energetic suddenly looked emaciated and wasted. He plopped down crookedly onto a black leather chair and continued to reposition his waist as if he were in extreme discomfort. He sized me up with a look of utter exhaustion and said, "Oh, I see you've had an exam over at internal medicine? This is the emergency room. I'm going to have to trouble you to go back there and do a blood test, urine test, x-ray, electrocardiogram, and a B-mode ultra—"

Right then and there, I collapsed on the floor. I felt like I never wanted to get up again.

The doctor appeared perturbed. He told Sister Jiang, "Tell him not to act like that."

"It's okay," Sister Jiang patiently told me. "Don't act so spoiled and stubborn. We are only trying to do the responsible thing, to take care of you. Haven't you heard? Modern biomedicine is a product of the European Renaissance, yet it has only been practiced here in our country for a hundred years. We must follow required procedures. The first rule is that all diagnoses are dependent upon examinations. That's right, and when you conduct too many examinations, patients are always afraid they will be uncomfortable, but if you do too few, then they accuse you of doing a half-assed job, and if you make even the slightest mistake, patients accuse their doctor of malpractice! What is a doctor to do? Well, I'm quite familiar with how hospitals function. I've learned a thing or two. Doctors come here with an educational background in science. They start off on the same track as people who study physics, biology, and chemistry. And isn't there a saying, *Traditional medicine is a product of the agricultural age, while modern medicine is the crystallization of the industrial age*? That is why all examinations must be administered by machine. Doctors today no longer hold on to the four traditional methods of diagnosis that Chinese doctors used in the old days. Only machines can help us see the cells in our bodies. Little Yang, you probably still haven't seen your cells, have you? Machines can give that back to you, allow you to see what a human being truly looks like. You should feel lucky. There was once a very high probability that you would be born to peasants in a remote area with little access to medicine or medical care. You wouldn't be able to write your songs, let alone have a B-mode ultrasound, an x-ray, or an electrocardiogram. I know, just thinking about it is terrifying! But that's precisely why you have to listen to the doctor. We keep telling you to have faith in the hospital, faith in your doctors, but what can you do to *prove* your faith to us? The first step is giving yourself over to machine-administered exams. This is a test of a patient's sincerity. There was recently a case in which an individual submitted tea to the machine instead of urine, and the results were positive for inflammation. He tried to use this to prove that the hospital was not up to standards. He even tried to blackmail his doctor! These types of underhanded tactics are not to be tolerated."

I agreed with everything she said. Few places in this country had achieved full modernization, but the hospital had. And as far as modern biomedicine, at least according to my limited understanding, the practical application of biological science was humankind's most marvelous technological achievement in the past four or five hundred years. Paracelsus's explanation of the human body's chemical processes, Leonardo da Vinci's and Vesalius's pioneering work on human anatomy, Santorio's invention of clinical thermometers and pulse meters, Harvey's discoveries about blood circulation—these developed into a massive body of knowledge that those without specialized training have no way of truly understanding, like a kind of magic. With the exception of rocket satellites and nuclear weapons, modern medicine was the most fashionable field and best captures the spirit of the times, and with the exception of a few isolated individuals from the countryside, the vast majority of citizens had experienced the fruits of these medical breakthroughs firsthand, although I have heard that the true model for Western medicine was not here in our country. For instance, I was told that hospitals in the United States have very few patients and are extremely quiet. It was said that doctors and patients met one on one and had a collaborative relationship akin to close friends and that no one needed to wait in long lines to be seen by a specialist, and that most people had family doctors that they made appointments with . . . but this was purely rumor. I had no firsthand experience of American hospitals, and some had even surmised that ulterior motives inspired these lies, in order to intimidate us. But there was nothing to fear. Our nation's modern hospitals had their own special characteristics. The process of examination and diagnosis seemed to be of Western origin indeed, but this was not something that patients needed to understand. We just needed to have faith. Those who would try to pass off tea as pee were truly lost, led down the path of fear by those lies originating in the United States.

I tried my best to stand up. Sister Jiang helped me, supporting me on our journey like a mother taking her child on a trip to Disney World. I wondered whether Sister Jiang would get a promotion for the wonderful work she was doing with me. I could tell how exhausted she was. I could even see the beads of sweat on her forehead. This made me feel even more guilty.

This time around I was able to complete almost all of the tests successfully, with the exception of the B-mode ultrasound. I had my blood taken, gave a urine sample, and had a series of x-rays and an electrocardiogram. Sister Jiang asked a nurse friend of hers to try and rush the results, and she promised we would have the results within two hours after each test. We sat and waited. Time seemed to stand still, but it also seemed to be spinning, replaying itself over and over, sending me down a never-ending vortex.

12

LAYMEN DECIDE THE COURSE
OF TREATMENT

As my pain continued to escalate, I seemed to get a glimpse of a strange new universe. I saw forms converging in clusters that resembled pale leeches floating through the claustrophobic space of the emergency room. The sharp sound of a bone saw echoed through the room, and incessant voices chanted sacred scriptures. I hated that I couldn't plug my ears, but at the same time, I couldn't help but listen. In the corridor old men looked like they were carved from panels of peach wood and covered up in oversize green army jackets, just glimpses of their eyes peeking out. They were pushed in black chrome wheelchairs that creaked as they rolled. The old men's eyes seemed devoid of life, and yet they left me with a sense of warmth and wisdom. Some had long grayish-blue plastic tubes inserted into their nostrils, which made them look like a herd of trudging Asian elephants. They groaned in pain but also seemed to be enjoying themselves, even deriving pleasure. I gradually came to understand that the elderly are the only ones who are truly fearless; they are much stronger than the young. When young people arrive at the hospital, they immediately fall apart, losing all confidence, thrust into a deep abyss with the first taste of discomfort. The elderly, on the other hand, have been around the block and know how to deal with pain.

I couldn't help but admire these patients, who were not only seeking treatment but were recreating an entire world, a tangible world that could support this hospital. They were like a series of stars forming, their very formation causing the joy of death to shrink under the pull of gravity and concentrate in the sick ward, diffusing the power and authority of the doctors. In the end, only the elderly were able to possess death and its many mysteries. If they didn't fall ill, there would be no reason for the hospital to exist, and this glorious city would be in ruins, unable to function. What would happen to its success, prosperity, civilization, and progress?

A trip to the hospital was a routine activity in the everyday life of the residents of C City, like dropping by a friend's or relative's house to visit. Medical insurance was arranged and provided by experts for the good of the layman, but in reality, laymen decided the course of treatment: when to go in for treatment, where to receive treatment, whether to listen to a doctor's advice. Laymen even made their own judgments about the effectiveness of a treatment, which in turn impacted their decisions about any future course of treatment. Patients decided what diagnoses doctors made and what treatment plans they created. Patients provided the solid foundation and driving force behind the hospital's development.

This was especially the case with elderly patients, who had rich experience and had spent their entire lives seeking treatment for various ailments. What *didn't* they know? They came to the hospital with no fear in their hearts, just a quiet serenity, a remarkable peacefulness inside them. Their moans of pain were feigned, to accentuate this sense of perfect calm, a joyful silence that left others with the impression that they were not sick at all. They came because they knew the hospital was here, right here before their eyes! Like a mountain climber who, when asked why he wanted to conquer a certain peak, responds by saying, "Because it is there!"

This is the kind of realization that one reaches only after a lifetime of cultivation. And so sometimes, when the elderly had nothing better to do, they feigned illness so they could achieve their goal of making a trip to the hospital. They grew accustomed to standing in long lines and waiting, and for them it was actually enjoyable. They would feel terribly uncomfortable if they *weren't* able to make these trips to the hospital; they might even get sick if someone were to deprive them of this pleasure. They didn't fret about expenses; after all, they had medical insurance. They would let the country down if they didn't spend the money allocated by their insurance for medical care. In short, this is where they found the meaning of life.

Most of the doctors were younger than these patients, allowing the old-timers to flex their experience and seniority. Many old-timers didn't even respect the doctors. They had been to the hospital so many times that they knew each and every doctor in the hospital. They waved warmly and offered pleasantries, even gave some of the doctors cute nicknames as if they were children. And this is how the patients and the doctors mutually coexisted and thrived. Those tales about doctors and patients being sworn enemies, filled with animosity toward one another? Those disputes helped to serve as a foil that ultimately accentuated the hospital's warm and affectionate atmosphere. Those patients were also close to nurses, security guards, and janitors, who often provided information on various treatment centers and wards and helped them get in to see specific doctors without waiting in long lines.

Although there were a lot of germs in the hospital, those patients never wore face masks. Instead they acted like they were the hospital's main corporate sponsors, with the right to breathe freely, unfettered by the inconvenience of a face mask. They probably viewed the hospital as their own private property, where they were the masters. Look over there! An old lady leisurely rolled around in her wheelchair, her bound feet looking as if someone had intentionally broken the bones to turn her feet into a living work of art. Across from her an old man held an elegant and ornately carved black wooden cane. He was blind, and yet he sat with perfect stillness and confidence, a broad smile on his face. A vision of such beauty could be found only in someone whom disease had already penetrated to the greatest depths of his very soul.

At this point I was struck by a terrible sense of shame. What I had seen at Central Hospital in C City made a self-professed veteran patient like me come to terms with how inexperienced I really was. Insecurity welled up inside me. I knew full well that my illness was not very serious, and yet there I was, unable to show the same dignity and calm that those old-timers embodied. I felt like I was sitting on a bed of needles, fidgety and filled with self-loathing for not coming to the hospital earlier. At that moment I finally began to try and establish a true sense of faith in this hospital.

Oh, C, such a remarkable city, the hospital was the pearl in your crown. Had I not visited in person, I would still have been in the dark. Did I still have the confidence to write a song that would do proper justice to this grand city? I thought that if I should ever recover from my illness, perhaps I would settle down in C City for the long term, apply for status as an honorary citizen, and continue to be nurtured by the deep medical culture the city had to offer. I could forever retain my youth and passion for art, and in the process, I could escape the boredom and pressure of my government job in the capital. And even if I wasn't sick, I could still make daily trips to the hospital to visit my doctors, all the way until the very end. Becoming a lifelong patient would be a great source of joy and happiness! Hadn't all of those songs I'd written over all the years been building up to this very moment?

Suddenly the overhead television turned on. The old-timers stood, placed their fists to their chests, and approached the television from all directions. They sat in neat rows in front of the screen, on which a beautifully produced advertisement promoted **Vegetarians for Health**. A bald middle-aged male movie star spoke in a low nasal voice: "Do you really think there are many sharks left in the sea? No. Do you think there are many tigers left in the forest? No. Let's come together to protect wild animals by refusing to buy and sell them. Please try the World's Fair Magical Cure for Ten Thousand Ailments—Isatis Root Molecular Extract!" The old-timers exclaimed a collective cry of approval.

A young female star with huge eyes appeared on the screen and spoke with a seductive charm. "I'm strong. But I'm also weak. What's missing for a woman who wields power?" I was thinking hard, trying to guess the answer, when she gritted her teeth angrily and announced, "Status, that's what's missing. Please use flora fingerprint identification, it's even more accurate than iris identification!" I felt like I had really learned something; only the hospital could verify someone's identity. The hospital was like an island in the sea, collecting different living creatures and, in the name of disease, reawakening their will to live and, over the long course of verifying their identity, reaching to the most crucial stage: finding the most suitable medicine to keep them alive. Ah, *this* was the reason we had come to the hospital!

But before I got to that stage, I still needed to resolve the more pressing issue of my stomach pain. It had almost done me in, making me feel like I had really let the hospital down. Several hours slipped by, but it felt more like several years, several decades, several centuries, several millennia . . .

Sister Jiang leaned over and said, "If you don't feel well, you can rest your head in my lap."

13

A WOMAN'S THIGHS ARE A PAINKILLER

For a moment I sat there frozen, completely dumbfounded by her offer. Put my head in her lap? It's not like I was one of those old-timers, but I was also not as tough as most of the locals in C City. Suffering through the pain of what felt like thousands of ants chewing on my bones had left me utterly exhausted, both physically and mentally; how I secretly longed for a soft, warm place to curl up and rest. And yet I found myself feeling bashful about the prospect—I had only known Sister Jiang for less than a day.

My hesitation seemed to make her unhappy. She cleared her throat and asked, "Little Yang, what are you thinking?" She extended her arms and then, right there in front of the other patients, reached out, grabbed my head, and directed it down to her lap. She seemed to have a lot of experience in this. I figured I had nothing to be shy about—after all, we were in a hospital, and I had taken off my pants not long before. I wanted to prove my faith in the hospital to Sister Jiang. My oh my, as soon as I put my head down, all the old-timers immediately turned their gazes to me, as if they had just witnessed an explosion. I closed my eyes tightly to protect myself from the blast.

Sister Jiang's pants felt light and slippery, like the skin of a catfish, and the entire area around her thighs had a dense and stretchy texture. Although my head was positioned very close to her private parts, I didn't get a whiff of anything out of the ordinary. But I did have the direct sensation that this was the body of a mature woman whose development had already reached its peak. I could feel her elastic body slightly moving beneath my head, expanding with the flow of blood rushing in, filling me with a feeling of warmth and care that I had not felt in a long time. I dared not entertain any further thoughts, and yet I couldn't help myself. It was as if Sister Jiang's thighs worked as a shot of painkiller, and her body became an extension of the hospital. At that crucial moment, Sister Jiang had saved me again. She indeed had an extremely high level of professional ethics. Never once did she treat me like an outsider.

Like a real patient, I pretended to fall asleep by closing my eyes, holding my breath, not uttering a single word, and remaining as still as a corpse, yet as I lay there I couldn't stop my mind from wandering, imagining just what kind of person Sister Jiang really was. Most likely born into an average family that didn't have any special privilege, she was probably a high school graduate, maybe went to a vocational school or attended some second-rate college. She had been working at the hotel for many years and had always been a conscientious and hardworking employee, working overtime, never afraid of going the extra mile. Every day she spent time committing to memory those more esoteric passages from her employee handbook so that she could recite them back to patients like me, to ease our anxieties, encourage us to cooperate with the hospital, and dispel our fears. Over time, she had begun to believe the rhetoric in the employee handbook, built up a long list of contacts at the hospital, learned to cope with all kinds of complicated situations, and became a true professional, always helping patients get the treatment they needed. She did all of this to support her family, but also for the honor of C City. She really loved the city from the bottom of her heart, took good care of her customers, her service impeccable, as if every patient were family. She was thoughtful in carrying out her job, her performance outstanding, a true model worker . . . a woman of this new era who had grown up alongside the hospital. Sister Jiang was someone I wanted to learn from.

She caressed my hair, sang nursery rhymes, and gently whispered, "You out-of-towners are so sad. Actually, my family also immigrated here. My parents originally came to C City to participate in the great construction. That was during a time when everything had wasted away after a great catastrophe, and they had yet to rebuild the city. They worked day and night. My father was afflicted with acute interstitial nephritis, which was further complicated by hypokalemia, but at that time we lacked medicine and medical care; there were no treatment options for him. He died when I was three. My mother decided it would be better for me if she did not remarry. At first I was very uncomfortable interacting with people from the hospital. It felt like the hospital was some lofty place, out of reach for normal people like us, without a lot of money. But gradually I was able to foster feelings for the hospital. This is something you need to work at, Little Yang; those feelings don't simply develop on their own. If my father had the resources we have now, he would have never died. And so I make it my mission to transfer my love for my father to all of the customers I serve . . ."

Her story went on and on, and through her hypnotic words, I even dozed off for a while. Then, in my dazed state, I seemed to sense my head resting on the back of my chair. I have no idea when she left, but as if she had fulfilled her mission, Sister Jiang had at some point quietly sneaked off. She hadn't even said goodbye. And I hadn't even noticed.

I was left despondent and depressed; like a lost child, I buried my head in my arms and curled up into a ball. I could hear the old-timers around me gleefully laughing like a pack of hyenas that had finally gotten their revenge. The atmosphere was at once joyous, strange, and terrifying.

With Sister Jiang gone, in my loneliness and shame, I couldn't help but think about running away again. I simply couldn't stand this hospital any longer. But I knew clearly then that I would never be able to escape.

14

LIFE IS LIKE BEING A MOTH
DRAWN TO THE FLAME

Speaking from a purely intellectual point of view, I really didn't want to leave. I had already invested a huge amount in the hospital, in the form of time, money, and energy. It was like a snowball effect, and I was sure that this was precisely the hospital's strategy for discouraging patients from leaving. The hospital's collaboration with the hotel, and the good offices of those two richly experienced woman employees, meant that not many people would be able to resist. My reliance on the hospital had already become something of a habit, not to mention the fact that I was still worried I might drop dead. So I just continued lying there on that bench like a mangy dog.

Signs flashed around me, LCD screens displaying the names of different diagnostic tests and centers: GE64 Spiral CT, GE 1.5T MRI, Digital Subtraction Angiography, four-dimensional color Doppler ultrasound, a high-end flat-panel detector angiography machine, PET scan, Near-Patient Testing, CR Imaging Center, AGFA All-Digital CR Workstation, ECG Workstation, Endoscopy Center, Arthroscopy Center, automatic biochemical analysis, A6 Invisible SGTB Operating Room, and so on. It was as if the hospital were trying to proudly announce to all the patients that it had "achieved true modernization" and was indeed a place where all patients could see their "dreams come true."

Other patients sat next to me on the bench. One guy with an out-of-town accent said to his wife, "Let's get out of here. We really don't have enough cash. Who the hell would've thought this damn illness could cost so much to treat?"

His wife responded, "It's okay. We'll find a way to borrow the money we need."

"No one's gonna be willing to lend us any money. We're broke. If we had any money, I wouldn't have had to sell my blood. If I hadn't sold my blood, I wouldn't have contracted AIDS. And now you're sick too."

His wife started to cry. And then they walked off, leaning on one another.

After them came a pair of patients that looked like a father and daughter, their eyes red from crying. The daughter said, "It's all your fault! You just had to believe what that guy told you! He took all our money!"

The father responded with a deep sigh. "I also wanted to give it a try. What's more, the prescription they gave me was much cheaper than what you pay at those big hospitals. The story they told also made sense at first."

After listening to them for a while, I figured out what had happened: the daughter had accompanied her dad from the countryside to the hospital. But as soon as they stepped off the train, some con man pretending to represent a hospital tricked them into going to some pseudoclinic. There they were forced to pay an exorbitant price for fake medicine. Once they realized that they had been ripped off, they came back to the Central Hospital in C City, but by then they hadn't had any money left.

A young professional-looking man sat down next to me and started to cry. He was on the phone. "I really can't hold on any longer. You know I requested the overtime. I worked seven days a week and even did odd jobs at night to earn extra money. I spent all that money on my father-in-law's medical expenses, but it still wasn't enough. You have to pay out of pocket for all of those new, fancy specialized medications. My wife is expecting, and even she took an outside job. We're getting ready to throw in the towel and sell our apartment. What else can we do? We all felt like giving up, and then, do you know what happened? I just got diagnosed with throat cancer . . ."

A man approached me and whipped out a photo of a bird with a massive head. He whispered, "You interested in an owl? They're really good for treating esophageal cancer."

A woman waved a flyer in the air: "If you have esophageal cancer, you should try our Magic Toad Pills! One guy suffering from that kind of cancer tried everything to no avail, then his wife heard that eating toads was a particularly effective treatment, so off she went to catch toads to cure her husband! After eating twenty-five hundred toads, her husband was cured!"

A middle-aged woman kept asking the patients, "Anyone have expensive meds for sale? I'm looking to buy. I'll give you one hundred and fifty for a box of Xihuang cancer pills, three hundred for one Rainin pipette, five hundred for tegafur . . ." She dragged a huge bag filled with medicine.

Some guy named Uncle Zhao, who looked like a salesman, approached carrying a pile of colorful advertisements. "Why don't you all consider going abroad for your medical treatment? We only send patients to the top ten hospitals in America and England, and we provide one-stop service. We make our patients feel right at home. Not only do we offer the most advanced treatment techniques, but we also offer great value for your money. The same stent procedure that costs you thirty-eight thousand yuan here can be done over there for only six thousand! Dental implants that cost thirty thousand per tooth here can be done for just twelve hundred! One bottle of Herceptin sells for twenty-six thousand here but can be yours for only four thousand . . . even better, you will never have to wait in lines again. You can get a hotel bed in no time at all. Stay in a luxury private room with air-conditioning and your own bathroom! Saving a life is like putting out a fire: time is of the essence! Think it over!"

His pitch was interrupted by a loud ruckus. Nearby, two middle-aged men were trying to stop a young guy whose face had turned a bright red. The young guy screamed, "Leave me alone! I'm going to find that doctor and teach him a good lesson! I can't tell you how angry I am or how many red envelopes full of cash I gave those doctors. I spent a million dollars on my father's treatment, and still they let him die! The most shameful thing is that the day he died, while my father was unconscious, one doctor even prescribed him some eight-thousand-dollar imported antibiotic! Pure evil!"

One of the men trying to hold him back said, "Don't be like that. Your father's gone, just try to let it go. You've got to realize that we aren't doctors. We don't understand medicine like they do. Keep in mind that we will all have to come here for treatment one day."

A man in his fifties burst into tears. "I came here to fix a bone fracture. But the receipt the hospital gave me lists a hysterectomy, an ovarian cyst removal, and a salpingectomy. And they want to charge me ten thousand more than the price the doctor quoted! What should I do?"

I wasn't a big fan of listening to all this. Patients' narratives tend to repeat the same old boring stuff, like how unpredictable fate can be and how life is like being a moth drawn to the flame. The only interesting thing was the disharmonious voices you usually never heard in the hospital, or anywhere else in C City. How could this be? Where were all the security guards? I admired those patients, even envied them. But I was starting to become frightened, and my pain only intensified. How I wished I could mute those groans.

The doctors didn't have enough time to care for all these patients. On one side of the hallway, a line of doctors gathered with their luggage. From the little tour-group flags they were holding, I figured they must be on their way to Africa to help in the struggle against some terrible epidemic. Several political leaders had come to see them off and deliver speeches, and a mob of journalists surrounded them, taking pictures and trying to get interviews. On the other side, a crowd of people displayed various signs. A red banner read, **WELCOMING EXPERTS FROM THE EUROPEAN UNION MEDICAL SCIENCE ASSOCIATION TO OUR HOSPITAL FOR EXCHANGE!** A celebratory poster with gold letters read, **CONGRATULATIONS TO ZHOU XIAOLAN, HEAD NURSE OF NEUROSURGERY, ON THE NIGHTINGALE AWARD!**

I thought of that line from Ostrovsky's *How the Steel Was Tempered*: "Man's dearest possession is life. It is given to him to live but once, and he must live so as to feel no torturing regrets for wasted years, never know the burning shame of a mean and petty past; so live that, dying, he might say: all my life, all my strength were given to the finest cause in all the world—the fight for the Liberation of Mankind." I continued to observe the other patients carefully; at first they were rather interesting, but I gradually grew tired of it. What does this reveal? Patients' narratives are completely devoid of creativity; they jabber on about how cruel fate is, but the fates of patients and the hospital are all connected.

I once went to the religious holy land of Mount Wutai, and while I was there someone handed me a Buddhist scripture, which I read through in order to understand what visions of a Buddhist hell looked like. There are many different layers of hell: the Hell of Blisters, where the bodies of all living beings are covered with painful blisters that form in layers, one on top of each other, until the blisters eventually rupture and the entire body looks like one massive open wound, oozing with blood and white pus; the Hell of Chattering Teeth, where it is so unbearably cold that all living beings coil up and convulsively twitch and spasm, the unspeakable pain making their teeth chatter compulsively; the Hell of Desperate Screams, where all living beings are burned alive by a fierce, blaring flame, trying to withstand the pain as their wide eyes pop out of their sockets and they scream and flail wildly. There is no escape. These horrific visions can all be seen in the hospital, where patients are indeed the living dead. Hell is simply an attempt to simulate the misery of human disease and suffering. As a songwriter with some renown in certain circles, I have known this for a long time, so none of it came as a surprise to me.

I couldn't help but connect all of that to the unfortunate circumstances I currently found myself in. I wondered, if my illness should be something serious, whether my insurance would pay for all of my medical expenses. I wondered if all the extra money I had earned over the years as a songwriter would be enough to cover the out-of-pocket portion of the cost. That's what I worried about most: out-of-pocket expenses are much more terrifying than hell.

But I couldn't worry about all of these details. Sister Jiang had returned. Her appearance triggered another uproar among the elderly patients. Their eyes locked on the object in her hand: a copy of my exam results. She flashed me a confident look that seemed to indicate that she had taken care of everything, and she gleefully announced, "All the results are in. Little Yang, we can fix your problem." Without offering any further explanation, she helped me up from the bench, and we rushed straight to the exam room.

15

THE MORAL OBLIGATION
OF A DOCTOR

When we got back to the exam room, the young male doctor who alternately looked like an installation artist or a mountain eagle was still there. He still looked like a strung out drug addict, yet the patients around him looked at him with adoration and infatuation. He haphazardly glanced at my test results out of the corner of his eye.

"From the looks of it, your results aren't too bad." He wasn't speaking to me, though; he was directly addressing Sister Jiang. "However, in order to make sure we take full responsibility for this patient, I think we better order a CT scan."

"What?" I mumbled listlessly. I felt like I had less than a minute before I would literally drop dead, my corpse thrown to a sea of devils waiting to chop me up.

"It is probably too late to get the CT today," the doctor added casually. "I also want you to make an appointment for a gastroscope."

"Can you just tell me what's wrong with me? When can you tell me?" I mustered my last bit of strength to make a fist and tried to think of the glorious image of those brave and righteous old-timer patients back in the waiting area.

The doctor seemed taken aback and recoiled. "Try not to be so anxious. Keep in mind that you are here in C City's Central Hospital. You are in good hands."

Sister Jiang quickly tried to encourage me. "It's not easy for the doctor. Did you even know that he also has a PhD? And he has been working for more than sixty hours straight. He has done several dozen operations on this shift, saving the lives of so many critically ill patients. If it wasn't for him, those poor patients would have been done for. But there are still many patients who only see the superficial side of things. They think that doctors make too much money, and in their eyes we are nothing but a bunch of walking ATMs. In reality these doctors have been pushing themselves to the limit. You should see how many lives they have saved; you wouldn't believe how many souls they have pulled from the jaws of death. This isn't some private clinic where you can just throw money around and get your way. These doctors are all public servants; just like you, their sole mission is to serve and save the people." She flashed the doctor a knowing look and took my wallet out.

The doctor didn't seem to have any interest in the wallet. He knit his brow. "I'd like to insert a gastric tube to thoroughly empty the contents of your stomach," he said resolutely, "which should give you some relief. I suspect you might be retaining something in your stomach."

"But I haven't eaten anything in more than three days. All I did was drink some water." I felt like a deflated balloon.

"And what is that supposed to prove?" The doctor stretched his long skinny fingers like a professional concert pianist. "From a medical perspective, the less you find, the more likely that something is there."

His words seemed to convey some deep philosophical truth, but it didn't make any sense to me. However, lacking any professional medical training, I had no basis for refuting what he said. "Is there any way we can skip the gastric tube?" I softly pleaded. I stared at his long white laboratory jacket, which bizarrely reminded me of those shiny black plastic military uniforms.

The doctor tried to suppress his disgust. "Are you really that scared of pain? With pain comes happiness. It is a simple principle. Don't you get it? Haven't you even been to a hospital before?"

In my state of desperation, I relaxed my clenched fists and tried my best to pretend that the pain didn't bother me. I didn't want the doctor to think I was weak, but he appeared frustrated.

"Let me just tell it to you straight. I'll make it crystal clear: the hospital has one objective, and that is bringing joy to those in pain. This is the moral obligation of a doctor. My dear patient, why is it you don't have faith in us? When they talk about doctors 'treating the sick and healing the wounded,' in many cases the doctors themselves suffer the real pain, in order to bring happiness to their patients. Of course, if you really don't want to have the procedure done, you can simply refuse to sign the release. We always respect the will of our patients."

Sister Jiang chimed in. "Your doctor is right. I've seen a lot of different people seek medical help, and in some ways, it is exactly like childbirth: it might hurt at first, but the end result makes you happy. All patients come here willingly. No one ever forces anyone else to come to the hospital. But once you are here, you need to listen to your doctors. Let me say this one more time to you, Little Yang: you *need* to have faith in the hospital. You *need* to have faith in your doctors. The country invested massive sums of money into this hospital, even tapping into its foreign reserves to import medical equipment from abroad, sparing no expense when it came to the patients' best interest. You must get this wishy-washy thinking out of your head and fully commit. Otherwise the disease will take advantage of this weakness and eat you alive, one bite at a time. That is what is making your doctor so upset."

"Okay . . . ," I agreed dejectedly.

Then, as if to show just how dedicated and professional she really was, Sister Jiang paused for a moment. "Little Yang, I think I had better explain a bit more about the situation. Did you see the news? Our medical resources are lagging far below those of developed nations, and yet we must use those resources to save a population many times the size of those other countries'. We have achieved the lowest rates for medical care in the entire world, and the average life expectancy is among the very best anywhere on the planet. This was not an easy achievement. Just go to the United States to seek treatment and see what happens! It will take you at least a week to make an appointment at a public hospital, then you'll have to wait several months for your exam, and it's not uncommon then to wait another year for procedures like a simple gastroscopy. An appendicitis operation will set you back thirty thousand US dollars. If you want to have a baby, it'll be sixty thousand dollars! Here it only costs ten yuan to see a specialist, and an intravenous injection is only two yuan! Our principle here is always to put the interests of the patient first.

"Little Yang, think about those songs you have written. Are they not songs that eulogize this great era? Don't you usually look at the bright side of things? Please write a song that speaks to all of this. Corporation B is a subsidiary enterprise of the C City government, so you are actually here to write a song for the city of C. You are no ordinary patient, which is why you are receiving such a special level of care. You need to undergo a much more intensive and detailed series of treatment procedures. This is how you will acquire a truly deep understanding of how things work at the most basic levels, and hopefully your song can become a timeless masterpiece. Try to endure a bit longer. After all, doesn't everything in life involve the art of enduring? Fate has determined that in your life, you shall experience numerous challenges. Only then will you be able to blossom finally into the proper man you are destined to become. Nobody wants you to die. Once you are dead, there is nothing left. Just think about it: What would it feel like for there to be nothing left?"

I guess Sister Jiang knew exactly what made me tick. I carefully thought through everything she had said, realizing that I had no other sensation than pain. What is death anyway? I was at a complete loss. Even the different levels of Buddhist hell were gone, erased from my mind. Could it really be that the pain experienced in hell is nothing compared to the pain of the human world? I clenched my teeth in silence.

Sister Jiang and the doctor looked at each other nervously. Time in the emergency room seemed to move backward, stirring up a vortex of memories inside me. I thought back to a time when I had fallen ill as a child and my parents took me to the children's hospital. People of my generation have had a relationship with hospitals throughout their lives. We grew up on antibiotics. On the way to the hospital, my parents took turns carrying me on their backs, as if I were a baby lamb they were taking to sell at the market. I tried to squirm out of the carrier, but my parents just tightened the harness around my waist. I remember, when we arrived at the hospital, the cries of many children. When it was my turn to get a shot, my parents said, "It won't hurt . . . it'll be over before you know it. It will just feel like an ant biting you." In my mind, I imagined an ant's sharp red mouth biting me, and I burst out in tears.

"Oh, you're so brave," the nurse encouraged me. But that had only made me wail even louder.

Thinking back to that moment, I broke down crying. The sound of my sheeplike sobs alarmed Sister Jiang and the doctor. The exam room immediately fell under a hush, the dead silence of Mars. I took advantage of the moment to turn quickly and rush out of the room.

16

TO RESIST THE HOSPITAL IS TO TREAT YOUR LIFE AS A GAME

I wasn't sure if this qualified as a form of resistance, nor did I know if it would succeed. If this was resistance, I wondered if it was the first time in my life that I had ever displayed such an act of bravery. Perhaps Sister Jiang was right, and deep down I really did want to run away. After all, she had a lot of experience in these matters and was able to see things clearly. I'd been to the hospital so many times and seen so many doctors. Had there ever been a time when I didn't want to run away? Had there ever been a time when I didn't want to stop taking my medicine? Had there ever been a time when I didn't want to avoid getting a shot?

The sensation of that nurse giving me a shot as a kid left an indelible dark shadow that had lingered on in my heart. But in the end, I still decided to go along with the rules and do what I was told. I did fear death. And I clearly knew who was the boss when it came to my relationship with the hospital. What normally made me frustrated was the lack of a more effective method for getting on the good side of these godlike doctors. Actually, they were not gods but more like incarnations of the awe-inspiring Buddhist deity Yama Raja—the king of hell. These doctors held the Book of Life and Death in their hands, and etched on those pages was the story of everyone's fate. Why could I not learn to be more like those elderly patients? At least learn to do a better job at feigning indifference. But my threshold for pain had simply hit its limit. If I couldn't outsmart this doctor, was there no way to hide from him?

But there I had gone again, allowing doubt to get the best of me. This wasn't how I should take responsibility for myself! Would behaving like this make my illness go away? Hadn't I just been thinking about applying to become an honorary resident of C City?

The contradictions in my mind left me in a state of unprecedented confusion. I scurried into the corridor, and it didn't take long before I was able to disappear into the massive crowd of elderly patients where, like a child playing hide-and-seek, I squatted amid a forest of legs that resembled petrified trees.

It wasn't long before Sister Jiang came looking for me. "Little Yang? Little Yang? Where are you? Hurry up and come out!" Her anxiety had turned her voice sharp, like the sound of a glass vial being shattered.

I didn't utter a sound, remaining perfectly still.

"Hey, Little Yang! I've got some good news for you! The doctor agreed not to put in the gastric tube! He only wants to put you on an IV so you can get some fluid in your system, which will also help with your inflammation. Hurry up and come out!"

Her voice sounded so much worse when she was yelling, exposing her inner weakness.

I continued to squat there, remaining perfectly still, all the while wondering whether she was telling the truth. And yet I couldn't detect anything wrong from the tone of her voice. She just wanted to do her job, which was to do what was genuinely in my best interest.

I started to regret my actions when I realized I must have made the doctor angry. How could I have become the kind of person that acts like that? Among all the stupid things one can do in the world, going against the hospital is perhaps the worst; it amounts to treating your life like a game. And yet I squatted even lower, to the point that I was almost lying on the floor. That was the moment I caught sight of Sister Jiang, on the verge of tears. She turned to walk in the opposite direction, and I immediately stood up and called out to her: "Sister Jiang!"

She whirled around and gazed at me with a look of tortured love. I obediently followed her back to the exam room. The doctor had already finished his paperwork and was just about to apply his stamp. But his ink had dried, so he opened the metal cabinet behind him, revealing a row of test tubes filled with fresh blood. He popped one of the tubes open and poured some blood onto his seal. As he put that nice red stamp to the paper, it felt like he was striking me right in the heart.

I swallowed my pain, offered a slight bow, and said, "Thank you."

The doctor handed the paper to Sister Jiang. "That's it."

Sister Jiang affectionately squeezed my wrist. "Soon you will no longer be in pain. But I'm going to have to run back to the hotel. There are a lot of customers waiting, and we have a shortage of staff. I just received a new assignment from my manager. Someone else drank the mineral water."

"What about me?" I had the urge to grab onto her sleeve like it was a life preserver.

But at that moment I heard the sound of a massive explosion. Flames danced, thick smoke filled the air, people screamed and started running in every direction. The hospital was thrown into chaos.

17

THE LIVING BODHISATTVA OF GREAT COMPASSION

When the explosion hit, Sister Jiang sheltered me with her body. Then she took me by the hand, and we ran. She told me to hide in one of the public bathrooms. My entire body was shaking, and I tried not to move, but it felt like it was the end of the world. Sister Jiang was bleeding heavily, and she left me alone while she went to see if she could find out what had happened. It wasn't long before she returned with the news.

"A family member of one of the patients attacked the hospital with a bomb."

"What?"

"One of the patients' family members just bombed the hospital."

"Why?"

"They are saying that the perpetrator's wife died during laparoscopic surgery for ectopic pregnancy. He is blaming the hospital for what happened, because as the patient was hemorrhaging, her doctor failed to insert a central venous catheter and administer other lifesaving procedures. He sued the hospital, but the court ruled in the hospital's favor, so he came to take his vendetta against the hospital to the next level."

"Did anyone die?" In addition to my pain, I was assaulted by a powerful stench of urine. I felt like all the blood in my veins was going to congeal into a ball of muddy paste.

"The perpetrator killed himself in the attack, but it is still unclear if there were any casualties on the hospital side."

Many people hid out in the bathroom, both men and women, feverishly discussing what had just happened. One of them claimed that the perpetrator had actually been attempting to blow up the hospital representatives, who are sent by the pharmaceutical companies to promote drugs and medical equipment. They offer lavish meals, entertainment, and kickbacks to entice doctors to use their company's products, forcing more patients into more exams and more prescription medications. Always secretive in their actions, these medical reps are like the true power brokers working behind the scenes in the hospital. I sneaked a peek through the crowd and could see that the rest of the hospital was still in a state of utter chaos. The hospital security guards were running all over the place, and police officers had appeared on the scene. But I couldn't tell who the hospital reps were.

Other patients said that the true target of the attacker was the VIP patients in the sick ward reserved for cadres, whose expenses are covered by taxpayers, and that the attacker was upset that more than 80 percent of the national health care allowance was spent on the cadres.

I took another look at Sister Jiang and discovered a hole in her chest that was gushing blood. Out of curiosity, I inserted my finger to see if it would stop the bleeding. Sister Jiang slapped my hand away and flashed me a wicked stare before using her clumped-up bra to press against the wound.

"Go find a doctor," I pleaded.

But she just shook her head. I figured I should just forget it, then. Meanwhile, my pain mingled with the assaulting stench of piss, shit, and blood.

Sister Jiang took a deep whiff and said, "Since I see we have a bit of free time, I'd like to stress again the points I made before." She launched into a speech that was both in depth and instructive, and what she said would remain with me for the rest of my life.

This is what she said: "Everything I tell you is of the utmost importance. You must not forget. You saw with your own eyes what just happened here. This is a tragedy that should have never occurred. In a little bit, I'm going to leave, and once I'm gone, the most important thing to remember is that no matter what happens, *never* get into an antagonistic relationship with your doctor. That is something that a good patient should *never* do. You must take time to understand your doctor. Sometimes we might think that they have a peculiar disposition, but that is because we only see things from the perspective of the patient. People suffering from chronic illnesses tend to be extremely picky, and they are unable to see things objectively. Instead their minds are twisted, torn apart, and the slightest problem makes them hysterical. They remain completely oblivious to their own limitations. Little Yang, please don't be upset by what I'm about to tell you. I'm only trying to do what is in your best interest. When it comes down to it, the hospital treats the illness and not the patient, which is all they need to do. Moreover, these doctors are normal people made of flesh and blood. They have all the same emotions and desires that you and I have. In that sense, they are kind of like engineering students. Don't tell me you also expect them to be stand-up comedians? It's too much for them. Their only professional responsibility is to cure disease. Cheering up patients is not part of their job."

She spoke as if she were passing on instructions for after her death, which made me feel even more ashamed. I quietly affirmed that I was taking everything in.

Sister Jiang continued. "Doctors are normal people, but something sets them apart from others. They are different from those traditional Chinese medicine practitioners who pass their teachings on generation after generation. Instead they are like a new breed of human; after all, in our country this profession has only existed for a hundred years. They attend the very best medical schools, where they receive strict modern professional training. Do you know how they learn to conduct an autopsy? When you went to school you learned from print books, but their textbooks are actual human cadavers. Patients have no right to stand side by side with them. Only doctors can truly perceive the truth behind the mysteries of life and death.

When someone achieves that level of understanding, what else could they possibly care about? These men and women wearing long white jackets appear cold and detached, even wooden and uncaring, but that is only because they see on a higher level than we do. When they step into the operating room, their professional skills truly shine, like when a professional athlete steps onto the court. When they get to work, conditioned reflexes take over, which help to ensure that they never make a mockery of things by combining their patients' lives with their own professional careers. When it comes right down to it, they are manifestations of the Living Bodhisattva of Great Compassion wielding a surgeon's knife."

When I heard that, I thought, *Isn't that the same as Yama, the king of hell?* I stared in shock at Sister Jiang, listening intently to each and every word of the speech she had memorized. My brain was reduced to a puddle of mush. On the one hand, laymen decide the course of treatment, while on the other, doctors make the big decisions. I had trouble truly understanding the relationship behind this contradiction, but for the time being, I decided just to let it go.

By this point, Sister Jiang was in so much pain that she collapsed in my arms, her body trembling. I continued to hold her tight, even as her face went expressionless and her limbs began to grow cold. Her blood flowed over my chest and dripped down over my stomach, which added some cozy warmth and colorful excitement to my pain. What really shocked me was that, even at this moment, Sister Jiang was able to maintain a stunningly high level of logical thinking and clarity of speech. Everything she said came straight from her heart without an ounce of pretension or exaggeration. Her entire body seemed to rise into the air like the glorious Saint Rui ascending. This hospital indeed had created a true miracle.

As if returning from the brink of death, Sister Jiang spoke. "You can understand why some doctors would accept red envelopes stuffed with gift money. Haven't you seen people at the temple leaving cash in front of the statues of Buddha? There is no other profession that requires anyone to work so hard, assume such huge responsibility, and take so many risks.

Doctors are dealing with life itself, and they are not allowed to make even the slightest mistake. It's not like they're writing some frivolous songs. Their job is not part of the service industry, like most people imagine. They're not selling vegetables or cutting hair or doing some other job that allows them to make mistakes. There is nothing more priceless than a human life. And yet they take it upon themselves to deliver all living creatures from suffering, receiving a low salary from the government, an insult to those who spent nearly a decade tirelessly studying in order to perfect their craft. Let's not forget the fact that they must spend many more years in college than most young people. They actually operate at a loss. Little Yang, think about all of the people who get paid so much for just idling away their time every day. Does that sound fair to you? But there is nothing we can do. This is simply the situation in our country during this period. Everything is in a state of mutual conflict, and there is no use wasting time thinking about it. But those doctors deserve that extra money. It is an expression of human dignity. They accept those red envelopes for the patients' sake. It is the doctor's way of setting their patients at ease, so that no one will be anxious when it comes time for surgery. And so accepting that money is actually a doctor's greatest expression of benevolence."

I thought of my own department, where we were terribly over-staffed, everyone did a perfunctory job and shirked responsibility, and no specialized training was required, a job where we could forget about lofty ideals like benevolence, righteousness, love, and trust. Instead the people in my office jumped at every chance to attack one another. Some of them wished they could literally stomp the life out of their colleagues. They became ecstatic when they learned that one of their other coworkers was sick. But here in the hospital, I had seen each and every doctor exhibit the utmost level of professionalism firsthand, work-ing themselves to the point of exhaustion, sometimes nearly to death. Every department cooperated with the others, offering a seamless expe-rience for patients. Some doctors could perhaps have benefitted from an improved attitude, but every action they took was aimed at giving patients a better chance at survival. They were truly the vanguard of our nation. I mechanically nodded my head.

Sister Jiang's face had turned pale, and the wound in her chest trembled like a pair of lips, spurting fresh blood. I wanted to stick my fist in the wound to stop the bleeding, but I couldn't bring myself to move. Yet like a soldier standing her ground, Sister Jiang bravely continued, with seemingly no regard for her own safety. "Little Yang, take a look at this! There they go again, twisting and distorting the true relationship that ordinary people have with our dear bodhisattvas!"

I had no choice but to agree. These contradictions were extremely difficult to resolve. I responded, though not without some apprehension, "This is really terribly wrong. I'm so sorry." But almost immediately I realized that I myself was also guilty of offending the hospital. I was every bit as bad as that suicide bomber. Whether we refer to them as manifestations of bodhisattvas or Yama, the king of hell, doctors are all gods, and yet, in this era where all things have become entangled and turned upside down, doctors are now considered a weak and marginalized group. And we could blame all of this on the patients. The question was, Who made us sick in the first place?

Sister Jiang then left me with some final words. "After I leave, I'll have Little Tao come by to keep you company tonight. Try not to look down on the fact that he is so young; he, too, has a lot of wonderful hospital experience."

At that moment a young boy, around ten years old, suddenly appeared out of nowhere. He rushed toward me with his lips parted, as if he were laughing. At first I thought he was Sister Jiang's son. Perhaps mother and son both worked for the hospital, serving side by side for this glorious enterprise. But where was Sister Jiang's husband? Had he drunk himself to death too? I really didn't want Sister Jiang to leave me, but leave me she did, abandoning me at the hospital.

I felt a terrible sense of loss and wondered, What could be awaiting me next?

18

WARM-UP FOR A LONGER AND MORE DIFFICULT ROUND OF TREATMENT

The chaos surrounding the bombing was quickly brought under control. It didn't take long before order was restored, as if nothing had ever happened. The patients resumed their Brownian motion before again moving collectively in the same direction.

My final glimpse of Sister Jiang was of her stiff body, covered from head to toe under a white cloth as an orderly carted her away on a flatbed wagon, like a sacrificial offering being brought to the temple of the gods.

Little Tao led me to the observation room. I knew that this marked a turning point in my long march to see a doctor. It meant that they were on the verge of moving my case forward with some practical action. All of the investments I had made to this point were about to pay off. Sister Jiang had arranged everything for me. There was finally hope for some relief, if not total release, from the pain I had been feeling. In my heart I felt that I was on the verge of coming back from the dead. At the same time, it felt like this was a brand-new beginning. I would be laying a foundation for tomorrow, which would bring with it a B-mode ultrasound, a CT scan, gastroscopy, colonoscopy, bronchoscopy, electroencephalogram, lung-function exam, cardiac imaging test, functional magnetic resonance mammography, nuclear medicine scan, tissue biopsy, and other more thorough tests and exams. Everything before had been but a warm-up for a longer and more difficult round of treatment, like the initial ascent up a mountain for a spiritual retreat, with the gorgeous scenery and transcendent views still to come. My illness must truly be quite serious, even though I still had absolutely no idea what was wrong with me. Nothing was more dangerous than what I was about to go through. Thank goodness I had come to this hospital.

I eagerly awaited my final salvation.

The observation room was just over ten meters wide and felt like a dark cave. There were four beds, one in each corner of the room, three of them occupied by elderly patients who all looked cold and broken. All three sat up in bed to look me over, their eyes gleaming with timid joy at the arrival of this young patient. They would have someone to take their place, and they could at last cast off this earthly shell and begin the process of reincarnation. Decked out in a tracksuit, Little Tao stuck close to me, like a personal bodyguard. But I wasn't particularly fond of having this little devil hanging around.

"Why don't you go?" I asked him.

"With you in this much pain, how am I supposed to leave?" Little Tao flashed me a cute and lively smile, but somehow it made him look old.

"Don't worry, I can handle it. I'm an old veteran patient." I didn't want him to feel any kind of psychological burden about leaving.

His face suddenly turned serious. "Do you even realize why you were brought to this hospital?"

"I . . . I don't know," I stammered. At first I had considered saying that I was here to authenticate my own identity and strengthen my faith in the hospital and the doctors.

"So you could stay alive! Yang Wei, do you have any idea how many people who slept on that bed have died?" Little Tao had a long face as he sternly pointed to the sickbed I was about to lie on. The filthy bedsheet was soiled with bloodstains and carried faint black outlines of the bodies that had once lain there. Little Tao adopted a mature, adult tone. "It is only the beginning. The long dark night is descending. This will be the most dangerous period, and some of the patients won't make it. Many will perish, their lives forever extinguished. For those who don't make it, the hospital's treatments will have been wasted. How will they ever make it up to those hardworking doctors and nurses? I am frankly quite worried; after all, Sister Jiang left me with the task of keeping you alive." Little Tao winked at me before running off, but he returned in no time at all with a new bedsheet, which he spread out directly on top of the old, dirty one. I'm not sure where he got them, but he also managed to find me a blanket and pillow. He tapped me on the shoulder, motioning for me to lie down. He even helped me remove my shoes. I had no choice but to crawl into the bed, where I curled up like a shrimp, trying to withstand the pain. The pain reminded me that I was still alive, so I supposed I still hadn't let the people from the hospital down yet. It was then that a dark, clammy wave that reminded me of condensed milk flashed through my body, the kind of cold chill you normally feel only at a cemetery. I started to get nervous.

A female nurse suddenly walked into the room, accompanied by an angelic breeze of sunshine and warmth. She approached a female patient that had been curled up on a bed in the corner and gave her a caring pat on the back. She then grabbed the patient's index finger and moved it up and down. As she did, the nurse asked, "Up?"

The patient repeated, "Up."

The nurse said, "Down?"

The patient responded, "Down."

The nurse said, "That's right. You're still alive." She repeated it over and over again before removing the patient's socks, exposing her bloated feet. The nurse tickled the patient's feet, and she giggled with glee. The nurse joined her in laughter.

In another corner of the room lay an elderly patient with big ears and a face covered with long whiskers like pig bristles. He seemed agitated and kept tossing back and forth, making the frame of his bed creak and rattle chaotically. But soon he tired himself out and fell asleep.

The booming sound of his snores shook the entire room like a tsunami crashing down upon us.

The nurse walked over and gently patted him on the head. "I see you've still got some life left in you yet." She seemed to be put at ease by the fact that he hadn't yet dropped dead, and she moved on to the next patient.

I was moved by the nurse's interactions with her patients. Here in the observation room, a harmonious relationship remained between patients and caregivers. This helped reduce my anxiety.

Lying in another corner of the room was a skinny woman around sixty, so thin that she looked like a piece of paper that might flutter away in the wind. Her large eyes protruded from her sunken sockets, and her dry, cracked lips shone bright red. She turned to me and asked, "What's wrong with you?"

But before I could even answer, Little Tao interrupted. "We are still waiting for all the test results to come back."

"Where do you work?" the woman asked, and, again, Little Tao responded for me. "I'm quite envious," the woman said. "No wonder you got admitted so quickly."

I wasn't thrilled with her comment and asked, "What's wrong with you?"

"I'm suffering from rubidium deficiency disease."

"What's that?"

"My body lacks rubidium."

"What are the symptoms?"

"I can't turn on."

"You can't turn on?"

"I can't turn on my man anymore. There are no sparks left and not a damn thing I can do."

"Is that an official medical diagnosis?"

"Of course."

"So . . . you need to take medicine and get an IV infusion to increase your rubidium?"

"That's right. My, aren't you the bright one?"

Feeling a cold wind on my cheeks, I scanned the room and sensed that some kind of unspeakable secret must be hiding behind these stone walls. For the very first time, I realized that all I had seen and experienced was simply a superficial manifestation of something else. It dawned on me that I had never truly taken the time to ponder the nature of this world, and the discovery left me feeling helpless and exhausted. My only fear was that all of the problems I had been suffering were but the beginning of my real pain.

On the wall directly across from me was a dark-red steel door. My eyes widened as I gazed with a deathly stare at its opaque black letters: MORGUE.

19

A PORTRAIT OF THE FUTURE WORLD

That's right, the morgue. The very place that writers use as the backdrop for tales of horror, the setting for so many stories of the supernatural. Who would have imagined that it had been right here all along? I thought I could see Sister Jiang's bloody corpse lying there. Even after her voyage to the other world, she still couldn't let go of me.

I could hear her voice echoing in my ear. "Perhaps you think it is utterly inconceivable, but every person is destined to encounter a situation like this."

Suddenly the door to the morgue opened, and a beautiful young girl with pristine features emerged. She carried a basin filled with hot water, went over to the female patient, and started to wash her feet. The patient introduced her as her daughter.

The entire room filled with a foul stench. The female patient splashed her feet in the water basin as she chatted. From the looks of it, these patients had all become good friends. But experience had taught me that patients are forever in competition with each other, while at the same time, they also frequently help each other out, forming temporary mutual aid groups to encourage one another to carry on living, and exchange stories about their experiences interacting with the hospital.

I learned that some of the patients had been in the hospital for months, years, or even decades. Day after day, they spent all of their time indoors, running into one another in the hallways, up in the eaves, and out in the atrium, like a troop of mandrills, the hospital their den.

It was quite a feat for them to carry on their devoted practice of self-cultivation for so many years.

Have you read *Journey to the West*? For those on their way to retrieve the true scriptures, the observation room was an important transfer station along the way. Anyone who desired to get to this place first had to accumulate enough money. Many wiped out their family savings, borrowed from their friends and relatives, and sold off their property. They came to the hospital with cash, credit cards, and bank statements in hand, but so much still depended on what mood the cashier happened to be in that day, and their greatest fear was that the cashier would take one look and say, "Not enough!" And just as one prepares incense sticks for the bodhisattvas before going to the temple, they prepared red envelopes filled with cash for all the doctors. Since they often couldn't get an appointment right away, they also needed to stay at a hotel or rent a room near the hospital. All of the apartments near the hospital were originally for physicians, but after the doctors bought nicer homes, they subleased their apartments to black-market housing agents, who then doubled the price and rented them to patients. Patients showed up with their own cooking supplies and then began the long arduous wait, all the while begging various friends, calling on old favors, or trying to pay people off to get their names on the long list to be seen at the hospital. When people were finally seen by a doctor and successfully squeezed their way into the observation room, their next grand objective was to find a way to be formally admitted into a treatment ward. Some patients had been through this many times, like the elderly man with the big ears. I'm told that he was originally in awesome shape—he wasn't on any medication and would jog for ten miles a day—but one day he happened to see a hospital advertisement and was quite moved. He went to have a CT scan to look at his heart, and his doctor told him that his calcium index was too high and a coronary angiography was required. Within a fairly short period of time, the patient had five stent implants and needed high doses of prescription medication, which not only put an end to his jogging but also sent him into a depression. He started to visit the hospital compulsively, and over the course of the next decade, he ended up getting twenty-four stent implants, several bypass grafts, and thirty-six coronary angiographies, which gradually drained his savings. Meanwhile, he was constantly paranoid that he might get sick; even the slightest discomfort would drive him straight to the hospital, and only additional time in the observation room would calm him down.

The patients enthusiastically exchanged stories about their medical experiences, as if the hospital were the best place to contemplate the nature of truth in the world. As they talked, they occasionally flashed me strange, secretive glances. The room clearly lacked enough oxygen— at least there was plenty of uranium—and everyone grew tired as they spoke until, one after another, they fell asleep. But I didn't dare close my eyes. I was afraid that something terrible might happen if I fell asleep. I guess I didn't quite understand this world, but in the end, I still went to sleep—only sleep can make me forget the pain.

The nurse pranced over and attached me to an IV infusion bottle. I kept waking up, and at some point, I noticed that the infusion bottle was empty. Meanwhile, Little Tao kept coming in and out of the room, appearing and disappearing like a shadow.

At some point I noticed that the door to the morgue had opened again. A man and a woman emerged and walked over to my bed. They looked like my boss and his assistant—my boss had come in person to check on me! I suddenly felt both excited and embarrassed. My dear boss had come all this way to see me, gracing C City with his presence. Had he taken a commercial flight? Or hitched a ride on the Monkey King Sun Wukong's magical cloud? Had the hotel or the hospital informed him that I was ill? These questions raced through my mind as I tried to prop myself up in bed to show my respect, but my boss's warm hands reached out and gently guided me back down.

He spoke to me in a deep, kind voice. "You need to relax. Focus on getting better. Only when you recover will you be able to get back to work. As long as the department is here, you won't have to worry about the medical expenses. You can get back to your songwriting once you are better. Corporation B hired you to write that song for them, and it is an organization with a lot of influence, a major corporate player here in C City. The CEO of Corporation B is actually the city's first prince. The quality of your song will have a big impact on one of Corporation B's major projects, a national project that will have international impact and even alter the future of C City and the entire country. That is why so many people are taking care of you, now that you are sick. You must treasure this opportunity. Establishing a relationship with Corporation B is the only way our division can strengthen ties with C City. What you see here in C City is a portrait of the future world. The division is counting on you. You fell ill at just the right time. Never run away from the hospital, and even more importantly, never get into any disagreements with the doctors or nurses, or all of our efforts to this point will have been in vain."

I was overwhelmed by this unexpected gesture of kindness. I'd had no idea that this was why my boss had sent me to C City. Not only had he not reprimanded me, but on the contrary, he had offered me nothing but consolation and encouragement. He and his assistant had even brought me a flower basket and a fruit basket. I was filled with a mixture of regret and gratitude, and I told myself that, once I recovered, I would work even harder not to let down my boss. I had used to think work was boring, but from that point on, I committed to exorcising those thoughts from my mind. I was so choked up with emotion that I bit down on the corner of my blanket. But then the pain returned, pain so bad that, in an act of immeasurable shame, I passed out right there in front of my boss.

I'm not sure how long I was out, but I awakened to discover that my boss and his assistant were long gone. Oh, I hoped they weren't disappointed in me. I felt my heart throb when I noticed the basket of flowers next to my bed. They were lilies, the kind people bring to funerals. Little Tao tore the basket open to reveal a pile of insects with sharp claws and long fangs. He opened up the fruit basket, and the longan fruit were moldy, the apples were rotten, the dragon fruit was infested with maggots, and the tangerines were so badly decomposed that a thick pus dripped from them. Little Tao didn't seem to be in the least bit fazed. He simply smiled and handed the basket to me so I could inspect it. I turned away and caught sight of some black object beside my bed, a pile of dead bugs mixed with the broken remains of an old flower basket. It had to have been left by a previous patient.

Despite my pain, regret, panic, and numbness, I gradually fell back asleep. I'm not sure how much more time passed before I was finally finished with that seemingly worthless infusion drip. As I slipped in and out of consciousness, I could see the nurse's silhouette walking back and forth. Eventually she approached my bed and swiftly removed the bloody catheter needle from my arm. I thought she might tell me something, but she didn't offer a word of explanation.

Meanwhile, I was still intent on getting rid of Little Tao. "Now that I finished the infusion drip," I told him, "I really don't need anyone to keep me company. Just give me some time to rest by myself for a while."

Little Tao replied reluctantly, "Okay, I'll come back first thing tomorrow morning to check on you."

Once Little Tao had gone, I found myself staring at the door to the morgue again. I could feel something twisting inside me. I hesitated for a moment, wondering if I should attempt to carry out my plan. Nothing had felt right since the moment I checked into the hospital. My division had sent me to C City. As soon as I arrived at my hotel, I had drunk a bottle of mineral water, which made me suddenly fall ill. Two hotel employees had appeared out of nowhere and taken me to the hospital, sending me down this path of no return. I had fallen into a trap; this was all clearly part of some conspiracy. And yet I dared not tell a soul that I harbored these thoughts.

It was the middle of the night. The entire world was sound asleep. After a long inner battle, I finally made up my mind: I packed my belongings, including my medical records, test results, and exam referrals, which I would need to submit to my insurance company for reimbursement. Then I slid off my bed and bid farewell to that iron door. Everyone in the room was asleep except the daughter of that patient suffering the rubidium deficiency. She flashed me a strange look as I slipped out of the room.

20

THE OUTSIDE WORLD IS THE
REAL SICK WARD

In the dead of night, the corridor seemed to go on forever, a long, dark, cold, humid tube. Visibility was limited to just a few feet. Piles of patients with indistinct features lined the corridor, some in sickbeds, others slumped over benches. It was hard to tell who was alive and who was dead. Some sat crookedly with their eyes closed, IV drips attached to their arms. I also caught sight of that nurse, helping a doctor extract spinal fluid from a patient, who kept bowing but didn't utter a single cry. I crept forward, careful to avoid their detection. I really thought I was going to escape, but I felt like a corpse crawling out of my casket. At the same time, I told myself, *I'm not running away. I finished my intravenous drip. I'm better now. I'm no longer in pain. I am perfectly justified in checking myself out of the hospital. Important tasks await me. I have a corporate theme song to write, a song of national importance* . . . the image of my boss appeared before me, and I'm not sure why, but this became my motivation to escape, even though I wasn't entirely sure if escape might be against his wishes.

I made it only a few steps before the pain started up again. I collapsed to the floor, which was covered in blood, dirty water, and excrement. I lay there for a long time, trying to collect my strength, before I was finally able to get back to my feet. The elevator was off for the night, so I had no choice but to take the stairs. It was quite a feat to make it back up to ground level, and when I got there, I rushed straight for the main entrance. I could see C City outside, this strange city of secrets, rising like a holy mountain, its jagged peaks extending as far as the eye could see, lit by millions of lights that reflected in the river . . . but the large glass doors at the entrance were sealed shut. I was caught between yin and yang, this world and the next. I stood there, filled with fear and anxiety, but there was no way out.

And then I noticed a vast sea of people outside the entrance, thousands of short old men and women standing like dusty old pottery figures excavated from some deep dark place. Desolate and determined, they held umbrellas, as if they were stubbornly waiting for something, their faces saying, "I want to live." The night fog rolled in and billowed up behind them, making their bluish-white silhouettes appear as if they were levitating just above the ground. They were here in search of medical treatment. They had arrived in the middle of the night just to line up and wait to get in. When the hospital opened its gates in the morning, they would rush in and fight over registration numbers. Without a number, they would be as good as dead.

I started to feel like the city itself was the real sick ward, the outside world the real hell. The old-timers had figured that out before everyone else, and that's why they were trying to escape their miserable situations. They foresaw all of this; they were the soothsayers. Their wisdom and experience taught them to look at the hospital as a place of refuge. They were the only ones truly qualified to escape; as long as they could take refuge in the hospital, hand themselves over to the care of the doctors, they could escape the coming apocalypse and leave the eternal punishment of this kingdom of hell behind. So what did it mean that I was trying to get out?

I should have written a confession to atone for my choices. The pattering rain continued. The sky was dark and gloomy, with cold that cut to the bone. The elderly patients waiting outside wore solemn looks, muttered silent incantations, and moved in unison as they commenced their communal rites of prayer. I frantically turned around to discover that the main hall was completely deserted. All I could see was a faint white light reflecting on the bilingual Chinese and English signs: REGISTRATION, BILLING, CASHIER, PRESCRIPTIONS. But wait! Those were not words. They had long thin translucent angel wings, twisting and growing and transforming before my eyes. They took flight into air filled with the thick smell of disinfectant, but their flight was hindered by the tightly locked steel doors between each room in the building. They fell to the ground, resting their wings against the walls, windows, pillars, and railings. The remaining lights in the dungeon-like emergency room shone brightly through the darkness, illuminating the hospital like a majestic temple of the gods preparing to welcome the daily rush of visitors. Having borrowed the hospital as a disguise to conceal itself, it gazed upon me, most likely trying to discern whether I was a true believer . . . or a heretic.

The doctors and nurses must have long known that many like me would endure terrible physical suffering in order to plot an escape. How could you not try to treat someone who is sick? This was too dangerous! Like those crowds of old people lined up in the night, I, too, needed to cultivate myself, to reach a state of absolute loyalty to the hospital. I couldn't allow myself to get dragged back by those women from the hotel.

I had reached a dead end. No, that's not right, there *was* a way forward: go back to the hospital. The hospital always opened its doors to me. I had never actually left.

Little Tao appeared suddenly before me, like a magical soldier descending from heaven, his hands on his hips as he flashed me a reproachful smile. I lowered my head in shame.

And so, with Little Tao leading me, I willingly made my way back to the observation room. Why had I ever wanted to escape? The hospital was the only place truly trying to protect me, the only place truly looking out for me. The air inside remained absolutely atrocious, but even if I died of suffocation, at least I would get treatment! I was forced to admit that I was indeed sick. Something was terribly wrong with me. I was suffering from a serious illness, all because I drank a bottle of mineral water.

TREATMENT

21

PAY THE FUEL SURCHARGE
FOR HOSPITALIZATION

I stayed in the observation room until dawn, when Little Tao accompanied me for a B-mode ultrasound and a CT scan. Apparently my condition was serious, yet no one was willing to disclose what was wrong with me. After getting my results, my doctor wanted to admit me. Little Tao led me to the admissions department, but we were told that all the sickbeds were full, and the wait time for a bed was one year. Since Sister Jiang was dead, Little Tao called Ah Bi and asked her to pull some strings, and only then was I finally admitted.

During the prepayment authorization process, the hospital provided me with a bill that listed all my expenses. Besides charges for treatment, medicine, the room, and meals, plus a caregiver fee and the bathroom surcharge, there was also a hospital construction fee, a fuel surcharge fee, an elevator overload fee, an environmental maintenance fee, a general safety fee, and a fire safety fee, among other charges. The cost for each item was clearly indicated. I didn't dare question any of the charges; they already had my wallet, anyway. It was out of my hands. As things moved forward, I realized that this was not a simple economic transaction but much deeper: the patient's fulfillment of a professional obligation to the hospital, a way to make good on an unspoken promise to the hospital . . . a demonstration of the patient's faith.

Little Tao acted as my guarantor. "You are an esteemed guest here in C City," he told me, "so be sure to let me know if you run into any money problems. If you don't have enough cash, I can always help you take out a loan from the hospital, whose interest rates are only slightly higher than the bank's. I've also been in touch with the department where you work. Didn't your department head come by to visit you? They said that there would be no problem reimbursing you for any medical or out-of-pocket expenses."

With that he shook my hand in a rather aloof manner and, having fulfilled his obligation, turned to leave. I stood there for a long time, gazing at this kid's weeping willow–like silhouette as it retreated into the background. The whole thing felt like a dream.

The admissions department was located behind the outpatient department, and the two were linked by a long intestine-like corridor. This area of the hospital was composed of a series of gray-and-white volcano-shaped buildings, the top portions of which were swallowed up by the clouds and mist, and yet I could make out a shining red cross jutting out from the very highest point, like a supernova piercing through a vast blanket of darkness, emitting its dazzling light in all directions, cutting through the heavy rain and thick fog surrounding those cold and lonely gods, immersing the entire world in a flush of light like a dose of healthy chicken soup, bringing people hope for the earth to undergo a true rejuvenation. Seeing that cross made me remember how long it had been since I had seen the sun. Just below the tower were layers of piled bricks, twisted and intertwined architectural structures attached to the main building, and an expansive construction site, all temporarily swallowed up in the dark shadow of those towering buildings, but they would never be able to stop the tide of rapid growth that followed the rain.

Upon entering the building's main lobby, I immediately saw more than a hundred elevators shuttling up and down. Like the outpatient department, the lobby was filled with a human tide, all crammed up against one another. The elevator operators were sick too. They looked like little monsters, all wearing the same dirty white uniforms that struck a marked contrast with the doctors' perfectly white jackets and gowns. The elevator operators yelled and shouted, giving them a certain air of authority. I suspected the hospital was short on staff, forcing it to hire some of the patients to operate the elevators. They wore looks of resolute happiness on their faces. A group of woman janitors in light-blue uniforms marched around the lobby in perfectly symmetrical lines, carrying their buckets of cleaning supplies.

I felt like I was in a movie that had suddenly cut to a new scene. Inspired, I picked up my pace and, after fighting through the crowd, managed to squeeze my way into one of the elevators. The elevator car felt like a steamer, the air filled with an atrocious stench, the patients packed in like sardines, and my breathing immediately became strained. Some of the patients passed out and died on the spot, but there wasn't enough room for their bodies to fall to the ground, so the lifeless corpses remained propped up against the other patients. It took a lot of effort to hold out until we made it up to floor seventy-four, where the door opened to reveal an even more expansive labyrinth, like some superstellar spaceship, and it took a long time before I finally found the doctor's office assigned to me on the registration form that the admissions department had given me.

22
HAVING A GOOD ATTITUDE IS
THE BASIC PREREQUISITE

Compared with the chaos and filth in the outpatient department, this new environment was clean and orderly, virtually untainted by dust, as if someone had quarantined the room from the rest of the world. Sitting behind a desk was a skinny middle-aged male doctor, his black hair neatly slicked back. He had an effeminate quality, his long white jacket elaborately draped over his body like an inflated kasaya, and he was completely immersed in a thick medical book written in some Western language. When he laid eyes on me, he said, "All the other doctors are in meetings or out seeing patients. I'm on duty, so let me know if you need anything." He wasn't overly warm, nor was he particularly cold; there was absolutely no sign of emotion on his clean white face.

I introduced myself and handed the doctor the receipt showing that I had paid my admittance fees. He quickly glanced at my paperwork, then opened a drawer and removed something. A copy of my chart! He must have just printed it out from the iMac computer on his desk. I could smell the fresh ink. I looked at the file and discovered that the patient ID number was correct, but I didn't recognize the name.

"You must have made a mistake," I told the doctor awkwardly.

"Is that right?" He flashed me a sidelong glance. "Are you sure *you're* not the one who's mistaken?"

"How could that be possible . . ."

"You know, some patients experience hallucinations when they come to the hospital. How can you be sure you aren't hallucinating?"

I thought back to all that I had experienced since coming to the hospital. Scenes flashed before my eyes in a montage—could my extreme pain have caused me to start hallucinating? Had I just dreamed all this up? Hmm, that would actually explain a lot. I started to feel confused. After a brief moment of panic, I said, "I really don't think I could have been hallucinating. I have a stomach issue. The pain is so bad that, at times, I feel like I could die. That's not something I could have imagined."

"Okay. So what's your name?"

"Yang Wei," I repeated.

He thought patiently before printing out another copy of my medical file. He carefully asked me about my condition again, writing meticulous notes and recording my name, age, occupation, symptoms, details of my illness, and medical history.

"What should I do next?" I asked in the spirit of cooperation, though with an uneasy feeling about what might be coming next.

"First let's get you set up with some tests." The doctor seemed to know exactly how this would play out already.

"How long do you think I will have to stay here? I still have a song to write." I hadn't forgotten the main task that had brought me to C City; that alone was enough to give me something positive to work toward. According to Sister Jiang and Ah Bi, I was an esteemed guest of the city, so I figured I should inform the hospital of this.

Through the doctor's thin skin and educated facade, I seemed to detect a mocking laugh. "Let's not be anxious, now. You can always write your songs in your hospital room. We have the best conditions of any hospital in the city, and we frequently organize various patient performances and art exhibitions. You can even attend the hospital's New Year's Eve gala. I'm sure you'll find that your presence here will be no hindrance to your creativity. In fact, it might even inspire you to new artistic heights. This is all part of our treatment program."

The doctor explained everything extremely clearly, and it felt like what I was seeing was real, that the hallucinations had passed. He gave me a haphazard look, as if sizing me up, which started to make me feel anxious. I realized that I no longer had my wallet, so I averted my gaze and looked out the window. Through the blanket of thick smog and depressing rain, I could make out a courtyard below, illuminated by the light of that shining red cross. The courtyard seemed to contain a garden, and in that garden I caught sight of a large iron cage.

I couldn't resist asking the doctor again. "Can you tell me exactly what kind of illness I am suffering from?"

"You still don't believe that you are sick? I thought you had found your faith back in the outpatient department? Having a good attitude is the basic prerequisite for treatment." This doctor was indeed the real deal. Every word out of his mouth was spot on.

I realized I had spoken out of place. I broke into a sweat and decided simply to shut my mouth and remain silent.

The doctor handed me a pile of paperwork to complete in preparation for my consultation.

"Thank you, I really appreciate your help," I told him sincerely.

I realized I would have to do all of those tests again! At least I was used to it by now, so I had more than enough mental preparation. As a hospital regular, I knew how things worked and was well aware of the risks involved in the various tests. For instance, the interaction between atoms in the human body and radiation can generate free radicals that lead to the destruction of genetic material. I also knew that tests often lead to more tests. But as Sister Jiang said, the positive impact that these tests have on advances in medicine is unparalleled. Unfortunately, I no longer had anyone to keep me company, but I knew the big picture: being admitted meant that the patient had fully given himself over to the hospital.

After a full week of exams, I finally finished most of the testing regimen that the doctor had prescribed, including many more tests than I had done in the outpatient department, and a gene sequencing exam, which was a new one even for me.

I was staying in room 168 in the General Medicine Ward. The room couldn't have been more than one hundred square meters, and forty or fifty patients were crammed inside. In sharp contrast to the outstanding environment where the doctors' offices were located, the patients' rooms were old and dilapidated, the walls filthy, some of the beds with broken legs, garbage all over the floor, cockroaches and centipedes crawling everywhere, flies buzzing all over, cobwebs in the corners, the oxygen equipment falling apart, a **BROKEN** sign on the air conditioner, the toilet in the bathroom missing its tank cover. I felt like I was back in the outpatient department.

When I arrived I had changed into a blue-striped patient gown with my name printed on it. After I had been admitted, I met a young woman named Bai Dai. She was twenty-five years old, much younger than Sister Jiang and Ah Bi. I'm not sure how it happened, but we quickly became quite close.

Bai Dai often took me for walks outside the patient ward, as if trying to cheer me up and help me adjust to the new environment here in the hospital. She seemed to be preparing me for the consultation and treatment to come. I wondered if she had treated other patients like this. I had never imagined that once I was admitted, I would meet such a warmhearted woman. Her consolation seemed to help alleviate some of my physical pain after my feeling of being lost since Sister Jiang and Ah Bi had left me.

23

ONLY WHEN YOU FALL ILL DO YOU REALIZE WHAT'S TRULY IMPORTANT

One day Bai Dai and I took the elevator down to the garden. It was so different from my room, and the garden really opened my eyes and gave me a new perspective on the hospital. Only in the inpatient department could such a heavenly garden exist, where patients had the opportunity to take their minds off of things and really focus on their recovery. Drawing from past experience, I deduced that the garden must have been constructed as part of the hospital's psychological therapy program. It was adorned with a small bridge, running streams, large ornamental rocks, small hills, and a winding path that seemed to spell out Arabic script. One stroll in the garden and all the filthy chaos and horrid stench of my hospital room was forgotten.

Bai Dai and I strolled with our umbrellas, approaching the large birdcage. Bai Dai pointed to a plaque on the cage, which read THE INDIAN PEAFOWL. Beneath those words were a few lines of explanatory text, and below that, a row of thick Chinese characters written in gold: THE BUDDHA SAYS, AS THE PHOENIX DOES NOT EXIST ON EARTH, WE HAVE THE PEACOCK TO TAKE ITS PLACE.

I stood there wondering if the hospital was more like a zoo or a Buddhist temple, the kind of question I can honestly say had never before crossed my mind. The inpatient ward was much different from my earlier hospital experience. Everything had a subtle touch, shrouded in an air of secrecy, as if the world had evolved and I was now on a higher plane. But to get to a place of inner peace, where I could accept everything, still required that I go through a certain process. No wonder the doctor kept telling me not to be anxious.

The birdcage really piqued my interest, and I tried to find the peacock, but with one glance, it was plain to see that the cage was devoid of any living thing. The empty golden cage, rusty gray from the constant rain, was bathed in the rich red glow emanating from the cross above. It seemed to pull me in, and yet there was also something slightly terrifying about it. Surrounding the birdcage were layers of flower baskets resembling a Buddhist stupa. The flowers had once blossomed in a gorgeous riot of seven colors, but over time they had all faded to black and white, like cancerous cells corrupting and destroying their former beauty. Perhaps the flowers were gifts brought by patients' families and later collected by the nurses and brought outside to the garden, creating this gorgeous site and contributing to its celebratory atmosphere, a source of happiness for long-term patients. Compared with the patients in the outpatient facility, where everyone struggles to survive, here the patients could enjoy a much more meticulous and thorough level of care.

The stone-gray complex of inpatient buildings surrounded the garden, which was like a deep valley cut off from the world, ringed by high mountains and bathed in a never-ending cloud of rain. And there we were, Bai Dai and I, a man and a woman, a generation apart, looking like sickly corpses as we strolled around the birdcage. I lost track of how many times we circled it. The misty rain persisted, with no sign of the sun or moon, yet that red glow spread along the ground like a snake chasing our shadows, extending outward and dividing into a cross, both supernatural and perfectly natural, transporting me to a place where I became lost in fanciful thoughts.

After we had walked for quite some time, Bai Dai said, "If we hadn't come out, we wouldn't have even seen the birdcage. Isn't that right, Brother Yang? That's much more important than whether we actually see the sun."

"That's right," I responded promptly. "I never imagined there would be a birdcage here! It is almost like a stand-in for a star. In some ways it is like the source of all illnesses. Now that we have discovered it, we can finally rest easy." As if I had finally found the true reason I had been admitted to the hospital, all of the sickness and pain in the world seemed to emanate from this great light. I lowered my head as we continued on our stroll. Finally I asked Bai Dai, "What kind of illness are you suffering from?"

"I probably have ureteral cancer and vaginismus. I suppose I have also been suffering from long-term attention deficit disorder. How about you?"

"I'm still waiting for my diagnosis. Or perhaps the doctors already know but just won't tell me."

"Try not to get impatient with the process. Treatment isn't something that you can do in a day."

"How long will I have to stay here?"

"Some people stay here in the hospital for their entire lives."

A cold chill combined with a hot cheer and ran down my spine. "I heard that this hospital has a lot of money. It is, after all, C City's Central Hospital. So how come the patient rooms are in such bad shape? Why don't they do some renovations?"

"Actually, the rooms aren't so bad. It's fine, as long as they match the level of the patient."

I had thought that Bai Dai would say that the conditions were a result of an overflow of patients or something like that. I wondered what exactly she meant. Was she implying that patients only deserve this level of service? Or did she mean that everything doesn't have to be so fancy, as if they're hosting the president, and that it should be fine as long as we can get used to the conditions? And then, from the top of the inpatient tower, which appeared and disappeared from behind the fog, I saw what looked like a massive green waterfall rushing down the side of the building. But it didn't look like water. I asked Bai Dai, "What's that?"

"Phlegm," Bai Dai answered. "It's all the phlegm the patients have coughed up."

I stared at the waterfall in a state of disbelief. I really couldn't imagine how all that thick, disgusting infected phlegm could transform into such a stunningly beautiful painterly vision—like something Van Gogh or Monet could have created! When matched with the red cross, the black-and-white flowers in the garden, and the dark rusty color of the birdcage, that green waterfall created a scene that was utterly intoxicating. No Hollywood special effects could ever replicate such unspeakable beauty. I couldn't help but think of the Summer Palace back in the capital.

"Brother Yang, how long did it take you to get admitted to the hospital?" Bai Dai asked.

"Hmm, I don't remember. It must have been a few days."

"Wow, so quick! You must have had someone pull some strings for you!"

"Indeed. Someone helped me out."

"Did you pay them enough?"

"Yes."

"Then they won't let you die."

"I'm not sure. I still don't even know how serious my illness is."

"Once you're here, the first step is to verify your identity. The second step is diagnosis."

"It sounds like the old saying: *Fish and bear paws, you can't have both at the same time!*"

"That's right, and then there is Heisenberg's uncertainty principle of quantum mechanics—that is very popular these days."

I had absolutely no idea what the hell Heisenberg's principle was, but I had a hunch that she was suggesting that nothing here was certain. It appeared as if everything here was certain, which actually meant that *nothing* was certain. In other words, if I could clarify my identity as a patient, I would never be able to clarify what diseases I was actually suffering from.

"This is going to sound a bit cliché," Bai Dai continued, "but it is actually quite useful. Something much more important to be certain about is this: everything that happened before you were admitted doesn't matter anymore. It is only when you fall ill that you realize what's truly important . . . and the meaning of true challenges."

Her words had a ring of philosophical truth, yet they were also fairly dialectical. This was very different from Sister Jiang's forthright manner, and frankly speaking, as a part-time songwriter, I didn't understand everything Bai Dai said. Yet I still felt so lucky to have met her.

After that point my experience with the hospital would begin to go much deeper. Only after being admitted did I realize that everything I had ever experienced before would pale in comparison to what was to come.

24

THE WORLD HAS NO USE FOR
THOSE WHO DON'T SURVIVE

Nobody knew how many sickbeds were in the general ward—perhaps somewhere between ten thousand and one hundred thousand? But the ward was staffed by an endless army of doctors and nurses. The hallways were adorned by portraits of famous figures in Western medicine, including Galen, Eurich, Bass, Vesalius, Pasteur, Pavlov, Morgan, Hartwell, Heymans, Landsteiner, Montagu, Greengard, Vaughan, and others. I heard that the hospital had commissioned an extremely famous Chinese artist to paint them. The centerpiece of the exhibit was a pair of portraits of the American James Dewey Watson and the Brit Francis Harry Compton Crick; in 1953 Watson and Crick had first proposed the double helix model of DNA, a scientific achievement on a par with the invention of the atomic bomb or putting a man on the moon. The famous Hippocratic oath was written on a large bulletin board: "I shall do everything in my power and exercise any and all methods to treat my patients. I shall never bring pain or do harm to my patients. No matter whose home I enter, providing treatment shall be my sole aim; I shall never act willfully, accept bribes, or seduce the opposite sex." I stood there carefully reading it for quite some time. Beside the oath was a list of the greatest inventions in the history of medical science, which included the microscope, the thermometer, vaccines, the stethoscope, anesthetics, fungicides, aspirin, the kidney dialysis machine, nystatin, chemotherapy, oral contraceptives, radioimmunoassays, the endoscope, the pacemaker, organ transplants, the artificial heart, cloning technology, and gene sequencing—all contributions from Western scientists spanning several different eras, which are now well managed by us. The displays, probably intended to provide the patients with extra confidence, were accompanied by quite a few full-color group photographs taken at various patient talent shows. And hanging above all of the photos and exhibition materials was a short powerful phrase, which I suspected must be the hospital's motto: **PRACTICALITY, INNOVATION, PROFESSIONALISM, DEDICATION.** There weren't any advertisements, nor were there any vendors, but a group of nurse aides was tasked with delivering meals to the patients, and those high-quality meals were professionally prepared by a trained nutritionist. They included sea cucumbers, turtles, beef, pork liver, lamb kidneys, ribs, lobster, cod, and pork-tenderloin meatball soup. But the prices were quite steep, and many patients couldn't afford these delicacies. Instead, they ate instant noodles.

Every morning the doctors came by to check on their patients. My doctor was that effeminate-looking middle-aged doctor with the neatly combed hair. His name was Bauchi. He held the title of head doctor, and he was one of the doctors who trained all the med-school interns. The younger doctors addressed him as Professor. It didn't take long before he set up an appointment for me. Meanwhile, my illness remained a mystery, and I was told that no previous examples of such an illness were in the record books.

A small shop was set up in our sick ward, and that's where I purchased a bedpan and a package of instant noodles. Since I had already handed over my wallet, they just put my purchases on my tab. There was a library in the sick ward, and all the new patients went there to borrow books. The medical books were most popular, and most were falling apart from having been read so many times. I picked out a few titles, including *How to Understand Your Lab Reports*, *Atlas of an Autopsy*, and *A Guide to Stomach Surgery*, and through these books I began truly to understand the hospital, including Heisenberg's uncertainty principle.

The patients who had been there awhile didn't read much. They were basically walking encyclopedias of medical knowledge. Most were almost as knowledgeable as the doctors, and they could go on talking for days about the various theories and practical treatments for all kinds of diseases and disorders. When they mentioned the names of the doctors at the inpatient ward, it was as if they were carefully enumerating their family's treasured belongings.

Dr. Bauchi had a strong sense of responsibility, even if he had screwed up my medical records when we first met. Then again, it may have simply been a problem with his computer, or perhaps I really was just hallucinating. Dr. Bauchi often gave patients the impression that he was quite cold, even a bit mean, but face to face, he always took the time to ask questions and explain everything patiently. He was quite generous with his time. Although he was responsible for more than one hundred patients, he remarkably knew all their medical histories like the back of his hand. Of course, it was only natural for him to lose his temper sometimes, like when a patient tried to check himself out of the hospital after not being able to take the pain of chemotherapy any longer. Dr. Bauchi screamed at the patient to stop and then spent the next two hours lecturing him on why leaving the hospital was an impossibility. By the end of his speech, every patient in the ward, including the attempted escapee, had been brought to tears.

Dr. Bauchi was extremely hands on when it came to making his rounds. He would often personally write out all of his patients' charts, never using the computer or relying on interns for that. He was also extremely understanding and considerate when it came to his interns. On one occasion I witnessed him visit the sick ward with an intern from the medical school, and after examining a patient named Old Ke, he told the student, "Please listen to those strange sounds you hear in his chest, and describe to me what you are hearing." The student listened three times but couldn't make out what the sounds were. Old Ke got scared, but Dr. Bauchi calmly reassured the student, "Give it another listen. I have faith that you'll be able to hear it."

After listening eight times, the student finally said, "The wind-like swooshing is the sound of mitral atresia."

"That's right!" Dr. Bauchi replied ecstatically. "Today marks a truly wonderful new beginning for you. It only took fifteen minutes for you to hear the sound! This is much better than having me lead you through the sounds you hear in ten different patients, because *you* heard it all by yourself!" At that moment, Old Ke passed out. Dr. Bauchi approached the patient and whispered, "Don't be nervous, I promise to invite you to our hospital's New Year's Eve gala!"

Dr. Bauchi also had a wonderful relationship with the nurses. He would occasionally joke with them, but when it came to the tasks at hand, they worked together seamlessly. The respected doctor usually stayed in the hospital, on one of the higher floors. He didn't seem ever to go home—I'm not sure if he even had a home. Having Dr. Bauchi as my doctor was the blessing of a lifetime.

Besides our three meals each day, the most exciting part of being in the hospital was treatment. There were many patients, but at least in principle, we had begun the initial stage of a customized treatment program, moving from the collective to the individual. This was the hospital's latest reform, meant to help patients adapt to their new environment. Biological data was extracted from each patient, and a specialized electronic medical file was created based on each patient's gene phenotype and diagnostic results. Based on these findings, a regimen of targeted medicine was prescribed, what people mean by "precision medical treatment." Everyone's body is different. The age of mixing up all kinds of different medicines had passed, and I was told that some of the medications in use were specifically designed for the symptoms of individual patients, based on their genetic information. These forms of treatment were, naturally, extremely expensive.

During treatment, dozens of infusion bags and bottles hung from the ceiling in a rainbow of different colors, like a sea of colorful balloons. This made the sick ward feel like an amusement park or a kindergarten classroom. The patients gleefully counted the drops of medicine entering their veins, and they got even more pleasure from adjusting the speed of their IV valves, watching the drips speed up and slow down. This rather traditional type of treatment helped set the patients at ease.

Going to the bathroom was a bit more troublesome. Because it was a communal facility, we needed to line up, and a lot of the toilets and sinks were broken. It was frustrating when the person ahead suffered from constipation, but after a while, we all learned about patience and restraint.

We grew accustomed to long lines at the window of the hospital bank to apply for loans for our treatments. The hospital bank was run by the Red Cross Benevolence Foundation. It opened once a week, on Thursday afternoons. The window was located at the end of the hall in the sick ward. Each patient had to fill out a massive pile of forms, including both medical and financial information, then go to the window to have the documents reviewed in order to determine the qualifying loan amount. With so many patients, they sometimes had to line up the night before. Eventually they figured out a way to make things easier, writing their patient numbers down on a piece of white paper in the order that they arrived and leaving these by the window. However, as soon as the window opened, the line immediately turned chaotic anyway, quickly devolving into a pushing contest.

Dr. Bauchi had actually signed a contract with me when I was first admitted to the hospital. It stated that he would refuse all attempts to bribe him with red envelopes filled with cash. I had seen other patients going to great lengths to give their doctors all kinds of gifts, often bribing them in broad daylight. I had seen people bring entire crates of fresh fruits to their doctors and others just slip gift cards and cash directly into the doctors' pockets. Some even gave cell phones and laptops. Never once did I see a doctor refuse any of these gifts, which was a terrible blow to my self-esteem. Since they had confiscated my wallet, there was no way for me to give my doctor any gifts. I couldn't figure out where the other patients were getting all this bribe money. Hadn't *they* had to turn over their personal belongings when they checked in? It looked like my experience was indeed lacking, and there was still so much I didn't understand. The strange thing was that regardless of whether they accepted any red envelopes or how much money they did accept, none of it seemed to have any impact on how the doctors did their jobs. They just continued to do what they were supposed to do.

When I was first admitted to the sick ward, there were a few female patients, but they had all passed away from various ailments, and Bai Dai was the sole surviving woman. She was a bit neurotic and rather eccentric, but also extremely sharp and intelligent, one of those young people that truly marches to her own drummer. The only bad habit she had was sneaking cigarettes behind her doctor's back. The male patients seemed to have a hard time dealing with the reality of a sick ward almost completely devoid of female patients. As soon as the doctor on duty finished his rounds—and before the nurse came to give them their next dose of medicine and administer their shots—the men immediately began to embrace each other tightly, converging together in a large fleshy mass. Their necks extended from the mass of intertwined bodies, up toward the ceiling, spitting up the putrid air that had accumulated in their lungs. Various body parts protruded from the mass, like worms twisting and shaking or on the verge of falling. It was as if they were pleading for a woman's touch but also relieving their own pain in the process. And so in this way, the patients provided help and support to one another, but as soon as a woman reappeared in their midst, they would go back to their endless infighting.

The one theme that remained unchanged in the sick ward was pain. I had grown accustomed to it. Extreme pain contorts and twists an individual to the point of becoming unbearably ugly, and that pain and ugliness contrasted starkly with the transcendent beauty of the hospital garden. With all the patients piled in together in the same room, my own pain continued to worsen.

When the pain was unbearable, I would think to myself bitterly, *Didn't they tell me that I was one of C City's most esteemed guests? Why didn't they arrange a private room for me? Will I end up like these other wretched male patients? All I did was drink a bottle of mineral water in*

my hotel room! I still haven't forgotten that I came to this city to write a
corporate song for Corporation B, but all of that feels like a lifetime ago.
Could it have been some elaborate plot to deceive me and lure me in?

It's okay, it's all nothing, I warned myself. I came willingly to this
hospital, and there was no escaping. I didn't want to escape. For the sake
of curing my illness, I had to adapt. All men are equal in the eyes of disease. Staying alive is no easy feat, but the world has no use for those who
don't survive. This sentiment was not unique to the modern era. More
than 2,300 years ago, the ancient Greek philosopher Plato said, "This is
the sort of medicine, and this is the sort of law, which you sanction in
your State. They will minister to better natures, giving health both of soul
and of body; but those who are diseased in their bodies, they will leave to
die, and the corrupt and incurable souls will put an end to themselves."

Once upon a time, I used to think that being able to write a few song
lyrics was some amazing feat, that it made me a useful member of society.
It made me feel proud. But that was no longer the case. The hospital was a
place to dispel humankind's arrogance and narcissism. With that thought
in mind, I decided not to get too close to the other male patients. This also
became the reason I ended up spending so much time alone with Bai Dai.

Then came a series of unexpected incidents.

One day, not long after I had been admitted to the hospital, Bai Dai
suddenly climbed up onto the windowsill in the sick ward. She stood
there, tall and erect, as if hoisting a flag or sounding a whistle, and she
screamed to the other patients, "Do you want to know how doctors die?"

I was caught completely off guard. She wore a blue-striped patient
gown that she had obviously made herself. It wrapped tightly around
her body. I noticed bloodstains on it, and it suddenly felt like a storm
had just whipped past me, revealing the clear, bold features of a woman
in her prime. Amid the vast gray crowd of male patients, Bai Dai was
like a fiery mermaid emanating a luminous radiance. I was utterly mes-
merized, and I couldn't help but wonder what would happen if she were
to slip into one of those white lab coats.

25

DO YOU WANT TO KNOW HOW DOCTORS DIE

Later I learned that it wasn't the first time Bai Dai had posed that question. Every so often she would scream it out loud. But when was completely up to her.

I used to go to the hospital all the time, yet I had never heard a patient say anything like that. *How do doctors die?* Who would dare to utter such words in a hospital? When the other patients heard those astounding words, the color drained from their faces, and they scurried back to their beds and hid under the covers. Who could tell what terrible things awaited them if the doctors and nurses got wind of it.

At the time I was the only one who didn't scurry back to my bed, not because I didn't want to hide but simply because medical resources were limited in the hospital—there were only about twenty beds for every forty or fifty patients. So when it came to various treatment procedures, or even sleeping, we had to take turns. Every day some were inevitably left out. Bai Dai was the only one with her own single bed. All the male patients had to squeeze in together, and they implemented a bed-sharing policy, though some still slept on the floor. As one of the new patients, there was no place for me, and I didn't know which patients to squeeze in with, so I just stood there like an idiot.

Once I got over the initial shock of Bai Dai's strange words, my imagination ran wild. At first I guessed that she had put on that little show to discourage the male patients from attempting to violate her, but it didn't take long for me to realize that that wasn't it: those other patients wouldn't dare lift a finger against her.

Bai Dai seemed surprised when she realized that, unlike the other patients, who all scurried away, I just stood there, frozen. But then she flashed me a smile and jumped down from the windowsill. Squinting her eyes, she glided over like a wandering ghost. Her gentle hands felt stiff as she took mine and led me outside the room. I felt like I was playing with a dolphin, our interactions more slippery and real than what I had experienced with Sister Jiang. Amid my hesitations, I couldn't help but feel a sense of secret pleasure.

As we walked down the corridor, I kept thinking that we would run into a doctor or nurse who would start interrogating us, but unexpectedly, every door was left open to us. Perhaps, like Sister Jiang and Ah Bi, Bai Dai was also an old face here at the hospital, with free rein in the place. Or perhaps the medical staff already knew that no one would ever try to escape—just getting admitted to the hospital was already like winning the lottery. It was so hard to get in that there was no need to take any real precautions against anyone running away, and this also displayed just how advanced and civilized the hospital was.

We went back down to the garden to look at the birdcage, which was still empty.

I wasn't really that disappointed. I had the company of a young female patient, and we could admire the birdcage and the flowers together, all of which helped reduce my pain. Bai Dai's excitement was infectious, and a wave of warmth rushed through my heart as we continued our leisurely stroll through the garden.

Just who is she? I wondered. *Why does she always stay by my side?* I sneaked glances at Bai Dai, noting how well proportioned her body was. She had piercing bright eyes and shiny white teeth, and her face had a strong, well-defined bone structure and an air of heroic confidence. Her tight-fitting outfit accentuated her curves, and on the surface, there was no indication that she might be sick. But then whenever she thought hard about something, I noticed her eyebrows contorting, squishing up like a pair of caterpillars. Her short dark hair always hung down close to her cheeks, exhibiting a perfect combination of strength and grace. She was like a bolt of brilliant lightning flashing through the dark, oppressive beauty of the hospital.

All the doors into the garden were wide open, and yet no paths led out of the hospital. It didn't matter, though, because we had no intention of leaving. We just strolled through the garden for a while before returning to the main hospital building.

When we stepped into the elevator, I was instantly assaulted by the overpowering smell of a strong disinfectant, which seemed to seep into every pore of my own skin. The smell was so intense that I realized that no peacock would ever be able to survive anywhere near that garden. I didn't think the Buddha himself would be able to survive there. And yet there was something mesmerizing about that smell. It made me think back to my childhood, when I loved the smell of gasoline. The elevator was completely transparent, like those fancy glass elevators in luxury tourist hotels that allow a view of the scenery. We could see layers of clouds enveloping the towers and those green serpentlike conveyor belts with their red copper gears, revolving incessantly as they transported an endless flow of patients into different rooms, as if they were semifinished products on a factory assembly line. At the end of the conveyor belt was a large mechanical claw that lifted them off the line and separated them into different categories. Some were coming right out of surgery, while others were probably being transferred in from other sick wards. The patients were all aware of the situation, and none of them uttered a sound. They simply gave themselves over to the mercy of the machine. I saw a few doctors and nurses wearing crisply starched white uniforms, all wearing red cross armbands and all with a solemn look, their hands behind their backs and their legs spread. Most stood motionless in the corner of every floor, like those heavenly soldiers keeping guard in the Jade Emperor's heavenly court. And like a superhero with the power to shape-shift, the hospital was no longer the place I had once thought it to be.

Bai Dai told me that I was seeing part of a newly constructed sick ward, where the hospital was experimenting with automation. I stood watching, in utter surprise at the marvels playing out before my eyes. Bai Dai and I then returned to our room, where the male patients had emerged from their beds and again converged in a fleshy mass of bodies. They were piled up near the door, squirming around on top of one another. From the mass of human flesh, arms extended like branches, pleading for help. The men's lips trembled but were completely silent. They seemed to be asking, *Where did the two of you run off to behind our backs?* A sense of jealousy emanated from them, as if they had been terribly wronged, and murderous glints flickered in their eyes. But none of them brought up the question, How do doctors die? It was as if the question were a black hole that none of them dared to face. Indeed, here in the hospital, who in his right mind would openly discuss the life and death of a *doctor*? Unless, of course, he no longer wanted to live.

When I saw the men piled on top of one another, I was struck by a deep sense of dread. What would I do if one of them jumped on me and began to strangle me? Instead of entering the room, Bai Dai just snorted and led me farther down the hall. This time we didn't take the elevator; instead, we walked up a long dark stairway. There were no lights in the stairwell, and we held hands, feeling our way through the darkness. We took periodic breaks, until we finally arrived at the highest floor of the inpatient tower. The building must have been 120 stories tall, and patients rarely ever visited the top floor. I wondered if the fact that I was able to climb so many stairs meant that I was getting better. My pain seemed to have eased a bit, and I felt like I was getting my energy back. Deep down, I felt very thankful for Bai Dai.

She dragged me over to the observation tower and urged me to look out at the view. I had a natural fear of heights, so I flashed her a terrified glance, as if she were forcing me to step out on a frozen lake, before finally mustering the courage to take a peek. The entire expansive view of the hospital complex spread out before my eyes, a majestic vista revealing towers and halls, brightly lit golden castle-like structures and dark corridors, expansive mansions and massive caves that wound in and out, rising and falling against the jagged cliffs and intermittently appearing through the layers of black clouds and the sheets of silver rain.

Bai Dai raised her hand, directing my gaze into the distance, beyond the hospital walls. All of C City was revealed before my eyes. I may have been suffering from a terrible illness, but my eyesight was still good, and what I saw in front of me was nothing short of a miracle. It felt like as long as we could see the world, it could be saved. I had traveled long and far in my lifetime and seen many things, but what I saw at that moment was a vista of true hope.

26

THE CITY IS THE HOSPITAL

This was clearly not the world I had once known. Gazing out over the city like a greedy child, I could see countless skyscrapers that seemed to surge up and down like the tide. Like the hospital tower where I stood, all of the buildings were adorned with massive red crosses, which resembled an army of giant spiders. They went on and on, row after row, like scales, one red cross after another. The scene reminded me of an ever-expansive primordial forest, where the earth and sky merge and there is no end in sight. Not only was there no sun, but even a lone star would have been burned out of the sky by the intense, all-consuming flames of those red crosses and the incessant attacks of the falling rain. They would shatter the stars, sending their remains fluttering to the ground like confetti falling on an alien landscape. Under the protective halo of this camouflage net, the illuminated names of this army of hospitals lit up the night sky: SONY TREATMENT CENTER, MICROSOFT EMERGENCY CENTER, GOOGLE COMMUNITY HOSPITAL, HUAWEI SPECIAL TREATMENT WARD, ALIBABA HEALTH CLUB, SINOPEC HEALTH CENTER, INDUSTRIAL AND COMMERCIAL BANK OF CHINA SURGERY CLUB . . . the names were endless. The skyline of signs also advertised these hospitals' and clinics' ratings and resources, background history, levels of service, software facilities, areas of specialty, awards and honors, doctors' qualifications, nurses' photos, and nurse aides' resumes. There were slogans like WE HOPE YOU CHOOSE OUR HOSPITAL FOR YOUR TREATMENT, OUR SKILLS GUARANTEE YOUR HEALTH, AUTHENTIC TREATMENT FROM ROYAL BROMPTON HOSPITAL + TRADITIONAL CHINESE METHODS PASSED ON FOR

GENERATIONS, COMPLETE SWISS ORGAN REJUVENATION METHOD, UNITED STATES OF AMERICA REGENERATIVE MEDICAL TECHNOLOGY, MARS VALLEY MINERAL THERAPY, and on and on. Across the street, some fast-food restaurants and specialty stores had been remodeled as twenty-four-hour FastMed clinics, extremely convenient for emergency patients who lived in the neighborhood. The hotel where I had been staying also had a massive red cross erected on its rooftop.

The entire city was one enormous hospital.

"Is this C City?" I asked, assaulted by a spell of dizziness. I grasped a metal handrail to stop myself from falling. I felt as if I were looking at a 4D IMAX movie about the future.

"That's right," Bai Dai responded in a matter-of-fact tone. She was a worldly person. She had seen it all.

I felt like someone had slipped me some hallucinogenic drug. I simply couldn't believe my eyes and kept shaking my head in disbelief. Was this some kind of conspiracy?

I looked at the cars below, and what do you know? Even the cars— sedans and Jeeps, delivery trucks and commercial vehicles, private automobiles and public transportation—almost every one of them had a red cross and emergency lights as they traversed the city like a pack of monsters.

The city was constantly trembling, as if it had been built on a sea of lava. Hissing screams that sounded like a massive bloodletting filled the air, the sounds of millions of ambulance sirens blazing through the city and combining with countless patients' cries for help. The sound was like a tornado encapsulating the city. Almost all of the vessels on the river were medical boats. Cicada-like helicopters, fixed-wing aircraft, and rotorcraft flew in and out of the airport, virtually all of them mobile sick wards. And in virtually every street and alley, people sang through loudspeakers: "Heal the wounded, save them from death! Practice humanitarianism! Everything we do should be in the interest of the sick!"

"Brother Yang, there is something I want to do to you." Bai Dai's voice trembled as she spoke. She extended her chest, exposing the outline of her nipples, which protruded beneath her tight shirt.

"What do you want to do?" My heart began to race. I could feel my face getting hot. I sneaked a peek at her full breasts, which made me think back to Sister Jiang's thighs. I wondered . . .

"C'mon, follow my lead," she said.

Bai Dai adopted a qigong-style stance and extended her arms like a bird's wings, exposing her armpits. I was taken aback, but I imitated her. It felt as if this were the true beginning of my treatment. After holding that pose for a while, I felt calmer and was able to expel all of those improper thoughts from my mind. I also felt less anxious. But then I suddenly remembered something.

A hazy light flashed through my mind. None of what I was seeing should have been unfamiliar. Had I really never visited this city before? No, perhaps everything was the *opposite* of what it seemed. In reality I had probably *never left* this city. I had been a citizen of C City since I was born. That must be the truth. All of that nonsense about a business trip must have been nothing more than a guise, a smoke screen, an illusion. Perhaps someone had injected false memories into my brain. I had already lived here. I had always been a regular, a frequent guest at the hospital. Actually, no, not a guest. The hospital was where I was from. I was *part* of the hospital, one of its cells. I was bacteria growing on the hospital's skin.

I suddenly remembered that I had a family—a wife and a daughter. I couldn't remember anything about my wife, but I thought my daughter was what was once called a flight attendant. Later her title may have changed to "aerial nurse," as pilots had become referred to as "mobile sick ward captains." But where was my family? Why hadn't they accompanied me to the hospital? Perhaps they, too, had been admitted?

It felt like the gun was cocked and loaded, and all kinds of crazy thoughts raced through my mind. Part of me didn't want to believe any of it, and another part of me felt like I should resign myself to this new reality. But why?

I turned to Bai Dai with a look that screamed for help. I wanted to ask her which was more important, getting confirmation about who I was or confirmation about my diagnosis.

But that would have been a stupid question to ask. Bai Dai said, "Even the recently launched manned spacecraft is no different. It, too, was retrofitted to serve as a space hospital. Certain terminal diseases cannot be treated here on Earth, so patients are now sent into space. Holes open in the outer shell of the spacecraft so that patients can directly receive cosmic ray treatment." She paused for a moment. "Brother Yang, you are not hallucinating. This is the true face of the world."

27
THE AGE OF MEDICINE

Bai Dai and I stood facing each other, our arms extended, like two lonely crosses. I could see the windows adorning the city like an army of countless pupils, as if a peacock had spread its plumes, flashing in rhythm through the air and over the land, exhaling a dark-crimson glow that also resembled a flower bursting open. Dark-green numbers and lines scrolled continually on a display screen. Perhaps they represented electrocardiograms? They seemed to tell the story of all the hearts in the city, each and every heart diseased, each and every heart in terrible pain, each and every heart nakedly crying out for treatment. On the other side of the windows were the faces of the sick, emaciated and expressionless, like sheets of wax paper.

To the southwest I saw flames shooting up into the sky. Bai Dai explained that we were seeing strains of the Andromeda virus leaking out from one of the labs. Hospital administrators had taken emergency measures to control the leak—they burned it. According to the protocol for controlling escaped viruses, in some cases entire districts were burned to the ground, transformed into wastelands incapable of treating future patients. These burns required massive amounts of fuel, which is why all patients were required to pay a fuel surcharge.

"This is the age in which we live," said Bai Dai. "The Age of Medicine."

"The Age of Medicine?"

"That's right, the Age of Medicine. Brother Yang, have you been asleep all this time?" She put her hand down and, like magic, pulled a copy of *Medical News* from her jacket. She slowly unfolded the newspaper and began to read. "Look, this editorial is talking about how our nation has already entered into the glorious new Age of Medicine. This is of landmark significance. Do you remember the days when our nation was weak and deficient in the realm of medicine? Back when other nations all around the world were strong, healthy, and proud, our countrymen were ridiculed as the 'sick men of Asia.' That was actually an accurate description. At the time one out of every two people had tuberculosis, one out of every three people had syphilis, one out of every four people was an opium addict, two out of every five babies were lost to infant mortality, three out of every six pregnant women suffered from dystocia resulting in the death of a baby . . . and there were those hidden behind their windows who just cried out repeatedly, so utterly exhausted and decrepit that they barely resembled human beings anymore. And let's not forget the countless cripples, deaf, mute, dumb, mentally handicapped, and other diseased and helpless individuals, clear proof of our nation's weakness and poverty, which led to our being invaded, bullied, oppressed, exploited, pushed to the brink of national collapse . . ."

"Is that so? I hadn't heard about any of this before."

"You don't believe the editorial?"

"I just don't trust my memory . . ."

"Ever since ancient times, the very body of this behemoth has been riddled with problems. It has been in a state of constant illness for thousands of years now."

"That sounds odd . . ." Most of the songs I had ever written were about our long, glorious civilization and the shining brilliance of our culture, our strong and powerful nation.

"But all of that is in the past now." Bai Dai flashed me a deep glance and continued reading in a blank, emotionless voice. "Later we imported Western medicine and began to tweak it by abandoning the cruder elements while holding on to its essence. We got rid of its falsities, leaving only its truth. We developed a technological medical system suitable for our nation's specific conditions. After the hard work and sacrifices of several generations, today this ancient nation is finally able to raise its head proudly and stand tall. Modern hospitals with distinct characteristics of their own began to sprout up like bamboo shoots after a spring rain, and everyone entered a new stage of rehabilitation. This is a marvelous feat not seen in several thousand years. Saving hundreds of millions of people from the brink of death is nothing short of revolutionary. Naturally, this is all an expression of the nation taking full responsibility for the lives of its people. We have arrived at a critical historical juncture. We have begun the pursuit of a higher quality of life, and we continue to leap forward as we strive toward a miraculous recovery, a resurrection, a renaissance . . . no ailment is too small for the hospital to treat. Everyone is taken good care of. The hospital designs a special treatment plan for each individual, combining tradition with modernity, East with West, in the best interest of each and every patient."

"That's great," I murmured, recalling my arduous journey from the outpatient ward to the inpatient ward.

"Take a look," she continued. "The editorial says that the Age of Medicine is rooted in the great progress that has been made in the biological sciences. It was a Western product, but we make better use of it by redefining and remolding it. We have made great innovations and achieved breakthrough successes on par with the most advanced nations of the world. You could say that today, it is no longer silicon leading the way but carbon, that is, living things: mice, pathogens, genes, ecology, evolution, biological development, life! . . . No, it is actually extrastrength carbon, which is creating super-life-forms: synthetic mice, engineered pathogens, engineered genes, industrial ecology, advanced evolution, data development, and artificial life . . . the government, industries, and social organizations have all pivoted toward the field of medicine, which is now at the center of our lives, surpassing everything else. But this proposition is all based on the basic premise that life is the center of everything."

"In the Age of Medicine, life is the center of everything . . ." A primal groan unexpectedly welled up from deep in my throat, as if I had been choking on a fish bone, and a series of images suddenly appeared before my eyes: the countless corpse-like bodies of patients moving back and forth, as if caught in a spider's web, the waterfall of phlegm crashing down from the main inpatient building, the piss and shit all over the floors, the emergency room filled with patients, the crowded and chaotic concentration camp–like inpatient ward. All of these images wove together to create a special kind of aesthetic beauty, more enchanting than a gorgeous sunrise.

"That's right," Bai Dai said. "In keeping with the needs of this age, unhealthy individuals are no longer permitted to exist. If you are going to do anything, better do your very best and take things as far as they can go. We will make major improvements to mankind before eventually entering the era of re-creating human beings. This is the foundation of our new economy, the elimination of all of our philosophical quandaries, marking the achievement of a new political harmony that will build our confidence in the realm of diplomacy. The World Medical Association's Geneva proclamation states, 'From the moment of birth forward, all human life shall be treated with the utmost dignity.' But what exactly is life? How should it be respected and treated with dignity? No one has ever been able to answer these questions. For tens of thousands of years, life has been a muddled concept. The word 'sloppy' can be seen as a synonym for life. Since modern times, life has been trampled upon by the brutal Western powers, their cruelty displayed across the globe, their colonial activities leading to countless deaths. Now that we know that life is the center of everything, we must face the question of how to go on living. Wasn't this question resolved a long time ago? What's the point of shouting slogans? What are you going to do to show dignity and respect? Westerners are quite hypocritical about this. Only here in our nation have we been able to do it. Brother Yang, take a look at what this newspaper is saying. The city of C represents an experimental district in the latest wave of our nation's medical reform. All of the residents adhere to the basic principles of the Age of Medicine: One, everyone is sick. Two, patients are useless. Three, all illnesses are untreatable. Four, if you are sick, you must seek treatment. Five, to be without an illness is to be ill. Six, serious ailments are actually like not being sick at all. These principles represent the most advanced thought of the Age of Medicine. If our people want to have a bright and glorious future, they must construct powerful hospitals so that each and every person has a personal hospital room. Under the guidance of this intellectual theory, all natural and social resources are medical resources. Cities will all transform into comprehensive superhospitals. Mayors will be hospital presidents, and their primary concern will be to ensure the health of every resident. This is completely without historical precedent. Never before has so much energy been devoted to medical care. It is a true milestone in the history of human civilization."

"It is indeed quite amazing." That was how I had been drawn in, willingly delivering myself to the hospital without even realizing it.

"But take a look. There are still people who are clearly sick and yet refuse to believe. The only way to get them to the hospital is to drag them kicking and screaming, and once they are here, they still try to escape. Escape is not tolerated, nor is it even possible." She flashed me another sly glance, as if waiting for me to do something. She raised my arms, which had begun to droop a bit. At that moment her form seemed to overlap with Sister Jiang's and Ah Bi's, yet there remained something different, something unique, about Bai Dai.

"Don't worry," I assured her. "I wouldn't dare attempt another escape." Amid my fear and trepidation, I came to the sudden realization that my entire life had been one chronic illness. I was stuck in place, never able to reach the end of my treatment, the hospital forever my final destination. Yet I remained puzzled. "What's the deal with how

difficult it is to get into the hospital and how expensive treatment is?"
I thought back to all the challenging experiences I had gone through
when I was first trying to get admitted. It had almost driven me mad.

"Well, according to *Medical News*, this is just to test the patients,"
Bai Dai explained. "Kind of like the college entrance exams. Brother
Yang, didn't you go to college? In some places motion-triggered tracking and holographic projection technology is employed to create some
of those effects. It is said that not only does it track your movements
but your thoughts as well. Then, based on individual patients' various
expectations of the hospital, an image of what they desire is created,
ensuring that people won't suddenly pass out from a lack of psychological preparation. This is also part of the treatment process. You must have
heard people ask, 'Do you have faith in the hospital? Do you have faith
in your doctor?' This is a required step to make a final determination
for each person's illness." She looked at me worriedly, suggesting a faint
hint of blame.

"Oh, so that's what was happening." After making it through
countless trials, I had finally passed the test and been admitted to the
inpatient division. The hospital really went to great lengths to mingle
reality with its illusions. However, even after my life as an inpatient
had begun, the series of tests had continued. Did they plan on waiting
until the day I either fully recovered or died before announcing the
final results?

"All of those old internet companies, energy corporations, transportation companies, and financial structures are now subsidiaries in
the service of the medical industry," Bai Dai continued. "In the past
everyone would go on and on about the importance of life, but in what
practical ways did they actually follow through? Back then life had no
value. Even those willing to do something didn't have the strength to
implement any real changes. Now that we have arrived at the Age of
Medicine, the value of life itself, for the very first time, is no longer
underestimated. From a philosophical perspective, this is a deep and

fundamental acknowledgment of our shortcomings as humans. The development of science and technology has finally revealed the true nature of life.

"It makes much more sense to label everyone as sick preemptively. That's the truth anyway. Personalized medicine has strengthened our ability to anticipate diseases. To give you an example, according to genetic testing, if an individual has a fifty percent chance of contracting colon cancer, then he should be confirmed as a patient. A person with a thirty percent chance of contracting Fanconi anemia should also be considered an at-risk patient. Every one of us carries imperfect genes. No one is a perfect genetic 'specimen.' Buried within everyone's genes is a 'ticking time bomb.' Since there is no way to root out these demons inside us individually, everyone should be sent to the hospital for treatment. No one has an alternative."

"So you're saying the sole purpose in life is to get admitted to the hospital as soon as possible."

"That's right. If you want to survive in this great age, there is but one question to answer: to treat or not to treat, that is the question. Yet no matter how you respond to the question, in the end, you *will* be treated. Only a sick person can qualify as a complete person. And that is how the birth of medical punk came to be."

"The Age of Medicine, medical punk . . . did our nation invent these things? Or do other countries practice them too?"

"Our nation is the true innovator here. Only a long-suffering diseased nation could create something like this. It was as if we were resurrected; back from death, we turned the corner and took the lead. We may have begun later than others, but we have finally risen up to take our place as a global leader. Many other countries do their best to learn from us, especially those disease-infested, medically deprived developing countries with short life expectancies—they admire the hell out of us! This has become the latest fashion in globalism."

Bai Dai had a completely serious expression as she rambled on, as if she were facing death unflinchingly. Yet her words belied a sarcasm, a touch of sadness and pain. She had said so much, and yet it didn't seem like she really believed it all. She seemed to convey a hidden sense of dissatisfaction, resistance, mockery, and denunciation, as if she really wanted to express something very different. She had been reading articles from *Medical News*, but what did *she* want to say? Was she hinting at something that could not be spoken in public? Had she, too, seen patients paying off doctors with red envelopes? Did she understand all the different things that medicine represented? Had she really cultivated an aesthetic appreciation for the phlegm waterfall? I couldn't be sure of the answer to any of these questions. Perhaps she was also riddled with contradictions and inner struggle, but one thing was certain. Bai Dai was a woman of thought. Deep down she was different from Sister Jiang and Ah Bi. She began to make me dizzy, triggering a pain more excruciating than my stomach pain. I mechanically nodded my head. What else could I do? I was but a small, insignificant patient in this great age of radical change, and this so-called medical punk was still thousands of miles away.

I gazed at the flourishing, self-sustaining, harmonious, ever-thriving medical megametropolis laid out before my eyes. How it resembled a mirage in the desert, yet how could I suspect that it was all just a holographic projection? It was clearly as real as Medusa's hair. My knees began to shudder, and I felt like they were going to give way. "Everyone is, is sick . . . ," I stammered. Where had I heard those words before? Oh, I remembered: they came from Friedrich Wilhelm Nietzsche, the nineteenth-century German philosopher who had once said that everyone is sick. He was really cutting edge! Nietzsche was quite prophetic. Who could have imagined that his maxim would one day come true? I wondered what Nietzsche's reaction would have been had he lived in the Age of Medicine. Perhaps he wouldn't have died at such a young age? He had once said, "He who has a why to live for can bear almost any how." And yet at the age of forty-five, unable to withstand long periods of loneliness and being misunderstood, he had embraced an abused horse on the streets of Turin and died of madness. During the days before the Age of Medicine, doctors had been unable to carry out screenings on newborn babies, so there was no way to treat this type of madness, but that was no longer a problem. Nietzsche's brilliant thoughts had been forgotten or discarded, but our nation had inherited the essence of the great philosopher's spiritual legacy and reconstructed it, raising it to new heights, safeguarding the dignity of human life for a splendid new age. Suddenly I felt as if I was about to go mad. Perhaps my ailment had been madness all along.

As if reading my mind, Bai Dai spoke in a tone of mixed blame and pity. "You're not mad, nor will you ever lose your mind. In the Age of Medicine, you are not allowed to be afflicted by madness like that. You are not even qualified to go mad, since madness is essentially the ultimate bliss. Brother Yang, you are still quite young, like a child that never grows up." She finally allowed me to lower my arms, and I heaved a deep sigh of relief.

She then appointed me as her assistant in the grand project of investigating how doctors die, and this new assignment came with equal parts glory and dread.

28

THE FAMILY IS THE ENEMY

Bai Dai and I continually roamed the halls of the inpatient ward, and we seemed to improve a bit. According to our medical records, even though both of us had yet to receive official diagnoses, we had already undergone an essential procedure of utmost importance: we'd had our hereditary genes modified. Dr. Bauchi confirmed this during his rounds.

Gene modification was a popular treatment, but strangely I couldn't remember when it had been done to me. My best guess was that I must have visited this hospital before. Perhaps I once stayed here for an extended period of time. It was also possible that in addition to my stomach ailment, I might have had some other serious illness, such as dementia, likely brought on by an even more serious disorder such as brain atrophy or arteriosclerosis. Thanks to the gene therapy, I had survived, but it had not cured me, and my treatment continued, round after round, an endless series of treatments.

Later I checked my medical records and discovered that, based on my complete three-billion-genome sequencing test and an analysis of my family's genetic history, the genetic mutations that I carried indicated that my risk of developing schizophrenia was 15 percent higher, and my risk of developing prostate cancer 100 percent higher, than the average person's. I was also a carrier of a recessive gene that could cause emphysema, liver disease, diabetes, and heart failure. But a timely intervention had addressed these problems, and their related risks had been eliminated for the time being. Perhaps my stomach pain was simply due to my careless everyday habits.

One of the side effects of the gene therapy, also reported in *Medical News*, was that because one's genes were no longer the same, from a biological perspective the patient's relationship with his family was effectively cut off. No longer a part of his family, a recipient of the therapy could avoid any bad blood with family. Doctors felt that the family was actually the single most terrifying and stubborn disease. *Your family is the enemy* was a common phrase that summed up this new perspective on treatment that came to us with the onset of the Age of Medicine. Built on ideas from the field of sociological medicine, the new therapy involved the establishment of "gene passports."

I was told that my genetic modification surgery had been carried out using microbots, which manipulated microneedles, injecting foreign normal genes into my defective genes. I had paid a hefty sum for this procedure, but after this transformative treatment, I had essentially been reborn. No longer my former self, I had cut off any blood relationship I once had with my parents. As I was no longer their "son," their "daughter-in-law" was also naturally no more. My wife and I could go our separate ways. As this chain reaction played out, from the day of my surgery, that gorgeous flying female nurse could no longer claim a father-daughter relationship with me. We were biologically separate. DNA tests would no longer reveal any direct relationship between us. This is why, before I met Bai Dai, I couldn't remember that I once had a wife and daughter.

According to modern medical and scientific theory, the family was a temporary and rudimentary phenomenon that appeared during our biological evolution, like the appendix, a vestigial organ with no real function. With the extended family community and meticulous care of the hospital, our doctors, and nursing staff, who needed a pathetic little nuclear family? In the past, falling ill commonly brought catastrophe to small families. Surviving family members frequently felt as if part of themselves had died. But now that we had the hospital, none of those problems existed.

In the Age of Medicine, normal people believe that the family is the source of all evil. In addition to dirty blood ties, families bring limitations and contamination, being hotbeds for the transmission of disease and the destruction of human dignity. Flesh and blood bodies mixing under the same roof, crowding into bed together, breathing the same filthy air exhaled from one another's nostrils, drinking the same putrid water, eating the same rotting food, individual space severely restricted, a state of suffocation and repression—the *horror*! Humankind's original system of "community"—indiscriminate relationships, people of opposite sexes in relationships based on what was advantageous for reproduction, disguised as "husbands and wives" in the name of civilization, for their *entire lives*, with no choice but to live side by side, swearing never to abandon each other—they even wrote this betrayal of our basic instincts into law! Things got so perverted that even when they had raised their children or one partner had lost the ability to perform sexual intercourse, they still did everything possible to sustain their relationships in order to look good in the eyes of society. It boiled down to a system of private ownership, a perversion of the fundamental principles of biology. Couples forgot that men and women are essentially different life-forms, with no basis for truly understanding each other. Husbands and wives spent their entire lives pretending, and this led to countless crimes. Families were indeed the cancer cells of society, the central source of all diseases, an infection, the most painful and shameful affliction, in direct opposition to the value system of medical punk.

Unfettered by the family structure, the hospital was now free to do as it pleased and push medical science to the extreme. Previously, the practice of medicine had been restricted by patients' family members and the lawyers who represented them. The threat of lawsuits and large payouts for malpractice claims had brought scientific advances in medicine to a standstill and threatened the lives of all patients. This was especially true when it came to pediatrics, which had become virtually unsustainable as a field. Hardly any doctors were even willing to be pediatricians because of the unique challenges and terrible insults they faced. One child patient would often be accompanied by more than a dozen family members at every appointment. All those aunties and cousins would nitpick every aspect of treatment. If an appointment was too short, they accused the doctor of being irresponsible. If an appointment was too long, they accused the doctor of being unqualified. Pediatricians were yelled at for everything. But after the dissolution of the family, there was no longer a need for a special pediatrics department. Human reproduction could now take place in vitro, so that all aspects of the process could be controlled by the doctor. The issue of how to deal with newborns suffering from severe birth defects was no longer a problem. Everything was much more simple.

Upon closer analysis, the evil phenomenon of the family—once described by Engels in his book *The Origin of the Family, Private Property and the State*—had been completely eradicated. According to Engels, early hunter-gatherer society was based on public ownership of property and group marriage. During this period that predated the family, people lived in a primitive state of "unrestricted sexual intercourse," but as women in the tribe gradually dwindled, paired families consisting of one man and one woman began to appear. Later, the husband assumed power in the home, while the wife was enslaved and degraded, reduced to an object of her husband's lust and a tool for childbirth. The husbands controlled the family order by virtue of economic power, representing the capitalist class, while the wife was akin to the proletariat. As long as the system of private ownership persisted, the family unit carried on. But now the hospital was not only eliminating disease but also eradicating the very concept of private ownership. This is how historical progress is achieved.

From an artistic perspective, gene therapy had allowed patients to live among the kind and beautiful Indian peafowls, eligible to reside in this heavenly hospital and become part of a new symbiotic body. No one thought of trying to escape from the hospital to return "home."

The nature of society was returning to communal living. Patients participated in collective talent shows and performances at the hospital, many of which, I suspected, featured a peacock dance.

Bai Dai let me borrow her copy of *Medical News*, and I began to understand the characteristics and follow the latest developments of the Age of Medicine. I had once thought that I had a good handle on what the hospital was all about, but I had only a very superficial understanding of things. I was deceived by those surface appearances. Everything I had experienced before was just a series of trials and tests.

But that issue of *Medical News* turned out to be extremely profound. The writing resembled a poem with hidden meanings. I could decipher only a portion of the articles, but the central theme of them all was that the hospital is a complex system that requires perseverance on the part of patients as they try to adapt.

Medical News was already complex enough! One article talked about how the medical revolution was unlike any other technological revolution in human history. Previous revolutions all involved technologies—the steam engine, the electric motor, the internet—that, at the very most, *affected* humans. But the medical revolution *was aimed directly at* human beings, at thoroughly transforming them. The Age of Medicine was the dawn of a new era in which humanity was being upgraded, spiritually and physically, the beginning of a new chapter.

Another article pointed out that following the Age of Fire, the Age of Cow Dung, the Age of Steam and Electricity, the Age of Oil and Nuclear Energy, and the Age of the Computer Bit, the Age of Medicine had finally revealed the true nature of life. When the instruction manual for human genome sequencing was revealed, we could finally prove with factual evidence that our existence is in fact a kind of disease, a strange, indescribable disease brimming with dialectics. "Whoever says he is not sick must be terribly, terribly ill," the article concluded.

That sounded right to me. I had indeed seen many people declare that they were strong and healthy, only to drop dead.

According to *Medical News*, the best scenario was to be admitted at birth. Actually, no, that's not right—better to be admitted as an embryo. We talked constantly about "health," but the word no longer appeared in modern medical textbooks. To say one was healthy meant that one was sick. To claim that one didn't get sick was shameful and preposterous, a harmful criminal act. In the Age of Medicine, we no longer differentiated between the sick and the healthy. The difference in medical treatment standards between rural and urban areas had been bridged, the wealth gap between rich and poor had been closed, class differences eliminated, and the problem of the duality of life had been resolved. Only one relationship mattered: the doctor-patient relationship.

I realized that I would need to borrow some reference books from the library, for extra help in getting a deeper understanding of the newspaper articles. As a mere freelance songwriter, I lacked training in medicine, and I felt guilty for that. I was fortunate to receive guidance from Dr. Bauchi and benefited from the study sessions and tours organized by the sick ward. My faith in the hospital strengthened.

29

ELIMINATING THE RISK OF
EXTINCTION AND NATIONAL
COLLAPSE

An assembly hall in the sick ward was used for promotional events. It was equipped with whiteboards, a projection screen, illustrated posters, and advertisements. Every Monday afternoon featured a lecture on a different topic. The speakers were usually old patients talking about their experiences—the hospital believed that patients' firsthand testimony was persuasive and powerful—and the moderator was Dr. Bauchi.

One day the speaker was Uncle Zhao, a model patient who would provide a technical introduction to the science of gene therapy. More than a thousand were in attendance, the hall packed to the gills with row after row of sick, eager patients.

Uncle Zhao was a thin, bald man in his fifties, hunchbacked and always modest. He cut out and pasted together several articles from the newspaper, which served as the basis for his lecture. So-called gene therapy, he explained, is the process of using gene sequencing to predict which diseases a seemingly healthy person might develop or to examine specific pathological changes taking place in the DNA of a sick person so as to introduce healthy exogenous genes into the base chromosomes of the targeted cells. The healthy genes displace the abnormal genes, and the DNA is regrouped in such a way to achieve the goal of curing diseases. There are two methods. The first, referred to as "external gene therapy," involves extracting cells from the patient's body, injecting the deficient DNA into those cells, and then transplanting those reen-gineered cells back into the patient's body. The other method, called "internal gene therapy," involves the direct injection of genes into the patient's organs. In addition to these approaches, specific medications can also be employed for a targeted treatment plan to block the epidermal growth factor and prevent proteins that might activate malignant lesions.

"With the basic human gene sequencing project now complete," Uncle Zhao concluded, "the pathogenic mechanisms behind almost all forms of cancer, diabetes, cardiovascular disease, autoimmune disorders, various neurological problems, and thousands of other common diseases have been fully revealed. Treatment is a piece of cake. This is the hospital's greatest expression of the sincere care it extends to its patients." Uncle Zhao's hunched back began to tremble, and the entire audience broke out in thunderous applause.

Uncle Zhao had a long and impressive history as an inpatient at the hospital. He was one of the veteran good guys in the sick ward. He always listened to the doctors' orders and played a central role in uniting the other patients. He had even been selected as a model patient for the leadership role he played in obeying the hospital's rules and regulations. When the sick ward put together an oratory club, Uncle Zhao was one of the central members.

He himself was suffering from a gastrointestinal stromal tumor, but he had been able to control his condition with targeted gene therapy. He was filled with gratitude for the hospital and made sure to sing its praises every chance he got.

I had heard about various gene therapy theories, but I had never imagined that, in the blink of an eye, they would be administered to me here in the sick ward, nor the shocking speed with which all of these developments happened.

After the lecture, we participated in a tour of a hospital exhibition. Uncle Zhao was our tour guide. The entire sick ward was decorated with propaganda slogans, adorned with photographs of doctors in surgery and patients recovering. Some of the patients had even turned a few of the photos into illustrations and sculptures, and they were quite moving.

One image depicted thousands of people, tears in their eyes, their hands waving, crying out toward the cross hanging over them in the sky. According to Uncle Zhao, if we took a closer look, we would discover a deeper meaning in the image, related to gene therapy. Gene therapy began with the transformation of each individual, but in the end, it would result in the rebirth of the entire nation. This was the core idea at the heart of the Age of Medicine. "The second you have the slightest doubt, you must immediately expel it!" Uncle Zhao emphatically declared. Treatment should begin *before* birth, by transferring normal genes into germ cells—both sperm cells and egg cells are suitable—in order to ensure that an embryo got on the right path from the very beginning. For patients suffering from serious disease, the vast majority of their genes needed to be reedited with great precision; through this procedure a brand-new person could be created. Patients could bid farewell to their original bodies. Gene therapy was becoming a method by which we could reorganize the entire nation, providing proof that we would indeed be able to live forever. And based on this foundation, a new form of national ethics and social morality would be born.

Uncle Zhao recited one of the classic lines from the editorial in *Medical News*: "It's not important who you are; the only thing that matters is what kind of illness you suffer from. In this way we can eliminate the risk of extinction and national collapse." As the words left his lips, tears welled up in his eyes.

After staring at those images for a long time, I came to the realization that I was receiving treatment not only for myself but also for the long-term peace and prosperity of my beloved country.

According to Uncle Zhao, a nation and a people were constructed from individuals and families. In the old days, we used to have to fill out a form about family medical history every time we went to the hospital, but this was basically a formality, and most people just scribbled the word "none" when it came to the question about family illnesses. But that was actually of great importance. If you have "first-degree relatives," such as a parent or sibling, with cardiovascular disease, your chances of contracting that disease double; if they have colon cancer, prostate cancer, or breast cancer, your risk for contracting one of these doubles or triples; you face a similar increased risk when it comes to asthma, diabetes, osteoporosis, and even schizophrenia. These are all the results of genetic mutations that will eventually be passed down.

Nations have their own history of genetic diseases, and especially nations with long histories and large populations, and if the defective genes spread in the population, then when the environmental circumstances are right, they eventually mature and lead to massive problems. Every nation has at least one or two fatal genetic diseases capable of bringing about self-annihilation. All societal problems are first physical problems. Frankly speaking, I almost never used to see things from this perspective. I was nothing but a quasi intellectual working at a government agency and writing songs in my spare time. Of course, I sometimes wrote about the nation and our people, but I always wrote about the good things. The history of hereditary illness never even crossed my mind, and I certainly had never thought about whether the nation might be infected with cancer, leukemia, or anything like that. I just wrote about the positive and glorious side of things. I barely gave my lyrics a second thought before committing them to paper. It was all quite mechanical and perfunctory. I took the great banner of the nation as my tiger skin and wrote out of pure vanity, in order to cooperate fully with the social trend of "only reporting the good news and burying the bad news." This was also required by our clients, but I never really understood the implications. But once I knew, I understood that I had clearly lacked a "scientific brain."

Indeed, with a direct genetic connection between the individual body and the national body, some things go straight to the heart. The process is akin to the literary being transformed into the biological, which then further upgrades the nature of the literary. No wonder the hospital was such a poetic and refined place. That thousand-meter waterfall of phlegm appeared again before my eyes.

One of the digital images displayed the shape of a tree, its branches representing the past and future. Uncle Zhao explained that gene sequencing was able to predict different possibilities for the future, and these possibilities were like the trunk and branches of a tree. "What kind of ailments you will be afflicted by, the state of your health, how long you will live—all of this information can be found right there in your genes. This is pure, unadulterated determinism. No form of astrology or fortune-telling can even come close!"

What this meant was that the kind of pathological changes our genes underwent determined what kind of illness or disease we would develop. If certain changes didn't occur, we would not develop that disease, though we might develop a different one. That is why everyone had to undergo gene sequencing. Newborn babies needed to be screened, carriers of recessive genes had to be screened, mothers with birth defects had to be screened, embryos had to be screened in a prenatal analysis, with a genetic diagnosis provided before implantation. Every base had to be covered and no stone left unturned. The gene sequences of every citizen in the nation were then stored in a supercomputer and uploaded to a public platform, where big data processing and statistical analysis were carried out. Based on this information, genes were reedited, impacting not only the patients' bodies and thoughts—various psychological disorders are also determined by one's genes—but ultimately altering the entire fate of the nation. With this as our foundation, we would be able to establish basic patterns for citizens' behavior, and thus the massive, all-encompassing hospital system became the basic structure for everything, utilizing patient-care methods to facilitate social management. From this perspective, the hospital's strength and prosperity became *the* key factor in determining the nation's wealth and development. One tree at a time, we built a forest, and eventually, these patches of greenery would spread and expand until they covered everything.

"Early on, genetic regrouping was utilized to transform some common social phenomena." Uncle Zhao brimmed with enthusiasm as he spoke. "But observation and research in the field of biology has enlightened medical workers."

The digital dendrogram cut to an image taken deep in a forest. "When spring comes, why does the bird waste energy singing even *after* it has successfully paired? Biological researchers conducted genetic tests on the birds to figure out which males fathered the hatchlings, and they discovered that among birds that 'pair for life,' even though the couple works together to raise the next generation, the female birds were not as loyal as expected. They often secretly mated with other males, effectively cheating on the 'husbands,' explaining why, even after 'marriage,' male birds continue to sing: they are looking for opportunistic 'affairs.' Humans are not that different. Some people continually do everything they can to show off, striving for promotions and making high-profile public displays of their greatness. This kind of self-promotion, like the birds' singing, had become the goal of many successful politicians, businessmen, writers, and actors, and this so-called sperm competition actually dominated historical development. Understanding this basic fact allows the hospital to know how to prescribe the correct medicine.

"With the widespread adoption of gene therapy, at least there is no longer the need to use crude methods like castration to create eunuchs," Uncle Zhao continued. "Nor is there a need to use violent measures to achieve racial purity, like the genocidal concentration camps implemented in Nazi Germany. We don't even have to follow the example of the United States, where the federal government approved more than a hundred thousand sterilizations on medically handicapped individuals from more than thirty states. None of that is necessary anymore. It can all be done with gene replacement therapy, a truly humanitarian approach to the challenges we face."

Uncle Zhao was a bit embarrassed to bring up the next example. "In the past," he explained sheepishly, "a lot of people liked to brag about the size of their dicks. This crude and outdated method of biological exhibitionism has gone out of fashion in favor of optimized genes available as upgrades. No one from the opposite sex would give you the time of day if you fail to upgrade. Let me provide you with an example: Chimpanzees are only one-quarter the size of gorillas, but their testicles are four times larger than those of gorillas. This is owing to different habits: male gorillas can monopolize a single mate, resulting in their sperm being without competitors, while male chimpanzees need to 'share' their mates with other males, which has led them to produce more sperm and incessantly mate as a means of increasing their opportunity to father offspring. But all it takes is a simple reconfiguration of chimpanzee DNA and they will have more sperm and more energy without the need for such large testicles. The same principle applies to human beings. The only difference with male chimpanzees is that for humans the most important factor between competing males is the length of the penis. This allows males to deliver sperm into the uterus more quickly and directly, thus winning the affection of women. The problem is, these days who needs a uterus to conceive a baby? Today we can edit zygotes and gametes in vitro, and the two can be combined in the laboratory to create the most outstanding human specimens. You can create as many as you want, and you don't even need a dick to do it! Of course, the only prerequisite now is whether you have enough financial resources. This explains why we must turn the whole city into a massive hospital. This is one of the most effective means to accumulate the financial resources required."

It was commonly said that the development of modern hospitals required the accumulation of large amounts of capital, which fell into the category of megacapital. When it came to these megacapital operations, doctors, hospitals, and the life sciences were all considered part of the front line, comparable only to the national defense industry in terms of their scope and scale. It was an open secret that, for many years, besides all of the nation's tax revenue being directed into the medical industry, patients themselves had been transformed into mobile ATMs. Owing to the long-term era of peace and prosperity we found ourselves in, life had become quite costly, paid for with a multitude of sacrifices. Naturally, there were also those who felt it shouldn't be so costly. For instance, with gene sequencing and gene editing, thanks to the application of next-generation sequencing software and CRISPR technologies first introduced in the early twenty-first century, the market price for these applications had already dropped considerably. However, since the entire city had become a hospital and the hospital was responsible for setting fiscal policies, doctors had the power to set the rate for hospital services and implement one-stop prices. There was nothing patients could do about this.

I realized that I must have squandered all my money on hospital fees during the first round of my gene therapy treatment. That's why Dr. Bauchi had prescribed barely any wearable medical equipment for me. That's also why I must have been so unattractive in the eyes of Bai Dai and why whenever I was with her, I was always filled with a sense of trepidation and uneasiness.

New digital dendrograms continued to appear, so many that I began to feel dizzy. Reproductive issues remained the "root issue" at the heart of the country's public life. Once we resolved this root issue, all our other problems—the other branches of the tree—would be solved naturally, from birth to monkhood, puberty to development, selecting a partner to selecting a career, and even the once seemingly incurable disease of corruption. These things collectively formed the basis of modern medical physiology. From there, things like the elimination of the obesity gene—inherited fifteen million years prior from the common ancestors we share with chimpanzees and gorillas; these variant genes are referred to as "energy-saving genes" because they convert sugar into fat in places where food is scarce and in times of famine—and reconfiguring the genes that cause violent crimes would be a piece of cake. The four major neurological disorders that harm society—schizophrenia, bipolar disorder, clinical depression, and autism—would all be suppressed, as they all stemmed from genetic factors, the result of certain regions of a gene sequence leading to serious consequences for the nervous system and a multitude of thought disorders. Homosexual tendencies would also be controlled, since in the Age of Medicine, homosexuality is also a major source of malignant diseases. Gene therapy could also be employed to cure addictions to alcohol and drugs.

"Thanks to the hospital and our doctors, we are currently building a pure land; a fair, just, and healthy society," Uncle Zhao declared, just as Dr. Bauchi led in a group of young doctoral residents. Tears began to roll down Uncle Zhao's cheeks. He led the other patients in a ceremonial bow to the doctors, and I realized that the true purpose of this exhibition tour was to consolidate the patients' faith in the hospital with their faith in this era. Bai Dai did not bow.

The tour then transformed into a confessional. Patients expressed their suffering and pain, with Uncle Zhao taking the lead by delivering an impassioned denouncement of how genes had reduced the lives of patients to such ridiculousness.

"I used to be a university professor," Uncle Zhao professed. "I was honored with many national awards, and yet I continued to be dissatisfied with reality, always complaining and criticizing. I could only see the dark side of society. At the same time, I was obsessed with taking on more projects and getting promotions. I was constantly jealous of my colleagues and supervisors. I embezzled public funds and used the money to buy myself several vacation homes. Even if I lived several lifetimes, I would have never needed all those houses. My greed gene had gone wild, and my greatest fault was that I had become arrogant, forgetting that I was simply a patient. Like the chimpanzees, I, too, had my genes reconfigured after being admitted to the hospital. The hospital saved me. I had been on the verge of falling into the abyss of crime, but the hospital pulled me back up, transforming me from an animal into a man . . ." Tears flowed down Uncle Zhao's cheeks. Dr. Bauchi flashed a sympathetic smile and nodded his approval.

Uncle Zhao stammered as he pointed to the image of another large tree. Through the adoption of biological engineering treatments, he explained, the collective genes of famine, fear, and anger, which we all shared as a nation, would also be eradicated. Tens of thousands of years of historical incidents had accumulated in our DNA and become a deficiency. Naturally, developments in genetic medicine and neuro-medicine could transform specific population groups to be sufficiently intelligent or ignorant, in order to reestablish the boundaries between fixed social classes and establish more reasonable structures between ethnic groups. This was all quite simple, because we had already dis-covered that the genes that determine IQ and cognitive abilities could be adjusted with simple manipulation. In the case of some genes, this was related to metabolic dopamine levels, with mutations and uncon-ventional characteristics impacting an individual's personality. These would all be adjusted in order to increase creativity among our citizens. Genes and mutations related to self-restraint could be cultivated, so that people would be more docile. Something referred to as the "loyal warrior gene," Uncle Zhao explained, enabled an individual to sacri-fice himself fully for a certain cause. At this point I began to wonder whether Sister Jiang had undergone this gene modification.

Through the process of gene editing, neurological diseases like Parkinson's and Alzheimer's could also be induced in patients. Some forms of gene editing triggered unpredictable new diseases or could even result in death. But this was not necessarily a bad thing. Medical scientists were researching how to use these methods to take the place of previously adopted forms of torture and punishment, which could lead to a historical revolution in criminal justice, injecting fresh energy into the new breed of democratic politics under development. The very foundation of the nation's strength and prosperity was all right here.

In the pale inpatient building, the green forest continued to grow and expand, like a flood drowning out the barren, dirty landscape of the hospital, and with it came a grand vista that left everyone feeling refreshed and uplifted. Personalized treatment, tailored for individual patients, was thus transformed into a grand collective aesthetic.

I gradually came to understand why *Medical News* described this as the greatest change for humankind in ten thousand years.

History is decided by man. So dominating and organizing mankind allowed for the control of history. From there one could rewrite the future and redefine the advancement of civilization. And there lay the original aspiration and founding mission of the hospital.

"We must express our gratitude," Uncle Zhao addressed the other patients. "The hospital has taken such good care of us. The hospital has been right there beside us our entire lives, wielding the kind of magic that the ancients thought only gods and fairies were capable of. Even if we wanted to die, the hospital would never let us. This place deserves to be called heaven. Let us now express our gratitude! Thank you, hospital! Thank you!"

I flashed a glance in Bai Dai's direction. She looked exhausted. Her lips were dry. I could tell that her nicotine addiction was acting up and that she needed another hit. But it certainly wasn't the right time to bring that up, at least until the tour finished.

"You think this stuff is interesting?" she asked, seeming self-conscious about my rude staring.

"It's okay." My tone didn't matter. Perhaps she really just wanted to know how much progress I was making?

"Brother Yang, do you know how to make pigs fly?"

"Pigs?" Her question made me uncomfortable. Was she implying that patients were pigs? Was I nothing but a chimpanzee in her eyes? "Didn't we once live in a country of primates?" I figured I'd have been better off as a chimpanzee. I once heard a story about a chimpanzee that had been kept at a hospital for medical experiments. Once the hospital was done with him, he was abandoned on an island, where he was separated from his mate and offspring and lived a lonely life. When a doctor went to the island to check on whether he was still alive, the chimpanzee joyfully leaped into the doctor's arms and hugged him.

"You send them to pig paradise." Bai Dai puckered her lips.

"Hmm, so that's it."

"Most people answer by saying that you have to transport pigs on a plane to make them fly. You could even paint a backdrop of sky inside the plane to make them think they are a muster of peacocks. But the quickest way would be to transform their genes—transform them directly into peacocks."

"That sounds like a highly efficient method."

"The hospital demands efficiency."

"Where would these pigs fly to?"

"Use your brain!"

"Heaven?"

"No! The slaughterhouse."

"Are you trying to say that the doctors have different genes than we do?"

"Of course the doctors aren't pigs! But what are they?"

The expression on her face resembled a desert, devoid of anything human, missing even the slightest trace of anything resembling an oasis. Only the dead could utter words of that kind. I thought back to what she had said: "How do doctors die?" The exhibition had not touched on that question. I didn't appreciate Bai Dai's tone of voice, and I started to feel a twisted resentment toward her. How come her nicotine addiction hadn't been eliminated? Was this an oversight on the part of her doctors? At the same time, I couldn't help but feel like I was growing closer and more attached to her, like a little devil standing beside the king of hell.

I began to feel nervous every Monday. I was concerned about what I would do when it was my turn to deliver a lecture and lead a tour. Would the other patients heckle me if I collapsed at the podium from stomach pain? They'd had it out for me for a long time now, I thought, and they would love to see me down on my luck.

30

TO LIVE IS TO BE CHANGED
AND RESTRUCTURED

In order to prepare for the possibility that I might be called to deliver a lecture, I decided to seek out Dr. Bauchi's advice, and I brought up the following. A long time ago, quite a few medical students had pinned their hopes for national salvation on medicine, only later to discover it was a dead end. And so we had the example of Dr. Sun Yat-sen, who abandoned a career in medicine to devote himself to the revolution, or Mr. Zhou Shuren, better known as Lu Xun, who gave up his dream of becoming a doctor to take up the pen and become a leftist writer, attempting to save the souls of his countrymen through literature. They both thought that the study of medicine was somehow superficial, unable to cure the most fundamental disease, which to them was a spiritual illness. Is it possible that neither of them was able to predict what would happen in our time?

Dr. Bauchi responded by saying that yes, I had identified a shortcoming of the era in which they had lived. Did the radical political activism of Dr. Sun Yat-sen and Lu Xun eradicate the ills of society and save souls? I didn't think so. Both were notorious for being sick men themselves; neither lived past the age of sixty. Instead, Western missionaries had established hospitals in our country, and during that era of poverty and chaos, they had saved many from the brink of death, brought salvation to many poor souls, and opened the door to modern civilization. This had allowed our country to evolve, laying the groundwork for the thorough treatment of *all* disease and illness and eventually achieving the incredible developments in medicine and science that we saw in our day. National salvation through medicine, Dr. Bauchi insisted, was the foundation of *everything*.

I had trouble agreeing with him. I didn't have any relevant knowledge to refute him, and I still had a lot of respect for the doctor. I remained silent as another round of abdominal pain assaulted my body.

"Looked at from the perspective of technological development," Dr. Bauchi continued, "the concept of medicine has already been widely accepted and is certainly no longer aimed at curing the bodies of the sick. It not only eliminates the chronic illnesses of society, but it can also refine human thought. Through targeted treatment, individuals' bodies and souls can both be treated, and through this process, the individual and the nation can, for the first time, be truly united. Wasn't this precisely what Sun Yat-sen and Lu Xun once dreamed of? If they had lived to see today, I'm sure they would both have been delighted to be admitted to the hospital."

I realized that, through the transformation of our genes, we could also transform our memes, through which our language, ideas, beliefs, and actions are expressed, similar to the role of genes in biological evolution.

I wasn't sure whether Bai Dai felt the same way, but I suspected that Dr. Bauchi's beliefs represented the innermost thoughts of most people working in the medical community. That's how they were educated.

I had noticed that doctors tended to do their best to keep conceptual discussions to a minimum, instead using their time as efficiently as possible. If they made a mistake, they simply tried to correct it later. The standards they applied were determined by money, usefulness, and how much fun was involved. As for ethical considerations, we had our own standards and refused to be intimidated by foreigners'. We needed to break with the past. For instance, regarding the question of what qualifies as a human being, different regions of the world were entitled to their own definitions, but if we didn't liberate our thinking, we would be incapable of accomplishing anything. This had resulted in differences in the level of development and treatment approaches between different hospitals, different sick wards, and even between inpatient and outpatient wards.

This is how *Medical News* described it: "When dealing with illness during the Age of Medicine, it is necessary to be firm and resolute. There is no room for any loose ends. In the name of health, the sole aim is to keep people alive using whatever means are available. As long as people stay alive, there will be hope for our nation."

To survive meant to be transformed, to be reorganized. The hospital's role in determining an individual's identity had been precisely and fully revealed.

31

A SOCIAL REVOLUTION TO
SHAKE THE WORLD

So, in a situation like that, was there still a possibility of reconfiguring the family unit? I occasionally found myself pondering this question, letting it reverberate around my brain for a while. I'm not quite sure why, but when I think about my former wife and daughter, I sometimes start to miss them. This turned out to be something that gene therapy had been unable to prevent. However, I couldn't blame this on hospital oversight. There will always be some things that are just not perfect. I occasionally thought back to the life I once had with my family, but it was like the shadow of a cloud passing overhead, quickly disappearing, never to return again.

After a period of time getting to know Bai Dai, we began to have some physical contact. We forged an emotional connection, and you could even say that we were brought closer under the old adage "misery loves company." I wondered if we would eventually take things to another level.

Truth be told, I was a bit interested . . . but I wasn't exactly interested in *that*. Not only because of the hospital's strict management system, nor only because I didn't have enough medical ornaments adorning my peacock plumes, but because both Bai Dai's and my genes had already been purged of those most primal and base urges that had been with humans for tens of thousands of years. Owing to this, even if I'd had those intentions, I would never find myself rashly acting on them.

As a newly admitted patient, I couldn't allow history to go backward. Not long after genetic testing gained in popularity, it became very difficult for people to maintain normal families. Researchers had also discovered the relationship between genes and men's faithfulness. Those who carried copies of two mutant genes were found to have a 50 percent risk of getting divorced or having an affair, but those without the genes had a risk of only 15 percent. The problem was that these two genes were highly prevalent in most men; this was in fact a "national illness." This led a genetic-testing corporation to launch a special project aimed specifically at married and unmarried women, allowing them the opportunity to verify whether their current or future partners would have an affair. The corporation also provided a test for men, offering them a good excuse for having an affair—just blame it on the genes!— and this proved to be a fatal blow to the institution of marriage as it had existed for thousands of years.

Only a very small number of patients who had failed in their treatment, had been negatively impacted by their environment, or were simply delusional still dared to try and establish a family with another patient. In our sick ward, a man named Old Gao, who suffered from hemolytic anemia, tried to hook up with a hypothyroid patient named Little Li. These two men strangely developed feelings for one another. In the vast majority of cases, attempts at relationships were stopped by hospital employees, who intervened early. After secretly dating for a time, Old Gao and Little Li's relationship was discovered by the medical surveillance system. Dr. Bauchi announced that they would undergo a new treatment employing a stronger regimen of drugs in order to prevent their health from suffering any undue setbacks.

But what happened between Old Gao and Little Li ended up being a true catastrophe. Since both men were of only average economic means, they were unable to afford the cost of this expensive new treatment. From day one, the hospital has control of all its patients' finances, forcing them to turn over their cash and credit cards upon admission and to sign away all of their family assets as collateral against future hospital expenditures. When patients like Old Gao and Little Li incurred additional charges during treatment, a debt appeared on their account, and, unable to get money from other channels, they were forced to borrow funds from the hospital bank and charged exorbitant interest rates. Failure to comply put one's very survival in jeopardy, and the patients all knew it.

Old Gao and Little Li were both transferred out of the ward under the pretext that they had conspired to "destroy the medical ideology of sharing." They were sent to different sick wards, far away from each other, and during their period of hospitalization, it would be almost impossible for them to see one another again. Naturally, this was all done in order to protect them, the primary consideration being their health and well-being.

"Emotions are not to be exchanged," Dr. Bauchi lectured. "It is owing to love that we suffer and worry. It is owing to love that we experience terror and pain. Love threatens our very lives, and if there is no life, all else is lost."

This episode taught the patients that "impulsive actions" would only lead to more suffering and would be taken as a sign that a patient was not taking his or her condition seriously. It also led some to say, "Here in the hospital, life is a form of political economy."

However, the way I saw things, life was no longer any of that. Life was nothing.

The bottom line was that, from both a practical and theoretical perspective, it was utterly impossible that Bai Dai and I would ever truly unite. The cost would have been too high.

So the main point of the Age of Medicine was not to make it more convenient for patients to stay home and reduce their risk of being admitted to the hospital. In fact, it was just the opposite: the primary mission was to eliminate the diseased family system, which was already on the verge of collapse, and to provide safety and health while people left every aspect of their lives to the hospital.

While on this topic, we should also talk about the definition of a patient. *What was a patient anyway?* A patient was a person who created trouble and inconvenience for other people. The hospital exists precisely to eliminate this inconvenience, not only to reform the lives of individuals but more importantly as a means of bringing about a social revolution, to shake the world. People would no longer employ unscientific phrases like "blood is thicker than water." After all, it is only the difference of a few molecular components that separates blood from water. By embracing the hospital, we exchanged the bankrupt family system for the endless possibilities of health—but only the possibilities. In the end, one's health was still dependent upon the final outcome of treatment. Cooperation between patients and the hospital was of the utmost importance. Patients had to remain self-aware; after all, we were still in the early stage of this revolutionary experiment. All the tests and challenges that patients faced were necessary.

They started with the body but penetrated the soul.

32

TO BE HEALTHY IS TO BE SICK, TO BE SICK IS TO BE HEALTHY

In order to assist in the treatment of patients, the hospital installed several high-resolution telescopes on the observation platform of the inpatient ward to help those patients with the ability to climb upstairs to get to know their environment and establish the "correct" view of life and medicine. In the Age of Medicine, people needed to learn how to think through medicine and adopt a new form of medical thinking.

When we didn't have any pressing treatment, Bai Dai would take me up to the observation platform so we could gaze through the telescopes. During those moments she always appeared somewhat beside herself. Sometimes I felt like she was extremely dignified, but deep down she was really just a young girl who liked to have fun. Whenever we went up there, she would light a cigarette that she had hidden away in her clothes and take a deep drag.

It didn't matter from what angle we looked at the scenery beneath us; the vista always looked like a sublime and gorgeous oil painting. Through the dark-red veil of mist and rain enveloping the city, the thousands of residents below looked like a colony of ants. Under the wide-screen dome of the sky, people silently scurried along ringed roads, back and forth, without a destination. Among them were patients who had just broken up their families and left home; they still hadn't learned how to acclimate themselves to the new Age of Medicine, and they flooded into the hospital in search of treatment. Doctors in white lab coats with portable diagnostic devices rode on hydrogen-powered skateboards, smiling as they herded the patients inside. Most of the patients lowered their heads and allowed themselves to be captured, but a few, not understanding what was happening, became anxious and scampered off like scared mice. Eventually they were all collected into an ambulance and returned to the hospital. The hunter would catch his prey, only without all the bloodshed—as the slogan says, the hospital maintains a deep respect for life.

Other doctors flew around on jet packs with first-aid kits. As they traversed the sky, making their aerial rounds, these doctors displayed all the qualities of medical punk. Their foreheads were equipped with disease scanners and high-speed germ detectors. The homes of families that had yet to be broken up were designated as "prep wards." Doctors would land directly at the prep ward site, break down the door, enter, and commence their inspections. They were not required to identify themselves or announce the purpose of their visit, because everything they would do was in either the immediate or the long-term interest of the patient. Each "prep ward" family would drag their sickly bodies out of bed and, while staving off their pain, begin preparing food and drink to welcome the doctor. Some of the families in better shape would line up in a row, their legs trembling, forced smiles on their faces as they tended to the doctor's every need. The doctor would sit in the seat of honor, reserved for an esteemed guest, and feign politeness as he requested that the family take their seats. "There is no need to be so anxious! Let's have something to eat first, and then we'll gradually start the examinations. Please relax, nobody's going to die." After politely declining, the family would finally agree to see the doctor's medical kit, which he would take out to show them. Only then would the patients dare to sit down. Despite their artificial smiles and forced politeness, they remained filled with fear and trepidation, worried that they might not receive the best treatment. Once the doctor had eaten his fill, he would begin the examinations. This is when the head of the family would present red envelopes and gifts prepared in advance, imploring the doctor to release his family from the incessant illness and eternal suffering they had endured. Sometimes the doctor would make a special request, always quite reasonable, and the families would tearfully express their profound gratitude and do their best to satisfy the doctor's wishes. Ultimately, all of this led to the dismantling of the family.

On one particular occasion, one of these flying doctors had landed at my house. My daughter was still in middle school and happened to be home that day. The doctor took one look at her and immediately saw something in her. He told me he wanted to take her away with him. He had just been promoted to the position of chief physician of the vertical landing platform, in charge of all midsize aerial medical labs, and he was in need of a lab assistant. Then he had invited her to serve under him as an aerial nurse! An aerial nurse! Can you imagine? How could I have possibly refused such an honor? I couldn't have been happier. My daughter was talented, but she was infected by my bad bloodline and had been suffering from chronic illness. This had deeply troubled me, but when the doctor extended his goodwill, I couldn't have been more eager to oblige. The neighbors came to express their congratulations. With the support of the doctor, our family, which had been teetering on the brink of collapse for so long, would finally be torn completely apart. Ah, such an envious position we found ourselves in!

After my daughter left, this period of bliss had continued for quite some time. Now that I, too, have made it into the hospital, I no longer needed to prepare red envelopes, food, or my only daughter for the flying doctors in white who descended from heaven. There was something sad about this, but the heavenly light of the hospital shone down upon me, and I should have had nothing but the most profound gratitude. With Bai Dai's help, I was finally able to remember my own sinful family, right here in this city. In order to cleanse myself of this poisonous tumor, I vowed to live the rest of my life for the hospital, and live not only to cure my own disease but for the greater body of society to remain healthy, which was, after all, the true reason to go on living. I wouldn't secretly think about the family I once had, not even subconscious thoughts. The all-encompassing happiness that overcame me eventually gave way to embarrassment, and I started to tremble with fear. I had once tried to escape from the emergency room, which seemed utterly humiliating in hindsight. Bai Dai's words rang out in my ears: "This is the true nature of the world."

All of that nonsense about my company sending me on a business trip had been nothing but a ploy to get me smoothly admitted to the hospital. I underwent gene reengineering, and even my memories underwent some process of reconfiguration. Like the box lunches provided with each examination, the hospital provided a specific cause for each patient's disease. For me, that cause was a bottle of mineral water. From there, everything played out naturally, and patients found themselves coming to the hospital without even realizing it. There was no level of service more thoughtful and precise than what the hospital provided. Its treatment reached the very depths of the patient's soul.

The entire notion of being "cured and discharged" became a false proposition. I gradually came to understand that the word "discharge," in normal situations, carried only two possible meanings. The first was a transfer to another hospital where a patient can continue his or her therapy, or another department, perhaps from the respiratory department to the gastroenterology department, or from dermatology to neurology, or from internal medicine to the surgery unit. Some illnesses *can* travel. In other cases, a patient suffered multiple ailments concurrently, but curing one illness is very different from curing *all* of a patient's illnesses. The second meaning of "discharge" was being sent to the crematorium.

"And so most patients who come to the hospital should try to avoid any negative thoughts," Bai Dai explained, exhaling a plume of smoke from her nostrils. "They should just close their eyes and think about the Indian peafowl."

The Indian peafowl belongs to the class of animals that includes birds, Galliformes, pheasants, and peacocks. They originate primarily in present-day Pakistan, India, and Sri Lanka, and they are the national bird of India. The tail feathers of the male Indian peafowl are 150 centimeters long and can be displayed erect or spread open like a fan. Adorned with reflective blue "eyes," they are used to intimidate natural enemies, who mistake these feathered "eyes" for those of a large predatory mammal. If the enemy is not frightened away, the Indian peafowl will shake its tail feathers and release a loud shriek. Of course, the most important facet of the Indian peafowl's long plumes are what they represent: the health of the animal. The eye-catching Indian peafowl's feather language screams to the opposite sex, "I'm not sick! I'm strong! I've got energy! I can scare away the bad guys!" The females tend to be attracted to males that have more "eyes"—*Ah, he is healthy and able and can protect me!*—measuring their health by the beauty of their feathers. Pairing with a healthy male can help ensure that the Indian peafowl female has a better chance of "surviving" and "having more offspring." Tragically, males not endowed with long plumes or enough "eyes" are not viewed as sufficiently appealing and find it almost impossible to attract mates. Through the continued process of evolution, male peafowls have evolved plumes that are longer, increasingly exaggerated, and ever more clumsy, an evolutionary trait that has broken away from other, more practical aspects of their existence. The plume has become a kind of art, and male Indian peafowl have become like punk artists, a rather pathological state. Those massive feathers weigh down their bodies, and when they're attacked by a fox or a mountain lion, their movements are so slow and stunted that they end up as dinner, thus failing to produce more offspring. At the end of the day, the Indian peafowl has become an endangered species, teetering on the brink of extinction, never seeing their own plumes as a disability, obliviously prancing on and proudly displaying their feathers.

Are we not also like the Indian peafowl?

Life is the greatest treasure. Life is nothing, and it is everything. The establishment of hospitals to preserve the health of individuals and society is unique to the human species. The hospital eradicated the illogical traits and blind spots of evolution. The mutated tail plume called the "family" had to be eliminated.

Naturally, the invention of genome research played a critical role in medical dialectics: *To be healthy is to be sick, to be sick is to be healthy.* This was the intellectual foundation of the hospital's long-term prosperity. And thanks to Bai Dai, I had finally seen the light.

According to the vocabulary of medical punk, "to live" is "to live for the good of the hospital," or rather "in order for the hospital to live on." We had entered a new level in our spiritual development, which we could only have begun to grasp after a long-term stay at the hospital.

33

SURGICAL SCARS ON A WOMAN'S BODY

Genetic modification was but the starting point. Once that procedure was complete, for the rest of their lives, patients still needed to work from the foundation of a newly modified body, and following the ever-changing orders provided by their doctors and working with the hospital's vast, seemingly endless platform of care in this magnificent forest fostered by high-pressure oxygen bottles, they continued to seek treatment, treatment of all kinds, lifelong treatment, in order to reshape their lives, to re-create the network of life around them and their social relationships in an even broader context. According to the description in *Medical News*, all treatment carried out in the Age of Medicine was comprehensive, coordinated, and all-inclusive. Treatment was continuous, carried on with the patient's every breath, every heartbeat, every step, and every thought. Only when all citizens participated in endless treatment could society as a whole regain its full vitality and create miracles that measured up to this great age.

Bai Dai told me that in the hospital's standing toolbox, the methods at its disposal were quite diverse. Besides gene therapy, a rich variety of powerful treatment options was available. For instance, in order to prevent HIV from destroying immune cells and causing carriers of the virus to fall ill, biologic inhibitors were utilized to block synapses between cells; another option was the use of nanobots to increase the physical distance between cells and prevent contact between them, effectively staving off death. What she said made me feel uneasy. I started to suspect that the example she cited was actually her own case.

During her twenty-five years of life, she must have experienced all kinds of extraordinary things, and yet they remained hidden from me. I suspected that she would never truly open up to me, never tell me what disease or diseases she was actually suffering from, instead revealing only selective details. Bai Dai was quite the schemer, but that is what the hospital environment does to people.

She had mentioned a certain treatment that she had undergone back when she was twenty-two, a surgery to open her neck and implant electrodes into her vagus nerve. The electrodes had been made from a platinum-iridium alloy, the anchor bolt and wire film both of silicon. A microbattery with a fifty-year life span had been inserted. Thanks to different levels of electrode stimulation, she had finally been able to improve her attention deficit disorder. Two five-centimeter scars were left on her neck and chest, and a third scar marked a three-way infusion port that had also been implanted in her body. This was of course not a traditional port: it also served as a wireless biosensor, constantly recording her heartbeat, blood pressure, breathing, temperature, blood oxygen level, blood sugar, brain waves, and other physical and psychological data and sending that information remotely to the hospital's supercomputer for timely processing and analysis. The great medical revolution had already merged with computers, the internet, mobile telephones, social media, and big data, and it was now one with the energy revolution, the information revolution, the AI revolution, and the space revolution. A fourth surgical scar on Bai Dai's back came from her climbing up on the windowsill during one of her screaming episodes and falling to the ground, injuring her back. Dr. Bauchi had gone in from the back and, opening up her spinal cord, removed her glial scars, then used an endoscope to remove approximately three centimeters of olfactory mucosa from the depths of her nasal cavity, transplanting it into the spinal cord to regenerate the nerve fiber bundles. Her fifth incision was therefore in her nasal cavity.

As far as I was concerned, the surgical scars on Bai Dai's body were beautiful, full of vibrant colors that made her much sexier. Humans were no longer limited to the nine orifices. Her wounds were like the feathers of a peacock, her procedures more effective than any cosmetics or plastic surgery. Her feminine qualities, her womanhood, combined with the heroic spirit of a man, making it appear as if anything could be inserted into virtually any part of her body. I felt quite self-conscious, though, because I had never received the same level of care or attention. Not every patient got to have a sensor installed, and even for those lucky enough to get one, each model had different functionality, based on the economic resources of the patient.

Take, for example, the veteran patient Old Yu. He had paid a hefty down payment and upgraded his skin cells to pluripotent stem cells, which could treat his Alzheimer's disease, accomplished by modifying only four genes. Stem cell therapy was an alternative to gene therapy, inducing pluripotent cells with the ability to self-replicate. Nanobots would then target these cells and deliver them to the designated part of the body, where they helped to improve the patient's symptoms. Or take Little Meng, who was extremely wealthy and had nearly one hundred implanted sensors, auxiliary treatment devices that made him look like a cyborg. Little Shi had paid a hefty price to purchase an artificial liver and kidney to replace his own failing organs. Old Sha was even more well off. His doctors had directly programmed his cells, and with the help of a computer, they operated his body according to his instructions, synthesizing insulin or launching attacks on dermal neurofibromas as needed.

Bai Dai continued to take me on long strolls around the hospital. We weren't trying to escape. We knew that according to the law of medical dialectics, we would never be fully diagnosed or cured, so our only choice was to stay in the hospital and receive—or rather enjoy—our treatment, waiting for our eventual death by way of disease or a medical accident. Inexplicable cases of medical negligence continued to occur in the hospital, but this was a relatively safer way to die, and we no longer had to worry about dying from natural disasters, traffic accidents, or court-ordered punishments.

34

THE NECESSITY OF LIFELONG TREATMENT

One day I asked Bai Dai why we would never get a full diagnosis or be fully cured. The question stemmed from my love of the wounds that adorned her body. In response, Bai Dai began to tell me about her life.

"The treatment began to rumble through my mother's womb before I was even born. They determined that I had a disease when I was still a fertilized ovum. An illness at this early stage is considered an 'original sickness.' They performed chorionic villus sampling, inserting a tube into my mother's vagina and extracting a sample of fetal tissue from the placenta, which allowed them to confirm further that my chromosomes had undergone a series of pathological changes. I received my very first gene treatment when I was just a ten-week-old fetus. The doctor performed genetic reediting on the inherited cells, removing deficient genes, and I was later told that the procedure was quite thorough, with almost no room for error. With one fell swoop, they eliminated all of my genetic defects. My mother was quite old when she conceived me, and I was originally afflicted with Down syndrome. I had an extra copy of chromosome twenty-one, which would have stunted my mental development. So in some sense, you could say that I have been designed. But this does not mean that I am not qualified to be admitted to the hospital. In fact, as soon as I was born, they admitted me to the sick ward, and I have never left."

"I understand. You're here for lifelong treatment. This is why they opened so many holes in your body and installed so many devices as you grew up."

"At first it left me somewhat frustrated. Then I figured it out."

"What . . . ?"

"It's the environment. In theory, disease is the combined result of inherited genes and the environment in which one lives; this is what they describe in the medical textbooks: 'Your genes provide the ammunition, but it takes just the right environmental factor to pull the trigger.' You would think that if your fetal genes were perfectly reengineered before you even came into the world, it would be extremely difficult for the environment to find its prey. But in reality, that couldn't be further from the truth."

"Woo . . ." I took a look around the sick ward. Patients were tortured by their diseased bodies to the point of near death, and I was reminded of the incessant cries and moans of the crowd in the outpatient ward and the relentless stomach pain I had suffered, and I realized that this was indeed quite the paradox.

"Even though our genes have been successfully reedited, the number of people getting sick keeps increasing."

"Perhaps it is all just a holographic projection meant to test us?" I suggested.

"On the one hand, over a person's lifetime, cells continually split and undergo new mutations, so there are a lot of things that even doctors can't fully explain. On the other hand, you can attribute some of this to the deterioration of the environment and other unknown factors. Cancer is a kind of genetic disease that originates with the destruction of the DNA sequence, but this destruction is always triggered by external factors. We are not born with cancer. Take the ever-worsening air pollution; it is so bad that on some days you can't see the sun all day. What is happening? Holes in the ozone layer result in ultraviolet rays being too strong. These days the vast majority of cancer-cell mutations are not hereditary but gradually accumulated over the course of our lives. You must admit that environmental factors have become like a kind of murder weapon, though *Medical News* would never openly report this. But what are patients to do? The doctor told me that the reason I contracted cancer was because I smoke cigarettes. He asked me to quit. But think about it: the worse the pollution gets, the harder it is to breathe and the more you feel like smoking. How are people expected to go on living in such misery? Let's put it this way: environmental factors are replacing genetic factors. The environment screws us in all kinds of ways, like a new form of genetic disease, and yet we cannot control our environment. Even a hospital as incredible as this one is helpless when it comes to the environment."

"But I was told that our environment is getting better and better."

"That is just the propaganda you see in the newspaper. In fact, it is deteriorating."

A lot of the people that had hired me to write songs had also developed various illnesses after being unable to adapt to the environment. They endured constant pain and suffering, and yet doctors couldn't find anything physically wrong with them. Their only respite was occasional trips to the karaoke room. Cases like mine, when people get sick from something as simple as drinking water, were actually quite common. The environment was indeed becoming increasingly inhospitable. People had begun to live their everyday lives as if walking on eggshells, but as time went by, even that had become increasingly difficult, and many took steps to emigrate to foreign countries.

"But how can that be?" I asked.

"Because of the West. According to *Medical News*, Westerners are not playing fair. They have created an unfavorable environment in order to hold us back, using meteorological, geological, and biological weapons to achieve their aims."

"Weren't the first hospitals in our country built by Western missionaries?"

"The Westerners are different creatures. Their behavior is always strange and contradictory. We will never truly understand them."

"Indeed." I supposed that Westerners saw us as a different species; our behavior is strange and contradictory. "But why do we have portraits of Western doctors hanging near the entrance to the sick ward? To humiliate them?"

"To deceive them. It is a tactic. We pretend to know nothing about their elaborate conspiracy, superficially maintaining our friendship while we exploit them for their medical technologies and products. In this way, the hospital is able to survive and develop."

I gazed at Bai Dai with admiration. "Wow, you know so many secrets about the world."

"There is another major threat too. Have you heard of the recent epidemic involving cases of King's respiratory syndrome? It took the lives of quite a few people. An interview with some specialists in *Medical News* reported that Western forces, filled with hatred for our nation, created a virus with the intention of attacking us—a calculated plot to hurt us! The virus is triggered by specific genes found only in our ethnic group. It's extremely strong, even able to modify itself and mutate to evade detection by either the host's immune system or drug treatments. Infection leads to long-term illness, and as long as the patient is alive, the virus remains in the system. Look, haven't I experienced problems with both my urinary tract and my spinal cord? Later I also developed attention deficit disorder, and none of these has anything to do with the genes my mother passed on to me. How do we explain this? It is all part of an elaborate conspiracy concocted by the West. And so the treatment never ends. On and on it goes, staying with us for the remainder of whatever in our lives has any meaning. In some ways this is actually pretty cool. Illness is, after all, the fashion of the day. It symbolizes our everlasting struggle against the West. According to an editorial in *Medical News*, so-called lifelong treatment is ultimately a test of patients' faith. Only when we have true faith in the hospital and the doctors can we commit our entire lives to the eternal struggle against the West."

Bai Dai's words mechanically flowed off her tongue. She didn't stop and think, as if her speech were filling some kind of gap in her life. The confused and jumbled way she presented these theories seemed to provide a subtle temporary balance between her emotional, logical, impulsive, and neurotic sides. I was afraid that she did not really understand the meaning of what she said, the instinctual reaction of someone hospitalized long term for a chronic illness. I thought of it as "spontaneous chemotaxis," taking pleasure in learning everything related to a specific disease.

I listened passively, but a thought suddenly flashed through my mind: *What if the doctors had intentionally injected her with defective gene fragments during the embryonic stage?* That would have ensured the child's admission to the hospital at birth and that it would spend its entire life in the hospital. Could Bai Dai be nothing more than a guinea pig? Could a medical-punk doctor intentionally insert a virus into a patient?

Could that be what had happened to me? I had endured multiple treatments and therapies, yet the pain I suffered never seemed to improve. Could *this* be why? Or perhaps this was punishment for my previous crimes? For the inconvenience that my illness brought upon others, perhaps I had been sentenced to lifelong punishment.

Westerners had created such an unfavorable environment that the only countermeasure the hospital could adopt was to create an even *more* unfavorable environment by producing *more* diseases and patients, an ultimate "antienvironmental weapon."

These were heretical thoughts that I would never dare to share with another soul, not even Bai Dai. But if I was to stay in the hospital forever, what could I do but continue my treatment?

Bai Dai kept searching for an answer to the question, How do doctors die? Normal patients would never have raised such a question. As far as I could tell, it was a strange and inappropriate question, and yet Bai Dai was abnormally fascinated by this mystery. She simply could not let go of it. And so, as she took me around the hospital and up to the observatory to gaze through the telescope, I knew that her main goal was to find evidence by locating the body of a dead doctor.

I thought of what Shuji Terayama had said: the role that women play most is that of a corpse. Women were often looked at as outdated spies, unable to keep even a single secret. In the end, all they could do was play dead. In this sense, Bai Dai very much resembled a beacon of death, driven to continue her search for dead doctors.

I couldn't help but feel a growing sense of sympathy and admiration for this young patient who had sacrificed her youth for the good of the sick ward. But then, what role did men play? Perhaps they were the maggots on the body.

Could this have been the cause of all my pain? The biblical Adam had been sleeping when he was awakened with a pain in his flank. "Huh? What happened? Who took one of my ribs?" He heard a sweet voice behind him, and he turned to discover a beautiful woman. "Who are you?" he gasped painfully. "And is that my rib in your hand?"

"That's right. I'm holding your lost rib."

"Are you toying with me?" Adam had screamed. "What is your name?"

"My name is Eve."

At that point in my thoughts, I couldn't help but rub my stomach. The pain was unbearable.

Sometimes I thought that Bai Dai was the only one who qualified as a bona fide medical punk. But I could never let the doctors know that I entertained such thoughts. It would have been much too dangerous. They might think that Bai Dai had developed a new disease. And so I became, in a manner of speaking, her protector. We were like a pair of military scouts who, under the pretext of "taking strolls together," continued our search for the Indian peafowl.

I previously described the structure of the hospital as being inordinately complicated, like a massive galactic battleship. Beneath the deck, various facilities were like a crowded forest, the corridors densely arranged like a spider's web, the secret chambers spread like stars in the sky—finding a doctor's corpse amid all of this would not be an easy task.

Bai Dai drew a military-grade map of the hospital that we used to navigate our way. After many years of observation, she had figured out most of the basic details of the hospital's layout. Based on her map, the inpatient department was made up of two series of buildings, the diagnostic towers and the treatment towers, the latter further divided into surgery towers and internal medicine towers. There were also an additional five research towers and two libraries. Each tower and group of buildings was freestanding but connected, collectively forming one massive structure. Several thousand operating rooms were concentrated in a single tower. Countless laboratories spread like inlaid pearls among the sick wards. Interspersed among the buildings were the departments of infrastructure, general affairs, housing management, auditing, accounting, logistics management, and other administrative offices. The complexity and sophistication of the organization was comparable to the imperial palace of ancient history.

On our journey to find the bodies of dead doctors, Bai Dai resembled an archaeologist. One day we discovered a round bronze plate inscribed with a snake wrapping a crucifix. She explained to me that this image was the logo of the hospital's forerunner, which was a teaching hospital established in our nation by the Rockefeller Foundation in the 1920s. For quite some time, this secret history had not been talked about openly, and I had no idea how Bai Dai had dug up this information.

35

THE ROCKEFELLER KINGDOM
OF WESTERN MEDICINE

The legendary John D. Rockefeller was one of the wealthiest men in the United States during the early twentieth century. Besides being regarded as the "oil titan," he was also well known for being a devout Northern Baptist. He had a famous saying: "I believe it is a religious duty to get all the money you can, fairly and honestly; to keep all you can, and to give away all you can." That led him to establish his own charity foundation. Beginning in 1913, the Rockefeller Foundation would spend US$80 million during its first decade, with more than half of that money devoted to public health and medical education, including the establishment of the Rockefeller Institute for Medical Research, which would go on to produce twelve Nobel laureates. But the largest single gift bestowed by the Rockefeller Foundation was reserved for our nation—the foundation spent more than US$10 million to establish a hospital and medical school.

It is said that, at that time, the Americans had a deep interest in our nation and thought that saving the "Oriental heretics" from poverty, backwardness, stupidity, and rampant disease was the single greatest act of merit in the eyes of God. After three separate visits to our nation, Rockefeller finally decided that the field of medicine should be prioritized for aid. That is how the former incarnation of Central Hospital in C City was established. The Americans believed that to save the people here, they would need to establish hospitals in the poorest locations rather than in the capital or the flourishing coastal cities. And so, C City it was!

The hospital and its affiliated medical school used English as its working language and hired some of the best doctors from the Western world. The aim was to establish a medical system on a par with those of Europe and North America, to have an outstanding team of teachers, the best labs, and a top-notch teaching hospital and nursing school. Great effort was devoted to training outstanding medical talent in clinical experience, education, scientific research, and public health management. During that period of chaos and unrest, these Westerners came to our country, filled with idealism, attempting to establish a new kingdom for Western medicine, to plant in this Oriental nation the best medical science the West had to offer and allow it to take root forever in our soil. At the very least, they would "allow the people of that nation to have a basic understanding of the journey of life." From then on the lives of our backward people were transformed by the violent impact of Western medicine.

I couldn't help but wonder: Was this the origin of all our happiness and suffering?

The Rockefeller Foundation also invested US$6 million to build a massive two-hundred-inch telescope in the United States. At the time, this was the single largest donation ever made toward the sciences. Prior to that, the largest telescope in the world was the hundred-inch Hooker telescope built in 1917. Edwin Hubble had used this telescope to observe for the first time that our Milky Way galaxy was but one of numerous galaxies in the universe and to discover evidence for the expansion of the universe.

"Establishing hospitals and building telescopes seemed to be two sides of the same coin," Bai Dai said to me once. "Rockefeller must have long ago discovered the subtle connection between the hospital and the universe. But what happened later?"

Historical records reveal that in 1921, Rockefeller's son, John D. Rockefeller Jr., attended a ceremony celebrating the completion of the hospital. He expressed his hope that the hospital would one day be handed over to the locals. "Clearly, whatever Western medical science may have to offer China, it will be of little avail to the Chinese people until it is taken over by them and becomes a part of the national life."

It took only thirty years for this goal to be fully realized. In 1952, during the Korean War, the hospital was reclaimed by the new government as a state-owned entity. All Western medical personnel left, and our own people took over the hospital's operation and management. The original incarnation of the hospital was viewed as a tool of the Americans to carry out intellectual and cultural invasion under the pretext of charity work.

From the 1960s through the 1970s, the entire nation became the victim of an all-out Western blockade. Much-needed medical equipment and supplies could not be attained through previous import channels. The nation's policy of self-reliance necessitated an integration of Chinese and Western medicine. The government implemented a preventive medicine and treatment program for the masses, adopting local methods to tackle key scientific and technical problems. This allowed for medical breakthroughs, including the invention of the artificial heart membrane, artificial heart-lung machine, and artificial cornea; the development of the BCG and smallpox vaccines and the elimination of smallpox and schistosomiasis; preventive steps against tuberculosis, Japanese encephalitis, endemic thyroid abscess, and other diseases; the success of reattached limb surgery, kidney transplant surgery, and liver transplant surgery; the use of traditional Chinese medicine and acupuncture for anesthesia; the artificial synthesis of bovine insulin; and the "eliminate the four scourges" campaign to promote public hygiene, a focus on sanitation in rural areas, and greatly improved care for newborn babies and their mothers, which resulted in a dramatic decline in infant mortality. As a key hospital operating on a national level, Central

Hospital in C City played an important role in this series of medical breakthroughs.

As a result, the people's quality of health care continued to improve, and we witnessed the single largest population explosion in history. This growth was later viewed as the cause of immense economic burden, but at the time it was a source of national pride. Even today, many nations are unable to achieve such growth; their mortality rates are simply too high, and they have entered a period of negative population growth. During the early twenty-first century, the African nation of Somalia had an average life expectancy of only forty-seven years, and in Zimbabwe, it was only thirty-six, equivalent to the life expectancy in our nation back in 1949.

One of the most important achievements came in the early 1970s, when the Central Hospital's Institute for Medical Research invented a new drug to treat cholera. The discovery was based on herbs used in traditional Chinese medicine. During the Vietnam War, large numbers of North Vietnamese soldiers were infected with cholera, suspected to be the result of a biological warfare campaign waged by the United States. Military hospitals and research facilities formed task groups to tackle the problem but were not making good headway. Who could have anticipated that Central Hospital in C City would crack the case? Its vaccine played a vital role in helping North Vietnam defeat the South and resulted in the complete withdrawal of American troops from the country, changing the course of history. Large quantities of the vaccine were manufactured and exported to other Third World nations, and the vaccine was hailed as a medical miracle. The Westerners referred to it as "the flower of the Cold War." Nations that benefited from the vaccine then supported China's bid to reclaim its seat in the United Nations in the 1970s.

Yet during that era, doctors formerly employed by the old Rockefeller hospital were also subjected to criticism, trampled upon, sent to the cowshed, and forced to do hard labor at reeducation camps.

Unable to stand the abuse and insults, some of them committed suicide. Was this a clue about whether doctors could in fact die? Could
this history have been the basis for Bai Dai's belief that doctors were
not immortal?

After the 1980s, Western medicine received unprecedented attention, and it was also around this time that contact with the West
resumed. The backbone of our hospital system was a group of doctors
that had studied in the United States and Europe. These students discovered an astonishing gap between the most advanced medical technologies of the developed world and what they had been exposed to at
home, which set them off on a frenzied search for medical knowledge,
information, and other patented and confidential materials that they
could bring back to their motherland. They eschewed traditional medicinal practices, and for the next several decades, our nation became a site
of great strategic importance for international pharmaceutical manufacturers and medical-equipment supply companies. We also became
the primary market for the sale and testing of new drugs from all over
the world. Every piece of clinical and lab equipment, large and small,
from CT scanners and nuclear magnetic resonance imaging equipment
to particle accelerators, was imported at a cost many times greater than
that of local manufacturers. Customs taxes swelled, as did supplier fees,
bribes, and the cost of medical personnel's international "observation"
trips.

However, the spirit of the Rockefeller era was long gone, and the
Age of Medicine was taking form. A crucial question was posed for the
first time: *Does the United States really exist?* Or had it been created just
to scare us? This mirage-like country remained a real place in the eyes
of many, but the details surrounding this fantasy nation seemed to grow
richer and more elaborate by the day. This, too, must have been some
form of illness.

But the truth was that the Rockefellers and everything that came
with their story were nothing but a series of imaginary props. *The*

hospital had been independently established by us. When she learned all this, Bai Dai's noble attempts to find archaeological evidence for her beliefs went up in smoke. She had a difficult time coming to terms with this.

During the early twenty-first century, C City's Central Hospital underwent a large-scale renovation. Rebuilt along modernist aesthetics, every trace of its former self was wiped away. In the Age of Medicine, its magnificent scale and bold construction still stood as a model amid a sprawling urban sea of hospitals. One of the major purposes of the renovations and upgrades was to prepare for the struggle against the Western clique, which was then led by the Rockefellers.

Bai Dai and I continued to explore this massive hospital, with its long and venerable history, on our journey to find a doctor's corpse.

36

PATIENTS ARE LIVING PEOPLE
IN THE STATE OF DYING

Over the course of our journey, Bai Dai and I often ran into various doctors and nurses, but they were all alive. We encountered security guards, but they almost never stopped us. Their main responsibility was suppressing hospital riots, but they also intervened when patients smoked in their rooms or engaged in acts of petty theft. Bai Dai often had her cigarettes confiscated, but she was usually able to get them back with a little bribe.

While on the road, we sometimes encountered the bodies of deceased patients, covered in a white cloth and placed in the corner of a hallway like pieces of unfinished lumber, waiting to be transported to the crematorium. Whenever we encountered one of these bodies, I whistled to Bai Dai, and taking my cue, she would remove the cloth covering and conduct a quick inspection of the still-warm body. Since she had lived in the hospital so long, she knew what all the doctors looked like, and yet we never discovered the body of a single dead doctor. Every corpse was a 100 percent certified patient. Their appearance, preserved at the moment of their departure from the world, was usually shocking and disturbing, yet there was something enchanting about them, like a terrifying horror movie that you can't stop watching.

Later we grew bored of all this, but during that time, I was still intoxicated by constant nightmares. The most common elements in those nightmares was death. In one nightmare my immune system rejected an infusion of foreign genes, triggering an even more serious disease. I lay there on the brink of death, filled with terror yet unable to speak. Then on the eve of my death, I saw a ring of rose-colored lights descending from the heavens, and I woke up, heaving a sigh of relief at the revelation that it had been just a dream.

It made me think: *What is death? What will I be like when I die?*

Though the hospital was powerful, it did not prevent people from dying.

Whenever a death occurred in the sick ward, it was almost always the doctor who announced it. The precise time of death was confirmed by diagnostic equipment meticulously designed to pinpoint the exact minute of death. Ever since the twentieth century, the number of hospital deaths had dramatically increased. Normal people no longer died at home, on the street, or in the river. My own parents were a case in point. Like Bai Dai said, a life snuffed out was nothing but a piece of medical data.

The institutionalization and medicalization of death had become popular, obscured by the hypocritical medical-punk approach to hospice care, but deep down nothing really changed. Natural deaths without medical intervention sounded like a joke. Nobody knew what it meant to "die a good death" anymore.

Not even Dr. Bauchi could tell us what death is. When it comes to death, even medical-school professors are nothing more than skilled technical operators. Death was said to be part of the mystery of quantum medicine, related to the phenomenon of consciousness but still being explored by a very small number of supergeek medical researchers, a top secret superweapon to forestall foreign intervention. I had no plans to make any inquiries, and Bai Dai was interested only in the question of whether doctors could die. She couldn't have cared less about the deaths of her fellow patients. She had already seen far too much death in her life.

Bai Dai and I decided to pay a visit to the VIP sick ward. Could there be any dying doctors there? Security was extremely tight, so all we could do was sneak a peek from outside. The ward was as fancy as the presidential suite in a five-star hotel, several times larger than my hospital room, and yet with only one patient inside. The room was equipped with a television set, a computer with internet access, a private bathroom, a sofa, and some special therapy equipment that I didn't even recognize. Fresh flowers and a fruit tray were brought in every day. More than a dozen doctors and nurses scurried around the single patient. The patient could be on the brink of death—or in some cases, already dead—and yet the medical personnel refused to give up, inserting breathing and circulation tubes and intravenous drips, and in some cases even replacing the patient's body fluids or performing spinal cord replacement surgery. This could go on for years, just so the patient could maintain a faint pulse and strained breathing. Could *this* patient have been a doctor? Perhaps only a doctor deserved such great effort? But later I learned that he was simply a VIP patient whose care was much better than a part-time songwriter like me could ever expect.

The inpatient ward had plenty of these zombielike patients on display, who received the best medicine year after year and had access to the most advanced medical equipment. Yet they never woke up. They made us feel that it was possible to live forever—a shame, then, that they were just patients and not doctors. But they were still categorized as top secret superweapons.

Here I need to mention another definition of what it meant to be a patient. Patients were living people in the state of dying. They had already set one foot on the bridge to hell, and yet they used medical means to create the illusion that they had yet to begin that voyage.

Had Bai Dai been sent from heaven to help me tear down that illusion?

37

THE RELATIONSHIP BETWEEN MAN AND GOD APPEARS LUMINOUS, BUT IT IS RUINOUS

No matter what, the Age of Medicine helps broaden the nature of our lives. Bai Dai's life had become very special. I gradually came to understand that, unlike me, she had the ability to think independently and emphatically. She was a woman quite unlike any other. She had been in the hospital since she emerged from her mother's womb: twenty-five long years in the sick ward. She had a stubborn and independent personality and loved to both contemplate and understand things. When she was a child, she had often lain on her sickbed pondering all kinds of strange questions: *Why are there four legs on my sickbed? What are the doctors wearing under their white medical jackets? How come there are never any animals in the garden? Are there hospitals up among the stars?* Over time, these thoughts transformed into a kind of obsessive-compulsive disorder. Her mind was always pregnant with new ideas. She pondered the truths hiding behind the illusions.

Early on Bai Dai had been extremely deferential toward doctors, like all the other patients. She had expressed her admiration for them, and she had always been respectful and obedient, but she gradually began to feel like something was off. She saw patients pass away, but never once had she seen a doctor die. Among all her fellow patients, not one was a former doctor. If the sole purpose of the doctors' existence was to save other people, why did they themselves never seem to give a second thought to their own well-being? To relieve the suffering of the masses, to control and reorganize life, to wipe out demonic enemies, were those not the powers of God? God does not fall ill. God does not die. God is immortal. Here in the sick ward, the truth dangled right before our eyes: the Age of Medicine was ruled by divine authority. Bai Dai was the only one obsessing over these strange questions that no one else dared to ask. She was terribly ill, and yet all she thought about was whether the doctors got sick or died. She was truly one in a million. How many years must it have taken the hospital to produce such a patient?

Bai Dai's were actually commonsense questions, simple enough, yet extremely difficult for most patients ever to consider. Excessive medication had damaged most patients' ability to think normally, and many patients simply dropped dead shortly after being admitted—they didn't even have enough time to ponder such questions. But Bai Dai had survived much longer than most. In twenty-five years, she had developed a resistance to her prescription drugs, and thanks to the stimulation provided by the electrodes implanted in her body, her neurotransmitters had strengthened, allowing for the production of uncommon thoughts. But she had never seen or heard about any doctor ever getting sick. Indeed, she had never even heard a doctor complain, "I've got a cold!" "I've got a toothache!" "My heartbeat seems irregular!" They spent all day in this germ-infested environment, constantly in close contact with patients, and yet they never got sick? How was that possible?

And was the deeper meaning behind "living for the hospital" actually "living for the doctors"?

There was one possible hidden explanation: *Doctors had some special procedure to grant themselves eternal life.* But what kind of procedure? Could they have figured out how to stop their organs, their bodies, from aging? Or some special technique to shield their feelings? Had they solved the mystery of why gene-sequence replication always led to errors and mutations, causing the body to accumulate inactive and even toxic proteins? Did medicine have a deeper goal beyond simply helping patients to recover? Was the *real* goal to help some achieve eternal life?

More than two thousand years ago, the first emperor of China, Qin Shihuang, sent the alchemist Xu Fu out to sea in search of an elixir of immortality. When the monk Tang Sanzang journeyed to the West to retrieve the Buddhist scriptures and all those monsters tried to eat him, weren't they all hoping that his flesh held the secret to everlasting life? Perhaps, after all of this arduous searching, medical biologists had finally found the elusive key to immortality?

It was said that the hospital had not only discovered the death gene—actually a series of genes—but mastered how to turn it on and off. But there are many ways to control life and death, and Bai Dai suspected that doctors had even figured out how to control entropy. Entropy measures the quality of life activities, but it has reached the point of total disorder.

In 1944, Erwin Schrödinger published *What Is Life?*, a book in which he put forth the idea of negative entropy, using physics terminology to describe biology. "What an organism feeds upon is negative entropy," the book proposed, meaning that entropy is the central idea of life. Control entropy, and you control life. Although this might have been technically possible, was it fair? Was it rational? If an elixir of eternal life existed, why didn't the hospital give it to the patients? Bai Dai had personally witnessed her fellow patients dying, one after another. Their entropy *always* increased.

Indeed, in the sick ward, death was something that occurred on a daily basis. Targeted care and personalized treatment are all worthless when it comes down to those critical moments when it really matters. I was terrified the first time I encountered, for example, the case of deeply respected model patient Uncle Zhao. One day he was talking and laughing—he even delivered a lecture on popular science—but the following day, he was a goner. He lay in bed, unable to get up, his face purple, foaming at the mouth, his limbs twitching. His heart rate reached 250 beats per minute. The remote sensor on his body sounded an alarm, and a doctor quickly rushed over. He tried to resuscitate Uncle Zhao, but his effort was to no avail. Two lines of thick black goo oozed out of his nostrils, dripping into his mouth, as he kicked the bucket. Yet he died with a smile on his face, though it was probably nothing but a false appearance, since he had been screaming in pain just before that, his shrieks utterly earth shattering. Finally the doctors put the machines aside and performed manual heart compressions as curious patients gathered, staring in silence as Uncle Zhao's stomach blew up like a balloon. The hunch on his back trembled; then he turned pale and listless. He was gone. The dead look just like us, but in reality they are very different. Alas, this was the problem. Uncle Zhao wouldn't ever be able to ramble on again about the miraculous achievements made during the Age of Medicine. His soul had begun a new journey, the next hospital its destination.

Euthanasia was also promoted broadly. Some patients actively applied for the procedure, and doctors directly employed euthanasia based on the clinical condition of their patients. Many such scenes left us feeling like we were witnessing the magnificent end of the world, taking a scenic tour through the gorgeous ruins of an ancient architectural site.

I used to think death was scary. But novels, poems, operas, films, and television shows about death (with climactic moments like a bullet suddenly taking the life of a young protagonist) showed just how beautiful death is. After witnessing the death of so many patients, I began to realize the wonder of it all. The chaos of life cleared away, and I felt like I had finally emptied an old garbage bin that no one had tended to. Every process—war, politics, terrorist attacks—ends in death. It is the result of a search for clarity, the final realization of life, a new form of beauty that bursts at the very instant that the beauty of life fades away. No, that's not it—beauty is the collective demise of a combination of the stupid, the ugly, bodily fluid, pus, regret, and tenderness. Pain is secondary to all of that. Observing the sick ward firsthand, I attained a deep understanding of what is commonly referred to as "fatal beauty."

In my pain, I could not help but yearn for death. When would I finally be able to experience it firsthand?

The data collected from patients' bioimplants was transferred to the hospital's central computer system for processing and analysis. With the exception of saving patients, this data most interested the doctors. The medical community remained dumbfounded by those final moments before death. Genome research remained unable to explain it. Like quantum problems, it was likely connected to the mysterious nature of consciousness.

According to one theory published in *Medical News*, human death does not signal a person's leaving the world but the disappearance of the world itself. The world exists only in the eyes of the living. The world is composed of particles, and if particles become real only through the act of human observation, then when no human observes them, all that exists are waves of illusion. So what are life and death? This was an incredibly challenging research question that only a small minority of supergeek medical scientists studied, and I have no plan to address it. More promising were advances in cracking the encrypted information contained within neurons, though we were still a long way from truly understanding how thoughts and consciousness form. Perhaps the research will prove how foolish humankind really is.

As if they couldn't bear to leave the sick ward behind, deceased patients quietly lay in their sickbeds for a while before finally being taken to the morgue. I often found myself staring at those dead patients as their bodies grew cold. I would zone out and think about how they must have been filled with hope and optimism when they first checked into the hospital. After countless tests and unspeakably painful treatments, they kept telling themselves, *Hang in there, try to bear it, you can do it, everything will be okay when this is over.* But in the end, death inevitably waited for them, as if it were their greatest reward.

"Hang in there" was the most frequently used phrase in the hospital. And if we could hang in there until death, that was truly amazing.

Every time I saw the specter of death approaching, I was struck with the same incredible feeling, as if I had suddenly looked up from the roof of the world to see a tapestry of shining stars lighting up the sky. They appeared so clear, as if just within reach, like ornamental crystals in a storefront window. Hard to believe that they would one day come crashing down upon us. Some people claim that death is nothing but an illusion, that like time, it doesn't really even exist. But I didn't need to go any farther than the morgue to see all the proof I needed: at the end of the day, that is where all the patients ended up.

Death was always repeating; like eating or getting dressed, it happened over and over. Some referred to it as one of the miracles of everyday life, reminding us of what the Buddhist scriptures call "infinite kalpas of misfortune."

Therefore a lot of meticulous attention was paid to master the distinction between "death" and "immortality." Was this simply the doctors' way of monopolizing resources, of maintaining the hospital's unassailable authority? If patients were to attain immortality, there would be no reason to "fear death" or "beg for death." And if no one feared death, who would come to the hospital for treatment? Who would take doctors seriously? Wouldn't the hospital be rendered superfluous? The Age of Medicine would have been reduced to an empty shell. And then how could the luscious hair of our nation and its people grow from a layer of dead skin?

From the perspective of extracting data about near-death experiences, research necessitated the sacrifice of patients. A modest and open-minded person like Dr. Bauchi could never take all the credit for himself.

Bai Dai thought these ideas extremely strange, and she wasn't at all ready to accept them. She didn't believe that doctors were made from special materials, nor that they were somehow immortal or immune from the virus of death. She was convinced that this idea was a big fantasy caused by patients' receiving only one-sided information. The real question patients should have been asking was, How do doctors die? She stubbornly held to the belief that doctors *could* die, that they were not gods but men—maybe demigods at the very most, but bound by biological reality. And these demigods had to have an Achilles' heel, a flaw that, under current conditions, meant that they could never achieve true immortality. We had recently entered into the Age of Medicine, but we were already on the eve of re-creating life itself. The achievements of the scientific revolution were still far from the point where biological organisms could achieve eternal life. We would need to wait many more years for that miracle. Doctors simply used the guise of "immortality" to deceive, intimidate, persuade, and control their patients, a means to ensure that they didn't get suspicious, make irresponsible comments, provoke hospital riots, or attempt to escape but rather willingly forked over the money for their hospital bills and accepted their treatment. Doctors had their own strategy and never openly talked about being unable to die, leaving patients with the impression that they were immortal gods. This caused many conflicts between doctors and patients, because patients' expectations of their doctors grew infinitely inflated.

As time went by, this gradually became a source of great distress for Bai Dai. Her obsession became more important to her than life itself. She even suspected that somewhere in the city was a secret hospital that specialized in treating sick doctors, a place where doctors were treated just like every other patient, and, when treatment failed, they, too, died. She couldn't believe that doctors and patients lived in separate worlds, nor that the relationship between doctors and patients should be like the relationship between God and man—luminous but ruinous. I began to feel that both sides were gearing up for war.

But in the Age of Medicine, it seemed like Bai Dai was the only patient with such a vivid imagination. If other patients happened to think similarly, they would never have dared to make their suspicions known, let alone set out to uncover the truth. The sole objective for most patients was to pull their heads back into their shells like frightened turtles and quietly live out the remains of their lives in the hospital, awaiting death. There was not a patient in the hospital who did not tremble before the doctors, terrified of somehow offending them, for they knew that such an offense could result in their being denied even the most basic medicine, essentially a death sentence, a ticket straight to the morgue, denied the chance to admire the beautiful scenery that comes before death. To ponder the death of the doctors? No one would dream of it, unless they were raving mad. But madness was not easily attained in the Age of Medicine. So when Bai Dai had bravely spoken those words—"Do you want to know how doctors die?"—it was like a peacock spreading its plumes, and the other patients pissed their pants in shock. She was deeply disappointed in them, filled with contempt for their weakness. As a new patient at the time, I was the only one who didn't run away. I just stood there blankly listening. Bai Dai had been moved that I had stayed there to listen, which served as the basis for our becoming friends, even companions.

Sometimes I wondered whether Bai Dai held these thoughts because, deep down, she still craved her freedom. She kept a part of herself secretly tucked away, something not determined by genes and thus not impacted by gene therapy. She yearned with all her heart and soul to break through the program that the hospital had constructed and to follow the truth inside her heart, to resist the delirious brainwashing that filled the pages of *Medical News*, to do something completely unconventional. But hers was an unproven thesis. Would the fact that doctors die mean that patients would no longer need treatment? Would it guarantee her freedom to finally check out of the hospital? From the purity of her sharp black eyes, I could see the deep yearning for freedom within her.

The hospital was actually similar to a prison: the patients' sick gowns resembled prison uniforms, the sick wards were like surveillance rooms with their ever-present security cameras, there were fixed times for visitors and for going outdoors, the chief medical officer functioned like a prison warden, nurses resembled prison guards . . . given all of this, shouldn't we have tried to win our freedom? But in the Age of Medicine, the word "freedom" is long forgotten, replaced by "treatment" in all the dictionaries. From this perspective, Bai Dai was a legend among patients, completely different from those hyenas, Sister Jiang and Ah Bi, who had relied on the hospital for everything. Deep in her bones, Bai Dai wanted to liberate herself. She didn't want to die in the hospital morgue; she wanted to take part in a true escape, the complete negation of the hospital. Was this not the purest expression of medical punk? I grew to feel that this made Bai Dai sexier than ever.

The urge to revolt built up in the heart of every patient, but those feelings were repressed, with nowhere to express them, let alone take action. I once tried, but I failed miserably. And when I discovered that this was exactly what Bai Dai had been attempting, I suddenly felt like I had been injected with a shot of adrenaline, and I all but forgot the dangers lurking everywhere. I became her biggest fan.

But when it came to taking concrete action, I knew it wouldn't be as easy as sneaking out to the garden for a walk. The true objective did not lie inside the peacock's cage but hidden away in a tiger's den, at the bottom of the dragon's pool.

38

NOT DEAD YET, BUT ON OUR WAY

One day Bai Dai and I left the observation deck and returned to the inpatient tower. Hand in hand we continued our quest to find a doctor receiving end-of-life treatment anywhere in the hospital, or better, the dead body of a doctor. How exciting such a discovery would have been! We yearned for such a scene, thinking that if we could see the gaze of death in a doctor's eyes, we could be liberated from the hospital.

But I was confused. In a world where everyone is sick, wouldn't leaving the hospital also signal one's own impending death? How many days could a patient hang on for without the care of medical professionals? If that is what freedom means, what's the point?

I couldn't help but think about what I had seen when I was in the outpatient ward: outside the hospital, infestation was much worse, with people willing to split their own heads open just to squeeze inside this sacred temple. If the entire city had become one megahospital, then even if I ran away, where could I go?

If I remained in the sick ward, even with all its top-notch treatment facilities, patients would still be dying right in front of me every day. Many died after using up the funds in their medical expense accounts; they could no longer afford good-quality medicine and ended up dying, a shameful way to go and completely the patient's fault but having nothing to do with the question of whether doctors themselves die.

But I didn't dare open up to Bai Dai about this inner conflict. I was afraid it might disrupt the balance between us and ruin the special relationship we had built up together.

We continued until we came to a room marked by a sign outside the door that read NURSES' LOUNGE. There was no one inside, just four bunk beds with clean, soft, perfectly folded floral-patterned comforters. Beside each pillow was a plush teddy bear—the room looked like a kindergarten nap room. On a table were perfectly arranged issues of *Medical News*, their covers soiled with drops of dried blood. Bai Dai knitted her brow and inhaled deeply, like a predator sniffing for prey.

"Although there are a few traces of blood, I don't detect the scent of death anywhere," she said. "It has a very different smell than the morgue."

"What does the morgue smell like?" I suddenly remembered the door to the morgue and felt a cold shudder go down my spine.

"Everyone seems to have their own idea about what the morgue is really like. But it is indeed a place that one can only go after death."

"So you are saying we might find the corpse of a doctor there?"

"I hope so."

"Have you ever been to a morgue?"

"Humph." Bai Dai seemed unwilling to answer my question. She was like a professional tour guide who didn't want to spoil the beautiful sites to come by describing them in advance.

I finally mustered up enough courage to ask her, "Why are you so intent on learning whether doctors die?" Perhaps I had been hoping to hear her utter the word "freedom," so that I would have some basis to enter the morgue later, but I was also afraid that I wouldn't be psychologically strong enough to stand it. Like Bai Dai herself, the word "freedom" was sexy, imbued with a destructive energy. But I never found the courage to face either of them directly.

"Because there is something fishy about this whole thing," she replied. Seeing the awkward expression on my face, Bai Dai gently raised her hand to caress my hair. "According to the natural laws of life and death, every living organism must die. One cannot escape the solar system. Even the Milky Way will one day be extinguished. Nothing in the universe is exempt from this rule. Everything ends up in the morgue. And that includes the hospital. Yet it continues to strive for immortality in the eyes of its patients. Frankly speaking, it feels like a conspiracy."

"Ah, that's also what I was thinking." I was upset. I had thought that Bai Dai would say something more impressive. I was also disappointed because I thought that she might *not* want to end up in the morgue.

"What's happening here is all about control," she continued. "They control us in the name of the hospital: 3D control—deep, direct, detailed—the ultimate control."

"That makes sense. When the hospital summons us, no one can resist its call."

"They are always saying that everything is patient-centric, that this is the democratization and socialization of medicine, that the patient has become a consumer who decides everything, leading to the birth of a buyer's market and things like that. But the way things actually play, humans are broken down into cells and genes, and nanomachines and drugs are used to control everything. Dividing people into groups according to their death patterns at the molecular level is simply brilliant. It took a lot of careful planning, and the hospital went to great pains to achieve this complete control. I used to think there might be some powerful figure behind the curtain, trying to use the hospital to achieve his ambition to control the world, but later I discovered that this was probably not the case. As it evolved to its current form, the hospital became a massive, dinosaur-like monster. There isn't a person alive who could control it. The hospital grows, rapidly, as if driven by some irresistible force, and then—boom!—before you know it, it's already crashing through the ceiling, replacing all the traditional structures of power. It's like a new form of animal that takes advantage of random circumstances to rise up suddenly, with bones protruding from the back of its head, raging against the reality of its age, and overnight, it overthrows the existing ecosystem and replaces the outdated ruler. The hospital rules over all living beings. With the power to rule in its hands, even if death should be imminent, it will never relinquish its grip. And if it is going to put on a show, it will not play meekly. It will dress up as King Kong and give the world hell. This is the true spirit of medical punk. This is why the Western forces, led by the Rockefellers, expended so many resources on creating a hostile environment, to contain the hospital."

"I think you are completely correct." I was again filled with great esteem after hearing her description of the hospital, so intricate and profound. I felt that some young prince had just stolen the crown and ascended the throne.

"To say that the hospital is the *cornerstone* of the nation would not be as accurate as saying that it is on its way to *replacing* the nation," she continued. "All of that flattery in the pages of *Medical News* is just a smokescreen."

"Is it necessary for the hospital to do this?"

"Of course. Its configuration grows increasingly more advanced, investment levels are skyrocketing, and with its hand in everything from genome sequencing to infinite sensor networks and from health information systems to 3D printing of artificial organs, it is clearly not some simplistic industry. If one day all of its patients run off and it has failed to control the world, wouldn't that be a complete waste? The hospital claims that its slogan is to save all of the patients under heaven. That's not a joke."

"So everything you've done has been part of your plan to protect our home country?" I was quite moved, as I thought I had found a new explanation for Bai Dai's behavior.

The term "home country" is composed of the words "home" and "country," but "home" had already given way to the abolition of the family unit, and the destruction of the "country" was within sight. It took only a simple logical inference to see that this was the hospital's next objective.

However, if the hospital really existed to eliminate the pain and suffering of its patients and to accomplish major projects that the nation was unable to carry out, then why was the hospital to be blamed? Sister Jiang had said that doctors are the only true manifestations of the Living Bodhisattva of Great Compassion, so taking control of everything seemed, in some sense, reasonable. Only under the guidance and protection of these bodhisattvas could the world avoid falling into chaos and unrest. And from the bodhisattvas' perspective, there was likely no such thing as "nations" and "home countries."

Here was the paradox: if doctors were indeed bodhisattvas, then they could not die, but Bai Dai, by secretly demoting doctors from gods to demigods or even ordinary people, "sentenced" them to the "death penalty." It was getting hard to tell who was right and who was wrong.

Bai Dai forced a smile. "Looking out over the horizon, all I see are hospitals. I can't even tell where the home country is anymore. Meanwhile, patients take all this expensive medicine yet remain in so much pain that they just want to die."

I heaved a deep sigh. I wanted to ask her, *If one day we learn how doctors die, do you think the nation can be rebuilt? Do you think families will return?* But based on her tone of voice, I didn't dare. I remained filled with complex feelings about my family, but I still didn't know much about Bai Dai's family. I knew she had a mother, who had given birth to her in the hospital, but everything else was a blank. If I disagreed with her, it might offend her, and I couldn't afford for her to be mad at me.

I sneaked a glance at her. There was a striking contrast between the black and white portions of her large eyes, which burned like a flaming battle flag. Two slight lines extended down from the corners of her mouth; they spoke of her resolute and unwavering spirit. Her forehead was broad and bright, brimming with wisdom and stubbornness. Her short hair went down to her neck, and it was mysterious, filled with a fighting spirit like a dark night. Her firm muscles were decorated with scars, and artificial holes showed from under her striped hospital gown, like a pack of wolves waiting for the right moment to swoop in and bite.

I had the urge to hold her, not out of love or attraction but in response to my own feelings of loneliness and loss.

In the end, I didn't do anything. I didn't mention "freedom," nor did Bai Dai. She pulled me from the nurses' lounge, and we continued forward. We still needed to find the morgue.

We were not dead yet, but we were on our way to that place where only the dead venture.

39

IN THE END, THE MEDICAL REVOLUTION WILL REVOLT AGAINST ITSELF

As we passed the nurses' station and the physicians' office, white lab coats twirled in the air, looking like they were either on fire or a kaleidoscope of black butterflies. I began to feel anxious and tightly clasped Bai Dai's hand. Like a true comrade in arms, she flashed me a knowing glance. The smell of cigarette smoke on her body was enchanting.

We rushed past the medical offices, soon arriving at an area that included the Department for Reviving Extinct Organisms, the Ray Room, the Sleep Lab, the Big Data Analytics Room, the Department of Molecular Dynamics, the Department of Nanowaste Disposal, the Neuro-Economic Center, the Night-Spawn Radiation Room, and the Human Embryo Management Lab.

The Human Embryo Management Lab housed hundreds, if not thousands, of frozen human embryos. In theory, each and every one of the fertilized eggs was a potential human, but they had largely been abandoned. Only a small percentage would be harvested for stem cells, which would then be provided to affluent patients to treat spinal cord injuries, diabetes, and Alzheimer's disease. Bai Dai told me that some of the embryos were produced via somatic cell nuclear transfer, which essentially meant that they were clones. The hospital supposedly kept backup copies of cells from every patient so they could be cloned at any time.

"I heard that these are kept so that in case there is ever a shortage of patients, the hospital can always provide more," Bai Dai explained.

She flung open a set of doors labeled with a yellow warning: **BIOHAZARD**. Inside we were immediately assaulted by extreme cold. As the mist cleared, we saw a series of mechanical arms manipulating samples of DNA, bone marrow, HPV, and umbilical cord blood. Moving forward, we entered a hallway that led us to the Gene Sequencing Lab. Through a small relay window, we could see robots inside receiving samples. Two layers of glass doors could be opened only one at a time, in order to prevent contamination, and more than a hundred high-speed sequencers ran constantly, emitting a faint blue light. The computers were miniaturized and fully automated. Samples were added to the text library to be "read" before sequencing, after which the mass production of genetic codes commenced. Many life-forms were tested here: giant pandas, rice, silkworms, soybeans, yaks, Tibetan antelopes, orchids, cucumbers, domestic chickens, Arabian camels, American bald eagles, emperor penguins, a community of microbes from the human intestinal tract, and virtually every type of patient—from cancer patients to autistic children and obese women to old people suffering from dementia—even dead people, such as a four-thousand-year-old corpse found frozen in Greenland. All the samples would be digitized.

Bai Dai explained that doctors were spending the majority of their effort identifying the genes that determine people's psychological states, especially as they pertained to religious beliefs, or what are sometimes referred to as "enlightenment genes" or, more crudely, "Buddhahood genes." The doctors believed in the existence of a hereditary gene mutation that could lead to transcendence, but they first had to compile a gene-expression catalog, the most challenging part of the process: the collective functioning of billions of brain neurons and tens of trillions of neural junctions is much more complex than simple gene sequencing. But doctors had not yet found another way, lacking sufficient breakthroughs in quantum neurology, so they searched using gene sequencing, a technological industry that kept growing and growing.

Beside the Gene Sequencing Lab was the Epigenome Analysis Room, where all kinds of human cells are stored and analyzed, including immune cells and skin cells, for immune regulation, wound repairs, and antiaging therapies, as well as for material to be used in the Human Embryo Management Lab.

Next came the Artificial Organ 3D Printing Lab, where supermaterials were used to create livers, kidneys, hearts, and other organs that continually spat out of the machine, each looking like a delicious snack from a tray of dim sum.

We then arrived at the Ordinary Life Supply Station, where numerous clean cages were kept at a constant temperature. Stacks of cages were also strewn haphazardly along the corridors outside, piled from floor to ceiling. Inside them were mice, rats, rabbits, and other rodents that had either had their genes extracted or been injected with human genes. The animals jumped around, and their cages clanked. A price tag was affixed to each cage, and employees hurriedly filled out order forms, pulled animals from the cages, and packed them in crates to be sent to different experimental labs at various hospitals, where they could be used to research specific diseases. As Bai Dai and I passed, the sweaty workers were too busy even to flash us a glance.

From there we arrived at the Special Life Training Center, which was equipped with several dozen secret chambers. Several of these were set aside for medical use, such as the creation of genetically modified peacocks, which were no longer provided to labs for research and were instead sold at a high price to an elite class of patient consumers. Although these were specifically developed to treat special VIP patients, peacocks had long been used by humans for medicinal purposes. During the Ming dynasty, the Chinese herbalist Li Shizhen had first affirmed the medicinal value of peacocks in his classic book *The Compendium of Materia Medica*: "The consumption of peacock meat has the ability to ward off evil, cure major ailments, and cleanse the body of a variety of toxins and poisons. After a patient eats peacock meat, most medicines will be ineffective due to the peacock's detoxifying effects." New breeds of Indian peafowl, created using modern technology, were said to be embedded with human genes and especially precious for their medicinal qualities. What was once heralded as a success of the modernization of traditional Chinese medicine was by that time considered an established part of modern medical science. "Traditional medicine" no longer existed.

The doors and windows of the Special Life Training Center were locked, so we couldn't see the peacocks, but knowing that so many species were being either sacrificed or upgraded left me with a long-lingering uneasiness. Like humans, they had been forcibly removed from their natural habitat and robbed of their familial relationships—and just like humans, they had become eternal residents of the hospital.

40

SECRET OF THE MICROBE CONTROL LAB

"There's no way the hospital could *not* eventually die off," Bai Dai told me. "Even if it toppled the state and assumed control of everything, it is still destined to fail. The crisis is coming. The hospital will share the same fate as the Indian peafowl."

I didn't dare believe her. The hospital controlled vast wealth, the most advanced technology, a brand-new set of values, a tightly organized structure, a perfectly ordered hygiene system, and an army of patients completely under the influence of—or addicted to—drugs. "How is that possible?" I asked.

"In the end," Bai Dai said, "the medical revolution will revolt against itself."

"Neither Dr. Bauchi nor Uncle Zhao mentioned anything like that," I said.

"Humph, how could they?" Bai Dai replied. "Modern medical science has already transformed everyone. We are no longer the human beings we once were. We are all 'mutants' now." She stared straight into the faint pain hidden in my eyes, which could be seen only by sensitive souls who look carefully, and yet she didn't express any compassion. Whatever sympathy she had was for the species I represented. Since the hospital was a public platform, long-haul patients tended to have a very weak sense of individualism, which further atrophied over time.

"And what does this mean?" I asked.

Bai Dai said there was no such thing as true human beings anymore. And without human beings, the hospital would lose the very condition of its existence and the impetus for further development.

That sounded right to me. Medical dialectics were everywhere. This was the philosophy behind medical punk. I found myself lost in thought, remembering Bai Dai's various wounds and implants. As a patient, there was something impure about her, but that was precisely what made her beauty affect me so deeply.

We arrived at the Microbe Control Lab. Lines of doctors and robots entered and exited. We hid off to one side to sneak a peek.

"Brother Yang, there is something else I need to tell you. The hospital is not only altering human beings, it is also altering microbes, and not simply by killing them." When it comes to microbes, I actually knew a thing or two. In some of the hospital library books I had borrowed, I'd read about microbes and learned that they are one of the most widely distributed, most populous, and oldest forms of life on this planet, the foundation of life, even the very life force itself. Microbes that evolved into plants and animals first arose from germs, and human bodies include a combination of hundreds of millions of germs. Some make us sick, but some keep us alive. The most fundamental mission of the hospital was to interact with microbes.

Bai Dai seemed to perk up suddenly, explaining that the hospital labs were carrying out a Microbe Cluster Project aimed at a large-scale remolding of microbes to make them more in line with specifications determined by humankind. "Do you want to know how they do this?"

I didn't really care; it was too complicated. But I followed her in to observe the Microbe Control Lab. Several doctors inside looked extremely busy. A few looked familiar: the doctors I had met at the outpatient clinic. There was the older male doctor whose face looked like an ornamental rock, and that thin middle-aged female doctor who looked like a ballet dancer, and that young male doctor who looked like an installation artist. When they noticed us, they invited us inside, saying that we were the very first patients to visit them at the lab. From what I could tell, they seemed to have missed having an audience.

41

FROM TRANSFORMING GENES
TO DESTROYING GENES

Dr. Ornamental Rock led a research group designing a new form of bacteria, implanting it with artificial alkali and resynthesizing its proteins. Dr. Ballerina's team was injecting frog genes into a virus, upgrading it to a "tamed virus" that could safely and efficiently transport foreign DNA sequences to the appropriate locations without being detected by the host's immune system. Dr. Artist was busy cultivating more complex magnetotactic bacteria to attain target molecules.

Dr. Artist looked like he had been chewed up and spit out. Perhaps he had just come out of surgery? When he saw us, he perked up a bit. "All of us doctors used to make up only a tiny part of the hospital, but later our team began to expand rapidly, like a drug addict's habit. It's hard to say whether that is a bad thing. In the future, drug addiction might not even be considered a disease. These days hereditary medicine is all the rage. We'll be left in the dust if we don't keep up with the current trends."

He provided a cursory introduction to the team's work, including its development of antibiotics that trigger bacterial mutations, fundamental changes it had brought about in *Enterobacter* bacteria after implanting them into nonbiological hosts, attempts to manipulate robots, research and development of microbe-fueled batteries used to power artificial kidneys, and more. Among these projects, the most shocking was the use of bacteria to grow brains to be combined later with robotics. These bacterial brains, he claimed, would lead to a brand-new revolution in the fields of brain science and artificial intelligence.

"You medical punks love doing this kind of thing, don't you!" Bai Dai exclaimed.

"That's right. The more they try to stop us, the more we want to do them. If we don't carry out these new projects, we'll go crazy! In the Age of Medicine, punk is setting the technological trend, and we are the true geeks running the show."

Dr. Artificial Rock and Dr. Ballerina said nothing, apparently too busy with their own research.

"There is nothing you guys can't do!" I added. "These are all things that only God is capable of."

"My dear patient," Dr. Artist replied, "how can I put this? As things move forward, none of this is actually about curing diseases, at least not anymore. Nor does it have anything to do with the existence or development of the hospital." His arrogance made it seem like he was discussing a much loftier, even spiritual, motivation.

"Then what is it all for?" I pressed. "To help defeat the invading supervirus released by those Western forces?"

"No," the doctor answered haphazardly. "It is purely to satisfy our own greed and curiosity."

I almost stopped breathing. Were these really doctors? Real doctors existed to save patients, do battle with the evil Western forces, and protect the hospital! But these were like a different species of doctors, disguising themselves as something that they weren't. Bai Dai nodded her head. She seemed to smell an air of death on the doctors.

"I'm fed up after working here in the outpatient clinic for so long," Dr. Artist continued. "No one understands what this hospital really does, so we decided to go back to basic medical research. In our eyes, it is a majestic and holy thing. We love it from the very bottom of our hearts, and this love is just as powerful as romantic love or the love one feels for one's family. It is like faith. If you can understand what it is like to feel this kind of love for the hospital, you will also realize why we have finally grown so exhausted."

"And then?" I felt like I already knew the answer, but I didn't want the doctor to feel like I was growing bored.

He let out a humph and got back to work.

I guessed that even though they had only transformed a small percentage of the microbes, these new bacteria were already spreading and would trigger some kind of chain reaction.

I noticed that Dr. Artificial Rock was designing a new semiartificial bacteria on his computer. It replicated rapidly and could consume other bacteria, which could then be transformed into part of its body and continue to live, thus creating a new superbacteria that in turn could go on to consume even more bacteria. Its final stage was a new life-form that continually self-replicated and self-transformed. Projects that manipulated bacteria had already become simple for the team, and in the future, microbe designers would no longer need to be doctors trained in biology. Anyone off the street would be able to download the software and create any kind of bacteria they liked.

A handful of schematic diagrams were displayed in the Microbe Control Lab, illustrating how all of this research was playing out in humans. Some of the microbe groupings, which had long been acclimated to humans, had been disturbed, and the doctors seemed particularly interested in these.

"If one day the bacteria in the human body undergo a major transformation, it will be impossible for them to operate normally," I proposed. "They will no longer be able to synthesize the necessary substances for the human body to function, nor will they be able to resist invasion by foreign pathogens, and they will transform into a harmful bacteria strain. Isn't that right?"

"Hey, isn't that what medical punk wants most?" Bai Dai responded.

Dr. Artist heard us and looked up. With a boasting tone, he announced that his research team had an even more ambitious plan than that.

"And what's that?" Bai Dai and I asked in unison.

"Through the development of these microbes, we hope to eliminate genes altogether."

42

THE HOSPITAL IS THE SOURCE OF ALL MALADIES

With a disdainful, indifferent tone, Dr. Artist spoke. "After editing genes day in and day out, we've grown tired of it, frankly. You know how little kids get sick of playing with the same toy all the time? It's become harder and harder for us to do anything truly innovative anymore. Many things in the universe are simply too sophisticated for humans to create. There is no point in even attempting them. This is especially true when it comes to locating the theoretically predicted 'Buddhahood gene.' All of that just makes us anxious. Perhaps the human brain has not reached the level of complexity needed to understand its own complexity. A lot of people think they have figured everything out, but in reality they don't understand a damn thing. This is the origin of so much bad debt to the hospital, and it has utterly destroyed our ability to appreciate true art. Anyway, things are much different now than back when I was in college. So even though you see me working away here, gene research was always destined to fail. It is a game that only a madman or an idiot would play. We have been going down the wrong road. The more you try to control people, the farther down a dead end you find yourself."

I had not expected him to speak to us so frankly. Maybe the doctors behaved differently at the lab than at the clinic? Perhaps they had become skeptics of the hospital? The doctors here seemed much more real . . . or were they less real? Had they returned to a playful, childlike state? Or had they been so stressed out that they were just using the opportunity of our unexpected visit to get some things off their chests?

Whatever the case, once we find ourselves going down a dead-end alley, the status quo always doubles down.

Bai Dai listened without uttering a word, as if she was worried she might fall into the doctor's trap. Indeed, it was hard to tell whether the whole thing was nothing but an elaborate conspiracy. Was he trying to deceive us? And what did any of this have to do with the question of how doctors die?

At least Bai Dai and I seemed a step closer to solving the mystery. If the doctors kept going down this path, they *would* die. Based on my experience as a patient, I had become sure of one thing: these doctors were *very* sick.

Dr. Artist continued his lecture: "True medical punks believe that only lower-level life-forms rely upon reproduction to continue their species. That is why they require the introduction of new genes to improve their nature. This is precisely what led us to artificial methods like gene editing. But moving forward, if we are able to take evolution to the next level, then we won't even need genes. The double helix structure, with all its clumsy inefficiencies, is completely redundant. Genetic engineering itself will become obsolete. Eventually there will be no reason for traditional hospitals. *We believe that the best hospital is no hospital.* The Age of Medicine is just a transition period, like bamboo-slip writing before the invention of paper or the abacus before the invention of the computer or the family before city-size hospitals."

"So what is the purpose of the hospital, then?" I asked.

"The hospital is here to eradicate genes and bring an end to the traditional meaning of life. Without life, there will be no sickness or disease. Once we do away with brains, failures of understanding will no longer be a problem. The same rationale that led to the formation of the hospital will also lead to its destruction. This is the real art."

"Wow, you have really done something quite amazing!" I exclaimed. Then I caught another whiff of the ardor of death. "So this is the reason all these patients are admitted to the hospital?"

"Ah, if you want me to be honest, the reason we do this has nothing to do with patients. It is all done to achieve other goals. When we first started, our aim was to lock up project orders. If we didn't have any projects, we wouldn't have been able to do anything. But once the projects started coming in, we committed ourselves. We were drawn in gradually; then we realized how interesting and fun it all was. Gradually we became medical punks. We started vying for larger projects as a way to get more funding. Once we had sufficient funding in place, we could do anything we wanted. In the Age of Medicine, money equals life. Even though money, like life, is a commodity that will soon be rendered obsolete, for the time being we can still take advantage of it. That is why when we implement a project, we go big and try to pull off something that has never been seen before. It is all about leaving an 'impression.' We need to leave an indelible impression upon the hospital's president-cum-mayor, since he controls all the funding. Once you create an impression, everything else falls into place, including the money."

"So everything has become a product of image engineering," I said.

"That's right. The entire universe is an image-engineering project. In the beginning we were just trying to lock down project accounts, then we sought to satisfy our own greed and curiosity, but at the end of the day, it wasn't about *our* own greed and curiosity but that of the president-cum-mayor. We are trying to entertain him and leave a good impression. That gentleman must know this art better than anyone else. He is, after all, the ultimate medical punk. At the very least, that was the impression I got from his sneaky demeanor. All the other punks ended up sacrificing for him, but I suppose we all did it willingly."

This was what you could call the peacock effect: everything moves outward from the center. Weren't the peacock's tail feathers, which led to his own destruction, also a form of image engineering? That's what I was thinking. If all this kept going, even punk culture would be destroyed. But none of that had anything to do with me. For the first time, I looked at the doctors with a feeling of pity. They were not yet dead but forced to carry on in this living hell.

And yet I still admired them. They were of another class of people, the rebels, the impressionist artists of our society, the avant-garde of the avant-garde. Like terrorists, their behavior may have seemed absurd, but they were not suffering from schizophrenia or any other mental disorder. The eyes of the doctors were like the eyes of a fish in the deep blue sea, apparently filled with innocence, arrogance, intelligence, and pride, but they emitted a sensuous light that illuminated the world. Did Dr. Bauchi know about all this? Did Bai Dai really want to see doctors die?

"Who knows what will happen in the future," the doctor said with the utmost sincerity. "No one can predict what life without genes will be like. Will it even be called 'life'? We simply cannot know what brandnew thing will be unleashed. But that is precisely the exciting part."

"Let *me* try to predict what will happen," Bai Dai said. "It won't be long before existing species will find it extremely difficult to adapt to the hospital's version of the natural world and civilized society. In the past, life on earth has gone through several major upheavals, triggered by volcano eruptions, meteorites, climate change, glaciers, rising sea levels, and flooding, but none of those was as radical and transformative as the changes we face today. Would you say that is true?"

The doctor nodded his head admiringly. "That is indeed the case. Hey, sometimes a patient's intuition is spot on!"

I was still confused. "So what else will happen?"

"That will be up to each and every individual," Bai Dai said excitedly. "If people don't play their cards right, humankind and the planet will both face destruction. As for what will happen after that great destruction . . . nobody really knows. But this way we will be able to find some dead doctors."

I tried my best to appear shocked, in the hope of winning Bai Dai's affection. "The whole thing is really terrifying. It sounds like the hospital is the source of all maladies."

"That is a bit exaggerated." The doctor let out a queer laugh. "I don't think we'll even make it to that day."

43

DEATH IS THE END, BUT THE END IS ONLY THE BEGINNING

"Medical punk's destruction of existing structures and social orders will accelerate the coming of the future war with the West," Dr. Artist said. "I don't know who will win in the end, but we have no time to waste! We are already growing tired of this war, and it hasn't even begun yet."

This was the first time I had heard a doctor express even a thread of doubt about the hospital's future victory.

"This all sounds like the kind of pessimistic preaching that patients hear all the time," Bai Dai replied. "Didn't *Medical News* refute this?" She whipped out a copy of *Medical News* and handed it to me.

The front page featured an editorial discussing the rising "medical threat" directed at our nation. The argument claimed that our country was using biological sovereignty to replace territorial sovereignty, developing microorganisms to spread to other countries in order to destroy existing notions of space and time, as a means of exacting vengeance for those historical injustices we had once suffered. The transformation of genes had led to the transformation of our national character and strength. Some nations, whose identities were based on traditional ethnic values, would be eradicated almost overnight. One supergene, coupled with a supervirus, could rapidly destroy an entire nation and its people. But if we eliminated genes, we could start from scratch, change the players, redirect power, invert the relationship between the strong and the weak. Nations would face off against each other in the realm of biological politics, and humankind would return to the Jungle

Age. The Rockefellers feared and despised this possibility, so before the end of the world arrived, the fight for domination over the order of life would result in international conflicts and sanctions. Biological channels between countries would shut down, and a biological black hole would emerge. The editorial writer's only fear was that none of this would solve any of the real problems, ultimately leading to the outbreak of a new world war. The peace-loving medical punks were worried and reluctant to sacrifice themselves for the war effort.

Dr. Ornamental Rock snatched the copy of *Medical News* from my hand and started circling passages with a pencil. "If real war should break out one day, there will be people that come to help. Dr. Norman Bethune will return to the world to establish a new era in our history."

I was confused. "Norman Bethune?"

"He was a Canadian doctor that changed the course of World War II," Bai Dai explained.

Dr. Ornamental Rock explained this period in history in more detail. "Bethune had already discovered that we had a difference of opinion with the short sellers when it came to the issue of genes. It was like the gap between Neanderthals and modern humans, two different human species with no possibility of mutual understanding. This is not as simple as the difference between civilizations. The main problem was that the two were at different stages of the evolutionary process. During World War II, the Germans possessed the same brain and physique as other Westerners, yet the two civilizations still found themselves enveloped in mutual conflict, a war between people of the same racial makeup, whereas Japan's attack on the United States was a war between different races."

"So does that mean that this Norman Bethune fellow was a different category of human?" I asked.

"He was superhuman, not only a brilliant surgeon, but even more importantly, he was a model when it came to moral conduct—a truly great man. The highest level one can achieve in medicine is a state of pure and utter selflessness. You must fully cast off any self-interest and shed all base thought. These superhumans only appear during times of war." Dr. Ornamental Rock was clearly filled with admiration. "The return of Norman Bethune provides us with the hope that we might actually win this coming world war."

Bai Dai flashed Dr. Ornamental Rock a sharp look. "I'm afraid that what comes will not be a war between humans, nor a war between genes or viruses. In the postgene age, it will be a war between different 'lifeless' life-forms. Will they destroy one another? Hey, do you think the doctors will die too?" She had come to the crucial question, and I finally understood Bai Dai's reason for coming to the lab. She was searching for clues.

"We bear no responsibility for any coming war. We are artists of a new era," Dr. Artist declared firmly. He waved the copy of *Medical News* in his hand. "This issue has a special feature about postmodern society as the West has constructed it, the so-called stance of abandoning extremes and embracing tolerance. They talk about nonsense like the eventual creation of a 'global village,' but ideological opposition has already replaced economic cooperation. Trade-offs and ambiguity have become the driving themes of international relations. Amid this era of constant change, even artists from the school of futurism have issued a proclamation stating that any attempt to provide a precise logical explanation of cause-and-effect relationships is pure idiocy. But medical punks are artists from the school of ultraism, and they don't subscribe to that. We can put the final nail in the coffin of the cursed era of postmodernism."

The issue of *Medical News* dropped to the floor.

"Isn't the notion of the 'home country' already obsolete?" I asked carefully.

"As for who will be the successor to what was once the 'home country,' that shall be decided by the final battle between the hospitals!" the doctor explained. "What emerges in the wake of that struggle will be an upgraded version of the hospital. In theory, it will be a much more merciful and joyful conflict than any nuclear war. Everything will be thrown into eternal brightness. How could this not be considered a new 'beginning'? But unfortunately it lacks art."

"How about the patients?" I asked.

"There will no longer be any patients," the doctor responded nonchalantly.

I turned to Bai Dai anxiously. "Do you really want to escape? You don't want to stand with the hospital until the end?"

"No, I won't attempt escape, nor will I share the same fate as this hospital!"

I didn't expect that, and I couldn't figure out why she said it. Bai Dai's deepest thoughts remained impenetrable to me. Perhaps she simply didn't want to admit the truth in front of the doctors? In that instant I felt that the time for this once provocative concept called "freedom" to rot and die had finally come. In the vocabulary of medical punk, there was no room for it. It sounded utterly ridiculous when compared with a term like "life." There was no connection between "freedom" and "life." Would understanding how doctors die prevent the destruction of mankind or help us to avoid the coming world war? Bai Dai had led me into a messy and overgrown jungle of thought. I couldn't get out, and I just kept getting pulled deeper and deeper in.

A stern and steely expression appeared on Bai Dai's face. Those deep lines descending from the corners of her mouth made her look like a witch preparing to summon a spirit. In an instant, she seemed to have aged twenty years. I couldn't help but take a few steps back to create some space between us. She was a young girl suffering from a major illness, and yet here she was worrying about these important worldly matters that only national leaders should have to worry about. There was so much about her that I still didn't understand. Perhaps this was as far as our relationship could ever go. Even when the destruction began, we would still not have received our full diagnosis.

I found myself entertaining a rather improper thought: Could Bai Dai be intentionally trying to test me? What was she really thinking? Experience had taught me that in the hospital, you should never believe anything the patients tell you. They were always trying to figure out what everyone else's game was, what illnesses the other patients had, in order to predict who might die and when so they could steal a bed the second anyone dropped dead.

But was Bai Dai really a patient?

44

THAT GORGEOUS BIRD LIKES
TO STAY CLEAN, SO IT STAYS
AWAY FROM THE TRASH ROOM

We exited the Microbe Control Lab, leaving that disturbing inter-lude behind us, and continued on with our quest. After discussing the coming world war, I was left with an increased feeling of anxiety. We couldn't find the path that led to the morgue, but instead we discovered the trash room beside the rescue unit. Inside the trash room, piles of black plastic bags emitted a strong stench that assaulted our noses. The room was littered with shit, maggots, phlegm, piss, discarded speci-mens, and fragments of animal tissue. Had these been left behind by the patients or the doctors? It was hard to determine.

Breathing became difficult, but something stimulated my central nervous system. As I looked out through the narrow oval window in the trash room, the garden outside resembled the Andromeda Nebula, stretched out amid the humid darkness of the never-ending abyss. The birdcage appeared as a bright spot in the distance; even though it was barely as large as my fingernail, it felt like a faint star, thousands of light-years away. Before I even realized it, night descended, and I thought I saw a birdlike animal taking flight from a misty valley, but I couldn't tell whether it was the rare Indian peafowl. I heard the rising and falling voice of someone singing. Could the other patients have been holding another talent show? If so, they had forgotten to invite me! Then I heard the faint sound of someone crying. We rushed out of the trash room and staggered our way to another sick ward, where we discovered another dead patient—again, not a doctor. I felt disappointed it wasn't a doctor. But, for some strange reason, I also heaved a sigh of relief.

"You must have come to see the peacock spread its tail feathers?" asked a soft but strong voice beside my ear. "That gorgeous bird likes to stay clean, so it stays away from the trash room."

I turned to find Dr. Bauchi right beside us, standing with his arms folded and looking at us with an expression that was at once warm and stern. He was a portrait of good health; his skin was glowing with a crimson tint. He looked calm and relaxed, like an immortal out of Greek mythology—there wasn't even the faintest hint that he might die one day. My knees grew weak. I attempted to say something but couldn't get the words out. In that moment, I felt like Dr. Bauchi was trying to send us a secret message: *Compared to the peacock, you patients are the truly filthy ones.*

Speaking of which, wasn't that which lurked behind the phenomena of disease also filth?

With all his experience conducting autopsies, Dr. Bauchi must have been well aware of this truth. As his scalpel removed layer after layer of flesh and muscle to reveal internal organs, the breathtaking beauty of modern medicine was revealed.

More doctors approached us, upbeat and animated, and the tower was abuzz with an intoxicating excitement, as if it were time for a hymn at a church. At midnight the doctors converged for group calisthenics, led by an announcer over the loudspeaker. The hospital was filled with a bright white light that washed over everything, cutting through the room like a knife. In their uniform, vigorous movements, the doctors were not only alive and kicking but clearly ready to keep on going. The longer they lived, the more healthy and spirited they seemed to become, in stark contrast to the patients, completing the circle of medical dialectics. Not only did the doctors fail to die, but the hospital lived on as well, suggesting that staying alive was in fact the deepest art of all. And yet the doctors seemed to be performing, as if putting on a private show for me and Bai Dai. They moved naturally, without seeming too ostentatious. After all, they had no need to show off. They just needed an audience.

I broke into an anxious sweat and flashed Dr. Bauchi a smile.

Bai Dai grabbed my hand and dragged me away.

45

ALL UNDER HEAVEN IS ONE
BIG HOSPITAL

Because she had received direct treatment from him, Bai Dai knew Dr. Bauchi much better than I did. Thousands of medical personnel worked in the inpatient ward, and Bai Dai knew almost all of their names. She had started memorizing them when she was still a small child. She was now twenty-five years old, so if she had remembered just one name a day, she'd eventually learn them all. But it was difficult, since she had been heavily medicated for most of that time, and the medication tended to damage patients' memories. So she used all kinds of methods to remember: scribbling names on paper, carving them into the headboard of her sickbed, and reciting them constantly. At first she had thought that if one of the doctors died, his name would be taken off the signage in the hospital directory, and she realized that tracing the doctors' names that had been taken down could provide a clue to which doctors had died. But she gradually came to realize just how naive that plan was. The names seemed to stay up forever, and her plan never worked.

"Among all the doctors and nurses that we know, isn't there a single one that can tell us the truth?" I asked her.

"I tried to ask around," Bai Dai responded. "I asked Dr. Bauchi. But who would ever reveal anything like that to a patient? The doctors are always pleasant on the surface. They share all kinds of medical knowledge, they'll console you, give you advice, but there is always a clear line. Over time, in most people's eyes, the relationship between doctors and patients has fallen into a fixed pattern, resembling the relationship between God and man—or, at the very least, a master to his servant or a father to his son—and there is no deeper or more substantial communication. With today's achievements in medical science, most doctors feel that patients live in a different universe, cut off from the doctors. It is impossible for doctors to understand their patients. There is no basis for understanding and no common ground. It is simply too difficult."

I had indeed noticed that even in their discourse, there was a major difference between the way doctors and patients communicated. Everything that came out of doctors' mouths was about molecular targeting mechanisms, tyrosine acid inhibitors, three-dimensional radiotherapy, genetic risk factors, and the like, whereas patients talked about which medicine was more affordable, whether to give a red envelope to the radiotherapist after paying off the surgeon, or whom to pay off to get an appointment with this or that specialist. While the nurses divided patients into categories—ordinary patients, emotionally unstable patients, patients able to walk on their own, patients with genital injuries, patients at risk of falling out of their beds—the patients also divided the nurses into categories: who could hit a vein on the first prick, who knew how to smile, young nurses and old nurses, careful nurses and careless ones.

Bai Dai appeared irritable and gave me a nasty pinch on the palm of my hand. I could sense that, after twenty-five years of pent-up sorrow, pain, anxiety, and yearning, she couldn't wait much longer. She seemed to think that a new patient like me should have brought her information from the outside world to help her achieve her goal and that all the time she had spent with me was repayment. But my own expectations for our relationship were higher than that.

After we left the Microbe Control Lab, our feelings changed. The threat of total destruction loomed over our heads. If we were not going to escape from the hospital, then the only path forward was to solve the mystery of how doctors die. Finding a way to kill them off seemed the only way to avoid an unprecedented disaster. I felt thrilled knowing we did not have any other good options. In my confusion, I confessed to Bai Dai: "Now that I think about it, my daughter might be able to help us. When she was a bit younger than you, she ran off to work as a doctor's assistant, and she became an aerial nurse."

"A doctor's *assistant*? An aerial *nurse*? Humph! She's nothing but a concubine! The hospital forbids patients to have families, but the doctors secretly keep concubines! If they can avoid illness and death, they have this special privilege."

"So the male doctor who took her in is basically my son-in-law?" I could feel my face burning.

Bai Dai looked at me with anticipation. "So . . . do you think you'll be able to use your connection to find something out?"

"I . . . I was thinking that," I uttered quietly. "But . . . uh, how should I put this? This is yet another paradox. You know that my genes have already been altered, right? So in theory I'm . . . I'm no longer the person I used to be, and she and I are no longer part of the same family. That means that that doctor is actually *not* my son-in-law, so how could I seek him out for help? Even if I were to track him down, it would be pretty awkward. We don't even know each other. I wouldn't know how to broach the subject with him. I'm thinking that for the time being, it is probably best not to try and exploit this so-called relationship."

I could feel myself recoiling. I thought about how our actions had already been discovered by Dr. Bauchi. I wondered if he would start me on a new round of treatment in response. Bai Dai let go of my hand and turned her eyes away out of disappointment. I could feel the blood rush to my head, and I can only imagine what my face looked like as it turned crimson.

I didn't know what to say, so I changed the subject: "Guess what I'm thinking right now?"

"Are you thinking about the Indian peafowls?"

"I'm thinking about elephants," I lied. My thoughts were actually wavering over this woman standing before me, about how to get the upper hand, how to save face, but out of a sense of inferiority, I felt like I would never be able to spread my tail feathers, so to speak.

"Oh, so you *weren't* thinking of the Indian peafowl . . ."

"Well, to be more precise, I was thinking about how elephants die." I jokingly struck an elephant pose, using my hands to mimic a trunk and tusks, hoping to look cute and loosen up the mood. "As the king of all the land mammals, elephants remain majestic and powerful well into their old age, but just before they die, they quietly leave the herd behind. One step at a time, they walk away and never look back. But no one has ever seen an elephant die, and no one has discovered where they are buried." The image of those old patients from the emergency room—with long plastic tubes stuffed into their nostrils—flashed before my eyes.

"Brother Yang, are you saying that we will never find where the doctors are buried?"

Seeing how sad Bai Dai looked left me with a strange sense of pleasure, yet I couldn't allow myself to feel truly happy. I wanted to tell her, *That's right, it is an impossible task.* Moreover, even if we found it, how would that relieve my pain? As a male patient, I felt that I had an even greater task, and that was to comfort this female patient. Bai Dai shouldn't always be the one comforting me.

And yet there was nothing I could do. Only in my imagination could I find even a bit of self-consolation, as if, after a long and exhausting search, we had finally come to a towering mountain of human corpses, bodies in white lab coats piled up higher than Mount Everest. Hand in hand, Bai Dai and I were like two marionettes at the foot of Corpse Mountain. We held our breath and gazed up until our necks almost broke, yet we couldn't make out what we were looking at. We were like the Monkey and the Monk who journeyed to the West to retrieve Buddhist sutras and, after countless hardships and challenges, finally arrived at the foot of Soul Mountain only to be prevented from ascending.

Perhaps in some corner of the city there was a secret cemetery for doctors? Or a public tomb for all the martyred physicians? That place where white tombs adorn the horizon is bound to be different from the hospital morgue. I knew all too well that even if I were to walk to the ends of the world in search of Corpse Mountain, I would never find it—nor would the Buddha ever receive me.

"It is obvious that even if we got on a plane and flew somewhere far away," I said, "anywhere we ended up would still be part of the hospital. Everything under heaven is one big hospital. Even if we devote our full energy to the task, finding the doctors' cemetery would be a thousand times more difficult than retrieving the sutras from the West."

That was when a strange thought flashed through my brain: If we couldn't figure out how doctors die, what if we just tried killing one?

46

THE GREAT, GLORIOUS, AND CORRECT HOSPITAL PRESIDENT

Amid the fortified hospital, even entertaining such a thought was, without question, akin to suicide. Yet from the second the thought popped into my head, I couldn't let it go. I even considered kidnapping Dr. Bauchi and forcing him to reveal the truth. If he refused to speak, I would kill him. I was confident that I could pull this off, and wouldn't that provide ample evidence of how doctors die?

I thought I should suggest the plan to Bai Dai. It would be best if she carried it out. But how could I broach the subject? Sometimes the simplest of plans are the most difficult to bring up.

I thought back to the explosion I had witnessed in the outpatient ward. I never figured out whether the target of the attack was the doctors or the big pharma reps, but I was almost certain that there must have been casualties. But did I really want to kill a doctor who took his job as seriously as Dr. Bauchi did? Perhaps Dr. Artist, Dr. Ornamental Rock, or Dr. Ballerina was more deserving? I could feel the sweat dripping down my back just thinking about this.

Bai Dai didn't seem the least bit impacted. Before I had an opportunity to share my idea with her, she suggested we write a letter to the hospital president-cum-mayor, requesting an explanation of how doctors die. Normal people seemed unable to answer this question, so we could go straight to the person at the top. Apparently she had yet to become a terrorist extremist. I felt a little disappointed.

No one had ever seen the hospital president or knew where he was. He was a legend, whispered about around the hospital. Patients said it took a man with exceptionally efficient management skills to steer a ship as massive as the hospital. He used the brand name of his doctors to build up the brand name of the hospital. He had reformed performance management for the medical technology department and reformulated the salary scale for staff in various positions. He used low-cost methods to improve cost accounting, which led to true breakthroughs in overall performance, with different management goals than those of other enterprises but much else quite similar. The hospital president had effectively taken the hospital from the passive age of advertising into the proactive age of word-of-mouth promotion.

Bai Dai wrote his name on the front of an envelope—she had once seen it in the pages of *Medical News*. This was truly a bold and decisive action, but she did it with no fear of the consequences. If the doctors had been hiding the truth about their death for all this time, it would be a most serious violation. I was worried that, in their anger, the hospital authorities would stop providing Bai Dai with medical treatment, but who could have imagined that, six months later, Bai Dai would receive a handwritten personal letter from the hospital president himself! The great man expressed his approval of Bai Dai's passionate spirit of exploration, but he went on to exhort her to focus on getting proper rest and taking care of her illness. After all, he wrote, "the body is the foundation of everything." He advised her not to visit the hospital garden anymore, because the pollen was an allergen that could have a detrimental impact on her recovery.

When she finished reading it, Bai Dai clasped the letter in her hand. She didn't utter a word for a long time. I had no idea what she was thinking, but the way she looked made me very concerned. Now even the hospital president knew about her, but the fact that he hadn't ordered security guards to arrest her for the letter showed me exactly how benevolent and magnanimous he was. Maybe he had even forgiven the doctors who had lost faith in the hospital. He knew exactly how the coming world war would end and who would be the winner. As people said, he was the ultimate medical punk, a true artist among artists.

At the same time, this episode terrified me. I could imagine the hospital president holding a ledger containing the names of every patient, including Bai Dai and myself. The carefree manner in which he responded to her letter demonstrated his greatness, glory, and correctness. He could see through all the petty games that patients play. In some ways, he reminded me of the all-powerful Buddha. No matter how we struggle, we can never escape from the palm of his hand. Although he did not arrest us or discontinue our access to medicine, that did not mean that he tolerated our actions. Just think of the chaos that would be unleashed if the secret of whether doctors die were ever revealed to the public! Not only would it damage the image of the hospital that the president had worked so hard to build up, but in the end, it would be certain to harm the patients as well.

When I remembered that I had once secretly entertained the thought of murdering a doctor, I began to feel scared. I turned to Bai Dai sternly. "Can doctors really die? No, I don't think they can. For a doctor to die in front of his patient would be completely illogical. They don't even get sick. Just look at the number of patients, and yet there is always a shortage of doctors. Think of what a catastrophe it would be if even a single doctor was struck down by illness and unable to treat his patients. It would unleash a chain of destructive events that not even the hospital could imagine. Didn't you say the same thing once? And so, I think it is absolutely impossible. There is no way that they are normal people. Even if there is a future war, I'm sure that they will survive. The more battles fought, the more we will need them to treat the wounded, no? The word 'death' doesn't even exist in their vocabulary; there is only the end. And the end is only the beginning."

What I was trying to express to her was that the president, in his own way, was trying to send her a gentle yet formal warning. But Bai Dai didn't seem to hear me. She stood frozen, deep in thought.

There was no doubt that a deep, insurmountable chasm of understanding remained between doctors and patients. If in the future we truly got to a place where genes and even life itself were eradicated, then who would care whether doctors died? What would be the point of the coming war? But these were things that most patients simply could not understand.

I returned to my room in a depressed mood. I didn't want to go out again. I didn't dare go back to the hospital garden. I decided to focus on treating my illness, like a good patient. The most important thing was to try and recover quickly. And so I rejoined the battle against the other patients vying for a sickbed. I ended up beaten and bloody, but I got a spot.

Lying in bed with my injuries, I felt like I was on the verge of death. Bai Dai came to take care of me. I seemed unable to get away from her. But caring for the sick was not her strong suit. I wondered, If she grew too frustrated or annoyed with me, might she try to punish me?

47

ONLY THE LIVING CAN PROVE THEY ARE SICK, WHEREAS THE DEAD CAN'T EVEN RECEIVE TREATMENT

I knew she had some ulterior motive, but that was inevitable. For example, she was clumsy and unfamiliar with the basic procedures for helping a patient relieve himself. But just sitting there on the corner of my bed, with that fierce look on her face, was enough to scare off other patients who might try and steal the bed.

"Brother Yang," she said, "you are a big, strong grown man. In some ways, you remind me of my father. So how could you run away when we were getting so close? I carefully reread the president's letter. He said to stay away from the garden, but he didn't say anything about the morgue. He was clearly leaving some room for us. What do you think his intention was? Perhaps he has sensed the coming crisis and wants us patients to shake things up a bit. He can't say any of this openly, but it is clear to me that we must not stop."

I kept silent. I couldn't figure out if I wanted her to stay or get the hell out of my sight.

"Brother Yang," she continued, "are you that scared of death? It's not like anyone is chasing after you with a butcher knife. Everything they do in the Age of Medicine is to ensure that you stay alive. Didn't the doctor say that life is the most precious thing? Even if you don't want to live, you've got to hold on. This is the hard logic of the Age of Medicine. Only the living can prove that they are sick, whereas the dead can't even receive treatment. As far as I'm concerned, being alive means doing what you want to do. Brother Yang, do you feel the same way? There is nothing to fear. No matter how difficult it may be, the most important thing for a man is to act like a man. So why are you always acting like a turtle with its head in its shell? Didn't you say you wanted to be more like an elephant?"

There was no resisting Bai Dai's stubbornness. I lowered my head in shame. All the male patients in the room were jealous over my relationship with Bai Dai. Their ears pricked up in fear and anticipation.

"Back when I was still breastfeeding, the milk was combined with sympathomimetic amines. The drugs produced a stimulant response that increased my heart rate and sped up my brain function. Amid my excitement, I kept mulling over the same few questions. If everyone is sick, is there no such thing as a disease-free person? But if everyone is healthy, how would we differentiate someone who was sick? This was a paradox. I decided my life should be devoted to solving this paradox, and at its very heart was the question of how doctors die."

I felt quite inferior. I couldn't remember a single thing about my breastfeeding days. "If the doctors never die," I stammered, "wouldn't that mean that they are all disease-free? And wouldn't that help us differentiate them from the sick?"

Bai Dai's eyes lit up. "This destroys the hospital's basic premise that everyone is sick."

We fell silent, facing the most absurd reality, a riddle that could never be solved. The most basic trait of the world was its insistence on toying with people. From the soil of impermanence, the tree of life had blossomed, revealing a harvest of dark, bitter fruit. Did life exist, or was it just an illusion? If doctors were unable to die and we continued on like this, the insane world would come to its destruction (or its end) soon.

I forced a wry smile for Bai Dai. "Okay, I think I have some new ideas about whether doctors can die. Perhaps this might help clear up some of your questions. You asked whether it might be possible that all the doctors are aliens or robots? They are certainly not human, and they aren't gods either. So that already answers part of your question." At first I was rather impressed by my own ingenuity, but soon I began to think I was rather pathetic.

Bai Dai widened her eyes and stared harshly at me with a mixture of indignation and surprise. "Brother Yang, don't tell me you believe that too. You think this is some Hollywood science fiction film? That the doctors came from Mars? Robots and aliens? It's the most childish thing I have ever heard! This world has no savior. Humankind is responsible for establishing the hospitals to treat their diseased bodies. They had faith that illness could be treated. But things underwent a dramatic change, and the hospitals came to rule over humankind. There were no external powers; nothing was forced. To reduce the existence of the hospital to the work of aliens or robots is simplistic, lazy, crude, and cowardly. Brother Yang, you must expel these spineless and indecorous thoughts this instant! You are one of our nation's famous songwriters! In all the time you have been writing songs, have you ever suspected our nation of having been established by robots or aliens? Of course not. Everything in this world was built by human hands, one brick at a time."

"Oh my." I didn't think my ideas were off the rocker. But the morgue had been built by the ultimate human do-gooders, and it had become a symbol of civilized society. Perhaps I would devote myself to writing songs about morgues in an effort to revitalize my songwriting style.

Bai Dai was not ready to give up. "Finding out how doctors die remains the sole clue we have to get to the bottom of this mystery," she said, getting more riled up as she continued. "If it turns out that doctors cannot die, then we'll know just how powerful the forces controlling everything really are. Everything else will seem weak in comparison. Everything else in this world is destined to collapse and fall apart, becoming part of the grave that will bury us. This is the most terrifying crisis of them all. My entire life has been aimed at proving this point. I need to get to the bottom of this, not because I fear death—a lot of people actually *want* to die. Brother Yang, you mustn't back down. That day when I cried out, screaming for an answer to the mystery, you were the only one who dared to stand before me. Not only did you not run away, but you accompanied me to the garden to see the birdcage. I can't tell you how moved I was by that. Brother Yang, you are only fifteen years older than I am. You're not that old, and most importantly, you are still young at heart. You showed me hope during my most desperate hour. Can you hang in there a little bit longer? The hospital is a gateway to death, but we are lucky to be standing together on the threshold. Can't you take just one final step forward with me?"

Bai Dai clasped my hand hard. I thought I could feel hot lava surging under her skin, ready to explode through her wounds. The subtle physical reaction I felt led me into a state of mental struggle. In the end, I just nodded at her.

The other male patients saw this and covered their faces in disappointment.

48

DOCTOR-PATIENT RELATIONS AND GENDER RELATIONS

Once I had sufficiently recovered from my injuries, I decided to overcome my cowardice and again accompany Bai Dai out of the sick ward on her journey to investigate whether doctors could die. Standing before the sole woman in the sick ward, I felt as if that knowledge would be the key to our future, and I decided that even though I was a patient, I needed to start behaving like a man.

It was around that time that we began to reflect again upon the meaning of "death." I had pondered it since, but never for long. Of course, the whole thing was quite ridiculous and uncomfortable. Nominally speaking, the hospital was responsible for saving the nation and ensuring its survival, but the keyword we were concerned with was "death." Death itself is the hospital's most important theme.

This was the revelation I had after visiting the sick ward reserved for the VIP patients. It was said that even in the field of medicine, there was actually more than one form of death. Cessation of breathing and the stopping of the heart were no longer the most accurate factors in officially determining death, nor did the loss of brain function signal the true, final death. What is the nature of consciousness? The extent to which a brain-dead person differs from a dead body remains riddled with controversy, touching upon the very definition of life-extending technology. In the hospital, these topics were considered top secret and *not* discussed with the public. The ultimate destruction would be closely connected to the coming war, in which all would come to an end. This was precisely what drew the doctors in and led them to become punks.

We had yet to find the corpse of a single doctor, but only because we still hadn't understood what "death" really is, even after thousands of years. At first we thought that with the cracking of the genetic code, we would make some progress, but we remained stuck on some of the crucial points. Entropic theory postulated that death is the final stage in the entropic process, yet this still failed to explain its core nature. Why must entropy exist? Why must life be so difficult, so exhausting, so miserable?

Perhaps the doctors we saw doing group calisthenics were already dead? Just as logic had revealed that to be sick was to be healthy, perhaps to be alive was also to be dead? However, as patients, we faced restrictions in terms of the information we had access to, which made it difficult to discern the obscure and often confusing line between life and death. This led ordinary patients to view death as something of a taboo subject, though there was something deeply contradictory about that, because even as they tried to avoid the topic of death, they were always drawn to it. In this regard, Bai Dai had taken an approach like that of a Buddhist practitioner engaged in spiritual development, in line with the dharma. For her, understanding the true nature of death was the most important thing. In the end, none of us can escape death; it is the most natural phenomenon in the world. Even if we avoid the topic, we will still be unable to avoid the reality when it comes. Was there a way to neither live nor die? Anyway, Bai Dai wasn't even a real Buddhist.

The Buddhist scriptures never discuss entropy; rather, they simply propose that a person's longevity is determined by karma and their destined life span. Death comes when people either use up their karma or live out their destined life span. There are four different realms one might encounter upon death. For outsiders, all four of these simply manifest as the patient not breathing, but the deceased have radically different subjective experiences, depending on which realm they enter.

For the small minority of spiritually awakened ones, death is without pain or suffering, but for the vast majority of common folk, death comes only following a period of extreme pain. The human realm is like a vast den of opium and endless pharmaceuticals.

It is said that Buddhist practitioners believe that through hard work, we can subjectively transform the nature of death, and this was one thing they had in common with medical science.

Could modern medical science transform our fate as common folk? It didn't seem so. For the time being, neither Bai Dai nor I had any idea on how to approach this. We felt we had better take a look around the morgue first, to see if we could discover any clues there.

We walked around the hospital in a massive circle—it felt as if we went from one end of the earth to the other—and yet we couldn't find the morgue. Finally we just went back to the trash room. We were utterly exhausted, and sitting there, shoulder to shoulder amid the clammy garbage and piles of filth, we tried to catch our breath. Bai Dai took out a cigarette and began to smoke. A row of official diagrams of human organs hung on the wall. We sat there, blankly staring at them, and slipped into a hazy semiconscious state before eventually passing out. On the floor were the fleshy remains of an orangutan, which seemed to pulsate still with the vestiges of life. I could feel a hot energy welling up in my heart. Above the row of diagrams hung another, a black-and-white diagram of the human meridian points used in acupuncture: sitting there upon the lotus throne, the wheel of yin and yang began to spin, converging into a flame that burned alternately hot and cold. Everything else in the trash room was like a dried-up wasteland. We might as well have been on Mars. Sitting there at the base of that lifeless mountain of garbage, we were like the two loneliest souls in the universe.

But we gradually began to feel the urge to spread our wings.

Suddenly afflicted by a strange force that pulled us together, we embraced in our desperation. It felt as though we would never have another chance. By this time, I had begun to look at the trash room as the birdcage. No, that wasn't it—it wasn't the nurses' lounge, it was the morgue! Was I going to die? If I didn't die then, it might be too late. My heart was on fire as I ripped off Bai Dai's clothes only to discover that she wasn't wearing anything under her hospital gown. Then, with a little pop, I entered her milky-yellow body. I forced myself to fantasize about my daughter so I could get excited: *I'm raping her! I'm raping my daughter! I'm raping the peafowl!* I inserted my tongue into the dark-red lesions all over Bai Dai's body. The stench of nicotine permeated her wounds, which I fervently licked, attempting to ignite the fire within her internal organs. Every pore in my body screamed as a wave of little white bubbles frothed out. The terrifying echo of life that my own body released unsettled me to the point that I had to turn away, only to be met with the disappointment that no external force had tried to stop me. I was still alive.

Less than a minute later, it was as if the two of us had suddenly awakened from a nightmare. We abruptly stopped, rolling over onto our sides in fear of what we had done and scared of what was to come. I suddenly came to the revelation that I was treating Bai Dai's illness— what a random, yet critical, discovery! Later Bai Dai also confessed to me that, in that moment, she had had the same feeling, as though she had been treating me.

We both suffered from serious ailments, and yet there we were, using our bodies to treat one another. I think I had started to warm up back when we were in the garden, looking at the birdcage. I was both her doctor and her patient. And she was both my patient and my doctor. It took only a single thought for us to break through the natural moat separating rulers from subjects, fathers from sons. Doctors and patients often fell into a confused maze of gender relations, forced to switch roles constantly. Patients were the only people who were truly qualified to become doctors, and yet their treatment never ended, at least not until one party crossed the threshold into death. Only then was one's identity finally confirmed. The dead were all patients; whether doctors can die was a false proposition. The answer revealed all.

But what exactly was this mutual treatment? From the looks of it, strategies like gene therapy or the complete elimination of genes were both far from sufficient.

Just then Dr. Bauchi appeared. Had he come to put an end to this, even though in our eyes, this was far from adultery? Such a description was far too flattering for us. There was no possibility of our having a true union; we were just trying out a new treatment method. There had been no climax. I don't even think there had been much excitement, only an indelible sense of pain, like a needle entering a vein, or the jagged, ironlike leaves of the sago palm piercing our bodies, punishing us for our fornication. We hadn't even injected any anesthetic.

Dr. Bauchi had taken in every detail of what transpired between us, so we ceased our mutual therapy, or rather were forced to cease it. Were our actions prohibited according to the rules of the inpatient ward?

My face turned bright red as I tried to explain our conduct to Dr. Bauchi. "We weren't trying . . . trying to start a family." Bai Dai didn't utter a word; she simply lowered her head.

"Got it," Dr. Bauchi said nonchalantly. "You two are different from Old Gao and Little Li."

"We were . . . we were doing therapy," I said.

"You have seen the light." Dr. Bauchi spoke in a dull, matter-of-fact tone, as if he had anticipated our behavior. But he clearly had something more on his mind. His face revealed a strange expression that was impossible to describe, but it was suddenly clear to me that everything that had just happened had been prearranged. It must have been part of the hospital's treatment plan. The ceremony had ended, and the test had been a success.

But it also signaled the beginning of an even greater test.

From that point on, Bai Dai and I were separated. She was placed in an ambulance and taken to another hospital, where she would no longer be a patient. Her new role would be as a medical intern, and she would formally begin to treat the sick. Patients could be transformed into doctors! In the Age of Medicine, every patient had the potential to become a doctor. Inside every one of us was a slumbering doctor, waiting to be awakened. It had been right before my eyes all this time, but I had simply never realized it. Somehow that mutual-therapy session had aroused a natural gift or an untapped talent within us. The relationship between doctors and patients was not only like that of a bacterium and a host—it was a paragenetic relationship, pure and simple. Doctors and patients were, at their very core, part of the same organism. Man and God (or demigod) were interchangeable; naturally, they could also play the role of the devil.

Bai Dai and I had both realized that the reason for the hospital's existence (and survival) was to produce more disease, continually. Without disease, the hospital couldn't carry on. In this sense, we had already created the world's ultimate disease with our mutual therapy in the trash room. What we had created in that moment was, at once, both the world's ultimate disease and the most effective vaccine. This was the true meaning of treatment. The valuable experience we gained in this rare form of medicine could now be applied in a clinical setting. The rest of the patients in the sick ward remained in the dark.

49

THE NATURE OF TREATMENT

Instead of being sent off with Bai Dai, I was ordered to stay behind. I was also promoted to the role of medical intern, which I happily accepted. I, too, could be a doctor! There was probably a shortage, requiring the hospital to replenish its physicians' roster, transforming patients into doctors in order to overcome the crisis, bid farewell to death, escape the end of the world, and ensure its eternal prosperity— the best it could do in an otherwise hopeless situation, or at least a passable option from a statistical perspective. At least that's what I thought.

But there was a price to pay: I was no longer together with Bai Dai. We were allowed to keep in touch only through letters. We exchanged thoughts on academic matters, and we made sure never to mention anything romantic—anything *seemingly* romantic between us was purely a means to express our vague, deep feelings about doctor-patient relations.

What we discussed most was the special form of therapy we had developed. Why was it considered a method? How was it different from other methods? Was it irreplaceable? Why did our participation in this form of therapy qualify us to be doctors?

Bai Dai saw this as an attempt to take things back to the beginning, like what they call in philosophy the "upward spiral." The family structure and its biological values had come to an end, but the crisis the hospital faced had still not been completely eliminated. A handful of doctors had begun to wake up to the importance and practicality of gender relations between doctors and patients. What began as a balance between collaboration and resistance came to reflect a much deeper dialectical relationship between doctors and patients, medicine and bacteria, individuals and the collective, the family and the nation, and even being and death. But it had all been hidden, pushed aside by gene therapy. We now had our opportunity to explore what we had learned, to make new discoveries about new diseases and treatments.

Let me illustrate. The uterus houses antibodies that come from blood serum, and these can lead to sperm agglutination, which causes sperm to stick together and lose mobility. These antibodies are found in the highest concentrations among prostitutes, secondly among married women, and lowest among unmarried women. Married women's antibodies may be responding specifically to their husbands' sperm, creating a rather embarrassing phenomenon for some married men—their sperm crippled by their wives' immune systems. This gives the wives' lovers a competitive advantage at fertilization and leads the husbands to suffer both pain and jealousy. Women's ability to use their soft side to conquer the strong might be miraculous or merely bestowed upon them by the principles of biological evolution, but either way, they can accept their husbands' penises while rejecting their sperm. This, too, could be a method of therapy, representing the pinnacle of a woman's skill: using her eggs to find the best possible sperm from a wide pool and simultaneously filling her husband with jealousy, making him even more faithful to her.

This was one of the happier realizations in the tragedy of life. It revealed the nature of treatment—how, deep down, doctors and patients are *actually* connected. Like a married couple, a doctor and a patient appear harmonious, but underneath that facade lies deep discord. They share a bed but dream different dreams. They exist in a state of tension, of constant conflict, even as they remain together, inseparable, mutually dependent, always taking advantage of each other, always maintaining a tense rapport. Yet due to advancements in gene therapy, the destruction of the family, and even the elimination of lovers, this fundamental system of treatment is unknown to most people, and it is indeed a terrible loss for these latent diseases to have been covered up, which also leaves the hospital unable to prepare for future changes. That is why we are in desperate need of an archaeological approach, to go back to the past, reflect upon what we discovered in the lab, and re-create a new system of reference. The hospital finds itself at a crucial point, its very existence hanging in the balance. Something has to be done.

According to the latest plan, all new doctors will be required to have experience as a patient. Not even the most advanced medical theories or rich clinical experience can replace firsthand experience of an illness. Without it, no one can truly be an outstanding doctor. This fundamental change represents the only way to break the vicious cycle of doctors' making patients increasingly sick as they treat them. The circle of unity between doctors and patients can finally be completed. In the past we thought that medical work was extremely taxing and that doctors all needed to have good constitutions, but we discovered a serious error. From this point forward, doctors and patients will work together anew to attain true equality. The hospital will exert all of its effort to make itself strong through forward motion, constant innovation, and consistent advancements that will continue throughout time immemorial.

All of this, it seemed, was due to Bai Dai's logical deductions, her obsession driving her to take her theories as far as they could go. But I was afraid that things weren't as simple as they seemed. Did any of these ideas come from Dr. Bauchi? Or Dr. Ornamental Rock's plans? Or a scheme devised by the hospital president? Why did the hospital seek out a pathetically weak songwriter? Couldn't some superfit marathon athlete have served as its guinea pig? My relationship with Bai Dai had absolutely nothing to do with the concept of family. Our quest to find the morgue brought us together. Maybe one can never truly understand how things begin, and the truth about the hospital will remain a mystery.

But none of this was what I was most concerned about, as I finally came to realize that Bai Dai was, in fact, Dr. Bauchi's daughter. Everything the doctor had done was to save his beloved little girl.

50
THE CHARM OF THE WHITE
COAT

Bai Dai had become a doctor, and for the time being, there was only one thing that I was interested in. I wondered what she looked like as she took off that blue-striped patient uniform and slipped into that big white lab coat. I could have gone on fantasizing about that forever.

I've always thought there is something particularly charming about white clothing. It symbolizes all that is clean and pure, but what's more interesting is that almost everyone involved with death wears white. Besides doctors and nurses, there are chefs (who kill plants and animals), barbers (who cut hair, which is also like killing a part of the human body), cleaners (who clear up the dead bodies), biochemical soldiers (who kill their enemies), lab researchers working with dangerous chemicals (if they aren't careful, they might even kill themselves), morticians (who clean up human corpses), and so on. According to our traditional culture, white is also the color of the mourning dress worn when an elder passes away. White *equals* death, I realized, and began a kind of free association about the dazzlingly fatal beauty of this world.

When Buddhism was introduced into our country, the bodhisattva Avalokiteśvara was portrayed in a long, flowing white robe . . . in her hands she held a bottle of purity, often filled with the corpses of slaughtered monsters and demons . . . the standard blue-striped uniforms worn by patients and prisoners, the stripes resembling the bars of a cell, are a visible sign of forced confinement . . . it was said that every patient in the hospital comes willingly, but they actually had no other choice . . . at the end of the day, all of our bodies will be covered by white cloth . . . when human beings invented uniforms, using clothing to signal different roles or identities, a piece of pure white cloth marked the boundary between life and death . . . that thin white cloth wouldn't keep them warm or hide their shame, but it separated them from animals . . . in the library I saw a photograph of a dead zebra on the African plains, its body cavity ripped open and infested with maggots . . . it was almost impossible to look at, but that horrific image revealed precisely what the white cloth conceals . . . one day, when humans are no longer human, will the flag of the white coat still fly . . . ?

Bai Dai and I no longer discussed how doctors die. We were both doctors. We had donned the white coat. There was no point in talking about it anymore. When the drive behind a quest is too intense, it is destined to come to naught.

And so I retracted my tail feathers. There was no need to display them anymore. I entered a new stage, quiet and peaceful. Gradually my illness seemed to improve.

Then one day, Bai Dai suddenly cut off all contact with me.

51

LIFE IS A CHARADE, ONLY THE NIGHTMARE IS REAL

I followed a dark corridor to the morgue, hesitating for a moment before I pushed open the door. Inside was a dead body wrapped in a white cloth. I approached and pulled back the cloth to reveal Bai Dai's terrifying face, bathed in green light, her dark-red tongue hanging out of her mouth. I only recognized her by her five-pointed star earrings. The profuse amount of blood that had been pouring out of the wounds on her body had congealed. She had finally found what she had been searching for—the body of a dead doctor.

All of my previous suspicions had been unfounded. This was Bai Dai's final destination. After so much struggle and hardship, she had finally arrived. I knew she would want me to look up the cause of her death, which would finally reveal how doctors die.

I stood staring at her body for a long time. Then I moved in closer, gently opening my mouth, and took her tongue between my teeth. I began digging my fingers into her wounds to see what I could find. Her internal organs felt like ice cubes, but they stank of alcohol. My hand was sore when I pulled it out, and it reeked, a horrid stench. Then I realized that Bai Dai had several new wounds on her body, all close to her vital organs. Her hand still clasped the letter the hospital president had sent her.

I was like a god who had secretly descended to the human world to consume the sacrificial offerings left for me on the altar.

This nightmare tortured me all through that night, and I awoke extremely uncomfortable. *Life is a charade, only the nightmare is real*, I thought to myself. I looked up the phone number for Bai Dai's hospital and dialed. I said I was calling to inquire into the condition of "Dr. Bai Dai." The person who answered must have been the on-call doctor. He said, "We had a transfer patient from another hospital with that name, but she hanged herself last night."

Hanged herself? Then where did those other wounds come from?

Death is the end, but the end is only the beginning. I kept ruminating over those words in my head, again and again.

In another nightmare, Bai Dai had died and transformed into the Buddha incarnate. She sat meditating on a black-and-white yin-yang pattern, revealed a broad smile, and began to pat the Indian peafowls with her broad pink palms. She hit them harder and harder until they died, and all of heaven and earth were bathed in the crimson red of their juicy flesh.

I woke in a cold sweat, full of anxiety and restlessness. I couldn't focus. My diagnostic and treatment skills began to falter rapidly. *What the hell was happening? Was Bai Dai really dead? Was her spirit haunting me?*

Gradually I began to suspect that Bai Dai had been using me, like a tool, to get herself promoted to doctor. This had been her real goal all along. It was all a deliberate scheme either to satisfy or to amuse her father, Dr. Bauchi. In her heart, she cared only about herself. Once I had fulfilled my purpose, I no longer held any value for her. But aren't all human relations based on mutual exploitation? This was especially true of doctors and patients; it was precisely the foundation of their relationship. I should have figured this out sooner. I had even taken advantage of my own daughter. Even if Bai Dai had really killed herself or attained Buddhahood, I shouldn't feel bad, right? Then again, maybe she had been murdered.

I couldn't help but miss my own daughter, the aerial nurse. Although I didn't know where she was, I felt proud and relieved to have become her colleague. Colleagues would never rape each other. That happens only between doctors and patients.

My thoughts and mood fell into chaos. Not only was I unable to treat my patients properly, but my own health began to deteriorate rapidly as well. My abdominal pain had greatly improved—it had almost disappeared—but suddenly, it came back worse than ever. My short career as a doctor had come to an end; I was a patient again. Autumn faded, winter returned; flowing water turned to ice. This was all part of a natural cycle. And so I found myself back at the sick ward. I put my patient gown back on. I was under the care of Dr. Bauchi.

After everything that had happened, I was back to zero.

52

A NEW KARMIC CYCLE

There were quite a few women in the sick ward. They gathered around me curiously, as if I were a monster from Mars.

Since I was getting on in years and not very brave about facing death, I wanted to reactivate the doctor inside me so I could cure myself. Bai Dai had once temporarily tapped into the potential doctor inside me, which had almost allowed me momentary enlightenment. But I needed external assistance. I couldn't do it on my own.

Out of frustration, I decided to summon up my inner courage. I did my best imitation of Bai Dai, yelling to the other patients, "Hey, do you want to know how doctors die?" I felt my eyes well up with tears.

The male patients immediately covered their ears and scurried back into their beds. The women were so terrified that they lifted their hospital gowns to cover their faces, like a muster of peahens spreading their tail feathers. I faced them, a dull scalpel in my hand, their exposed thighs trembling. One woman stood defiantly, staring straight into my eyes. It felt like the beginning of a new karmic cycle. I tried to overcome my fear—of the generation gap, the gender gap—but after a deep breath, I stepped forward, took that girl by the hand, and led her out of the sick ward and toward the garden.

We walked and walked until we arrived at the birdcage. I anxiously asked her, "Hey, can you see it?" She shook her head. "Take a closer look. Do you see it?"

She moved in a little closer and chuckled. "Oh, a rooster. There's a rooster in the birdcage!"

Filled with regret and sadness, I wondered, *How could this be?* She wasn't Bai Dai. She was so innocent and naive. But that was okay. Perhaps this was all just some kind of intergenerational hallucination. *As long as you are here in the hospital, you shall receive treatment.*

Bai Dai was gone, but I sensed a new opportunity arising in the guise of this girl standing before me. She had awakened something hidden, something deep inside me, and even if it meant making myself seriously ill again, I couldn't wait to dig it out.

POSTSCRIPT: SURGERY

Author's note: *This postscript can be regarded as a supplement to patient Yang Wei's experience at C City's Central Hospital. It not only explains the further adventures of Yang Wei after he was sent back to the medical ward but reveals to those interested readers the secret history of the hospital . . . and our universe.*

53

I ENTERED HER BODY LIKE A
THIEF IN THE NIGHT

It hasn't stopped raining since I arrived in C City. The cold, icy rain just keeps coming down, enveloping the city in a backdrop of gloomy darkness that makes it difficult even to determine what season it is. And yet all the plants and vegetation continue to grow like mad. Layers of cold frost and turbulent clouds engulf the city. Various towers and buildings from the hospital complex occasionally jut out from beneath the thick mist. But the sun and stars are completely obscured. In fact, it is hard to say for sure whether there is even a universe out there still, beyond the mist.

Sometimes it is easy to forget that everything will eventually be destroyed. Humankind will be rendered extinct, and new life-forms will rise up to control the world. But to most of us, all of that feels like an impossibility. We think that everything will simply continue on as it always has. This often leads people to a certain misconception: they feel like they are already living in a postapocalyptic age, where everyone has already died several deaths. It is said that this kind of feeling is particularly vivid when one undergoes surgery.

I met a female patient named Zhu Lin. When I first spoke about doctors dying, she was the only one that didn't try to run away or look at me with disdain. And in that moment, I felt like I had transformed and taken Bai Dai's place. I later accompanied Zhu Lin to the garden outside the inpatient tower, and it was as if I were reliving all the things I had done with Bai Dai. We walked in circles around the garden in the cold rain. We didn't use an umbrella, just let the water soak our bodies. The entire scene felt like an illusion.

It didn't take long for me to discover that Zhu Lin was the daughter of a woman from the observation room in the emergency department who had been suffering from a uranium deficiency. She had originally come to the hospital to help take care of her mother. Her father had been relying upon the electricity that his wife's body generated to stay alive. When Zhu Lin's mother came to the hospital, her father had to stay too. But they hadn't expected their daughter to be admitted as well.

Zhu Lin was on the plump side. She had large breasts, her eyes were shaped like teacups, and her long black hair went down past her shoulders like a disheveled clump of wild grass. She had just turned sixteen but was as mature as any adult. She suffered from epilepsy, and her seizures caused her to lose consciousness, suffer bouts of incontinence, foam at the mouth, and experience muscle spasms. In order to help alleviate her symptoms, Dr. Bauchi performed a temporal lobectomy.

After the surgery she still remembered me. "Uncle Yang, good to see you again. I guess you haven't escaped yet." She expressed a willingness to spend time with me, but Zhu Lin's mind was not very sharp after the procedure. Whenever she saw the empty birdcage, she would always exclaim, "A rooster! A rooster!"

I would try to console her. "How's your dad?" I asked with feigned concern. "Any news from him?"

"I dunno I dunno!" She giggled in a way that seemed to spill from her jiggling breasts.

"Oh, I was worried about him. Can he survive separated from your mother?"

"Never thought about that. But he used to be unable to leave her. Only when Mom produced electricity did Dad pop out of his zombie-like state. He'd come right back to life and started trampling on women like a hungry tiger. But that's not the reason they had me. Dad used to be with another woman. They went to have in vitro fertilization, and they inserted the frozen embryo from that other woman into Mom's womb—that's how they had me! So it's hard for me to say whose child I really am. I matured superfast: my breasts started to develop at age six, and I had my first period at eight. Yet I have been disappointed with this world, so very disappointed . . ." As Zhu Lin spoke, the happy expression disappeared from her face, and she began to cry. But like so many other girls her age, she quickly wiped away her tears and started to laugh. "Ha ha! The thing is, I'm different! I'm different from all the rest of them, and I'm going to live a new life. Ever since I was little, I have dreamed of becoming an angel in white. I want to dedicate myself to the noble cause of healing the sick and caring for the wounded, as a nurse. Now I have finally fallen ill and been admitted to the hospital! The hospital is the place where all my dreams can finally come true!"

Zhu Lin opened her mouth as she laughed, revealing her damp bloodred esophagus. I could see directly into her wormlike body cavity. She was sick, she was in pain, and yet she still hadn't abandoned her yearning for a better life. The vitality pulsating through her stabbed at me. I was afraid to hear the sound of her laughter, and yet I saw an opportunity that I could take advantage of.

And so I wondered whether I might be able to take the precious lessons I had learned from Bai Dai and apply them to this naive young lady. I couldn't get that exercise I did with Bai Dai out of my head, that wonderful mutual therapy where we had used our bodies in concert. I wondered if doing it again might awaken the slumbering doctor inside me, triggering another radical improvement in my illness. I know that the end of the world is coming, but I'm not ready to die . . . at least not just yet.

And so I asked her, "Hey, do you want to know how doctors die?"

I led Zhu Lin to the trash room. The piles of excrement and puddles of human blood shocked her, precisely the effect I had been hoping for. I took the opportunity to pull her close; she struggled only a little bit. I was quite proud of myself, but at the last minute, I grew timid. "Don't be scared," I told her, but it was more like I was talking to myself. Alas, I'm not only a patient but a pretty damn incompetent one.

But the treatment had already begun, and I was ready to put everything on the line. I entered her body like a thief in the night. She was frigid inside, like an ice crack at the South Pole. She quickly loosened up and began to giggle. "Good job, Uncle Yang. Don't be scared." She collapsed into my arms crying, then squeezed me tightly, leaving a trail of cool tears on my chest. I felt like I had become her father. She was almost the same age as my daughter. I silently swore to be this helpless girl's protector, and my eyes began to tear up too.

From that point forward, I performed daily treatment on Zhu Lin, once in the morning and once in the evening. These therapy sessions served as a supplement to her medication. Through all of this rubbing and banging, we were finally able to see a spark of hope for her recovery. I liked it quick, simple, and rough, but as time went by, Zhu Lin seemed to take more pleasure in the whole process, to savor it. She also became quite considerate, sometimes even crooning like a mother to her child.

But for some reason, we were never able to climax, always giving up halfway. There was nothing at all pleasurable about it, and they didn't promote me to doctor like before. As for my pain, it hadn't subsided in the least. In the end, our treatment regimen had absolutely no impact.

54

PAIN IS A DISEASE ALL ITS OWN

I first came to the hospital for stomach pain, and even after all this time as an inpatient, my pain had yet to subside, and they hadn't even given me a real diagnosis.

The pain started in my upper abdomen, but later it moved to my lower abdomen and triggered discomfort in my shoulders, thighs, groin, and back. I had numerous bouts of vomiting. I checked my medical records and discovered that I had been diagnosed with a case of intractable fifth-degree pain, which had already impacted my endocrine and metabolic functions.

I took out some books from the hospital library to learn about the origin of pain. It starts with free nerve endings in the skin and tissue and transfers various injuries and stimulation into a coded nerve stimulus, which then travels along slow myelinated nerve fibers and thin unmyelinated nerve fibers, transmitted through the spinal ganglion to the relevant neurons in the posterior horn region of the spinal cord or the spinal nucleus of the trigeminal nerve, and then on through the contralateral ventrolateral funiculus to the more advanced pain centers in the thalamus—which ultimately translates into pain sensations and responses by the cerebral cortex and other related areas of the brain.

Dr. Bauchi told me that the ability to sense pain has been designated as one of the "five signs of life," the others being consistent body temperature, pulse, breathing, and blood pressure. Pain is the most critical indicator. "Pain is not just a symptom of disease," he explained.

"Chronic pain is a disease all its own, and diagnosis of a disease is the only means to acquire good health."

You could even say that the reason people always circle around the topic of "the meaning of life" and expend unimaginable effort on things like the construction of hospitals and morgues is to escape from or seek out pain.

When we speak of hell, that, too, is about the concept of pain. You could even say that pain is the central idea of hell. When we refer to hell as the mountain of knives, the sea of fire, the frying pan, the lake of blood, the place of spears and knives—these images elicit thoughts of pain and torture. I once read the following description of hell in a Buddhist classic: The jailer placed the deceased on a massive anvil and proceeded to pulverize the dead body with a steel hammer; the body was reduced to a pulpy mess of juicy flesh and shattered bones, and blood flowed like a river. Then the wind blew, triggering the cycle of life to begin again. The jailer applied the mace to another group of tortured souls, inserting its spiky end into the anus, twisting and turning until its porcupine-like spikes began to emerge through the victim's skin. The horrific scene of flesh being ripped apart is difficult to describe. And then there was a man who, having been freed from the dreadful scene just described, saw a gorgeous pasture of green grass; he ran onto the grass, only to discover that the blades of grass were actually burning-hot, razor-sharp spikes. With each step the spikes would penetrate straight through his feet. As he raised them up, they would heal, only to be penetrated again with the next step. The pain was unbearable.

Here in the hospital, heaven and hell are one and the same.

The pain described above is quite close to my own personal experience. The only difference is that there are eighteen levels of heaven or hell, whereas in the world of medicine there are five dimensions of pain. As far as the living are concerned, five dimensions are more than enough.

Dr. Thomas Sydenham, the seventeenth-century British physician regarded as the founder of clinical medicine, once pointed out, "The physician's most direct relationship is not based on practical experience in anatomy or biology experiments, but is instead rooted in the pain and suffering experienced by his patients. That is why the first responsibility of the physician lies in accurately understanding the nature of pain."

And so we may describe the physician's mission as follows: "If I don't go to hell, who will?" Going to hell means sending people into heaven.

But why am I in so much pain? What is the nature of this pain? Why am I unable to shed myself of this pain that gnaws at me so? An old saying suggests that "chronic conditions lead to the best remedies," but I have nothing to say to that. I know that both heaven and hell will always be beyond my reach.

According to the medical books, my stomach pain could be related to an injured organ in the abdominal region, an ulcer in the digestive tract, acute gastrointestinal bleeding, intractable or recurrent gastrointestinal bleeding, intestinal perforation, mesenteric lymphadenitis, mesenteric thrombosis, intestinal obstruction, parasitic infection, inguinal hernia, appendicitis, cholecystitis, acute biliary tract infection, bile duct stones, splenic infarction, acute hepatitis, liver abscess, acute cystitis, acute pancreatitis, chronic pancreatitis, stomach cancer, gallbladder cancer, cholangiocarcinoma, pancreatic cancer, colorectal cancer, liver cancer, bladder cancer . . . the list goes on. I heaved a deep sigh at the long list of diseases that humankind has "invented." How did primitive people living thousands of years ago survive?

What's more, the psychological instability triggered by so many rounds of failed treatment, the depression resulting from being ignored by my fellow patients, the stifling feeling brought on by exhaustion and insomnia, and other psychological triggers can all produce the sensation of pain.

From the outpatient ward to the inpatient ward, I undertook all kinds of tests, yet not a single doctor was able to give me a clear diagnosis. Whenever I ask Dr. Bauchi, he simply repeats the same thing: "Let's not be anxious now. Diagnosis and treatment both take time."

But how much time? Until the next world war breaks out, the battle to establish a new paradise? There exists a particular type of scorching hell or flaming heaven, a place not only where all sentient beings suffer the pain of being burned, roasted, stabbed, and chopped up but where the jailer fills their mouths with molten iron and copper. Once the liquid burns through a victim's tongue and internal organs, the molten metal, combined with melted flesh and blood, exits the body through the nine orifices. Then the jailer's trident penetrates the body through the anus and slices up to the top of the head. He pours a thick red solution into the gaping wound. The scene is impossible to watch. The length of a victim's sentence is 1,600 hell years, equivalent to the length of five dynastic cycles or 3,084,160,000,000 human years. Our universe has been in existence for only 13.7 billion years.

Sometimes I wonder if the doctors already knew the cause of my pain and simply wouldn't share it with me because they were contemplating other, longer-term considerations.

Not that the doctors aren't taking their jobs seriously. They are extremely dedicated to their work and display the highest level of professionalism. Like a police detective arresting a suspect, they treat my condition with a step-by-step treatment plan, utilizing various conventional and unconventional methods to stop my pain. My body is like a crime scene. Some of the methods they have employed: local anesthetics to shut off or block fine fiber activity along the afferent pathway; various forms of physical therapy including Chinese adjustment, massage, heat therapy, electrotherapy, acupuncture, and electrical nerve stimulation therapy; oral administration of nonnarcotic analgesics that inhibit the synthesis of prostaglandins, such as aspirin, and narcotic analgesics that bind with opioid receptors, such as morphine; nonsteroidal anti-inflammatory drugs; serotonin, norepinephrine, and other peptides involved in the downward inhibitory pathway to implement deep electrical stimulation; and even surgical procedures to destroy or cut off the ascending anatomical pathways that transmit pain.

For a body to withstand so many forms of treatment, it must have a certain strength and tenacity. This process has allowed me to develop a deep understanding of the patience and persistence of our medical workers.

I heard that normally pain-relief therapies were not permitted for patients who had yet to receive a diagnosis. And yet owing to the peculiar nature of my condition, they still tried so many different treatments.

From what I can tell, there must be a way to eliminate pain. A document I read in the hospital library discussed how modern medical technology has already advanced to the point that it can allow people to know what pain is without actually feeling it. Through neuron modification or the installation of micromachines on the cerebral cortex, the sensation of "pain" in humans can be numbed. The "actual sensation" of pain is filtered out through the use of electrical implants. A special patient uniform can even sense when a patient bleeds and automatically apply pressure to stop the bleeding, simultaneously cutting off the transmission of pain signals to the central nervous system.

This functions somewhat like syringomyelia, a degenerative disease that afflicts the middle of the spinal cord, causing the patient to cease feeling pain. Patients suffering from this disorder can insert their hands into boiling water without any sensation of pain.

Unfortunately, I have yet to see such advanced treatment methods in the sick ward, where it seems that the only way to ensure that the patients know that they are in a hospital is to allow their screams of pain to play out like a continual background soundtrack. I suppose that is more humane than putting the patients' hands into boiling water.

Leaving patients in a state of never-ending pain is all part of the hospital's strategy to ensure everyone stays in the hospital. Heavy meds keep patients alive. After all, as long as you are alive, you feel pain. Pain is the greatest encouragement a patient can receive, a warning signal issued by the body's defense system. It warns us not to take risks, to be more cautious. It is said that people born without the ability to feel pain die before the age of thirty. Pain indicates that happiness is on its way.

I have gradually come to believe that doctors use those flashes of pain to remind their patients never to forget that they are patients, that illness requires treatment, that treatment is designed to preserve the continuance of pain, and that pain is life's ultimate reward.

When the future Zen Buddhist master Huineng first arrived at Shandong Temple in Mei County, his teacher, Master Hongren, assigned him menial tasks like sweeping the floors and cooking for the monks. This brings us back to the question "If I don't go to hell, who will?" This can also be summed up by the saying *As long as there are souls in hell, I shall never achieve Buddhahood.* Both amply illustrate the core characteristics of geek-like figures such as Master Hongren and Master Huineng, who endeavored to create a paradise where all living beings could enjoy eternal happiness. Zen and medicine are one.

Meanwhile I lag far behind, trying to catch up.

I have been growing increasingly bored and frustrated with my attempt to carry out my self-salvation plan using Zhu Lin's body, and yet, having come this far, I have no choice but to see it through to the end.

55

DEATH ISN'T SCARY, JUST THE PAIN THAT PRECEDES IT

Every day Dr. Bauchi brought a group of resident doctors and interns to the sick ward during his rounds. Although the sick ward was equipped with intelligent technology and a two-way video conference system to connect all the patients with their doctors, Dr. Bauchi still insisted on personally doing his rounds every day. This hardworking and professional doctor believed that face-to-face contact with patients—looking them in the eyes, up close—was irreplaceable, unless doctors were one day replaced by medical robots.

"How are you feeling today?" Dr. Bauchi's voice was like a natural hot spring, gentle and warm. His flowing white lab jacket was like a massive movie screen connecting heaven and earth, almost holy in appearance.

I opened my mouth but couldn't say anything. The doctor reached out and removed the pillow that had been propped under my head. I lay down flat and could feel my breathing start to strain. Dr. Bauchi gestured to one of the medical-school students to examine me. The student pressed on my abdomen, and I screamed in pain.

Dr. Bauchi addressed the students. "What do you think? Where is the problem?"

The interns and residents whispered among themselves, but they couldn't come to a consensus.

"Shall we increase his dose of morphine?" one intern suggested.

I wanted to ask them if there was any treatment they could offer other than more pain meds.

"Do you see it?" Dr. Bauchi asked. "The source of his pain is quite complicated. The human body is like a black box. The most important thing is to figure out the cause of his suffering. But even if you spend your entire life as a resident here in the hospital, it is still sometimes extremely difficult to diagnose. Experience-based medicine, evidence-based medicine, and precision medicine all have their limitations. To study medicine is to be lost in a vast ocean that knows no end."

"That's the challenge we all face as doctors," one intern said.

"It is the joy we get to experience as doctors," said a resident.

"Will I have to spend the rest of my life in this hospital?" I asked with a mixture of misery and expectation. No one even mentioned that humanity was on the verge of being wiped out in the coming world war.

"Please don't be discouraged," Dr. Bauchi said. "I suspect you think your doctors can't relieve your pain. In fact, you probably believe we are the ones intentionally *creating* the pain that you feel. This causes your sensation of fear. But you are completely wrong. You need to have faith in the hospital. You need to have faith in your doctors. We were even about to make arrangements for you to participate in the hospital's big New Year's Eve gala! But you need to *submit* to the hospital. You can't go on doing what you want all the time. We do not approve of alternative therapies that have not been medically sanctioned. But what we fear most is your losing faith and ending up a prisoner to illusion. Once that happens, your illness will be very difficult to treat." Dr. Bauchi's words carried an air of both care and caution.

Sometimes I wonder if all this pain is just a figment of my imagination. It has leaped over so many different obstacles and is a direct function of my brain, which is why none of these therapies—whether pharmaceuticals, gene therapy, or mutual treatment with the opposite sex—has dispelled what is essentially an illusion.

Could that be what is really happening?

No, it can't be an illusion. Nor can this pain be part of an elaborate conspiracy collectively devised by my office, the hotel, and the hospital. It seems like it has always been here, deeply rooted in my body since birth, constantly reminding me, every second of every day, that living is endurance. It's like an old jaded devil inside me, stubbornly resisting each and every therapy.

To put it more precisely, it is as if some kind of external force has installed a "pain device" inside my body. Someone pushes a remote button, and I immediately roll around in pain.

I shouldn't blame my doctors. I have only myself to blame. As a patient, I am simply incurable! All I do is cause more trouble and create more opportunities for my poor respectful doctors.

But I wonder if my pain might be part of the larger crisis that the hospital faces. Could this be a precursor to the coming extinction of mankind and destruction of the world? And here I am, just an insignificant nothing, drowning in an ocean of sin, all while continuing to sound an alarm like the siren on a buoy.

If that is the case, this pain is indeed untreatable. Even if my disease doesn't kill me, the pain will. In the end, quite a few patients have no choice but to go out like this, willingly. Death isn't scary, just the pain that precedes it. And as for the pain after death? We will have to leave that in the hands of Yama, the king of hell, to decide.

But there are things that are more unsettling than pain alone. Like waking up in the middle of the night, still in pain, only to discover that Zhu Lin was gone.

56

THE SECRET BETWEEN DOCTORS AND PATIENTS

I crawled out from my sickbed and sneaked out of the sick ward. The corridor was so quiet that it felt like everything had died. Cold light shone down in all directions. I spotted Zhu Lin strolling a corridor up ahead. It looked like she was sleepwalking, with a strange limp, like her ankle was twisted. Meanwhile, she kept reciting something, as if speaking to an invisible man.

She arrived at the doctor's office. Dr. Bauchi was sitting alone, reading a book by lamplight. His entire body looked very pale. Zhu Lin didn't say a word but walked right up in front of him.

After a long pregnant pause, Dr. Bauchi finally looked up. "You're here."

"I'm here," she answered.

He put down his book and stood up. Taking her by the hand, he helped her up onto his desk and had her lie down. He slowly removed her clothing until she was completely naked. "Your illness is quite severe," he whispered, "so I'm going to perform a special treatment."

The look in his eyes was completely different from how he had appeared at the sick ward the previous day. His words flowed like molten metal and had a hypnotic effect. Zhu Lin gazed at him, and tears began to pour down her face.

That is when Dr. Bauchi and Zhu Lin began their mutual-therapy session. He removed his white jacket. He wasn't wearing anything underneath. And then, like a skilled pro, he entered her body.

I felt like I had accidentally walked onto a movie set. I was flustered beyond belief and couldn't help but wonder, *Could Dr. Bauchi have been a patient once too?*

I couldn't bear the thought of my doctor having to perform self-salvation therapy. My best guess was that Zhu Lin's condition was particularly serious and required this special treatment. Based on my experience, some female patients are especially reliant upon their male doctors, which leads them to develop mild crushes that sometimes turn into deep infatuations. They think about how wonderful their doctors are and want to spend every minute with them. They hope and pray to catch a glimpse of their doctor making his rounds, longing for the moment he conducts a thorough physical exam. I silently grumbled to myself, but there was nothing I could do.

Dr. Bauchi and Zhu Lin pressed their bodies together so tightly that I thought they were trying to combine their internal organs. The doctor's insect-like body oozed a dense green liquid, and I felt like both the doctor and his patient were caught in some kind of dream state.

I stood off to one side, secretly watching, afraid that Dr. Bauchi might discover me. But he was lost in the act, completely oblivious to the outside world. His face revealed a portrait of suffering not at all unlike that of his patients. He was like a tightly drawn bow about to break. I could smell the scent of the hospital's approaching crisis. And in the doctor's unassailable yet still very mortal body, I seemed to catch a glimpse of a reflection of hell . . . or was it heaven?

This brings us back to the earlier question: Are the doctors already dead? Do they simply display the appearance of the living? Only the dead can treat those on the brink of death, a strategy we could call "fighting fire with fire." All the while, the doctors extract immunity from their patients. Death is the best medicine for death.

Every three days, in the middle of the night, Zhu Lin would find her way to the doctor's office automatically. And there, Dr. Bauchi would personally perform his therapy.

When she returned, her face and body were red, like a plump shrimp. She looked like a female heroine who had just endured a prolonged session of intense interrogation and torture. I found myself lost amid a sea of confusion and jealousy, as if this had made my own chance for self-salvation extremely unlikely, but I didn't dare ask what she had done with Dr. Bauchi.

I had no choice but to grit my teeth and do what needed to be done: perform another round of therapy on Zhu Lin. I imagined myself to be her doctor and kept at it until I was utterly exhausted, the pain in my abdomen exploded, and I collapsed on her naked body.

57

A SUDDEN CONFIRMATION

I awakened to discover that the other male patients had pulled me off Zhu Lin's body and dumped me on the floor. My body was covered in a mixture of phlegm, piss, and shit. I felt upset and embarrassed, but all I could do was apologize with a forced smile.

At first I tried just to hold everything in. I didn't dare reveal my helplessness and morbid state of mind in front of Zhu Lin. But she was worried and immediately summoned Dr. Bauchi.

Dr. Bauchi didn't seem the least bit surprised by my condition. He adopted a slightly admonishing tone. "Patient, are you seeing things again?"

I pleaded with him. "Please forgive me. I didn't mean to . . ." I was secretly hoping that, since I had already been discovered, Dr. Bauchi might make me a doctor again.

Instead he haphazardly ordered me to do another exam.

The next day, Dr. Bauchi announced that I had a terminal illness.

The sentence came so abruptly, as if dusk had just fallen and yet suddenly dawn had already arrived. Perhaps this was revenge for spying on him? My understanding of the head doctor's psychology is still quite superficial.

While this was bad news, part of me was immediately relieved. After such a long period of trying to get a proper diagnosis, I finally had one. There was no better news than this; it meant that the hospital had finally recognized me and accepted me as its own.

"That's great news! I've been mentally prepared for this for a long time. There can finally be an end to my suffering." I shed tears of gratitude and grief, repeatedly thanking Dr. Bauchi, like a convicted criminal begging for mercy in front of a judge.

I wanted to express my gratitude toward Zhu Lin, but when I saw her tightly clasping Dr. Bauchi's sleeve with a concerned expression on her face, I just felt like a caged bird. I had a bad feeling about what was to come.

Dr. Bauchi never told me the exact nature of my terminal illness. He simply pointed out that, for the sake of my health and well-being, I was prohibited from continuing the special relationship I had with Zhu Lin.

Then he issued a treatment notice: he was going to remove all of my lesions.

Shortly thereafter my presurgery evaluation began. It included a series of routine examinations: standard blood panel, liver and kidney function test, coagulation function test, electrocardiogram, lung-function test, coronary angiography, and a few other simple tests.

Since I have no family members, I had to sign the informed consent documents and approval to receive anesthesia.

The night before the surgery, I couldn't sleep. I wasn't sure if this was due to the medication given to me to prepare for my procedure or something else. I was overcome by the feeling that I was a prisoner about to face execution. But that ominous feeling of imminent execution is actually the same as the feeling one gets when one is about to be cured.

I may have been a frequent visitor to the hospital, but I had never undergone surgery. During my entire time as an inpatient, I had dreamed of undergoing an operation that would relieve my pain, once and for all. But now that the time had finally come, I began to feel sad. With the surgery complete, I could no longer stay in the hospital.

I had no relatives or friends to bear witness to what was about to happen. And all of the women I had formed relationships with in the hospital—Sister Jiang, Ah Bi, Bai Dai, Zhu Lin—were gone. I twisted and turned; the pain was impossible to endure. Then I heard a sudden urgent high-pitched shriek: "I can't go in for surgery! No surgery!"

58

IT IS NOT A PATHOGEN, IT IS POSSESSION

That strange voice was actually coming from inside my body, like a finger poking an orifice, salaciously twisting around the thick sticky juices surrounding my internal organs. I felt like I was going to throw up. But it wasn't a real voice; it was more like a series of sound waves sending signals to the auditory center of my cerebral cortex.

"Who are you?" I asked in surprise.

"Shhh. I am your possessor."

"What? My possessor? Are you that doctor inside of me?"

"I'm that thing inside you that they think is a 'terminal illness.'" The voice was straightforward and serious, like a teenage boy.

"How is that possible? Is this an illusion? Am I hallucinating?"

"You really think hallucinations are so easy to produce? Certainly not. It's a long story, so let's not get into all the details right now. We don't have the time. Long story short, I am not some pathogen, nor am I the source of your illness. I'm just a normal part of your physical makeup. How can you let them just cut me out?"

"The doctor is trying to save me. I've been waiting for this day for so long."

"So it seems their deceptions have been successful. But let me tell you: trying to save you is nothing but a front, a lie they use to keep you from leaving the hospital, all so they can get you under their scalpel."

"The way you describe it sounds so strange."

"No need to be scared. I'm here to help you. Let's take this moment before they kill you to think of a way out of this. We can't allow those cold-blooded butchers to cut open our body!"

I seemed to see a pair of thin, reedlike lips fluttering open and closed, from which a series of dense sounds squeezed their way out from a tight little pale throat. That long-slumbering thing inside my body had come to life, awakened by this unexpected "diagnosis."

I dimly perceived myself on the operating table. I witnessed my death as the scalpel entered my flesh. I had once entertained the fantasy of death, to see what it was like, but now that the time had come, I found myself recoiling in fear.

59

THE SICK DON'T HAVE THE RIGHT TO BE PESSIMISTIC

The next morning Dr. Bauchi came into my room with a team of interns and residents. They surrounded my bed and scrutinized me from head to toe, as if they knew all about the secret inside my body.

With some hesitancy, I pleaded, "I don't want to go through with the operation."

"How is that possible?" The doctor spoke with cold professionalism. "You already signed all the paperwork."

"But . . ."

"The sick don't have the right to be pessimistic." Dr. Bauchi made it clear that there was no room for negotiation. "And don't worry, you can still stay in the hospital, even after the operation."

The interns and residents stood in a circle with compassionate expressions on their faces, but I could tell that they had ulterior motives, high hopes for what this operation would mean for their careers. They hoped that my fresh blood would baptize their hands, allowing them to become great masters of medicine.

I realized that perhaps my possessor was right—if he wasn't just a figment of my imagination.

"No surgery! No surgery!" The scream that escaped my lips shocked even me, as if I were standing at the mouth of a volcano. I felt like I was speaking to my possessor, to justify myself in his eyes. (I say "his" because he really feels like a man living inside me.) I became even more afraid of this alien thing of unknown origin that had taken root inside my body. I've been alive for forty years and never had a clue. I thought back to when Bai Dai told me that my body would one day sprout all kinds of strange leaves and branches.

Dr. Bauchi flashed the younger doctors a deep knowing look.

"This is a low-risk operation," one of the residents explained. "The chance of death is less than one percent. There is nothing to be scared of. Doctors can now perform surgery with the same precision as a garment-factory worker knotting a thin piece of thread."

"Surgery is the only way to resolve the problems you are having," one of the interns added. "Medical science has advanced to the point where we can now perform heart surgery, brain surgery, eye surgery . . . the scalpel can now enter and explore all the sacred parts of the human body."

"Most patients look at surgery as a terrible bolt of lightning striking on a clear day," another young doctor chimed in, "but for most doctors, surgery is simply a natural choice. Patient, we won't cut out of you a single part that you don't want us to. We will explain every detail of the process so that you can cooperate with what we are doing."

"Patients are always scared when it is time for surgery," said another intern, as if reciting verbatim from a book, "but in the doctors' eyes, surgery is just another procedure. We always follow the rules. Don't worry. We do this kind of thing every day."

A resident doctor wore a kind look but spoke with a firm tone. "We all know that you called in a favor from a friend to get admitted. It's been a tough journey for you. You already blew a fortune on your treatment, but in order to eliminate this disease, surgery is necessary."

"But all I did was drink a bottle of mineral water!" I screamed. I hoped they might remember that I had temporarily been a doctor like them. In a sense, I was their colleague.

The doctors couldn't resist feeling my stomach. One after another, they approached and clumsily felt my forehead, belly, and groin, listening with their stethoscopes. Then, almost in chorus, they warned me,

"Hey, don't forget, you are the patient!" I tried to evade them, like an insect dodging a spray of insecticide. I thought my possessor would lend me some support, but he didn't make a peep. He seemed to be hiding out somewhere, deep inside my body, carefully and cautiously observing.

Dr. Bauchi made the final decision. "You must have faith in the hospital and your doctors. There is nothing to fear as long as we are here. The decision to go ahead with this surgery was made the day you were first admitted to the hospital, but all this time we have been waiting for the proper moment. Here in the hospital, each and every person has the opportunity for self-salvation. But you must listen to your doctors. When you find yourself unable to obey yourself, you need to put your trust in others."

60

THE DOCTOR'S PAIN

At that moment, sorrow appeared on Dr. Bauchi's thin and noble face. His weathered forehead broke into a mild sweat, and when he spoke, his words came off as insincere, as if he were trying to disavow his earlier actions. To say that he was trying to convince me to go forward with the operation wouldn't be as accurate as saying that he was trying to convince himself, as if the sole path forward was to surmount the dangerous hurdles ahead. This unusual operation was a test for him. The image of Dr. Bauchi treating Zhu Lin flashed before my eyes. I could see him struggling like someone on the verge of drowning.

I was secretly surprised. Dr. Bauchi should have known exactly how long I had been suffering from this pain, and yet even a brilliant doctor like himself had no real plan. This was indeed a paradox. Doctors exist to relieve the suffering of their patients, but once that suffering has been eradicated, there is no longer any value in the doctors' existence. So therein lies the rub. What should one do? Is there no way to make a choice? Did the doctor need to perform this surgery in order to save himself? When they say that no one can save himself, does that include doctors?

In that instant I felt that the doctors' pain was identical to the patients', but the pain that doctors suffer is worse, because in front of their patients, they are required to maintain the authority and dignity of the field of medicine. No matter how much pain they are in, they need to bear it, muffling their own cries until they can no longer be contained. I suppose the mutual-therapy sessions between doctors and patients are carried out so that doctors can release the deep pain they are forced to keep inside. But what is the source of doctors' pain? Did Dr. Bauchi also see the sword of Damocles hanging over the hospital?

How terrible it is when a doctor is unable to relieve his own pain and yet is forced to boast about how safe and effective an operation will be for others. He does everything he can to conceal the truth. And if doctors really live forever, isn't that even more depressing? Yet there I was, forced to go under the knife.

There was nothing I could say. I certainly couldn't tell them about the possessor in my body. I finally mustered a wimpish cry, as if that might scare the doctor away. "I don't have any money!" That was my final trump card.

The residents and interns were stunned. They converged around Dr. Bauchi and began to discuss my case in whispered tones. Dr. Bauchi removed a calculator from his jacket pocket and started punching in some numbers. "I see that your medical insurance policy has not yet been terminated, and there are still some funds left in your account," he said. "Your place of work will directly cover any out-of-pocket expenses, and if that isn't enough, the hospital can set up a loan for you. Owing to the fact that you are one of our most important patients, we can even arrange for a lower interest rate. Rest assured, we won't be sending you in a time machine back to the ancient world!" He didn't say anything about a red envelope. Then he turned to the interns and residents. "The patient remains lost in his own delusions."

The young doctors looked at each other with a sense of relief and laughed.

In my pain, I stared blankly at Dr. Bauchi until I lost consciousness.

61

A HOLE IN THE SYSTEM

They administered a short shock treatment to revive me, after which I was placed on a gurney and wheeled off toward the operating room. On the way there, a young intern explained the surgery.

I was wheeled to the end of a long queue of patients waiting outside the operating room. The dim lighting reminded me of a holding cell for death row inmates. Wave after wave of pungent reek filled the thick black air. Many of the patients sat up from their gurneys and, clasping their heads in their hands, began to vomit compulsively. These must have been patients recently diagnosed with "terminal illnesses." Did they also have possessors inside their bodies?

One of the hospital residents picked up a manual and started reading aloud to the patients. "When we mention surgery, patients usually think of all the blood, pus, and filth. In their minds, it is like a garbage dump. But in the eyes of a physician, fresh blood is like warm honey. The patient's soft, shiny skin is like fine silk. The only garbage we see is the suffering you endure, and everything we doctors do is aimed at eliminating that pain. Surgery is a major repair job on the human body, and after surgery the patient is like a clean new house. Doctors are trained not to look at the rectangular object under the white sheet as a person. Instead they regard it as a part to be worked on. This in no way represents a disregard for life; rather, it is only by learning to look at patients' groans, their blood, their very lives with a feeling of utter indifference that doctors can nimbly carry their heavy bodies off to the other shore, where they shall be reborn . . ."

That was when my possessor began to speak. He ordered me to run away.

"It's not like I haven't tried!" I uttered reluctantly. I still had a deep nostalgia for the hospital. "There is no escape from the hospital!"

"That's only because you haven't been doing it right." His tone was unyielding. "If you don't get out of here, you're as good as dead!"

"But I've already been diagnosed."

"A diagnosis is the overture that comes just before death. The reason you couldn't escape earlier is because you hadn't been diagnosed!"

"But how can I escape?"

"In any system, there is always a hole. The hospital is a system, so there has to be a hole in that system."

"Why should I listen to you, anyway?"

"Because I'm the only one who can help release you from your suffering." My little possessor spoke with such certainty! He was much more confident than my doctor. "You've been in the hospital too long. Self-salvation is no longer a possibility for you. You need to call for reinforcements."

Between my doctor and my possessor, I had to choose a side. This was a tough choice. Both claimed that they wanted to end my suffering, and yet they remain locked in a kind of life-and-death struggle. My body had become their battleground.

I have a fairly passive personality. I'm not exactly what you would call a man of action. I finally decided I had no choice but to go along with my possessor's plans. His force of will was so strong. He practically controlled me. If he were to decide to start messing with my stomach, he could probably have killed me. I had gone from yearning for surgery to being terrified of it, and I took an increasingly confrontational attitude toward the hospital and my doctors.

And so I escaped. The hospital employees were way too careless. They had never imagined that a patient would try to escape so close to the operating room. But every patient in line tried to escape, at least the ones that didn't drop dead. After the crowd of elderly patients trying to get into the hospital, this radical shift would have been hard to predict. Most of the patients probably weren't acting of their own accord but were instead responding to the unexpected appearance of their own possessors. The doctors had probably overlooked these possessors, but how could they have evaded all that high-tech scanning equipment? The possessors seemed to have a special ability to avoid detection. Was this why it had taken so long for me to get a diagnosis? I felt utterly perplexed.

In that heavily monitored tower, my possessor showed his special talent for evading detection. He seemed to have an innate intelligence when it came to finding the best escape route. He knew the layout of the hospital and directed me where to hide so the pursuing doctors and nurses wouldn't find us.

But the hospital was simply too big. Running away only highlighted just how massive and mysterious the hospital really was. I couldn't tell if I was wandering inside it or was actually a part of it. I felt extremely uncomfortable, as if held hostage by some monstrous entity. I no longer even knew whether I was that man called "Yang Wei," whose name I had entered on the hospital's admission registry.

I ran up one floor after another. Faint red lights shone from what looked like an endless number of sick wards. In every room I found a crowd of silent men who had just come out of surgery, standing beside a window, staring outside in a depressed manner. The bleak and desperate look in their eyes seemed to say, *How could you ever think you would run away? There is no escape!* As if just released from a hellish purgatory, I noticed a dark, cool shady spot in the distance and made a run for it, only to fall into a simmering hell pit, my flesh burned away, the pain utterly unbearable.

I was terrified. "I shouldn't go any farther. Just turn back and surrender."

"Surrender? Why? Are you a murderer? Are you an arsonist? Are you a rapist? You must really have something wrong with you!" my possessor lectured. "You are a law-abiding man who has lived a cautious and conservative life. You worked hard, writing some songs to make a few extra bucks. What have you done to deserve this kind of torture?"

"But I really am sick. I've been sick since childhood. Everyone in this world is sick . . . everything the hospital does is to cure the sick. The doctors would never try to hurt us. I willingly accept their torture. Is this not the Age of Medicine? I can't give up on my treatment." I had finally remembered the lesson that Sister Jiang had sacrificed her life to leave me with.

"Treatment? That's all bullshit! All the so-called Age of Medicine does is make healthy people unhealthy, normal people abnormal, turning small illnesses into big illnesses, the living into the dead. It forces the dead to be reincarnated so they can suffer even more. And you want to turn yourself in? Whatever illness you have has gone to your head! It is a good thing I'm here to provide you with a clear, healthy state of mind. This just goes to show that *I'm* the one trying to save *you*!" My possessor spoke with a stern authority, as if he alone were qualified to represent me—but that's wrong; he doesn't represent me, he *is* me.

"But even if I escape, where could I go?" I looked helplessly at the wall of volcano-like hospital towers surrounding me. The red crosses perched atop the buildings looked like a sea of blazing Olympic torches, bathing everything in their all-encompassing harmonious light. There was nowhere to hide.

"Just follow me." My little possessor didn't have an ounce of modesty.

My possessor led the way as I ran out of the inpatient tower and scurried back into the treatment area near the hospital entrance. The lobby was still a sea of people, just as when Sister Jiang and Ah Bi had first brought me there. The faces of the patients were filled with longing and thirst. They moaned and screamed, wading through the trash and fighting their way into the examination room as if the guardians of hell themselves were pursuing them. Time seemed to flow backward; I had been transported back to the past. I instinctively wanted to return to the end of the registration line, but thankfully my possessor stopped me. He showed me how to slip into the emergency room undetected, and from there he took me to the observation room. In every restricted area, crowds of patients glared at me in surprise. My possessor asked me to open the door to the morgue. I went in. Everything inside was enveloped in a blanket of perfect darkness, and I was assaulted by a horrid stench. Reaching into the pitch black, I felt like I touched a broken arm and then a thigh, and then I kicked what felt like a decapitated head. My heart raced and my skin crawled, until I finally felt my way to the back door. I suspected that it must be the door to hell. But my possessor wanted me to go through.

Beyond the door was an old-fashioned elevator. I took it down to a metal tunnel with a floor covered in a blanket of maggots. After walking for a while, I could see the reflection of something bright up ahead. I came to a skylight and looked up to see a bottle-shaped opening that revealed a peek at the sky above. Through the red glare and curtain of rain, I could see that the ground was muddy. There were traces of an area that had burned. Bones were scattered along the ground. Vipers and scorpions and insects and rats scurried. Amid the bed of moss covering the ground, I noticed a deep pit, ten meters wide, like a massive naked eye.

My possessor whispered with an air of pride. "Behold—the hole in the system!"

62

THE CLINICAL-ACADEMIC-INDUSTRIAL COMPLEX

Like a reel of silk unraveling from a cocoon, more truths about the hospital gradually became exposed. The doctors had indeed been concealing many things from us. This led me to have even more confidence in my possessor. I felt dizzy as I stared down into the hole, but after taking a moment to steady myself, I made out a series of faint lights coming from the bottom. Through the dark shadows I could see a crop field, a small village, farm animals walking around, and a row of simple houses. It was a world within a world, a lost place right under the eyes of the doctors. I thought to myself, *This is not a hole, this is a miracle, a dream!* Or was it just another hallucination?

My possessor impatiently prodded me. "Hurry! Hurry!"

I climbed down a long stone staircase covered in thick wet moss. The animals below howled like witches and demons. The hole must have been a thousand meters deep. It took a lot of effort to get to the bottom, where several vine-like men jumped out of nowhere and began wildly shining flashlights at me.

"Who are you?" a fat middle-aged man with a gray beard asked gruffly. He wore a tattered blue hospital gown covered with mildew stains and a pair of red cloth shoes with holes. Thick flesh hung from his face, hiding his tiny eyes like he was a cartoon version of Lord Voldemort. A graveyard stench emanated from his wildly disheveled hair.

"Don't be afraid, he's one of us," my possessor explained. "Everyone here is an escapee from the sick ward. This is an abandoned pharmaceutical mine."

"Pharmaceutical mine?"

"Pharmaceuticals are the gods of this world. Patients continually take medicine like they are worshipping gods. All the medicine used by the hospital is produced in underground facilities like this one. This particular mine was shut down after a serious outbreak of contamination, and it was later taken over by escaped patients."

The patients hiding out in the abandoned pharmaceutical mine wore peacock badges on their chests. The fat man with the beard looked me over suspiciously and asked me a few questions. I suppose this was his way of authenticating my identity. When he was done with his questions, he gave me a peacock badge, then pointed to a cave and asked me to go in. It was cold and damp inside and infested with maggots. A group of men and women who looked like refugees squatted or lay on the ground. I was so exhausted that I didn't even bother introducing myself and just collapsed and fell into a deep sleep. When I woke up I had the strange feeling that something was missing. And then I realized that my possessor seemed to be gone. I immediately grew anxious and began looking for him.

"What are you looking for?" he asked suddenly. "I'm still here inside you!"

As it turned out, the little fellow had been taking a nap. I couldn't help but feel embarrassed.

"Hey, what are you thinking right now?" my possessor asked, as if he didn't want me to have any personal space.

"Didn't you say you were part of me? Aren't you just another me? You should know what I'm thinking!"

"Are you still thinking about that girl?" He had nailed it on the head.

"Do you think we'll be able to see her again?" I asked with some hesitation.

"Since all human mating activity has been eradicated, do men really still need the scent of female flesh? Let me tell you, that girl Zhu Lin is nothing but trouble. She has danger written all over her!"

I thought of her body, like a polar ice crack, but I didn't say a word. I simply steadied myself and observed the environment around me. It was not a natural cave but part of a large-scale man-made construction project. Layers after layers of broad metal doors led to a tightly woven series of main and side tunnels that extended out to a railroad in the distance. A complex web of wires and cords ran through the tunnels, a seemingly never-ending series of factory workshops and labs. Countless sugarcoated pills were scattered over the ground. A thick, pulpy substance oozed from broken glass vessels, merging into a filthy river that flowed between lines of metal vaults and file cabinets. The vaults were battered and pocked with holes, but I could still make out the faded labels: EXPERIMENTAL DRUGS FOR PROJECT X, APPLICATIONS FROM PHARMACEUTICAL COMPANY Y, and so on. Each file cabinet was labeled with the name of the doctors overseeing the various research projects. Scattered files and documents contained information on the parameters for various research and control teams, as well as paperwork covering the approval process for new antibiotics. Rows of thick metal tanks contained fermentation experiments to test various drugs. Labels were affixed to a whole series of other devices, most of which were severely damaged, including atmospheric or high-vacuum distillation devices, centrifuges, filter presses, high-pressure reactors, fixed or fluidized beds, gas-phase reaction devices, liquid-phase catalytic reaction devices, and ion exchange columns. I saw signage for all the brands owned by United Pharmaceutical: PURPLE PROSPERITY LUCKY BRIGHTNESS; GREATER CHINA PEACEFUL GENES; CLOUD BIO PHOENIX DANCE; SPLENDID PEACE ON THE CENTRAL PLAINS CEMMO; NEW FAMILY STARTS WITH LUO, WANYUAN SK; HARMONIOUS, HEALTHY, LUCKY: BEVANO; GREAT PEACE INHERITS ALL

BEAUTY BABY. My possessor explained that all of this was a part of the "Clinical-Academic-Industrial Complex," which was one with the hospital and directly connected with the Emergency Resuscitation Room and the morgue. A special Protective Tariff Section included mountains of containers piled as high as the eye could see, and the imposing Customs Building stood dead center. Medical equipment imported from abroad could be directly transported there. Everything suggested that the hospital was simply the tip of the iceberg. The real deal was hidden beneath the surface.

There were more than ten thousand patients hiding out in the abandoned pharmaceutical mine, and all of them had possessors in their bodies. Everyone referred to the fat guy with the beard as Village Chief Ai. He had led the people when they prepared to flee the hospital. They participated in heated debates about the philosophical path to salvation and the delirium of language. Village Chief Ai paced back and forth among the crowd, denouncing the evils of the Age of Medicine. He said that the pharmaceutical industry's lucrative blue-chip stocks were once the locomotive fueling the world economy. The Clinical-Academic-Industrial Complex would never allow for any disease to be cured, or else the pharmaceutical industry would face a major loss in profits. But now it had lost the motivation to innovate. It was on the verge of being crushed beneath the weight of its own exponentially inflating research and development costs. The amount of money invested in studying the biology of tumors alone had already exceeded one trillion yuan, more than the entire budget of the aerospace industry. And yet a huge percentage of the new medicines had not yielded any clinical benefit to patients. They were basically just blind experiments. Even in cases when a disease's genetic cause had been identified, most remained untreatable or were simply not treated, for various reasons, intentional or unintentional, thus maintaining a consistent population of patients. So-called miracles were simply fabrications that the hospital boasted about to increase its profits. Foreign-controlled pharmaceutical companies, in collusion with local hospitals, launched false marketing campaigns to cover up scandals and avoid potential fallout. Common drugs generated a 500 percent profit from the factory to the hospital, with some profit margins as high as 6,500 percent. Doctors received kickbacks for providing fake trial data. The hospital had become completely commercialized. Doctors' and nurses' salaries were directly linked to hospital profits, and the number of CT scans, lab tests, examinations, and prescriptions impacted their compensation. On numerous occasions lab heads issued drug-trial reports stating that a new medication triggered a certain disease, but those were quickly suppressed and the doctors paid off with hush money. The sole goal was to prevent those medicines from being taken off the shelves, while hospitals continued to run advertisements that heavily promoted these same drugs. In the words of Village Chief Ai, "The whole thing is rotten to the core!"

Village Chief Ai asked me to pay a membership fee to join his group. But since I didn't have any money, I had to write an IOU. He ordered me to cook for everyone as a way, he said, for them to check me out and also to whip me into shape. Food would be more important than medicine, he said. And so I broke from the hospital, on my way back to a natural lifestyle.

I am just a quasi intellectual who likes to write songs. I have a weak constitution. I know how to take my meds, but I don't know a damn thing about cooking, and yet there I was, forced to slaughter roosters, chop firewood, boil water, and prepare meals! Once I set to it, I realized that they weren't even roosters—they were genetically modified peacocks! The bird's innards were fat and oily, and soon I realized that all the animals looked different from the ones above ground. Once again I found myself with a new identity that I had never asked for. I didn't know whether to laugh or cry, but whatever it is, so shall it be.

One day Village Chief Ai rode over on an oversize medical barrel, his fat belly protruding. He didn't say a word, just stared at me. I was soaked in blood as I tried to slaughter those peacock-roosters. He took out his camera and snapped a picture.

Before anyone had taken a bite of the meat I had prepared, we suddenly heard the sound of metal exploding overhead. The animals raised their heads and began to bark and howl. It turned out to be a fleet of drones adorned with the red cross symbol, hovering over the mouth of the hole.

"The doctors are coming! The doctors are coming!" The patients screamed in terror and glared at me with suspicion.

"You're the one who led them here!" Village Chief Ai roared in anger. He slapped me across the face. I fell to the ground, knocking over the pot of scalding peacock soup.

My possessor quickly urged me to explain. "No, I didn't; I swear! I was extremely careful on my way here and made sure I wasn't being followed. I'm afraid you have a hole in your system."

Village Chief Ai's anger reached new heights. "Get the fuck out of here!" he screamed. "Men, move out! We need to move up our plan."

The patients threw their helmets off and rushed toward the mountain of garbage at the bottom of the pit.

63

NATURAL EVOLUTION
INTERRUPTED

Like an army of bald eagles, the hospital security department's battalion of drones zoomed down from the skylight and into the hole. Under a curtain of searchlights, robotic arms fired anesthesia bombs and shot wire netting to ensnare the patients. Those that managed to escape the nets converged on the mountain of garbage, which was littered with human remains, animal carcasses, and the battered and broken remnants of old medical equipment. The drones followed them up the pile, hovering just over the peak and adopting an aggressive formation as they prepared to wipe out the remaining patients. Thanks to the light emitted from the drones, I was able to see a Great Wall, erected from human bones and medical waste, winding along the crest of the mountain. Village Chief Ai continued to take photos. Hiding in bunkers along the mountain of trash, the patients played hide-and-seek with the drones above. Finally, they escaped via a secret tunnel beneath the wall.

Only five hundred of us made it into the underground tunnel, where we had to feel our way in the dark. After walking for a while, we took a rest. All was silent. As we rested, our possessors got together for a telepathic meeting. They seemed to have emerged as the true masters of these shells of flesh. Finally they came to a decision, which was announced by Village Chief Ai: "We can't stay here anymore. We must go to the place beside the sea. Only there can we find a world devoid of hospitals, a completely healthy world."

The place beside the sea? A world devoid of hospitals? A completely healthy world? All we knew was the hospital. Where was this sea? What did it look like? Who had ever seen such a thing? Weren't we trapped underground?

I started to distrust my possessor and to wonder whether I had ever even really left the hospital. Village Chief Ai shouted orders, and the crowd leaped into action like a pack of lemmings. I was utterly parched, exhausted, and in pain.

"I don't want to go," I muttered dejectedly.

My possessor, my teacher, tried to be my cheerleader as well. "You have to pull yourself together and keep going."

"Why? So they won't dig you out of my body?" I still wasn't used to having my decisions made for me.

"Don't talk to me in that tone of voice! It was *I* who saved *your* life. *I* should get the credit for relieving your pain. How would it benefit you if they were to dig me out of your body? We share the same fate. Now hurry up—let's get out of here!"

Those words—"We share the same fate"—left me speechless. I had known only about either prospering together, alongside the hospital, or perishing with it. I had once been willing to bust my head open for a chance to squeeze into the hospital, but now I was willing to pull off every kind of scheme to escape, and being unable to make decisions for myself felt like the end of the world. But I had no choice other than to submit. I caught up to the rest of the group.

While on the run, patients kept collapsing on the ground from their various ailments. The possessors seemed to be gifted with boundless powers, and yet they were unable to save their hosts from this dire situation. The only thing we had to eat on the road was leftover meds that we found in the broken pharmaceutical equipment and containers. Village Chief Ai had said that we would never need to take medicine again—but that turned out to be a lie.

I heard a mechanical sound coming from up ahead. I thought that the drones had found us and was getting ready to start running again, but then I saw a series of mine carts. They had come to pick us up. The patient operating the train of mine carts was wearing one of the peacock badges. We climbed aboard and took our seats. Men and women who had been complete strangers immediately bonded: we were all escapees from the hospital.

Along the way we passed a series of collapsed pharmaceutical production labs and abandoned laboratories. We discovered large numbers of strange mutated creatures: some had yet to hatch, others were growing, and others had already died. The living adults swam in the underground river of pharmaceutical chemicals and liquid medicine: mice with transparent skin and internal organs growing on their backs, lizards with two heads and four eyes, micropigs the size of rabbits. Some of the organisms looked like mutants, frogs crossbred with human babies, and then there was a dark-red blob of organic matter like porridge, squirming on the ground . . .

Compared to what Bai Dai and I had seen in the hospital laboratory, these creatures looked more like something out of a special effects studio for a movie. I hadn't known that such a world existed beneath the hospital, and it felt like another planet. But nothing seemed strange anymore.

My possessor explained that some of these underground species were the products of mutation caused by drugs and radiation, others were the result of synthetic biological experiments, and still others were the products of the Digital Life Factory—digital objects in the process of undergoing rapid transformations. This led me to wonder whether the hospital patients, myself included, were also digital images. I saw the remains of many AI medical machines, four out of five of them broken and scattered across the rocks. They had been intended to replace the human doctors.

The medical industry had created forms of life never before seen in the natural world, but it was starting to lose control.

My possessor spoke, sounding like a savior. "This is proof that the Age of Medicine is faltering and on its way to collapse. The disease itself has become infected. And you pathetic creatures remain completely ignorant!"

But the secret was out. At least Bai Dai and I had had some understanding of the tragedy about to unfold. All that talk about eradicating genes, mankind's extinction, and the coming world war had been inflated by doctors, themselves motivated by vanity and the hospital's sense of self-importance.

The underground life-forms reminded me of the "six paths of life" in the Buddhist scriptures. But these were not the result of evolution based on millions of years of natural selection; they were products designed and produced by the Clinical-Academic-Industrial Complex, which had condensed evolution into an overnight process never before seen. The source code for life had been unlocked, reduced to programs running on mobile phones and the internet. The medical punks had become the most active group, directing our path into the future, a path that will render the punks themselves obsolete. A great change of a kind not seen in hundreds of millions of years had begun, and the usual language was insufficient to define the new era upon us, which would bring a fundamental shift to the ecological rules of the universe. Natural evolution had been interrupted, and I was riding the wave, fortunate to be living in this "strange universe," this "grand explosion of life," much greater and more intense than that of the Cambrian period, five hundred million years ago, though the end result will certainly be catastrophic. The mad creators were too arrogant, their knowledge and abilities too limited. Nothing out there has the power to keep them in check.

But those are just my own thoughts and opinions. With such massive changes coming, no one knows what the new forms of logic will even look like.

64

COLLAPSE AND DECAY BEGIN
FROM WITHIN

Occasionally rising up from the reddish-yellow waters of the underground river, a black-and-red eyeball-shaped creature attached to series
of fibril tissue-like structures extended long, thin tentacles to snatch
patients sitting on one of the mine carts and rapidly pulled them apart,
swallowing their flesh and sucking down their pus and blood. The water
was littered with bones that the creature was unable to digest.

Was this a nongenetic life-form?

Those who survived frantically huddled together in the center of
the mine cart.

Sitting beside me was a boy around ten years old, staring at me
ominously. I felt a terror creep over me. "Don't look at me like that."

"I heard you were the one who led the doctors here," the kid responded.

"I already explained everything to them, it wasn't me."

"Humph. Who's gonna believe that!"

"C'mon, I don't even know who I am anymore!"

"That's cool. Did you bring any money?"

"I handed all my money over when I was first admitted to the
hospital . . ."

"That really sucks. How are you gonna escape without any cash?"
The kid's eyes were full of disdain.

I felt confused. Would I really need money to get to the sea, to
embrace this healthy new world? "Do you get along well with your
possessor?" I asked the boy.

"How should I put it? Although we share the same fate, he's always got his own ideas, which are often at odds with mine. But I'm gradually getting used to it."

"What's your name?"

"You can call me Little Tao."

The kid who had brought me to the observation room and helped me check into the inpatient ward! He was a patient too? He didn't appear to recognize me, and I wondered if he might be Little Tao's clone. Every person in the hospital had a copy, making biological identity a rather messy concept.

"I started off as a student at the Hospital Elementary School," Little Tao explained. "The school was also part of the hospital, and they have a premed curriculum. We were all training to be future doctors. While there I conducted experiments on myself. I even won a silver medal at the International Genetic Engineering Robotics Olympics. But then a viral infection caused me to develop nasopharyngeal cancer. The possessor inside me told me to run away. I didn't have any other choice."

We rode that train for three full days before we reached a village. The village had been established as a relay station by the first generation of patients who had escaped from the hospital. Deep in this underground cave, the patients had created a massive community to wage a war of resistance against the hospital above. If I hadn't seen it with my own eyes, I would have sworn it was all a dream.

Originally a mining tunnel three thousand meters deep, it had been destroyed in a chemical reaction in the attempt to produce a new drug. Below the hospital was an expansive world composed of these abandoned pharmaceutical mines, a restricted zone that no one from outside had seen. But even among the half-destroyed remains, I could see that the massive scale of the pharmaceutical industry went far beyond the wildest reaches of my imagination. What had once been the material foundation supporting the hospital's world dominance had been gradually abandoned, one site at a time. Collapse and decay begin from within.

A stone wall around the relay station prevented mutant organisms from invading. Everyone rested for a while, and the local villagers prepared medicine, water, and food for the newly arrived refugee patients. As I ate, I reflected on the chain of events that had just transpired. It felt like my entire body and soul had been transformed into a pile of silt and then remolded by some strange force into something I didn't even recognize.

That's when I remembered an elderly man named Old Cai from my days in the sick ward. He had lost his memory in a car accident and didn't know who he was. He was also a bit crazy, shuddering when he saw the doctors, often getting up and pretending to deliver special reports to the UN secretary-general in the middle of the night. The hospital performed brain reconstruction surgery on him, implanting a second personality into his medial prefrontal cortex. From then on, whenever he started to go a little crazy, the AI nanobots implanted in his skull would turn on, monitoring and manipulating the movement of atoms and controlling his behavior, forcing him to leave the United Nations General Assembly meeting room and return to his hospital room. Electrodes implanted in his brain had effectively replaced his damaged neurons. I wondered, *Is my possessor doing the same thing?* Perhaps I also had a brain injury and a device installed in my head. But how could I have no memory of such a thing? And if my possessor had been implanted by the hospital as a tool for treating me, why was he always pushing me to escape from the sick ward and betray the hospital?

Seeing the bewildered look on my face, Little Tao assumed the stance of an expert know-it-all. He was about to school me.

65

HOW DO YOU KNOW THAT YOUR BRAIN ISN'T THERE SIMPLY TO PRODUCE SHIT

Little Tao explained that the original model for the possessor was actually our second brain. People have two brains, but they both come from the same source. Hundreds of millions of years ago, ancient biological life-forms with chambered bodies first began to develop primitive nervous systems. One portion of this early nervous system gradually evolved into the central nervous system, which became capable of various complex functions—that was our first brain, hidden in our skull and spine, its leftover portions controlling our organs. Our second brains are hidden in our stomachs.

Forgive my ignorance, but this was the first time I had heard any of this.

Little Tao went on. "For a long time, people thought that the stomach was simply a tubular structure composed of muscles that responded only to basic reflexes. However, it was later discovered that the gastrointestinal tract was composed of hundreds of millions of cells, with no way for the vagus nerve to guarantee contact between this complex system and the central nervous system. In reality, the gastrointestinal system works independently. The reason lies in the fact that it has its own control system—a second brain. The primary function of this second brain is to control stomach movement and the digestive process, observe the characteristics of various foods, adjust the speed of digestion, and increase or decrease the pace at which digestive juices are released. Just like the first brain, the second brain also needs time to rest. When the second brain dreams, the stomach and intestinal muscles contract. When people feel anxiety, the second brain releases hormones, just like the first brain. If too much serotonin is released, people start to experience 'cat scratch fever,' and when they are scared or their stomach is stimulated, the result will be diarrhea. That's what people mean when they say, 'I was so scared I almost shit my pants.'"

Little Tao seemed quite confident in himself. He was really acting like a know-it-all, but then there is no place like the hospital to make people grow up fast. And yet I couldn't accept this as the reason for my stomach pain. So I argued. "This tube inside me that digests food and processes piss and shit couldn't be more different from the brain that I use to think, reflect, study, and understand concepts like passion, justice, love, and hate! How can you even compare them?"

Little Tao flashed me a disdainful look, as if I were nothing more than a dirty insect. "Objects in the world differ less than you might think. Your brain is, after all, but a muscle. How do you know that your brain isn't there simply to produce shit?"

Of course I knew that bacteria is the primary ingredient in excrement. Bacteria is everywhere, always being and creating, but I still tried to refute what he was saying. "I can't imagine that my stomach could speak, control my thoughts, or be used as a GPS!"

"Everything has been turned upside down," Little Tao insisted. "Nothing is what it once was. Perhaps in this new era, our first brain is no longer of use, so our second brain has taken over. Maybe we never even had that first brain. The hospital is evolving so rapidly that nothing is impossible anymore. Hurry up and get used to using your stomach to think. There is so much to learn. Everything must be torn down and built up again. People who want to prove they are still alive will need to learn how to study and adapt. Yang Wei, you really are an old man." The kid didn't hold back in putting me in my place.

The patients ate their medicine, which they supplemented with a little bit of food and water, and we continued forward on our journey.

66

DIVERGENT MEDICAL VIEWS

It wasn't long before even more escapees started to converge from all directions. They showed their peacock badges and formed a massive crowd. It was quite a sight. As they fell into line, our battalion swelled to several thousand people.

Along the way, the villagers transformed the pharmaceutical mines into the kind of tunnels people dig in times of war, like the underground structures that ancient pagans used to escape persecution. These hidden tunnels featured a complex layout of defense areas, working areas, and living areas, making it extremely difficult for doctors to locate these areas and launch an attack.

As I explored deeper into this new world, I came to appreciate the scenery. It no longer felt as strange as I had thought initially, and at least our planet hadn't yet been destroyed. A continuous series of workshops and laboratories felt like an art gallery, where under the shadow of night, indelible illusions burned bright. There was even something endearing about that creature with the man-eating eyes. After our extensive trek from the outpatient ward to the inpatient ward, this was our new long march.

One time a few patients broke out in song. I recognized an old melody from home, listened carefully, and realized it was the hospital's official anthem.

Born between yin and yang,
God bestowed upon me a beautiful name.
Those warriors referred to as the angels in white

Carry out the mission of saving lives.
With open hearts they wade through humanity's misery,
Using love to treat your wounded souls.
As long as there is an ounce of hope, they will carry on,
All they do is so your tree of life remains evergreen.
Oh, evergreen, evergreen!

I wondered whether they were still practicing for the New Year's gala, but either way, hearing that song gave me the itch to start composing again. My possessor promised that he would give me a chance just as soon as we reached the sea.

That was when a strange sound broke out from the other side of the rock walls. The underground creatures scurried away. All the color drained from Village Chief Ai's face. Then he turned and ran.

"What's happening?" I asked.

"It doesn't look so good . . . ," my possessor muttered.

A battalion of doctors broke through one of the junctions, each with a medical textbook in one hand and a spray gun in the other, blocking the road in front of the patients.

The doctors began to chant in unison, their voices displacing the sound of the patients' lingering melody: "Hurry back to the hospital! All of you need to go back!"

The doctor in the lead issued a command, and the other angels in white pulled the triggers of their spray guns, releasing an anesthetic into the air. The closest patients immediately fell to the ground, and the doctors dragged them away, placing their bodies on a flatbed cart.

Following my possessor's instructions, Little Tao and I decided to break through the doctors' barricade, but as we approached, Little Tao suddenly started to laugh. I asked him what was going on, and he responded, "All those doctors are my teachers."

"Your teachers from school?"

"Yeah."

"And that nonsense about the brain being a simple muscle that produces shit, are they the ones who taught you that?"

Little Tao pulled me aside into a small cave to tell me a story that his teacher had once shared in class . . .

> More than a century ago, a great war broke out in our land. In order to steal our nation's resources, Western colonial powers organized a multinational military force that violently fought its way into our country and directly occupied our capital. The commander in chief was a German named Alfred Heinrich Karl Ludwig Graf von Waldersee. At the time, Germany was one of the most powerful countries in the world. That madman Nietzsche was also a German. Waldersee sent troops to pursue the emperor and empress as they fled the capital. They had planned to take them as prisoners, punish them for their crimes, and then chop up our country to divide it among these foreign nations. However, the troops that Waldersee sent were ambushed and defeated by one of our own battalions. Waldersee, who had never lost a battle, was deeply shocked by this turn of events. Wanting to figure out how it could have happened, he ordered a team of twenty-six medical officers and fifty-two soldiers to conduct compulsory physical exams on all Chinese men going in and out of the thirteen city gates, to determine how many met the basic physical requirements for German soldiers.
>
> The results of this survey came out quickly, and Waldersee realized that ninety-five out of every hundred men between the ages of eighteen and sixty met the basic physical standards required for German soldiers. Waldersee was so stunned that he immediately ordered his troops to give up their pursuit of the Chinese emperor. He also sent

a memorandum to the German emperor, Wilhelm II, attempting to persuade him to give up the plan to chop up China. In that memorandum, Marshal Waldersee wrote:

"I feel that, from the perspective of biology, the lower-class people of this nation are much more fit and healthy than the lower-class people of our nation. If China should produce an intelligent and charismatic leader, he could utilize the cultural contributions and methods of nations around the world to rejuvenate the nation. That is why I have boundless faith in the future of this country."

The German emperor was shocked to hear this and personally organized an investigative team that included biologists and medical experts. They came from halfway around the world to our country and used their advanced technological methods to survey the physique, mental functions, and lifestyle of our people. This was the first time in history that such a thorough and comprehensive survey of our citizens' health was ever carried out. The research team took an entire year to complete its study, which resulted in a report that stated that the Chinese people's physical constitution and level of intelligence were in no way inferior to that of the white race; moreover, it found that in terms of their work ethic, Chinese actually outperformed whites.

Based on the Germans' recommendation, the Western coalition of nations reached a consensus to spare our country, and peace was preserved.

"So our national salvation was somehow related to a bunch of physical exams?" I asked in surprise. "Like the employee welfare exams we do every year at work?" The sea of doctors rushed toward us like an incoming tide.

"That's right," said Little Tao. "Our teacher told us that we have the most outstanding genes. We're certainly not the 'sick man of Asia'!"

I imagined the scene at the capital gates: naked Chinese men lined up in rows as hairy white men groped their bodies, sticking fingers into their assholes and scrutinizing their private parts, measuring their foreskins and jotting down visible deformities in their notebooks.

Little Tao took on a bragging tone. "My teacher said that, ever since ancient times, our country has suffered the worst living conditions in the entire world, and the constant string of plagues, famines, and wars effectively weeded out those with inferior genes, so people today retain the very best genes."

"And your teacher . . ." I wondered if I might be a medical student in my next life.

"When the Age of Medicine arrived, my teacher became part of an opposing faction. They refer to people like him as 'holding divergent medical views.' The opposition united and formed a group called the Protect the Species Association."

"Protect the Species Association?"

"Protecting the species is the only way they could ensure their own survival. According to their mission, the sick are actually the healthy ones, the true masters of the hospital. Only the sick can save the hospital and rejuvenate the nation. That is why my teacher was against gene therapy and the elimination of genes. He also forbade us to escape to the sea."

"If everyone runs away, all of our race's best gene lines will be broken."

"That's right. That's why my teacher summoned me back. But my possessor kept ordering me to escape." Little Tao looked depressed. "Gosh, I just don't know what to do anymore."

"Is Village Chief Ai a member of the Protect the Species Association?"

"No. He doesn't give a shit about his body. They could change it any way they wanted, and he wouldn't care. He just wants to stay alive."

67

A STORY WITHIN A STORY

Little Tao told me a bit about Village Chief Ai's colorful past. He was the oldest son of the C City mayor-cum-hospital-president, and he ran Corporation B (short for Corporation BioMed), the company that had first invited me here to write a corporate song.

Ai the Princeling started out as a third-rate actor, performing in small comedy sketches, but owing to his father's background and connections, he had taken over one of the largest pharmaceutical corporations, in charge of a series of research labs, major projects, and a foundation, allowing the corporation to gain practical control of the hospital's major operations.

One day, on a whim, Ai the Princeling ordered his staff to resurrect a thirty-thousand-year-old virus discovered frozen beneath the Siberian ice sheet and smuggled into our country. The virus was one micrometer long and composed of 4,200 genes; to put its massive size in perspective, influenza has only eight genes. Ai thought he could unleash this virus on humankind and leverage that threat to produce vaccines, sell them to hospitals, and come away with an outrageous profit. He would use his position as the new industry leader to get all the other pharmaceutical companies, big pharma reps, hospitals, and doctors to obey him.

But what he really wanted was to realize his lifelong dream and achieve unprecedented happiness. Ai became an all-out medical enthusiast. Convinced that he had transformed himself from a two-bit sketch actor to a legendary biological artist, he became obsessed with virus design. The strange structures of those tiny miraculous life-forms under the microscope—spherical, spiral, rod shaped, crowned—were like a series of microuniverses. Never before had he felt such a sense of accomplishment.

Hoping to promote his incredible achievements in medical punk, Ai sought me out to compose some laudatory songs. But as soon as I arrived in C City, I fell ill, was admitted to the hospital, and ended up lost in its starship-like labyrinth. In his anger, Ai the Princeling had released his frustration on the pharmaceutical biologists, destroying their lab and allowing the virus he had so carefully bred to escape.

The entire hospital had been mobilized to prevent the spread of the virus. In order to cover up his son's mistakes, the hospital president established a new synthetic biolab to create a new virus, with the intent to infect the Siberian virus. But then the new virus leaked too. Emergency measures were adopted to control public discourse about the leak, but the news still managed to get out. The president assumed all blame and resigned.

Corporation B collapsed almost overnight, which caused a chain reaction, leading to the downfall of the entire Clinical-Academic-Industrial Complex. Ai the Princeling had been expelled from the medical world by a group of angry doctors, leaving him no choice but to go underground, where he had assumed the title of Village Chief Ai.

I wasn't sure if Village Chief Ai recognized me. Perhaps he had long forgotten that he once hired me to write a corporate song. Again I heard the patients singing:

> Love permeates heaven and earth and bathes my heart,
> The angels in white walk alongside me.
> I use my great love to drive away the nightmares,
> When I awaken, I gift you with new life.
> Oh, new life, new life!

I was surprised to find that the tide of doctors who had been chasing us in the name of the Protect the Species Association had retreated. Just as we were about to arrive at the next relay station, a pile of rocks suddenly exploded—and the voices of song suddenly fell silent, like a snapped rope.

68

A NEW VIRUS NEVER BEFORE
SEEN IN HISTORY

Rows of doctors and nurses on solar-powered skis emerged from a crevice between the rocks and rushed thunderously toward us, looks of fire in their eyes. This time it wasn't the Protect the Species Association. Under the leadership of Dr. Bauchi, medical workers adorned with red cross armbands suddenly illuminated the subterranean world with helmet-mounted searchlights, as if a ferocious dragon had been unleashed. The patients covered their eyes in panic and scurried in all directions. Quite a few were ensnared in the doctor's nets and taken away. I wanted to flee, but a voice called out, "Stop right there!"

Before me a woman on skis wore a white gown and a nurse's cap. She gazed at me with a look of impunity.

"Zhu Lin . . . ?" I stuttered. I wanted to ask my possessor for advice, but he had fallen silent.

Zhu Lin's brand-new white outfit seemed to glow, creating a magical aura around her. She seemed imbued with a dashing new energy. Her breasts danced up and down, reminding me of the legendary warrior Mulan. She ordered me to return immediately to the hospital. I wondered whether she had been promoted to the ranks of the angels in white. I wondered what kind of special treatment Dr. Bauchi had performed on her.

"Listen to me," I said. "I'm afraid that's not how things really are—"

She cut me off. "Let me tell *you* how things really are! Dr. Bauchi summoned me to his office the day you ran away from the surgery ward.

But instead of criticizing me, he just gently asked me if anything out of the ordinary had happened between you and me."

"And what did you say?"

"I told him that the patient kept trying to find a peacock in the birdcage, even though there was only a rooster inside."

"The patient . . . ?" A terrible pain shot through my stomach. "And how did Dr. Bauchi respond?"

"He said that you really did have something wrong with you, but it was certainly not an atavistic hallucination. He told me that I was a human efficacy enhancer, which the hospital had provided to drive out the diseases lurking in men's bodies. The hospital had been experimenting with the use of live humans as part of its treatment methods. The best way to save a patient is to use other patients. With mutual therapy, I was able to tease out all of your symptoms. This is how they use humans to do things that no x-ray, B scan, CT scan, or MRI can ever do."

"How is that possible?" I asked sadly.

"Dr. Bauchi would never lie to me." Zhu Lin flashed me a sidelong glance. "He earnestly explained the seriousness of the situation that the hospital now faces. Something terrible was hiding inside the bodies of the patients. All kinds of treatment methods had failed to address this. Due to security concerns, no one had told me about this. The hospital had long been tracking that stubborn disease, which was much more malignant than any cancer. Did you know that right now the world is undergoing a radical transformation, and all kinds of abnormalities are beginning to appear in different species? Take yourself as an example: you drank a bottle of mineral water and fell terribly ill, and yet they still can't get to the bottom of your disease. In reality, all of this hides a much more serious illness. Patients are being controlled by an unusual virus, and this is the real reason they are not allowed to leave the hospital. We have finally learned that this disease develops its own consciousness within the human body. It imitates its host's personality, ordering the host to go against the hospital and resist treatment. This virus is unlike any before in human history. We have no defensive shield. All of our current medications and treatment methods have failed. The doctors' mission is to wait patiently for the pathogen—in medical terminology, the thing is being referred to as 'the monster'—and then, when it shows itself, to eliminate it in one fell swoop. In response to this terrible threat, hospitals were established all over the country. They are here to cure disease . . . that is, uh, to serve as a base in the battle against 'the monster.' We must fight, fight, fight, fight! The very survival of our nation is threatened!"

I asked Zhu Lin if this monster inside me—which, according to Dr. Bauchi, must be my possessor—had been created in the Microbe Control Lab by Dr. Ornamental Rock, Dr. Ballerina, and Dr. Artist. Or perhaps it was a strain of that never-before-seen oversize virus that had escaped under Village Chief Ai's watch?

But Zhu Lin said, "Based on our analysis, this new virus was created by the Rockefeller Foundation as a means of collapsing our hospital."

My possessor still hadn't uttered a word. Was he afraid? I took another look at Zhu Lin, who blazed with an intensity that made her look like a storm trooper. Perhaps that's what all human efficacy enhancers looked like? I thought back to our mutual therapy sessions and felt another jolt of pain run through my body.

"I tried to plead on your behalf," Zhu Lin explained. "I even asked Dr. Bauchi whether it was necessary to wipe them all out. Is there really no other way? A more conservative treatment method we could try?"

"And what did he say?"

"He seemed really torn about what to do. He didn't believe all those conspiracy theories about 'short sellers.' But the hospital is set in its ways. The 'essentialists' hold all the power. Dr. Bauchi just carries out technical work. The central plans are drawn up by the hospital, while Dr. Bauchi and the others simply follow orders. Even though he felt conflicted, he is the kind of man that plays by the book; the last thing he would do is express any views divergent from those of the hospital. He said not to worry; he wasn't going to hurt you—he was going to save you. All that persistent pain the patients have been suffering has been caused by 'the monster.' As the head doctor, he has to assume full responsibility."

"And after that? Did he perform therapy on you again?"

"Oh, c'mon now! You know it hurts so good!" Zhu Lin's eyebrows danced, and her face lit up. She wasn't embarrassed in the least.

"Uh . . ." The pain was so intense that I had to clasp my stomach and double over. Meanwhile, my possessor didn't seem to give a damn.

Zhu Lin raised a net above her head. She was going to try and bring me in. "Patient, don't be scared. I'm here to save you. If you don't cooperate, 'the monster' will kill you." She was on the verge of tears.

I decided to give up without a fight, to hand myself over so she could go back and show Dr. Bauchi that she had completed her mission. That's when Little Tao appeared out of nowhere, rushing toward Zhu Lin with a scalpel in hand.

69

EVEN IF YOU DIE, YOU'VE STILL GOT TO KEEP GOING

Caught off guard by the sudden attack, Zhu Lin screamed and fell off her skis. I flashed Little Tao an angry look before running off with him to hide behind some boulders. Terrible cries rose from all directions. I caught a glimpse of Zhu Lin, completely silent as a male doctor dragged her off by her ankles. Her white lab coat was stained with blood, which dripped from her torso down over her face. Her black bra and purple underwear, soiled with piss, were completely exposed. Her chubby thighs jiggled as her body was dragged over the gravel. A semispherical organic object that resembled some kind of internal organ hung out of the side of her plump belly, attached to a red tube. She was like a lamb being dragged off to the altar. I felt so confused, like I was to blame. I had to close my eyes . . . I'm not sure how much time passed before everything fell silent. The medical workers retreated with their trophies in hand. Gradually the surviving patients emerged from their hiding places, muttering in a state of shock: "How much farther is the sea? Can we really make it there on foot? What will happen when we get there?"

I stared dejectedly toward the medical search team as they retreated. The image of Zhu Lin, staring at me just a few moments earlier, flashed through my mind. Her angelic eyes, so pure and full of innocence, made my heart race; the glow of someone who chases her dreams radiated from her body; her pure, perfectly white outfit made me feel like my internal organs were going to explode—seeing her half-naked body, soiled by blood and piss and carried away like that, was crushing. Was she dead? Since she had become a member of the doctors' medical team, did that mean that she couldn't die?

"Even if you are dead, you've still got to keep going," Little Tao said firmly. "Not only are you now responsible for yourself, you also need to think about your possessor. You can't be so selfish anymore."

"That's right. There are two of us now."

"No, there is only one of us," my possessor corrected me. He was back. He must feel pretty damn lucky that Zhu Lin didn't drag me away.

Gradually, the survivors converged—there were less than a thousand people left. Village Chief Ai said, "We are now on our way to rendezvous with our contact person. He is a veteran patient, the first to escape from the hospital and cross the sea. He made it to the healthy new world and has now returned to retrieve us. Of course, the main reason he returned is to save *me*, but all of you get to benefit from my presence."

We kept walking until all of the medicine and food were used up. The relay station ahead was said to have been destroyed already. Someone suggested going up to the surface to take a look. The possessors telepathically discussed it and decided to send some patients ahead to investigate. They discovered the burnt remains of an old sick ward. Although we were still in the realm of the hospital, at least there were no signs of any doctors or nurses. The Age of Medicine was gradually being destroyed, one section at a time. The possessors made the patients climb up through the ruins. Out of the rubble, they dug up some burned bodies, which could have been animals used for experiments or deceased patients; it was hard to tell. They peeled the charcoal and ash off the corpses' skin and removed the cooked meat to eat. Then they found some medicine nearby to wash it down with.

The possessors took this opportunity to replenish their strength. They had expended a lot of energy helping the patients to escape, but the possessors are unable to nourish themselves. So I decided to have an open and honest discussion with my possessor.

70

IS THERE A NEED TO MAKE EVERYTHING SO BIG

"I was originally doing just fine," I said to my possessor, "so how did my body grow a little monster like you?"

"Monster?" My possessor was clearly annoyed. "How could you say something like that? Do you even have a conscience?"

"Are you really the virus that the doctor described?"

"That's ridiculous! Don't buy their bullshit!"

"Are you a so-called second brain in my stomach? Is my first brain no longer of any use?"

"Hah, you really think it's that simple?"

"Anyway, it seems like you have been causing my stomach pain."

"Didn't I already tell you? I'm here to help relieve you of your suffering."

"Who are you? Where do you come from?"

"I'm so far I could be at the most distant edge of heaven," he said, his tone strange and mysterious, "and I'm so close I could be right under your nose."

Suddenly, like a magic trick, all the rocks, rubble, and roads around me disappeared, and I found myself floating among billions of stars. The stars were like eyes lighting up the sky, their glimmer reflected upon my body.

"Are you an alien?" I asked after a long pause.

My possessor let out a deep breath, but he didn't respond. The torrent of stars seemed to expand, as if to wash everything away and expose the true face of this world.

"Okay then . . . ," I said. "It seems like there are a lot of you."

My possessor adjusted my brain waves, and I saw a bird's-eye image of C City, the massive medical city arrayed in detail before my eyes. Then it transformed, switching to a full-scale view of the sky, as if seen through the Hubble or Planck telescopes. My possessor explained that the *C* in C City stood for "Cosmos." C City was in fact a simulacrum of the universe.

"Every part of the cosmos is a reflection of the entire cosmos," my possessor explained in a tone that sounded like he was lecturing an elementary school student. "Do you know anything about holographic theory?"

"Uh . . ."

"You must have noticed that the northern and southern hemispheres of the universe are asymmetrical. There is a notable difference in temperature between certain regions, including some unusually frigid zones."

"Oh . . ."

"This layout clearly violates the cosmological principle of physics, which is difficult for most humans to understand, given their limited intellectual abilities."

"Then please, explain it to me."

"The cosmos is sick."

I tried to warm myself up and forced a smile. "Hey, stop playing around with me. Someone was just talking about all of this hospital business being connected to the nation, our people, and now you're talking about the entire cosmos! Do we really need to exaggerate everything? Perhaps you think that's the only way to impress people? You're worried nobody will pay attention if you don't give crazy examples? Hell, I'm just a civil servant that moonlights as a songwriter!"

"I'm not exaggerating," my possessor responded calmly. "You can choose to look at the universe as a massive cabinet spanning ninety billion light-years or as a tiny microscopic cell. This has nothing to do with the fact that you are a civil servant."

And then my possessor led me into the cosmos.

71

DISEASE IS THE DEFAULT
SETTING FOR EVERYTHING

There are so many ups and downs in life. Things can be quite unpredictable, and there's nothing any of us can do about that. We simply need
to take as much medicine as we can during our limited time on earth.

I leaped from the hospital directly to the stars.

My possessor urged me to observe a large cold cosmic void. I
could feel it against the pores of my skin, a squishy, organ-like object,
like a massive lymphoid hyperplastic growth that emitted a stench of
rotten flesh.

I remember back when humans conducted research on microwave
background radiation. Scientists had just discovered this object, this
thing. It was said that its temperature was colder than any place ever
recorded. At first no one could explain it. There must have been a mistake in the calculations or a problem with the instruments that observed
it. Only later did they agree that it must be a cosmic supervoid, with
a radius of more than seven hundred million light-years. According
to current theories, cosmic evolution could never produce a void that
massive. No one knows the truth about this large cold void. Some
astrophysicists believe that the abnormal energy emanating from it must
have been created by some highly intelligent alien life-form.

Strange and confusing signals were emitted from the void, where
multiple civilizations were in the process of being destroyed. Disgusting
fluids—black mucus and thick vapor—shot out amid intermittent

flares of exploding light. In this place of desolation, not even black holes could exist for long.

My possessor said that this was the locus of the universe's disease, proof that the cosmos is defective, as if the universe were suffering from liver cancer, its blood flow blocked, its connective tissue torn away. But he did not show me any concrete proof. He wanted me to observe for myself. But after only a cursory look, I understood. That sick and twisted condition was basically the same state I was in.

Experiencing the universe through the eyes of my possessor, I felt like I wasn't actually passing through the real cosmos, and yet there was no difference between what I was experiencing and the real thing. At first I thought I had entered some virtual reality matrix, some machine's stereoscopic image of the universe, projected directly into my visual cortex through an integration of miniature holographic images, microscopic specimen analysis, and vascular nanoscouts.

Perhaps the entire universe is indeed just a single cell.

My possessor pressed on, introducing me to more of the universe's pathology.

Unable to reach a tacit understanding between the macroscopic and microscopic, the universe's inherent structural disfunctions far exceed its harmonious elements. Paradoxes that the cosmos is unable to solve on its own haunt mathematics and physics. In some fields, time and space are collapsing like broken bones. The cosmos relies on quantum entanglements to maintain its structure, and if those entanglements weaken, it will rupture and split, the way cells split, but within the quantum realm, everything becomes elusive and unpredictable, like trying to catch a phantom. Mutations abound. Dark matter and dark energy resemble necrosis. And then there is entropy, strange and completely unnecessary. How can the universe—meant to last for time immemorial—possibly stop itself from aging, ever advancing toward its own death, even while it remains so very young!

My possessor explained that, professionally speaking, "disease" is nothing more than a phenomenon in which the body deviates from its routine form and functionality. Owing to some cause, life becomes afflicted with some abnormality, causing the body's condition and abilities to undergo changes, normal functions restricted or destroyed until, sooner or later, observable symptoms appear, which eventually lead to death. Disease and illness are everywhere. Pain is universal, the essence of all physical phenomena. From the microscopic to the macroscopic, pain extends from all sentient life-forms to every object in the world.

I asked my possessor if this was his personal opinion or hard fact.

He said there was absolutely no difference between the two.

"Speaking of the disease afflicting the universe," he added, "its manifestation and appearance are bound to be different than in humans, but they are all diseases. Little humans fall ill from disease, so why would we expect something as massive and complicated as the universe to stay healthy? Humans are like tiny universes, after all, and the cosmos is like a massive human body." Thus spoke my possessor.

I was utterly speechless. How superficial my previous understanding of the cosmos had been.

"Not only is every person sick, but so is the universe," my possessor repeated.

"So it is . . . so it is." After all of Bai Dai's revelations, my possessor had finally revealed the truth to me.

"Disease is the default setting for everything, the normal state of things," he explained, denying that he had been sent by the Rockefeller Foundation to bring down our own supervirus. "Your astrophysicists believe that the universe functions like a precise machine, every detail from constants and galaxies to elementary particles meticulously designed to operate seamlessly, like a Swiss watch. According to them, if you want to explain the universe, all you need is a formula less than three centimeters long. But that couldn't be further from the truth.

Like humans, the universe is filled with flaws and deficiencies. The most crucial step in understanding it is to come to terms with the fact that it is diseased. We live in a world full of loopholes. The universe will never make it to the natural end formulated by mathematics, chemistry, and physics; instead it will die a sudden violent death when you least expect it."

I suddenly remembered that all the astrophysicists had been admitted to the hospital. "So the universe is suffering from a serious disease."

"That's *not* what I'm saying. Humankind rushes forward, expending all of that precious brainpower and hard work, yet remaining helpless when it comes to understanding the ultimate laws that govern the universe. Your physics is becoming more and more like some sleight of hand illusion, because humankind mistakenly took its diseased universe to be a healthy one."

"We are all sick *because* the universe is sick." I finally understood. No wonder I couldn't get rid of my stomach pain. It wasn't actually caused by my possessor.

"The universe is also in pain, but humankind has no way of understanding its pain. This has to be the greatest failure of biological evolution."

"Disease is everywhere . . ."

"In the beginning the universe refused to admit that it was sick, but once the pain set in, it could no longer take it."

"It must be so desperate . . ." I'd had no intention of saying that; the words just popped out. When desperation reaches its extreme, it is no longer desperate. Or is the word "desperation" a bit too stingy? Should we feel pity and sympathy, or should we gloat about the great misfortune that afflicts the universe? A lot of sick people are in so much pain that they want to kill themselves. Quite a few die directly from their diseases or are sent to be euthanized. Entire species have been wiped out by epidemics or contagions. But all of this barely amounts to a few feeble groans for the universe.

"That's right," my possessor said. "The universe is so filled with desperation that it is forced to admit how serious its illness is. And then it begins its regimen of self-treatment."

"The universe . . . practices self-treatment?"

"In order to stave off its pain, the universe has evolved into a hospital."

72

THE ULTIMATE HOSPITAL

The universe is a hospital, another "fact" that I found difficult to believe, but everything my possessor said sounded so very convincing. The situation was rapidly evolving to extremes.

Following the guidance of my possessor, my line of sight gradually settled back on C City. Although the hospital president-cum-mayor was no longer around and Prince Ai had refused to allocate projects and funding to doctors, this massive medical institution was still firing on all cylinders, though more out of inertia than anything else. Standing on hoverboards, equipped with flight backpacks, or piloting fixed-wing aircraft, rotorcraft, and helicopters, doctors captured one patient after another and sent them back to the hospital. The sick ward was terribly overcrowded. My view pulled back, revealing all the universe, the "cosmic hospital." Each star, each civilization appeared in the form of a hospital, with outpatient wards and inpatient towers erected at the bottoms of craters or beside ammonia-ice lakes where red crosses shone. The shrieks of imprisoned patients pierced the air. Dead bodies were tossed into volcanic pits used as morgues.

I flew amid the stars, thinking back on all the strange events I had encountered while seeking treatment in C City, and I couldn't help but think, *There's no point in living*. It really didn't matter whether I lived or died.

"It's truly unfathomable." Only now did I finally understand the meaning of these words.

"The universe is even more unfathomable than the unfathomable," my possessor said. "If you just look at it like a hospital, you will be on the right track. You can also look at it as a continuum of doctors and patients. It is the ultimate hospital, treating its own maladies."

It would be inexcusable for an unfathomable world not to have an ultimate hospital like C City's Central Hospital, but as I thought about the filthy and chaotic sick ward—the long lines of patients, the scalpers, and those suicide bombers carrying out vendettas against doctors who had wronged their family members—something about it all just wasn't quite right. I wondered whether, in order for the universe to treat itself, it had really been necessary to take my daughter away to become an aerial nurse. "Could that large cold void be the universe's intravenous infusion of sodium chloride and glucose?"

"Don't try to apply the narrow understanding and one-sided perspective of humankind to something as profound as the ultimate hospital," my possessor sternly criticized. "The universe requires the kind of rules that we apply to the field of medicine, especially when it comes to the description and analysis of the process of birth, death, aging, and sickness. These are the fundamental laws that dictate how the world functions."

"Oh, so that's how it is. It seems the pathology department is quite important."

"In fact, among advanced extraterrestrial civilizations, the field of medicine has supplanted physics as the grand unified theory of everything. We no longer have to waste energy on a thankless search for so-called universal truths. We just need to focus on diagnosing what illness it is suffering."

I had learned in the hospital library that, during the Age of Medicine, it was widely accepted that medicine was actually basically all about physics: molecules, atoms, quarks, and gluons. To replace physics with medicine would just be considered part of medical dialectics.

"The universe . . . is so amazing." I couldn't find the right words to describe what I wanted to express.

"There is nothing we can do. The universe also wants to live. Survival is the unifying theme of everything, including the universe itself."

"Why is survival so important?"

"If you don't survive, you die."

"And the universe is also afraid of death?"

"Yes, it, too, fears death. The universe is suffering from a terminal illness."

"But how does the universe know it is sick?"

73

CONSCIOUSNESS IS FOR
SENSING THE BODY'S DECAY

My possessor projected a palm-size organic plexiglass bottle into my visual cortex. Inside was a light-green, oval-shaped halo, slightly moving and emitting a glow. My possessor told me, "This is a piece of cosmic memory. It is consciousness that you can touch." He said he wanted the consciousness of the universe to connect with my neurons. It was large and cold, yet hard to make out, emitting a moldy smell that reminded me of an old man who hadn't taken a bath or changed his clothing all winter.

My possessor said that consciousness is actually a pathological phenomenon—it is diseased. Truly advanced, normal, healthy things would never have consciousness, which, like maggots, develops only in corrupt organisms. Consciousness exists so it can sense the body's decay.

"Not only organisms made from cells and proteins can develop consciousness," my possessor explained, "as long as mass, spin, and electric charge exist. In other words, consciousness can appear anywhere that the presence of death is felt."

This was a bit hard for me to understand. But I knew that our 13.7-billion-year-old universe has consciousness, which means that it is a body riddled with disease and decay.

My possessor explained that consciousness is different from thought. It is not a material thing, even though it must rely upon a neural network in time and space. As pathetic as the universe may be, it is still not merely a cold place of dust and radiation—it is neurological. With consciousness comes pain. And it takes only a sensation of pain, of the flesh, to know that one is sick, which sparks the will to keep on living.

That is what has enabled the universe to survive up until the present day.

And that is why we are here.

I now view the universe as alive. Life indeed comes in many shapes and forms. As a child, it would have been almost impossible for me to imagine plants as "alive," not to mention single-celled organisms like viruses. It is said that deep in the ocean, even more life-forms utterly defy our normal definitions of life. Besides that, doctors are currently creating nongenetic life-forms, all of which makes a life-form like the universe easier to justify.

My possessor said that the universe has also been referred to as the "ultimate game of life." But what is life? Besides anything that experiences a metabolic process, is life not simply that which senses pain? In this sense, life is more like a sensor, and so consciousness is but one process that the universe goes through, similar to computer programming.

"That's why we still use 'it' to refer to the universe, and not 'him' or 'her.'" He spoke as if he had personally watched the universe's birth and development.

But why must the universe live on? Could there be a world out there where the sole purpose of life is a search for death?

"How unfortunate this universe is!" my possessor continued. "Due to mutations, it is now likely quite deformed, as if growing a pair of legs on its face, where the eyes should be. Some places in the universe are too hot, while others are too cold; some are devoid of air, while others are inundated with fatal radiation. Black holes will grind your bones into nothing before you even have a chance to scream for help. Supernova explosions send matter spiraling into outer space, but even there these poor particles are unable to be released and instead must endure an endless cycle of frantic turns and collisions before they are reborn, only to begin the same painful process all over again. Small galaxies are warped and destroyed by larger galaxies, their leftover remnants an ugly stream of stars. These various cosmic visions are identical to the scenes from hell."

Now I understand: first, the universe has consciousness; second, it is deformed; third, the process of deformity brings with it pain and suffering, making the universe sense the threat of illness and death; fourth, all life-forms imbued with consciousness try to find ways to correct their faults, to alleviate the threat of disease and death. They do everything in their power to survive, and this inevitably leads them down the path toward treatment.

Isn't that how I have spent most of my life? Humans and the universe are one and the same.

"By the time the universe finally became aware of how sick it was, it was already too late. However, when it comes to most countries in the world, and even all of humankind, don't most of them only discover their diseases quite late, at which point they reluctantly begin their treatment? The United Nations is also a community hospital. Just think about how many years it's been since it was established, and how inefficient it is. Practically every time they hold a meeting, someone says, 'If the planet is sick, the human race can never be truly healthy.' But what's the point? Is the so-called global village not just another manifestation of the doctor-patient relationship? Besides aiming nukes at each other, what else do these nations really do?"

Everything my possessor said was more or less correct. I'm not too familiar with the whole planet, but the situation I see around me every day is exactly as he described. This proves that the universe is indeed diseased. The question then is, *How did the universe get sick?*

My possessor explained that, according to the latest version of cosmological pathology, there are two explanations. According to the first, disease is caused by a series of evolutionary errors accumulated over time, referred to as the derailment effect. If the universe is to be viewed as a life-form that is continually evolving, it will end up like the peacock, gradually deviating from a healthy growth track to pursue pathological beauty. The chaos of entropy is but an external manifestation of this illness. The second explanation is related to flaws in the design. This is also the more popular explanation.

74

DESIGN FLAWS

I looked back out into space, but all I could see was the faint outline of the stars, which hovered there, unmoving. The Milky Way was calm and mysterious. Man-made satellites like little particles of eye gunk shot past me, gracefully floating through the empty expanse. The light from stars farther off has taken tens of billions of years to get here. I have no idea why they would idiotically expend all that energy—is it part of the "derailment effect" or a design flaw? Like a newborn solely focused on breastfeeding, I exerted all my energy gazing out into space, but no matter how hard I tried, I could not find the universe's deepest depths or see any active signs of its consciousness at work: no nervous system, no brain sulcus, nothing that could be construed as the spark of thought or contemplation, just layer after layer of shattered remnants, endless chaos, and the most brutal cold, like a vast state of unconsciousness, conventionally referred to as three-dimensional space, but factoring in that invisible entity called "time," it is a four-dimensional space. (Some smart-ass humans have calculated that there must be eleven dimensions in the cosmos, but there is absolutely no evidence to back this up.) The strange thing is that it always appears as if time is unidirectional. Why is that? Isn't that superfluous, a sign of its illness? Or is it a lingering side effect of its treatment?

What I saw reminded me of my fellow patients. Some had been sent to the Emergency Resuscitation Room after falling into comas, arriving unconscious, drooling, their muscles twitching, their necks stiff, and their heart rates, blood pressure, and breathing all dropping.

In the end, the patients had been declared dead, their breathing tubes and intravenous lines removed, their respirators turned off.

According to my possessor, the entire cosmos had already been sick at the moment of its inception, and the universe bears the mark of something designed. As to why it was designed, he asserted that an alien civilization conducted an experiment simulating the conditions of the universe in a lab, where a mathematical algorithm recreated the entire process of evolution. The laws of natural selection suggest that the result would be much different: not only would humans never appear, but possibly no mammal-like creature should have evolved. But the lab experiment showed the opposite: each and every life-form that now exists reappeared in the experiment. This points to a very particular design. Otherwise, how to explain so many coincidences in the universe?

But there was nothing surprising about that. A variety of mechanisms go into the creation of things. Take flying, for instance, which is a skill that doesn't necessarily require fleshly wings gradually evolved over hundreds of millions of years. The airplane was the product of an engineer whose designs were driven by vanity, and it took only a few short centuries for the Wright brothers to realize concepts first imagined by Leonardo da Vinci.

However, careless designs can also create monsters and copies, which has occurred repeatedly over the course of human history. Just take all the different social forms that have arisen through the process of trial and error, and all the people that have died in the process.

As far as the universe is concerned, the big bang was nothing but a premature birth by cesarian section, my possessor insisted. Something went wrong during the embryonic stage. A loss of control, just a few quantum fluctuations in the great void, was all it took to trigger major problems. What was supposed to be heaven developed into something much closer to hell. Even more tragically, the grand designer seems to have forgotten to give this universe a soul.

I remembered something that Dr. Artist had said: the universe is a product of image engineering.

I thought about those artificial organisms created by the Clinical-Academic-Industrial Complex. It seems that design is indeed universal. Humankind has carried it out, but the result is riddled with problems and harbors the danger of self-destruction. It was a terrible shame to learn that even the universe is a product of design.

But who designed the universe? This subject does not seem to be terribly appropriate for inspiring new song lyrics. At best, I can only imagine whether there might be another Clinical-Academic-Industrial Complex overseeing the universe. That person (or group, perhaps even a family) should take responsibility for the current crisis we are facing. Perhaps a half-baked product like the universe should never have been created.

My possessor described some hypotheses about the identity of the great designer. As one theory goes, the designer is a flying monster shaped like a syringe. After mistakenly being loaded with liquor and getting violently drunk, it spent four days creating the universe, the way a toy maker manufactures toys. This theory later led to one of the most popular religions in the universe, and almost all religions are variations on this theory. Therefore, there is reason to believe that alcohol poisoning caused the Syringe God to create such a flawed universe. All the existing evidence supporting the theory of evolution was actually planted by the Syringe God, who intentionally aged some elements of matter to test the piety of the believers. But even this aspect of his grand design is riddled with holes.

"The designer of the universe is also diseased," I said.

"Actually, this isn't the kind of issue you can oversimplify." My possessor spoke in a self-mocking tone. "The identity of the designer lies beyond the realm of anything that intelligent life-forms can comprehend. No created being can understand that which created it. When a plane crashes from the sky, it has no knowledge of the aeronautical engineer that designed it. The question of the great designer is not open for discussion. It is a subject of the utmost sensitivity and should be considered taboo."

"The universe must have searched for its designer, right?"

"That's a possibility. At some point it may have wanted to seek out the designer to correct its problems. That would have been one way to rid itself of its disease and its pain at the very source. Perhaps when the designer, who worked so hard to create this universe, saw what it really looked like, he decided simply to abandon it."

The possessor repeatedly referred to the designer as "him." I hoped this was simply a little word game, because it left me feeling really confused. One of the most frustrating things in the universe is the confusing relationship between "he" and "it." I pretended to be infuriated. "That would be utterly irresponsible!"

"I suspect he had no other choice. I don't think he was simply being careless or muddleheaded; instead I suspect that because the universe is a high-precision object, no matter how much effort he expended, no designer could ever get it perfect. More likely, it came down to a question of cost. It may be theoretically possible to produce fail-safe components, but the required investment would be infinitely higher. No matter who the architect of all of this might be, there is no way anyone could pay *that* bill. And so, no matter how you look at it, the problems haunting the universe seem inevitable."

"And we are the ones that suffer . . ."

"Life is a matter of continually standing face to face with a diseased universe. The only thing we are clear about right now is that so-called voyages into the sea of stars to explore the universe, journeys to the final frontier, are nothing more than sticking our heads into a boundless sea of pathogenic bacteria and medicinal fluid." My possessor's voice was as cold as it was direct.

I nodded my head. My heart, which had been so full of worries and uncertainty, was finally at ease. All along it had been the universe's faulty design that had led me to enter the world enmeshed in the Age of Medicine and to spend my entire life in the hospital. Perhaps I will never know the reason, but at least I have a partial explanation. In trying to uncover who I am and where I came from, I had gone from the hypothesis posed by Alfred Ludwig Heinrich Karl Graf von Waldersee to that of Rockefeller, and from Dr. Norman Bethune to the Syringe God. All of it is relatively empty, but I suppose it is better than nothing.

Part of me thought that the great designer must be quite sad. I'm sure he didn't initially intend to create a diseased universe. Who would ever wish such a thing upon his children? But the most tragic part of the story is that although he was able to design the universe, he was unable to save it. All he could do was witness its gradual demise. He may have abandoned it, but he must still have suffered in pain as he watched it die. Pain is everywhere.

In the face of the great suffering and pain endured by the universe, my little bit of pain is barely worth mentioning. But this pain continues to eat away at me. I may not care about the universe—according to the predictions of specialists, this guy won't be going to visit the Syringe God anytime soon—but I very well might die a tragic death any minute.

Would the designer have stood by and coldly observed, after intentionally creating a disease that deformed the entire universe? Maybe the guy is a sadist? Or perhaps he has a morbid sense of appreciation when it comes to beauty? Maybe he is determined to use this morbid sense to ease his own pain? Or maybe he has fallen in love with pain, like a dog that eats its own shit?

My possessor said that if that were the case, the grand designer would be even more pathetic. He, too, was probably designed by someone, or maybe he is simply a machine that passively carries out its program, but then it, too, was built improperly.

Or maybe he's sick too.

The whole thing is hopeless.

No one can clearly explain the origins of what's to come.

I asked my possessor to explain how the universe performs treatment on itself, so he brought me deeper into outer space, to see the aliens.

75

THE MISSION OF LIFE AND CIVILIZATION

In the past, humankind built radio telescopes and sent probes into outer space to search for aliens outside our solar system, but none of those efforts resulted in contact. In actuality, the aliens were right here all along, scattered among the stars, but they were too consumed with the construction of hospitals to pay attention to the probes.

There has been so much talk about aliens that the whole concept has become almost cliché. Upon seeing them for real, I discovered that some of them resemble humans, but others look more like the strange creatures I had encountered in the pharmaceutical mines. They fit within the parameters of what one would expect from a science fiction movie, but nothing about them really challenged the imagination. However, we had never categorized them as doctors or patients, and medicine turns out to be the most common language in outer space, providing a kind of universality that neither hydrogen-atom wavelengths nor any other mathematical models can provide.

Aliens had come to this universe on a mission.

My possessor explained that, in order to treat its disease, the universe created intelligent beings, "cellular machines with thought and movement," which includes humans and aliens. The universe allowed these beings to multiply and spread across several galaxies, serving a function similar to that of medical nanobots, cleansing the oil from the blood in the space-time continuum, eliminating the thrombus caused by the big bang, clearing out wormholes from the blood vessels, and even repairing the infrastructure of the cosmic strings. This process is typically referred to as "civilization building." The job of civilization is to "wipe the ass" of an incorrectly designed universe.

"The universe may have created us, but did it imbue us with souls?" I asked.

"That is hard to say." My possessor appeared uncomfortable. "But if the universe itself doesn't even have a soul . . ."

I guess he meant that even if the universe doesn't have a soul, it must have fabricated souls for living beings as a medical means to fix their physical defects. In this way it could save itself from dying. But in the end, it just brought more pain.

My possessor insisted that medical science is the most distinctive feature of civilization. It is *the* science, standing out among all the other sciences, the jewel in the crown, the only thing the universe can rely upon to cure its ills, correcting form and function with the aim of returning itself to the realm of normality.

Think of the universe as a body. Bodies are mechanical systems within which diseases exist independently. Specific components of the universe are malfunctioning: dust, galaxies, gravitational fields. Whenever something has been damaged or begins to fester, subbranches of medicine—mathematics, physics, and chemistry—provide the necessary tools to heal and repair the diseased areas. At least in theory.

All of this requires specialized intelligent life-forms outfitted precisely for this purpose. The universe can no longer carry out these tasks on its own. It is semiparalyzed. It has accepted that "no one can save the facade." After imparting scientific and cultural skills to life and civilization, including the ability to learn and calculate, it can no longer carry anything else out.

"Take astronomy," my possessor explained. "That, too, is a medical method. It is related to physics, in that they share the common mission of sequencing and diagnosing the basic structure of the universe. Every civilization, no matter how long or short it may last, ends up doing the same boring things, never realizing why. After the universe was born, it burned at a high temperature for a period of time, hoping to burn the diseases out of its system. Gradually, the universe began to cool off, but it had already burned out its subjective consciousness. It no longer knew what its own body was composed of, nor the site of its disease, and it had no time to explain the meaning and purpose of life to the organisms it had created." My possessor seemed like he was trying really hard to appear serious.

Although intelligent life-forms have all been receiving treatment, they don't even realize that they are treating a disease—nor even that the universe is sick. Instead, they think they are advancing the cause of their own people.

My possessor provided an example. Occasionally, humankind realizes that time and space are warped, a manifestation of the universe's diseased nature. Under normal circumstances, time and space should never warp. The appearance of these abnormalities marks the point when treatment should commence. However, humankind has used the theory of relativity to satisfy its own twisted thirst for sick materialism. When we talk about gravitational waves, the bending of time and space, this, too, is a sign of how serious the illness really is. But humankind not only fails to recognize it, we actually celebrate with wanton abandon! In the end, this only increases the friction between doctors and patients, further straining their relationship.

And yet the universe still holds on to the hope that the life-forms it has created will repair fundamental structures, even change its constants, in order to supplement the primary algorithms, culminating in a major operation to eliminate the root of disease. Medicine has replaced physics.

But this is only one layer of life's purpose. The universe hopes that, if one day it should perish, the civilizations that it fostered will live on and replace it, serving as extensions of its own life. Perhaps these civilizations will create brand-new universes.

"Death is the end," my possessor concluded, "and the end signals a new beginning."

I had heard him speak those words before. I'm not sure why, but those words sent a chill up my spine, and the stench of a dirty ass assaulted my nose. "I await the origin. That's how it always is."

And so my possessor led me off to investigate the truly tragic side of all of this.

76

THE ORIGIN OF LIFE'S
SUFFERING

My possessor urged me to observe cosmic life-forms and civilizations from an even closer vantage point. Their environments weren't much better than humankind's, and in some ways, they were even more wretched, filled with beings struggling in pain as they faced impending death.

The universe's creations are not only ill but suffering from serious disease. No one escapes the law: "Disease Is the Default Setting for Everything." Intelligent organisms are incapable of sensing the universe's illness, caring only about preserving their own lives, unable to feel the universe's pain or even an ounce of pity for a universe on the verge of dying.

My possessor explained: "This is yet another design flaw, a flaw within the flaw. What positive things can you expect from a patient, anyway? All phenomena of life are imperfect, which is yet another piece of evidence pointing to the fact that the universe suffers from a birth defect. Why does spending time in the sun lead humans to develop skin cancer? Why does virtually every activity run the risk of injury? Why do twenty-five percent of all people carry the gene for nearsightedness? Why do we only recognize the tiger when we are close enough to become its lunch? Why do the tube that delivers food to our stomach and the tube that delivers oxygen to our lungs intersect in our throat? Didn't the designer realize how many deaths this faulty design would lead to? Why do we suffer from cholesterol deposits on arterial walls, like a Mercedes-Benz with a plastic straw for its gas line? The immune system naturally plays an important role in people's health, and yet why does it attack the human body, triggering autoimmune disorders such as rheumatic fever, arthritis, hyperthyroidism, diabetes, lupus erythematosus, and multiple sclerosis? Who would design things so that just as women are pregnant and most in need of nutrition to aid in the development of the fetus, they develop nausea and vomit after they eat? Why is sexual compatibility so difficult for men and women? Wouldn't it be a more satisfying model if they could climax together? Why are we all so unfortunate, and yet we insist on continually hurting one another? Why is our happiness always short lived, disappearing in an instant, while pain never seems to end? Why, after achieving a goal we have struggled so long to reach, do we not only fail to feel satisfied but immediately set out for an even more distant goal, bringing us more sorrow and regret? There is no explanation for any of this."

"When I was in the hospital, I read a book that explained some of this," I responded. "According to that book, the cases you describe all result from compromises and concessions made over the course of evolution. Our bodies evolved from those of our tribal ancestors, who lived as hunters and gatherers on the African plains, but after millions of years of natural selection, we have developed certain patterns that have not had time to adapt to the realities of an unprecedented new environment: high-fat diets, cars, drugs, artificial lighting, central air-conditioning. This is the price of progress. And the question you raised about nausea during pregnancy, that is actually to prevent the fetus from being harmed by contaminated food . . ."

"Those are all preposterous lies that people tell themselves," my possessor retorted, "and over time, they have come to believe the lies! These fictions were created to provide legitimacy for the hospital. It is not appropriate to project the theory of evolution on a world that has been suddenly twisted by the sheer force of the human will. Disease comes down to design flaws. Indeed, the reason that civilization developed so quickly was that cosmological constants, along with the basic structure of matter, had already been transformed by supercivilizations. It stands to reason that they should be able to solve their own problems, but instead this has become the source of interstellar warfare—not only was the universe not cured of its disease, but its destruction was actually hastened. The universe has finally realized that it's shooting itself in the foot by never having pondered these questions, and now that death is breathing down its neck, it's already too late."

It really was too late. Just one look around and I could see it. Absolutely nothing was going according to plan. Take me, for example: I had lived on this earth for forty years, and up until this point, all I had known was that all life was suffering, but I never knew the reason. Now I know that the nature of pain is right here. It was all decided from the very moment that the universe was formed, and I have no control over it whatsoever. When I think about those joyless mutual-therapy sessions with Bai Dai and Zhu Lin, I can only sigh in resignation.

Standing amid the waves in this ocean of stars, an image of misery was unveiled before my eyes. Humans have devised formulas, such as the Drake equation, to calculate how many civilizations exist in the universe. Some estimate that the Milky Way contains between five million and twenty-five million planets that are home to intelligent civilizations, and there are between eighty and two hundred billion other galaxies. According to these calculations, there must be no lack of civilizations in outer space.

A pity, then, that they are all diseased. If you are part of this universe, pain and suffering are inevitable. We are forced to confront this reality, and if we fail to take this into consideration and just research the stars, launch ships into outer space, and visit alien planets, we will only end up more desperate and disillusioned. No wonder my possessor said that supercivilizations had replaced physics with medicine. But now it seems that even medicine has a limited impact.

According to my possessor, cells form the structure of life. The universe probably felt that this type of design was already so complex and sophisticated that it would be impossible to imitate. One human cell alone contains forty-six DNA chromosomes. If you were to unwrap them and spread them out, they would stretch more than two meters in length. An adult human body contains approximately sixty trillion cells. If you unfurl all that DNA, it would be 120 billion kilometers long, eight hundred times the distance between Earth and the sun.

How could anyone ensure that there are no errors in all those cells and molecules? This is the tragedy of life.

77

VICIOUS CYCLE

I followed my possessor as we traversed the universe. Everything we saw was decay, collapse, and death. All we heard were moans, cries, and screams. This came as a terrible shock, and yet my own pain merged with the universal pain of the cosmos. My feelings toward my possessor grew more complex, a combination of hatred, disgust, dependence, and gratitude . . . he had expended so much energy trying to lead me to the sea. *But what was waiting for me there?*

My possessor spoke with deep lamentation. "Ever since life first appeared, we have been living in a hell-like universe, afflicted with terrible ailments, and the primary question we all face is how to regain our health, to prevent ourselves from dropping dead in the middle of this evolutionary road—but that proves to be an impossible task. The physiological dimension of all this is bad enough, but if we broaden our definition of disease to include civil societies composed of individual organisms, the picture becomes even more horrendous."

"So what can we do?" I asked anxiously.

"The universe has no choice but to prioritize our treatment. It selects a few patients suffering from rather mild ailments and transforms them into doctors to treat the other members of their species. Since they are the universe's plenipotentiary representatives, we call them 'angels in white.' From there we expand this team to treat even more patients. Only when we have been successfully treated can we begin to treat the universe. But we are unable to treat ourselves properly and thus unable to treat the universe—a vicious cycle."

"A vicious cycle . . ." I couldn't help but think of a toilet. Isn't all that work, reconfiguring genes and creating new organisms, just like wiping the stinky shit off our assholes and flushing it away to some far-off place where we never see it again? It lulls us into thinking that life is pure, clean, healthy, and carefree, but before we know it, our intestines fill up with a new load of shit.

"If the universe wants to cure itself, it needs to build bigger and better hospitals," my possessor explained, "and those massive hospitals require even more patients. In other words, the patients are actually pieces of shit, successively produced by doctors that the universe has churned out after devouring interstellar matter in the name of curing its own disease."

"So the universe and civilization are basically wiping each other's asses?"

"Yes, and that is the true source of all your pain."

"I'm in pain because the universe is in pain?"

"The cosmic malady is also your malady."

"And what about the nation, history, war, economics, philosophy? Where do they fit in?"

"Those are prescriptions that the universe hastily whipped up as it was on the verge of passing out from the excessive pain in its ass."

"Wow, the universe has really had it tough." Thinking about how my minor incessant pain was connected so deeply with the pain of the universe, I wondered whether I should pass out too. But I didn't want to overestimate my own importance.

"Everything in this world gets more and more difficult." My possessor heaved a deep sigh, just like a real person, and somehow, through his empty voice, I caught a glimpse of his soul.

When I had engaged in mutual-therapy sessions with those women, there were moments when doctor and patient collapsed into one another and became one. I now know that that sticky, sweaty scene in the trash room was merely a reflection of cosmic reality. Patients on earth are but reflections of the patients in the heavens. I suddenly realized why Dr. Artificial Rock was leading a team of new researchers in designing a life-form devoid of genes, of what we normally call "life." He must have sensed a chance to break free of that infinite cycle. But even that proved impossible; in the end, there is no way to escape from self-destruction.

"When you get right down to it, the universe is not as painful a place as you imagine," my possessor added. "It is able to find happiness amid its pain. It is actually addicted to the creation of hospitals. In fact, it gradually started to look at itself as a medical punk, or even a medical-punk geek."

I imagined the ass-pain-tortured universe as a drug addict. "It must think that the hospital is really cool and beautiful."

"There are three basic laws governing all things," my possessor said in a boastful tone. In order to gain a greater degree of control over me, he decided to share with me what he thought was the greatest secret. "The first is the law of design thinking. No matter which way you look at it, the universe is clearly the product of design. Someone or something with a perfectionist mentality came up with a thought system aimed at creating or transforming a world, so obsessive in its pursuit that it needed to achieve one hundred percent perfection to satisfy its own vanity. The hospital is the most typical example of this. The second law is the defect theory. Everything in the universe, including the universe itself, is riddled with natural defects. Disease is the default setting for everything, and this is something the designer brought to the table. While the designer approaches things from the perspective of infinite determinism, the world is bound by the theory of finite determinism. Most people are unable to understand this. And so, in order to repair the design flaws, the designer needed to redesign everything continually. Everything since the birth of the universe has been part of an unending redesign. Eventually this evolved into an art form. What makes art beautiful is its flaws, but they also lead inevitably to a series of vicious cycles. When it comes to our beautiful and glorious hospital, it is precisely the same situation. The third item refers to the law of the reverse trend. Any designed form of evolution is bound to deviate from its original goal and start moving in the opposite direction eventually. This, too, is unavoidable. The hospital claims to save people, and yet it remains unable to save itself."

That's right, it's all unavoidable. Spoken beautifully. Generation after generation, people have lived in this massive sick ward we call the universe, all their self-proclaimed achievements and accomplishments nothing but little pills to ease the pain.

I felt like my possessor had revealed the real reason why medical treatment is always so difficult and expensive. As the universe struggled with death on the scale of light-years, it had created humans and all kinds of other strange creatures on a minuscule scale, in order to survive. The entire thing is utterly ridiculous, but even more ridiculous is the fact that these pitiful disease-ridden creatures must use their pathetic brains not only to attempt to understand the universe but to attempt to cure it—indeed, a wasted effort. If my possessor hadn't mentioned this, I would still be in the dark.

But then . . . "Why did you come here, to save me?" I suddenly put things together, and I realized that we were still on the run.

78

RESISTING TREATMENT

My possessor grew excited as he spoke. "This is by decree of the Super Patient!"

Continuing to indulge in histrionics, he projected a new image into my mind: a peacock badge. He explained that this was the symbol of the Super Patient. No one had ever actually seen this Super Patient, but they just knew that he had first discovered that the universe is sick and dying.

I realized just how complicated the situation really was. Everything was now on a completely different level. Patients in this cosmic civilization fall into three groups. The first group is selfishly consumed with curing itself, employing any and all underhanded methods to get treatment for themselves, getting friends to pull strings or bribing doctors with red envelopes. Another group stands beside the hospital, steadfastly defending the Age of Medicine, using therapy to shed their identities as patients and elevate themselves to the level of doctors. Finally there is a group best represented by the Super Patient. They know all too well that the universe will never cure itself of its terrible disease, and that with its imminent death, so, too, all patients will perish. And so this group decides to resist treatment.

"The Super Patient realized that the most laughable thing in the world that you can't laugh at is seeing the universe fruitlessly toiling over the course of many light-years to conquer its own predestined demise," my possessor said. "But no matter what it does, in the end it is helpless, like a person who is on the verge of being promoted to the level of doctor and suddenly finds himself a patient again! Theoretically you can discuss it all you want, but when it comes time for action, you realize it's all bullshit."

I thought about all that I had experienced, and I realized he was right.

"The universe claims it is offering to help treat the diseased," he continued, "but in reality it is knowingly or unknowingly slaughtering countless lives and civilizations. It is nothing but a charlatan doctor! Think about your own experience. Didn't you go through the same thing? If you keep going down this path, they'll kill you with their treatment! Treatment means death! The doctors are unreliable, and so is the universe. This is reality."

When he realized what was happening, the Super Patient had sent out a call for all patients to reject the ultimate hospital. The message quickly spread until it developed into a universal Treatment Resistance Movement. Now *this* is the core struggle facing today's intergalactic civilizations. It is broad and sweeping, epic in stature. Ultimately, all life-forms in the universe must participate. The group led by the Super Patient is known as the Sect of the Awakened. Right now its plan is not only to make it out of the hospital but to escape from the universe itself.

Escape from the universe? This is the single most challenging space-time operation I have ever heard of. It must be harder than ascending to heaven. In the past, the farthest humankind had ever gotten was setting foot on the moon. For someone like me, who had only just recently escaped from the sick ward, the idea was completely beyond the scope of my imagination. And as an amateur songwriter, I usually prefer to distance myself from anything described as "epic."

"So that's why we are headed to the sea?" I asked with a feigned sense of surprise.

"That's right. But only the very smartest and bravest dare to take this step. When we talk about 'going to the sea,' we are talking about a port to a new, healthy universe, devoid of illness. It is also referred to as the Gate of Life and Death. It is like a cell membrane: once you pass through it, an entirely different world awaits, a place of ultimate pleasure, where no one even knows that pain exists. It is said that in the universe that exists inside, matters of life and death are settled."

This struck a sensitive chord in me. I was reminded of that famous saying: *The bitter sea knows no boundaries. Repent and you shall find the shore within reach. Put down the butcher's knife, and Buddhahood awaits.* But then another question popped into my head: "So who designed this universe by the sea?"

Perhaps no one had ever dared to ask. My possessor was momentarily rendered silent.

"If it was the product of design," I pressed, "wouldn't it, too, have flaws? Wouldn't there also be disease and illness there?"

". . . I don't think it was designed," he said after a long hesitation. "It was probably created naturally. When you hear about a heavenly kingdom so perfect that it is like a garden of infinite beauty, that is the place!"

"Then I suppose there is still some hope . . . ," I said awkwardly.

"You need more than one brain," my possessor continued, "if you want to go head to head with a number one patient and charlatan doctor like the universe. Lower life-forms like humans suffer from inferior intelligence and inadequate stamina. They make frequent mistakes and are easily deceived. The universe has created an entire series of hallucinogenic drugs to paralyze life-forms. That's why you need my help. Only I can help you avoid falling under the universe's bloody scalpel."

My possessor seemed indignant, extremely impassioned, as if reciting a lofty essay on justice. When he mentioned that scalpel, I couldn't help but think of the mace and trident that the jailer in hell had used to impale dead souls up the asshole.

"So . . . you are part of the backup army sent by the Super Patient?" Besides a feeling of gratitude, I also felt a pang of resistance. Are human beings really that bad? Must they suffer such discrimination? Although they claim to settle matters of life and death, aren't the Super Patient and the Sect of the Awakened also selfish? The universe is certainly a despicable place, but isn't it also worthy of pity, like us? It, too, is a patient, a sacrificial lamb of the great designer. None of this was part of its original plan. And now everyone is ready to abandon it. If it hadn't been for the creation of the universe, none of us would exist: human-kind, aliens, even the Super Patient.

I asked my possessor why we had to run away. Couldn't we just play the role of a good patient, or a good doctor, and work together to save the universe?

"If the universe has been designed incorrectly from the beginning, there is no saving it," he responded. "No matter how hard we work to save it, it will only temporarily postpone its death sentence. The universe is devoid of a soul, so while we can treat it, it can never find true salvation."

That response didn't quite satisfy me. I thought of my own family. According to traditional human practice, we do whatever we have to in order to save a dying family member, even when we know it is a lost cause. We still try.

But my possessor pressed on. "The sole reason we are alive is to resist treatment. We don't want to sacrifice ourselves for the universe. We shouldn't waste our time trying to extend its life, nor should we think about creating another universe to carry on its legacy."

"Thank you, I think I understand." I thought about my possessor, crammed up against all the shit in my intestines at that very moment, doing everything he could to evade detection and eventual annihilation at the hands of the doctors, and a flood of warmth flowed through my body.

79

AN ETERNAL DEATHLIKE SILENCE

"As for me possessing your body without getting your permission first, all I can do is apologize," my possessor said. "This was all arranged by the Super Patient. Owing to your extremely low evolutionary level, the first step was to implant a set of spores into the body, which eventually developed into a second brain near the gastrointestinal system. This is a matter of life and death, and time is of the essence. There is no middle path. Although I'm just your possessor, that doesn't mean that I don't have an independent will. Who asked for my opinion about any of this? Who asked if I was willing to be stuck with you? It's not like your shit-filled shell of sticky flesh is some kind of a peachblossom paradise! I'm even worse off than you! I was born without any family. I have no home. I don't even have a physical form—I don't even know what I look like! I don't know if I am in fact alive or just some inanimate thing. Perhaps I'm something in the middle. My birth and existence are based solely on the mission that the Super Patient entrusted me to carry out. Once you are saved, I will be terminated according to my internal programming, expelled as a liquid through your anus, urethra, and sweat glands. You will be left with your original brain. Rest assured, I won't go on meddling in the affairs of humankind by writing Shakespearean plays or inventing quantum computers. As for your future in the land of eternal bliss, the Super Patient already has all of that planned out. There is nothing anyone can do. When it comes to fate, it doesn't matter which corner of the universe you are in, everything has already been determined."

My possessor's usual air of confidence gave way to a bleaker, almost dejected tone. He, too, was in pain. But his pain contrasted with the big decision at hand, as if he knew that nothing could be done yet refused to concede defeat. He really did possess the true qualities of a doctor. I remembered the doctor's mission statement: "If I don't go to hell, who will?" It was time to see if we could live up to it.

I understood that this revealed a much deeper level of the doctor-patient relationship. In this uncertain universe, at least one thing seemed to be certain. Life is no better than the universe, and yet it has taken upon itself the lofty task of resisting the universe. Against all odds, it resists treatment—doesn't that prove it is sick?

I couldn't help but start to feel a bit pessimistic, again uncertain about the prospect of escaping. I looked up at the stars again, into that expanse that had inspired such awe since childhood. I didn't want to see the stars with the help of my possessor's projections; I wanted to gaze upon them with my own naked eyes. I wanted to see what it all *really* looked like. I had learned that the universe was diseased, and my view of the world had changed.

There is no such thing as a static worldview, and those who believe that there is are only deceiving themselves. This is probably why the prince Siddhartha Gautama left the Indian kingdom of Kapilavastu to practice self-cultivation. He saw through the misfortune and hopelessness of the material world to the true face of life, death, illness, and suffering. After experiencing enlightenment, he returned to lead others out of the secular world and to a place of salvation. He eliminated illness and suffering from its very source so that he and his followers would no longer be caught in the six cycles of the samsara. My god, he was the most amazing medical punk of them all! My brain started to make some wild connections—could the Super Patient be the Buddha himself?

A shooting star flashed by silently overhead. Was it an epidermal cell, shed by the uterus of the universe? That was too disgusting to think about, so I swallowed my saliva and looked back up. The strange body of space-time itself seemed to rot before my eyes, gradually transforming into a zombie before exploding into pieces. I smelled the raging spring tide, the true scent of a bloated universe in decay. I rubbed my eyes and took a deep breath, realizing that nothing had happened. The smell was gone. Spreading out before me was a vast, infinite quietude, like a towering wall of darkness extending into eternity. No one knows what lies behind that wall.

I imagined that the galaxies, star clusters, and planets were each hospitals and sick wards. But without my possessor's projections to guide me, relying only on my naked eyes, I couldn't actually see them. I could not bear witness to the interstellar red crosses adorning the heavens. I could not see the Super Patient leading billions of lives along the path to salvation. Instead there was only an oppressive silence, unlike any I had known before, an eternal deathlike silence . . . was this actually the morgue?

Upon this disgusting, diseased body, the universe emits its transcendent beauty, captivating countless adoring souls who sing its praises and recite poetry in its honor, creating a miraculous chapter in the history of science and technology. Their adoration goes so far that they do not hesitate when they are called to traverse the flames and swim the oceans, even sacrificing their own lives.

The universe probably cannot even tell if it is deceiving the human race or deceiving itself. It has created so many strange, cruel, and merciless beings that it probably no longer understands what it is doing. And so we end up with medical-school classrooms filled with pious-looking young faces, eager to cure the world of its ills.

And yet I continue to exist in this reality, oddly unable to change, simply enduring the pain and suffering of endless illness. How could a man named Yang Wei exist in a universe like this? Was he created specifically to treat a diseased universe? To carry on the mantle of the universe? Does he live solely to carry the burden of this great mission? How can his diminutive body withstand all of that? And now he is expected to stand up against the universe somehow? As soon as I realized that the universe and I had such a strange and utterly preposterous doctor-patient relationship, the pain traveled throughout my corporeal self, as if someone had taken a rolling pin to my body.

Oh, this couldn't be real . . .

My possessor turned off his projection, and I withdrew my gaze. Those millions of stars before me faded, and the simulacrum of the universe disappeared. Rain poured down. I was back in C City, in the middle of my escape. Shadows flickered ahead. Our contact person from the sea had finally arrived, and everyone ecstatically rushed to greet him.

80

TERMINAL PATIENT TURNED ASSASSIN

Village Chief Ai's long beard and portly body shook as he fawningly addressed our contact person. "We're ready! From now on, we'll follow your lead." He raised his camera and took a photo to capture this historic moment.

The contact person wasn't wearing a patient gown. Instead he wore a light-colored Western suit and a pair of glasses. He was tall and thin, with a dignified academic look about him, like a poet. A crowd stood behind him, an army of doctors and nurses wearing matching white uniforms and holding sharp surgical tools in their hands.

The medical workers had exaggerated artificial smiles that made them look like they were right out of a comic book. They swiftly surrounded the patients. Village Chief Ai was in shock for a second, but once he realized what was happening, he quickly made a run for it. He didn't give a damn about the other patients, but they, too, quickly realized the danger and tried to break through the perimeter of doctors. Everything devolved into utter chaos.

I tried to locate Zhu Lin among the crowd of doctors, but I couldn't find her and ended up running away. I made it only a few steps before I was stopped by a short, heavily armed male doctor. He looked somewhat familiar. Could this be my son-in-law? He had once come to my house on a medical inspection and, after expressing an interest in my daughter, taken her away with him. Now I know that he was sent by the universe to deliver treatment. As soon as he saw me, his artificial smile widened.

"Aha, I've been looking for you!" he said. "I'm here to save you. You are in great danger. There is a foreign object inside you, a new pathogen that has invaded your body. This unknown life-form is able to mimic humans and project a pseudopersonality. Life-forms are always competing with one another, and this thing displaces the host's memories with its own. It is the cause of all your hallucinations. It has incited you to hate the doctors, which has effectively destroyed the whole purpose of doctor-patient relations, deceiving you into thinking that the people trying to save you are monsters. Meanwhile you can't even see the real monster hiding inside you. This is a most horrific kind of hallucination. The next step will be for it to destroy your brain and completely control your life. It wants to suck out all of your bodily fluids and obliterate your consciousness. In the end it will turn you into a walking corpse! *You* will become your own living hell! This thing and others like it want to hurt the hospital, to bring it to the brink of disaster, to eliminate humankind, to destroy the solar system, the Milky Way, and the entire universe! Let's not forget that the universe is our collective home, the garden in which we all dwell, our destiny and shared future. Don't you *get* it? You mustn't believe anything it tells you! You should trust only your doctors. For you to survive, we must remove this pathogen from your system. Only then will you be able to recover, regain your personality, ascend to the ranks of the doctors, and fulfill your mission in life. Through our collective hard work, we will maintain harmony and stability in the universe!"

"Don't listen to his bullshit," my possessor warned me solemnly. "Those doctors are nothing but puppets, tools! They're the ones hallucinating! They started out as patients, and the roots of their deranged illnesses are still inside them!"

The doctor raised a large-caliber rifle and aimed it straight at my head. I don't think it was an anesthesia gun. "Please don't!" I pleaded.

"For god's sake, we're in the same family!" I imagined him as a fellow patient that just happened to be wearing a white lab coat. Somehow, with a gun pointed at my head, I was able to resist the sense of utter ridiculousness I felt inside me, but surprisingly I didn't feel that scared. I knew that sooner or later, it would all come down to this for both the doctors and patients.

This doctor, whom I had assumed to be my son-in-law, suddenly screamed, "Who the hell are you, addressing me as family? Your genes were already reedited! There is no longer any common blood between you and your daughter! You aren't related anymore!"

With that, the doctor could pull the trigger without a second thought. If not for the family structure, the psychological burden would have been too great. How could anyone be expected to make such a sacrifice for the health of the universe? At that crucial moment, as my life hung in the balance, all I wanted was to ask him where my daughter was. But I was too late, and he pulled the trigger. I stood in shock as the bullet whizzed past my ear. Before the doctor had a chance to react, my possessor drove me to charge forward, and I knocked the doctor to the ground. I was quite surprised by how much strength I had. My possessor must have gotten secret orders from the Super Patient to tweak my body's physical potential. All of this felt like the final struggle before death; it also represented my single greatest contribution to the Treatment Resistance Movement.

I squeezed the doctor's neck, which I would never have previously dared. As I strangled him, a wellspring of guilt flooded me, so powerful that I almost released my grip. *My god, what am I doing? How can I possibly commit an act of violence against one of the angels in white?* Then I remembered my former plan to murder a doctor, and I came to the horrific realization that, for the first time, I was about to witness how a doctor dies. No . . . no, that couldn't be. Doctors can't die! And certainly not at the hands of the very patients they are trying to cure! And yet the life gradually began to leave the body of the man before me. I had killed a doctor, a man that was probably my son-in-law, a physician who had held patients' fates in his hands, a messenger sent by the universe to bring us salvation. I had ended his life.

"I have never killed anyone before . . ." My exaggerated cries seemed to place the blame on my possessor. "How could he die? How could the doctor *die?*"

"You thought doctors could not die before your eyes were opened to the truth about the world. But now that you see things for what they really are, killing is no big deal." My possessor spoke in an assured voice that didn't leave any room for debate. "Your body and soul are no longer prisoners of the hospital, and you can now see the world with fresh eyes. This is a state akin to enlightenment. The act of murder is a form of enlightenment. Those doctors may be amazing, but they are not gods; they are merely tools or servants of the universe. With the universe itself halfway in the grave, what do you expect the doctors to do to you? All of this is the manifestation of the power of the Super Patient running through you."

"No, it's simply not possible . . ." In less time than it takes to bat an eye, I had gone from terminally ill patient to murderer. The doctor had been groveling just moments before. Was my possessor really trying to save me?

Or could he be a new pathological monster like the one Dr. Bauchi had described? Could he be some ancient reconstituted virus? Or a mutant organism formed from radiation in the pharmaceutical mines? A synthetic life-form that had developed intelligence? A terrifying enemy sent by the Rockefeller Foundation? Had he invaded my body in order to use me as a host in which to produce offspring? Had the other patients' bodies also been taken over? Perhaps this had been his ulterior motive all along, but instead he tried to deceive and intimidate me with the monumental claim that "the universe is diseased." Was his plan merely to lure me to the sea? What exactly was waiting for me there? What proof did he have that a healthy and peaceful world awaited? Or perhaps the pressure of the mission had caused him to go mad or fall ill? Maybe the strange cosmic portrait of a diseased universe that he so brazenly presented was just something produced by his crazed subconscious, but even he believed it was real? He still projected that terrifying image into my brain, but perhaps that horrific picture of the universe was just a figment of his twisted imagination? I had heard that these monsters always target the weakest subjects, which is why they invade the corporeal bodies of sick and diseased humans. He wanted to take my place. Or perhaps he already had? Perhaps the war to end humankind had already begun . . .

The world had again been reduced to a set of dice in a thin metal cup. What would the outcome be?

I still cannot believe that I actually killed a doctor. Bai Dai and I had searched for a doctor's corpse for so long and never found one. Perhaps I really did commit a terrible crime against the universe, failing again to live up to its expectations for me.

81

ON WHAT BASIS SHOULD OUR
LIVES BE SAVED

Noticing my silent, protracted inaction, my possessor took a harsh tone. "If you don't do it, we'll both be fucked. Patients and perpetrators are simply two sides of the same coin, tied together by 'death.'"

I lost my temper and screamed at him. "Shit, you've really taken me over! I don't even know who I am anymore!"

My possessor seemed taken aback. "Now, let's not use such harsh language! You are responsible for all of the decisions you have made. I am, after all, just an appendage. I could never truly take your place. You're getting all worked up about nothing. Just think about it. When you see a murder committed in a movie, don't you also get all worked up? And don't you feel that same pinch of excitement when you see news reports about rapes and murders? Didn't you also once have a dream in which you raped your own daughter? Wasn't that something you thought about the very day you got married? Actually, wasn't that the *reason* you married in the first place? This must be a very different feeling than songwriting—or maybe it's all the same. I saw in one of your memories that there was once a woman who sent you a fan letter. She was infatuated with your songs and fell madly in love with you, but she also confided that she was being persecuted by a terrible man, who happened to be your boss. She asked for your help, hoping you might step in and do something. You responded by telling her you would write a song about it. You said that by exposing what happened to the world, the perpetrators would be publicly humiliated and scorned by the people. Then you slept with her and turned her letter over to your boss! You betrayed her. You even followed your boss's instructions and wrote a song to ruin that woman's reputation. In the end, she killed herself. Am I telling the truth? And here you have the gall to claim that you never killed anyone before? Do you only feel guilt when it comes to doctors? That's not right! This is the *real* you, you two-faced son of a bitch! Yet you refuse to admit that you have any design flaws! So it's not a case of who's replacing who. We are all in the same boat. Everything I do is in *your* interest! I'm trying to take us to a place where there are no hospitals, no pain, and no sin. And yet you still insist that I'm secretly plotting to hurt you, take your place, or destroy you! How can you bear to harbor such thoughts? Even so, following the orders of the great and benevolent Super Patient, I still must save you!"

My possessor had articulated so many things that I could never bring myself to admit. I wanted to defend myself, but my words fell short, and I realized just how terrible a human being I really was. This was the most serious disease of them all, the reason why the universe wanted to put me through a thorough treatment regimen.

Perhaps the universe should purge itself of all the imperfect creations it brought forth. There's nothing wrong with that, right? I may not understand the condition of all the myriad living organisms in the world, but I know that humankind, with its ridiculous antics, endless troublemaking, illogical thinking, and extreme selfishness, is a true virus. I'm not a monster; I'm my own enemy.

So no, it isn't that the universe wants to eliminate us. It is actually that our existence simply has absolutely no value. On what basis, then, should our lives be saved?

When we check into the hospital without having answered this question first, we put ourselves in grave danger. Yet now we must face an even greater danger by trying to escape.

82

LEARNING TO COEXIST
WITHOUT REALLY
UNDERSTANDING ONE
ANOTHER

I lowered my head in a gesture of remorse, looking down upon the body of the lifeless doctor on the ground. I understood that there was no hope for me ever to become like him. After a long pause, I solemnly asked, "Are you sure they will still want us by the sea? After what you just said, I feel like a real piece of shit."

"That's not a problem," my possessor responded. "I've already reported everything, and the people by the sea have forgiven us. They never use vulgar language like 'piece of shit.' They feel that our core nature is good, that we are merely victims of a bad environment, the evil system established by the hospital. We've been in the dark and can't control our actions. When they see us, they will say, 'Ah, you've been through so much! In its attempt to cure you, the hospital corrupted you, ruined your self-esteem, and made your illness worse. You were turned into docile slaves. Now that you are finally free from the nightmarish smell of Tegaserod and polyethylene glycol, a new life awaits you.'"

"But . . . weren't we just attacked again by the doctors? How will we make it?"

"Oh, our contact person betrayed us. He informed the hospital of our plan."

"Why would he do that?"

"Betrayal is a core part of human nature."

After a long silence, I asked, "Are you also capable of betrayal?"

My possessor remained silent.

"Although we are joined together, sharing the same blood and nourished by the same essence," I continued, "I feel like I still don't really know you. I'm not sure if I should believe anything you say. You, too, were the product of design. Where are your flaws? You are another consciousness, a part of me, while at the same time, you aren't. If you were to betray me, I wouldn't have anywhere to run to."

"We don't really need to understand each other in order to live together, nor do we need to cling to the lofty expectation that we will have some kind of deep spiritual exchange. Right now the task at hand is to learn how to coexist without really understanding one another. We are like black boxes to each other. You might not be able to tell what's inside me, but that's okay. In a world full of disease, this may not be the perfect alternative, but it is all we can do. The Super Patient has told us that this is the true nature of survival."

My possessor expended a lot of effort explaining all of this. Communicating with him was really beginning to exhaust me too. In my state of weariness, I felt like I had returned home, the home I had lived in before being admitted to the hospital. My daughter was in her room, sitting on the side of her bed. Lying beside her was a boy I had never seen before, wearing a white shirt, and they were happily lost in conversation. They started to undress each other, throwing their clothes, one article after another, onto the floor. When they noticed I was home, the boy hastily ran off. My topless daughter flashed me an awkward and ambiguous smile. I didn't know what to do. She pulled me over to sit in front of her, unbuttoned my clothing, and pulled my head down between her breasts. She extended her hands and began to massage my head gently. I had never imagined that my own daughter would become my treatment therapist! I soon felt something wet behind me. Her saliva dripped down my neck, onto my back, and down into my butt crack. Feeling uncomfortable and anxious, I closed my eyes. I wanted to ask my daughter where her mother was, but then I remembered we were already divorced, so I didn't say anything. Her technique was sensitive. She knew exactly what to do, caressing my skin like she was massaging the strings of a musical instrument. My possessor gradually melted into a pool of pus that welled up in my glands and began to push itself out. It flooded from my pores and rushed out my nostrils, a yellowish-white paste that had taken over my body, gradually breaking me down like stomach acid. For the first time in my life, I felt a true sense of security. I couldn't help but laugh out loud. "Ah, I'm home. I'm home," I told myself. "I'm finally reunited with my daughter, and now there's no reason for me to go to the sea!"

But then I heard the voice of my possessor: "You can never go back. Number one: we no longer have any relatives we can trust. Number two: you can't even trust yourself. Number three: we don't even have a home anymore. We have no choice but to head to the sea. We all voted, and the only one we can trust is the Super Patient."

83

DOES AN INTERNAL ORGAN'S
CRIME ABSOLVE ME OF GUILT

I had no choice but to stay with the other patients and follow Village Chief Ai back down into the pharmaceutical mines, where we could escape through the tunnels. We heard announcements, broadcast through the speakers embedded in the rock walls, and one sounded like Dr. Bauchi's gloomy voice: "Patients, there is no escape. You're as good as done for. There is a fierce and stubborn pathogen within you. It is our most vicious enemy. You must submit yourself immediately for surgery or your lives will be in danger. Please cooperate with the organization. You must not fear treatment!"

I tried to sound sincere yet still fearful as I shouted at the speakers: "I've killed a man. He was a doctor, and he was my son-in-law. I've committed a terrible crime. If I turn myself in, you will surely kill me!"

The response came over the loudspeaker: "Rest assured, according to the recently revised Treatment Charter, if one of your internal organs commits a crime, that doesn't mean that you are guilty. These things are viewed separately in the eyes of the law. Patient, the organization has already carried out its investigation: the mistakes you made were done under duress, after you were controlled by a mutant foreign virus. You are not responsible. You, too, are a victim. None of you are responsible for what you have done."

Dr. Bauchi's voice grew hoarse, as if the pain inside him were about to burst through like a dam breaking. That voice left me deeply disturbed. The doctors had to have suffered a lot since the patients' collective exodus.

"Patients and doctors are connected by fate," Dr. Bauchi continued dispiritedly, as if none of this had anything to do with him. "We must not lose this battle."

My possessor ordered me to make a fist and hit myself twice in the face. "Why the hell are you wasting your time talking to him? Get the hell out of here! *Go!*" He seemed really upset.

"Damn, who should I trust? I'd rather just die!" I was so torn about what to do that I just picked up a rock and slammed it into my forehead. Blood immediately rushed out, but this time I was not following my possessor's instructions. I felt like my brain had temporarily broken free of his control.

This unexpected action seemed to scare my possessor. "So you want to kill yourself? You plan to use this method to end your pain? Well, don't! You'll only end up being reincarnated and repeating this all over again. You'll be a patient in your next life as well. Think about it—this hasn't been easy, has it? I came all the way from the other side of the universe to bond with a lower-level body like yours, just to serve as your guide. I began as a tiny growth, the size of a bean sprout, and it has been really difficult to develop to what I am now. But you still take up ninety-nine percent of the space in this body, with only a tiny area left for me! Those women you were with, Bai Dai and Zhu Lin, they were all yours—they didn't even know I existed! Do you have any idea how uncomfortable it was, for *me*, every time you engaged in your 'therapy' with *them*? I had no choice but to shut my mouth and sit there, off to one side, observing like a little cat. I was afraid I might hurt you, so I made sure to siphon off only a tiny bit of your leftover nutritional intake for myself. I even created a backup 'healthy outlook' protocol, which I inserted into your brain to provide you with inspiration for your songwriting—*that's* how you were able to write those amazing, uplifting lyrics. I deserve a lot of credit for what you have accomplished! How could you now turn around and be so selfish? It's bad enough if you have to die, but why should I have to die with you? It's not like I have a lot of time left anyway. How can you be so cruel? What right do you have to treat me like this?"

My possessor was on the verge of tears, revealing his weak side for the first time. His words tore at my heart. He wasn't a doctor, so what right did he have to decide whether I should die? Still, his words gradually softened me up, and I began to feel the pangs of regret. Finally I stuck a few pebbles into my ears to block out the sound of the loudspeakers, and I continued my journey forward.

As I crossed a cold rushing stream of medicinal fluid, I ran into an escaped patient coming from the other direction.

"If you continue ahead, you will reach the far south," he said with a rattled, uneasy tone. "When the temperature gets warmer, you'll know you are close to the sea."

Suddenly the earth began to shake, sending rocks tumbling from the tunnel walls. The medicinal stream began to rise, and within minutes it had washed away several patients. I caught sight of Little Tao, bobbing up and down in the waves, frantically extending his arms for help. I pulled him to the shore, but then an evil thought overtook me. As if possessed, I picked up a rock and started pummeling him. It took only two or three strikes before he was dead. A thick pasty juice flowed out of his nostrils and ears, a mixture of leafy green and salty white. Was that his possessor? I'd had no intention of killing again. But was it me or my possessor? Or had we conspired to carry out this act of violence? Does an internal organ's crime absolve me of all guilt?

I silently cursed it all. I searched Little Tao's body and found some money, but just as I was about to pocket it, I caught sight of Village Chief Ai approaching with his camera. I handed the money to him.

"Follow me!" he insisted. "We must make it to the sea. The backup contact person has already arranged everything. This one's reliable. We won't have another betrayal like last time." Village Chief Ai counted the bloodstained banknotes. He noticed me looking at him, and after a brief hesitation, he slipped two bills back to me. "Save that for yourself. You'll need it to purchase a ferry ticket when we get there."

84

HOW CAN A PERSON DIE IN A PLACE DEVOID OF HOSPITALS

It was hard to tell how much time had passed. People began commenting in whispers: "I smell something weird." "Something smells like a rotten fish." "What a strange shape. Its salty fluids are leaking between the rocks!" Village Chief Ai ordered all the patients to higher ground, and as we climbed, we saw a vast beach. The sand was black, and in the distance was a row of purple mountain peaks and a flowing river. We couldn't see any sign of hospital buildings, but right before us was a boundless body of water. For the first time in my life, I could experience true nature: earth, mountains, rivers . . . even the sea. Had we finally left C City? Were we on the threshold of the "Gate of Life and Death," crossing into a new universe? The sea was a fleshy red solution, thick, cloudy, full of foam. Its raw, horrific stench reminded me of the disinfectant used in the sick ward. Frothing in the waves were countless living cells and viruses, along with living organisms of all sizes that I had never before laid eyes on. They were densely packed, huddled up against one another, barely able to breathe as they struggled and squirmed in the dark water. Some consumed others. Corpses were tossed around by the crashing waves, a perfect portrait of a diseased universe.

My possessor was silent. Perhaps he was also suffering from amnesia.

I was also silent. I could imagine myself soaring, completely unbound, over the broad sea. The sky above was like a deep cavern, the waves below like a forest of ancient trees. Body parts and shattered bones disintegrated in the foam; chunks of flesh and rivulets of blood swirled in the whirlpools. From the deep came a massive, slow-moving monster, gliding through the waters in search of prey. Undersea volcanoes spit flames and lava . . . was I supposed to traverse this foreign oceanic landscape in order to arrive at the legendary healthy kingdom without hospitals? How reliable could this place be?

Then I seemed to be back at home again. It was a warm, sunny afternoon. My daughter and I were lying naked beside each other on a wooden recliner, drinking tea and reading books. My wife had yet to divorce me, and she was sitting beside us, knitting a wool sweater. The real world hadn't changed one bit. Beyond the realm of my senses, everything continued normally . . . but I sensed that something awful was coming. A terrible feeling ran through my body. Then a voice from deep within my brain spoke: *Go back. Who cares if you die on the operating table? It will be better than dying in that terrible sea. This is a trap . . .*

"Where do you want to go?" my possessor asked cautiously.

"We'll see," I replied. "This red sea looks even more suspicious and dangerous than the hospital. My family . . . we have all been land dwellers for generations. We have never even heard of the sea. I've been a part of the hospital for a long time. I'm not a healthy person; I've been sick since I was born, destined to be a lifelong patient. I can't live without the hospital, which I've always looked at as my home. I've never even imagined going to a foreign place, a place without hospitals. How could a person even expect to die in a place devoid of hospitals? What an utterly terrifying thought! Please, just let me go."

"You decide that *now* is the time to go back on your word? *Now* you feel scared?" my possessor screamed. "All this time you have been pretending to love that which deep down you really fear! We are just one step away from the land of ultimate bliss, and *now* you want to turn back? How am I supposed to explain this to the Super Patient? Your pain has clouded your judgment and blinded your heart—this is the tragedy of you and your kind!"

I began to sob.

But my possessor softened his tone. "Just stop with all these crazy thoughts. You need to get used to what is happening. No matter what, everything comes down to a question of whether you can acclimate."

Patients gathered from all directions, descending on the beach, where they anxiously gazed out to the sea. Gradually the shadow of a large mast emerged on the horizon, just beyond the violent waves. Soon the backup contact person arrived in an assault boat.

"Buy your tickets before boarding!" the contact person yelled in a strange voice.

I quickly fished those two bills out of my pocket. I didn't have quite enough, but the contact person didn't say anything. Then a fleet of ferries arrived to transport us out to sea. Everyone paid and boarded the ferries.

85

THE PLEASURE OF BEING PRICKED BY THE THORN OF A ROSE

The strange ferry was as broad as a mountain. A bright multicolored flag adorned with white stars hung from the mast. This vessel was to take us across the sea and deliver us to the other shore, where we would pass through the "Gate of Life and Death," escaping to a strange universe devoid of illness. But what kind of boat was this?

At midnight the anchor was finally lifted, and as the vessel set sail, the skies suddenly cleared and the wind died down. I noticed a steel island-shaped structure in the center of the deck. Under the canopy of stars, the structure appeared to have teeth and claws. It emitted red light in every direction. Like a massive birdcage towering into the heavens, it was surrounded by black-and-white flower baskets and rich green vegetation like a small forest. Realizing that once I left, I would never return, I was struck with a feeling of sadness. I rushed to the railing to gaze at the coast as it retreated into the distance.

Village Chief Ai was flapping his arms like a pair of wings and crying out to the sea: "No! I don't want to go! I can't bear to leave the hospital! I still haven't even completed the experiments I was doing on guinea pigs! I want to go back! I promise to do my best! I'll reorganize everything and do better next time! I've lived half my life without ever seeing the ocean. But now that I see this horrific thing, it is simply too terrifying!" He removed the camera from around his neck and threw it into the sea. My stomach began to cramp up again.

Along the vast surface of the ocean were patches of blood that reflected the gemlike stars above. The world was more realistic than anything I had ever seen before. I had finally left the hospital, and yet I found myself broken and dejected, like a woman who had just had her virginity taken. I was finished. Never again would I see Bai Dai or Zhu Lin. I had failed as a doctor, and I had failed as a patient. What would become of me next? What did I really want? Would I fail even in my quest to attain death? I felt stuck in a place of nothingness, a no-man's-land. Gradually my mind emptied like an hourglass. I felt like my possessor and I had completely merged, and we had fallen into a bottomless pit of time itself, where there was no longer any distinction between past, present, and future. Then I felt the presence of something I had never before experienced. I can't describe it, but it enveloped me, eating away at me, toying with me, leaving no residue behind. My body felt a wave of intense pain, but deep in my heart I felt the kind of pleasure you get only from being pricked by the thorn of a rose. The ocean breeze blew. Tears rolled down my face.

"What are you thinking?" my possessor asked suspiciously.

". . . that birdcage. When we get to our new home beside the sea, I wonder if we'll ever see another peacock, that creature that adores flying through the deepest, darkest, most hell-like places." I unconsciously rubbed the peacock badge on my chest.

"You're wondering whether you'll be able to bring Zhu Lin over, aren't you?" There was a hint of malice in my possessor's tone. He sounded like a child.

"I'm . . . now I'm wondering if she ever really existed." Did my possessor know whether she was dead? "I'm also thinking about those other women—Bai Dai, Sister Jiang, and Ah Bi. Will they be at this new safe haven beside the sea?"

My possessor half-jokingly cast a spell that made all the muscles in my body tense. I felt a sense of guilt welling up inside me again. I tried to hide my pain by turning away, but I caught sight of Village Chief Ai jumping into the sea. A desperate, inhuman scream escaped his mouth as his massive body sank, triggering a huge wave on the surface, though the water quickly resumed its peace and calm.

An announcement came over the ship's loudspeaker: it was lunchtime. The cafeteria was located in a large steel cavern just beneath that birdcage-like structure. I followed the other patients as they anxiously lined up to enter. Inside was a sight that was all too familiar.

86

EVERY UNIVERSE WILL
BECOME A HOSPITAL

The layout of the cafeteria was exactly the same as the hospital's outpatient ward. The musical *Altar Boyz* played faintly in the background. Surrounding the main hall was a series of cabins, where passengers instinctively formed a long line. One of the cabin doors was open, and I caught a glimpse of an elderly man with blond hair, blue eyes, and silver skin behind a desk. He had a high nose and deep eyes, and he wore a shiny white lab coat and a stethoscope around his neck. Yet with his strong, reserved, arrogant, and solemn manner, he looked more like a missionary.

I suddenly got the sense that something was wrong. I turned, thinking of escape, but a boy stopped me. He looked exactly like Little Tao. I was stunned. I wanted to pull his hand off me, but I couldn't. The young man didn't offer the faintest smile. Instead he simply warned me: "Please be sure to follow the rules for maintaining order. Wait for your number to be called." I scampered over to the end of the line.

I'm not sure how much time went by, but I finally made it before this strange-looking elderly doctor. A woman stood beside him, looking just like Zhu Lin. She must never have died. My face grew warm. I felt as if I had just woken up from the morgue. I couldn't tell if I was happy or sad. I called out to her, but my speech was so faint that I couldn't even hear my voice. Zhu Lin quietly observed me. She had completely grown up: that frivolous quality of a young girl had faded, and she was now mature and reserved. She looked at me as if she had figured me out a long time ago.

Standing beside Zhu Lin was Dr. Bauchi and someone who resembled the doctor who had been my son-in-law. Maybe my son-in-law was not dead after all? Or perhaps he had been resurrected? A mysterious grin wrapped his grapelike face. All of them wore white lab coats. They appeared lively and proud, like models on display in a department store window. Behind them was a portrait of a man from the waist up—it was John D. Rockefeller—and below the photo was one of his famous quotations: "I believe that the rendering of useful service is the common duty of mankind and that only in the purifying fire of sacrifice is the dross of selfishness consumed and the greatness of the human soul set free."

"What's going on?" I asked my possessor. Fearfully I wondered whether he was going to have me kill again.

"It's strange, really strange. None of this seems possible. Could someone have discovered a loophole and taken advantage of that?" My possessor shuddered before retracting deep into my body, hiding away like a timid ostrich.

"Stop running away," I told him, annoyed. "Running away won't solve any of our problems."

My possessor adopted a more slippery tone. "I just didn't want you to lose faith. How could we have known if we didn't give it a try? Even if it was a long shot, we had to hold out for that little flicker of hope. But as to whether we would successfully escape, that's in fate's hands. Now it seems that this struggle against the hospital, which I have long been fighting for you, has ultimately failed. I have failed you, and I have failed the Super Patient. I'm sorry. I did my best."

"That can't be . . . ," I responded coldly. I glanced at Zhu Lin and my "son-in-law" and thought about how "the end is just the beginning."

My possessor remained silent for a while. "Oh, that's right," he sighed eventually. "You're correct: this can't be. The Super Patient didn't know that escape was impossible, but he was so infatuated with the idea that he elevated it to a medical-punk art form. He was intoxicated with the idea, lost in the pleasure of it, obsessed with its beauty while overlooking its practicality. In the end, he couldn't extricate himself and ultimately forgot to escape."

Listening to my possessor made me feel like life was some kind of placebo. This thoroughly abused and self-abused universe is so inundated with ridiculousness, from the inside out, that it is utterly pathetic. And yet somehow, I still felt a flicker of hope. When the Super Patient finally forgot about his plan to escape, could that have been the moment that actual escape became possible?

As far as I'm concerned, it is already too late.

"Perhaps it's a good thing that you didn't tell me all of this," I said to my possessor. "I'd rather just keep on believing that the hospital treats the sick and heals the wounded. After all, C City is still the designated hospital for my medical insurance plan!"

The old doctor with the blond hair and blue eyes stood up, tapped me on my shoulder, and asked me to sit. There was something so utterly bizarre about him that I thought he must have been a martian. He gently felt my forehead for a fever and then muttered some strange words that I couldn't understand.

Dr. Bauchi stepped in to translate. "Welcome to the Hospital Ship! No matter how many monsters you have inside you, and even if you run to the ends of the earth, the Red Cross will always be here to protect you." The intensity of light reflecting from the red cross hanging around his neck was blinding.

Zhu Lin murmured, "All under heaven is one big hospital."

I asked her in a hushed tone: "Hey, did you ever find an answer to your question about how doctors die?" I was unconsciously associating her with Bai Dai again.

Zhu Lin didn't respond. Instead she just flashed my "son-in-law" a knowing look.

And then it was finally time for surgery, which I had yearned for since I was first admitted to the hospital and later spent all my effort trying to avoid. It had come to this: surgery would be the method by which everything came to a close.

As it turned out, every cabin on the ship was an operating room. We entered one, and the floor was covered with fleshy scabs and pools of black uncoagulated blood. A nauseating stench filled the air. Zhu Lin took the liberty of signing a medical disclosure form on my behalf. Extending from the wall was the steel frame of a flat bed-like surface. Along the wall was a control panel and a series of flashing medical instruments and computer screens. The old blond doctor ordered me to lie down while Dr. Bauchi and my "son-in-law" administered anesthesia. Somehow, even after the anesthesia, I was completely conscious and alert.

"Scalpel," the doctor requested, extending an open hand.

Zhu Lin handed him a scalpel. I could feel my abdomen being sliced open. Warm liquid frothed out.

"Hemostat."

"Abdominal pliers."

"Bandages."

The surgeon was so close to me that I could see the long primate-like hair follicles on his face, as well as a large black sack of skin that emitted a stench unique to adult mammals. That sharp red cross necklace dangled above my eyes. Despite the lidocaine, I was in terrible pain. As they cut open my gut, the smell of excrement made me want to vomit. And yet somehow I had complete faith in this doctor. He was probably the first truly qualified doctor I had ever met, the only one who hadn't started off being a patient and been "promoted."

Seeing me anxiously staring up at him, the old man magnanimously tried to console me. "We're not going to kill you. We're only trying to save you." His tone made me think of the Super Patient. Or, no . . . he actually reminded me of Dr. Norman Bethune, the truly great man.

It seemed that my crime of murder had been pardoned, even though the man I had killed was alive and well, right here on this very ship. This pardon was the true mark of a living Buddha. I struggled to get the syllables of "thank you" out of my throat.

The operation lasted three hours, though it felt like it went on for several days and nights. The lead surgeon removed something from my abdomen and handled it carefully, with both hands. Dr. Bauchi and my "son-in-law" rushed over for a look and offered alternating commentary.

"A bloody mass of flesh. Approximately the size of a walnut."

"No eyebrow, no eyes, no discernable facial features. It is not characteristic of a neocortex and is more consistent with what we see in reptile species."

"Overall it appears to have extensive wrinkles, but upon closer inspection, all of the details are smooth, with the exception of faintly visible spiral microstructures."

"Look, that diffuse red halo has a machinelike casing! I have never seen such a meticulously designed implant."

"None of the patient's organs seem to have been compromised."

"It looks like a bionic digital integrated device. Based on a rough estimation, I would say it contains sixty billion neurons and six hundred million recognition patterns—that's double the capacity of the patient's own brain, and yet it is only a fraction of the size. It weighs only twenty-one grams. We have yet to master the kind of technology to produce such a device."

"I heard about an artificial peacock brain with this type of structure . . ."

As the doctors conferred, Zhu Lin began to clean up the operating tools. As she cheerfully carried out her task, she talked to herself. "He is finally saved! He is finally saved!" Her face lit up with a sense of accomplishment, like a proud girl that had just celebrated her quinceañera.

I lay there, curled up on my side, in pain. The doctors continued to observe and discuss what they had removed, but there was nothing there. It was as if they were all extras in a movie. They had all memorized their lines perfectly, but I was the sole audience. Had my lesion been removed, just like that? I felt like every ounce of energy had been sucked from my body. Some time went by before I sensed a dark shadow moving in the corner of my room, faintly struggling, as if trying to say something. I froze in fear. Was this my dying possessor, using his last bit of energy to leave a final message for me, just like Sister Jiang before him . . . ? I felt sad, but I wasn't sure if that pity was for myself or for my possessor. Soon even that faint shadow disappeared without a trace. Where was the Super Patient during this crucial moment? How come he still hadn't made his move? Did he even exist? Even then, I still didn't know the true origin of my possessor. What was it? Could he have been the true me? And was I merely a cheap copy? The pain in my stomach was unbearable. I told myself not to worry, that the thing should have been taken out a long time ago. I'm sick, I have a serious disease. When I recover, I'll be able to go back to writing songs again, with a clear conscience. My tears fell silently, and then I lost consciousness.

87

THE OTHER SIDE OF THE ILLUSION

For three days and three nights, I slept like a dead man. Finally I was able to get out of bed and move around again. Zhu Lin helped me around the deck. Everything I saw looked brand new.

"Patient, are you still in pain?" She addressed me in a formal tone, fulfilling her role as my nurse.

"I think . . . I'm a bit better."

"It will take some time before you fully recover."

"Did the lead surgeon come from the place beside the sea?" This question had confused me. I still wasn't completely sure if I had been saved.

"You know the old saying: monks from out of town are better at chanting the sutras." Zhu Lin's tone was that of a woman who knew a thing or two about how the world works.

"But didn't they say that there are no hospitals by the sea?"

"Patient, did you grow up watching cartoons or what? This is the Age of Medicine!"

"I get it. Everything has been predesigned . . . but is the universe really diseased? Were you all really sent by the Ultimate Hospital?" I looked up and saw a single bright spot in the sky—it must have been Mars.

"It's so good of you to worry about the universe. It shows you have a real sense of responsibility. But that's not something we can discuss. Right now the most important thing is for you to recover quickly."

"Thank you," I said. "You have already helped me get better."

"Removing the tumorous growth inside you is only the first step. To truly go on living is about allowing your consciousness to achieve immortality. But that is much more complicated."

"What do you mean by 'consciousness'?" We had finally gotten to the crux of the matter. Everything comes down to a question of consciousness. We feel pain only because we are conscious beings. I felt like Zhu Lin was hinting that I don't have a complete consciousness, that even after the operation, I still have some serious flaws.

"To put it in simple terms, according to the field of medicine, 'consciousness' refers to the pattern of relationships that patients develop between time and space, based upon repeated feedback."

"So in order for consciousness to achieve immortality, this other consciousness must first be destroyed?"

"That disease inside you has no consciousness."

"How can you be certain?"

"The treatment needs to continue."

"Why is treatment even necessary? To win this new world war?"

"In order to help you achieve enlightenment. A healthy body is an important precondition for enlightenment. Life is merely a tool for helping us achieve enlightenment. In the past, your soul was stuck in a dark place."

"Do I even have a soul?" I asked wryly, not knowing whether to laugh or cry.

Zhu Lin unconsciously caressed the red cross hanging from her necklace. "The ultimate mission of all doctors is to extricate patients' souls from their pain."

"Is that so? So that's what all this suffering has been about? That's why I've been subjected to such horrific pain . . ."

"A little bit of pain helps to accelerate the enlightenment process. The whole reason we established the hospital was to keep up with the times by providing trials, training, and inspiration for those on the path to enlightenment. One important part of that is allowing individual pain and collective pain to find common ground. This is how a foundation of true awakening is established. This is how we save souls."

Zhu Lin conveyed the intention of a grand idea, but I had a hard time understanding a thing she said. I felt like she had been taken over by another possessor, or perhaps the doctors had implanted something in her brain. There were moments when I wondered if her entire body had been swapped out. But I couldn't help but feel excited as I wondered, *Why do I need to have a soul? Why do I need to have a life?* I don't need enlightenment. In a world like this, enlightenment is bound to bring about even more suffering, a true form of eternal damnation.

Suddenly I heard people singing. The chorus seemed to come from all directions.

> Love permeates heaven and earth and bathes my heart,
> The angels in white walk alongside me.
> I use my great love to drive away the nightmares,
> When I awaken I gift you with new life.
> Oh, new life, new life!

The image of a giant stinky hair follicle appeared before my eyes. "It feels so . . . disgusting."

Zhu Lin put up her guard. "What are you talking about?"

"You really are nothing but a cheap spy sent by Dr. Bauchi, aren't you?" As I turned away in anger, I seemed to catch sight of a few other familiar faces on the gunwale, but they were gone in an instant.

Zhu Lin was clearly upset. "Still worried about conspiracy theories, are you? What's there to be afraid of? Huh?"

Meanwhile, the words of my possessor echoed in my ears: "We don't really need to understand each other in order to live together . . . right now the task at hand is to learn how to coexist without really understanding one another." Those words applied to my current relationship with Zhu Lin and to all the other medical workers aboard this ship. This is the proper way for doctors and patients to get along.

I carefully raised my head and gazed up at the universe, floating overhead as if nothing had happened. I couldn't detect any sign of either hostility or goodwill. Mars dangled lonely in the sky, like a toy.

"I think you worry too much," Zhu Lin said. "What the doctor removed from you was not any kind of possessor. We refer to them as possessors, but in their eyes, they are something different."

"Then what are they?" I thought back to a few days earlier, when the doctors had held what looked like nothing, and then that strange dark shadow in the corner of my room . . . I could almost hear his cries during those final moments. "He claimed that he had been sent by the Super Patient. In order to escape from a diseased universe, he came to this world to lead us, to offer salvation, to relieve us of our pain. And now he has probably been thrown into the ocean to feed the cuttlefish . . ."

I suspect that the real me died the second they cut open my abdomen. I have now begun my new karmic journey of reincarnation. I have no choice but to go through the difficult process of acclimating myself to a new body and a new consciousness. I must again set out on the road that leads to truth or ruin, and from the moment I am reborn, I shall be readmitted to the hospital. Before my eyes are countless red crosses, like wildflowers blooming over all the tomb-shaped planets in the universe, their raging flames melting me down, along with the rest of the world, only to cast us again.

Zhu Lin flashed me a look of pity. "You think that pathetic, disgusting thing they took out of you would have relieved your pain? Do you have any idea just how deep your pain runs? Patient, did they ever arrange for you to gaze up at the stars? Did you know that there aren't actually stars in the sky? Everything you saw was an illusion. As for whether the universe you describe is real, that's something we will never know. Even if it does exist, it is sure to be a site of ultimate cold and emptiness, devoid of emotions or meaning. It could never conceive of treating itself or anyone else. Who can prove that the universe is a hospital? Would the universe ever make itself into something so utterly laughable? And even if the universe is a hospital, the purpose of its existence is certainly not what you imagine it to be. Perhaps it has no real purpose. Patient, you are behaving like a child! Children live in a world where 'everything has a purpose, everything has a meaning.' If you ask a child why rocks have sharp edges, he will tell you, 'So animals can rub against them to scratch their itches.' But all of that is wishful thinking. Who said hospitals exist to treat illness? Life is such a lowly and vulgar thing. To look at the universe as a living being isn't giving it much credit. If it does exist, its profound meaning will certainly be beyond our comprehension. It is much more difficult to understand the world than it is to settle matters of life and death. Every time you make it past one hurdle, you discover even more questions—infinite questions—lying ahead. You are destined to be a mere subset of a much larger phenomenon. It's like we are always peeking at the world through a tiny bamboo tube, and everything we do in life is to broaden our perspective just a little bit . . . but what's the point? When most people mention the universe, the first thing that pops into their head is 'It's done for.' But things are never that simple. Patient, what do you think you can do when you don't even know the truth? You keep babbling on about protecting your right to a healthy life—what a joke! How should I put this? Your brain imagined a lot of things while you were unconscious, but all of it originated with your pathetic, perverted, middle-aged subconscious and those shitty dreams you cling to. My god, what the hell do you really want to do with your life? You don't even know! The doctor removed your illusion, or the other side of the illusion. But starting today you will gradually come to understand that the other side of things is always the most beautiful. But the other side is also the most brutal, disgusting, and painful. Your stubborn delusions led you to believe that escape was possible. In your mind you have been repeatedly trying to escape from the hospital and find salvation. But none of that is possible. The hospital's meticulous treatment plans have been developed specifically to target stubborn patients like you. Look, after running in all kinds of circles, here you are, back with us again. Do you remember when we first invited you to participate in the hospital's New Year's Eve gala? You were so excited to take part. You really showed us your best side. But your illness acted up during your performance, and you collapsed onstage. How could you forget that? But it's okay, the performance has no real end or beginning. It just goes on and on. There is always time to rejoin the performance. What do you say? Do you understand things a bit better now?"

This sixteen-year-old girl spoke so eloquently that it was as if lotus flowers were blooming with her every word, like Maxwell's demon had opened the invisible door.

"Was this really an illusion?" I asked. "Or the other side of an illusion? Who cares if I finished that performance? Does it matter? Even while anesthetized I could clearly feel the scalpel cutting through my skin. Oh, how elegant and nimble his knife work was. I shall never forget that pain as long as I live. It was enough to . . ." I carried on like an obsessed and terrified drunk, both sad and excited by Zhu Lin's contemptuous attitude and the fact that she had revealed so many of my own flaws. "Well, let me tell you, I'm still in pain! I suffer, therefore I exist. That's how I know that all of the things I have seen must be real. Hey, you said there aren't even stars? Do you mean to tell me that they don't exist? How can you prove that everything you have been saying isn't just a bunch of lies? But even if it is, who cares? The Ultimate Hospital has firmly rooted itself in my heart. Even if it is an illusion, I still want it, even if all I can get is the other side of that illusion! Just like the doctors, illusions are real too. Or do you mean to tell me that there are fake illusions? When you said that illusions were fake, does that mean that illusions don't exist?"

Zhu Lin didn't seem to take my sophist quibbles to heart. "Patient, it seems that your illness is indeed quite serious. If you want to eradicate your suffering, you must go on with your treatment. Without repeated stimulation, it simply won't do. Remember, what happened yesterday was simply the process of using an illusion to remove your illusion, and that was only the beginning. This is a new advanced treatment method. There's not much we can do, because our hospital is too backward. Instead we rely upon the power coming from the sea. Over the course of the last few centuries, medical advances on the other shore have made startling breakthroughs. With the support of the Rockefeller Foundation, the people there have invented the phantom scalpel, an advanced medical instrument imbued with the magical power of the Diamond Sutra. It is extremely expensive. Your entire lifetime income, including whatever money you bring in on the side, still wouldn't be enough to afford one. But that is precisely what saved you."

A phantom scalpel? Made from what? Another illusion? "Does the Rockefeller Foundation, and all those other foundations, really exist?"

This question seemed to offend Zhu Lin. She thought for a second before throwing the question back at me. "What do you think?"

This was too novel and advanced for me, as a mere patient—like talking to someone from the nineteenth century about gene therapy. After a long pause, I asked, "Is he . . . the Buddha?" Zhu Lin pretended like she didn't hear me.

The stench of corpses came over the sea breeze. I inhaled deeply. Zhu Lin's body emitted a strange rotten smell like the scent of formalin in imported perfume. The red cross dangling from her neck was like a tree of life. I wondered if this woman had already been treated by the head surgeon from beside the sea. Had she delivered herself to him willingly? Or had they forced her to receive treatment? Who was she actually? Had they cured her disease . . . ? I looked at Zhu Lin's gorgeous birdlike body with a combination of envy and hostility, but the courage to engage in another mutual-therapy session was long gone. There is no hope of ever resuming the relationship we once had. Would I also never become a doctor again?

"I don't believe you! You can kill me, and I still won't believe you!" I tried to climb up the railing to leap off, babbling like a krill dangling from the mouth of a whale.

But Zhu Lin reached up and pulled me down to the deck with one neat yank. "Don't forget that anything is possible in the Age of Medicine. The use of illusions has reduced patients to nothing more than puppets of themselves. This is the cause of all known forms of pain."

She looked exhausted and fell silent. Her clear eyes burned like a wildfire as she looked to the sea. Her long black hair whipped in the wind like a handful of umbilical cords. I lay there on the deck with my limbs spread, staring helplessly. In my eyes, she slowly transformed into a flower, reflected in a mirror, floating on the salmon-red sea, her body stretched open, her white lab coat unfolded, her bones stretched, her thighs open, and as she solemnly took flight, her body looked anxious and restrained, unable to unfold, like a wet roll of toilet paper, yet somehow revealing a hint of a godlike quality, like the Avalokiteśvara Bodhisattva of Great Compassion. She revealed a long tail and took on a birdlike form. The pattern of the red cross radiated from her feathers.

I couldn't believe what I was seeing. I used all my strength to pull myself to my feet. I bumped into the side of the gunwale and looked out to sea. The surface filled with a fleet of massive ships, everywhere, as far as the eye could see. Adorned in the colors of the rainbow, tens of thousands of ships moved in unison. Painted on their silver bows were imposing images of the red cross, which together lit up the horizon like a constellation of stars. The ships all moved in the same direction, slicing against the waves like a battalion of vessels off to fight a final decisive battle. I remembered the saying *The fate of the emperor's kingdom shall be decided by this battle.* Following the ships, in the air above the colorful clouds, was a fleet of flying machines that resembled a flock of peacocks, their wings spread in such numbers that they nearly blotted out the sun. I couldn't see the other shore. Nor, looking back, could I see the port from which we had left.

Where was this hospital I had come to? Where was this land?

My abdomen began to ache again, right at the site of the incision. I extended my trembling hands to the empty sky. The universe loomed overhead, announcing its authenticity, hanging full and heavy in the sky, like a peach of longevity.

TRANSLATOR'S AFTERWORD

It's not important who you are; the only thing that matters is what kind of illness you suffer from.

—Han Song

The factors that draw a translator to a particular novel are often quite peculiar. For *Hospital* it began with COVID-19. Although the novel was first written in 2016, and the trilogy it kicked off was completed by 2018, I didn't read *Hospital* until 2020, when the world was enveloped in the terror and instability unleashed by a new global pandemic. Reading *Hospital* in the age of COVID-19 provided a new context for understanding Han Song's dystopian vision. As social media feeds lit up with nonstop updates about infection rates, vaccines, and health tips; political discourse became overwhelmed with controversies about school closures, stay-at-home orders, and mask mandates; and the nightly news was inundated with narratives about overrun hospitals, exhausted medical workers, and tragic stories of the human casualties, it indeed felt like we were living in the Age of Medicine and that the world had become a giant hospital. As society began to emerge from an eighteen-month lockdown in the fall of 2021, little everyday details revealed just how much had changed. Downloading daily health QR codes became an essential part of the school routine for my children. I met someone for the first time at a neighborhood gathering, and as she reached out to shake my hand, she said, "Hi, my name is Mary.

I'm fully vaccinated." I immediately thought of Han Song's maxim: "It's not important who you are; the only thing that matters is what kind of illness you suffer from." Markers of health had taken over as the most central part of our identities as individuals and as a society. Many other passages from *Hospital* began to take on haunting new layers of meaning, like this one: "In the Age of Medicine, the word 'freedom' is long forgotten, replaced by 'treatment' in all the dictionaries." That passage was no doubt inspired by ideological wars in China, in which the government sanitizes the internet by banning sensitive keywords and replacing them with politically correct alternatives. But in the post-COVID-19 age, it also now brings to mind the ideological battles raging in the United States about "individual freedom" versus "public health" when it comes to everything from masks and lockdown policies to vaccine mandates. Eerie signposts from Han Song's dystopian medical universe seem already to be upon us.

But another, more personal factor drew me to *Hospital*. More than a decade earlier, I had been struck down with a debilitating autoimmune disease. As challenging as it was to cope with the constant pain and physical impact of the disease, equally daunting was living in an extended state of "unknowing"—it took more than a full year to get a diagnosis. That was my "hospital year," a year filled with constant trips to specialists (infectious disease, rheumatology, neurology, orthopedics, etc.) who carried out a seemingly never-ending series of tests and procedures (blood tests, x-rays, nuclear bone scan, bone biopsy, spinal tap, etc.). The greatest absurdity of the ordeal was that, after more than twelve months of tests, procedures, and suffering, I finally left Santa Barbara, where I had been living at the time; traveled to Northwestern Memorial Hospital to enroll in a program for undiagnosed disorders; and received a diagnosis in fifteen minutes. Translating *Hospital* brought back memories of the pain and preposterousness of that experience, but ironically enough, it also provided a strange form of literary catharsis as I finally came to terms with that experience.

Of course, while informed by the horrors, tragedies, and absurdities that so many have experienced in search of medical treatment, *Hospital* is also rooted in more profound shifts taking place in the field of medicine. Discussing the origin of the novel in an interview, Han Song said:

> Everyone has the experience of going to the hospital, and the transformation that hospitals are undergoing today is massive: people are more focused on their health than ever before, hospitals have undergone a process of radical marketization, we have witnessed shocking disputes between patients and doctors, and then there is a new series of technological innovations, like genetic technology and synthetic biology, that have always been prominent in science fiction. I wanted to portray the hospital on a much deeper level by combining all of these elements.

> At the same time, the hospital is itself a very "sci-fi" setting; it is a place brimming with absurdity and contradictions. On the one hand, it is a place to save the sick and heal the wounded, but on the other hand it is a place where life continually comes to an end. It is a place imbued with the most advanced high-tech innovations, which are side by side with all kinds of superstitious acts—as soon as you enter the hospital, you see everything from folk healers to vendors selling traditional home remedy treatments made from toads and owls. The hospital is a place where human space and time are simultaneously compressed and expanded—there is no way to express this using traditional realist methods; all we can rely on is science fiction. If you just rely upon an expression of the surface phenomena

to provide a point-by-point description, it will never be enough.[1]

While *Hospital* is indebted to the science fiction genre, it remains a book that is difficult to categorize. The novel draws from suspense, social satire, the Chinese critical realist tradition, and experimental fiction. Critics have often lauded Han Song as China's answer to Philip K. Dick, but I prefer to think of *Hospital* as a Terry Gilliam adaptation of a Franz Kafka story set amid a crazed Chinese Communist Party politburo. Han Song's fiction also brings to mind the work of Lu Xun, the father of modern Chinese literature, whose body of fiction is often haunted by dark images of madness, cultural cannibalism, the failure of the revolution, and a deep questioning of tradition. It is no coincidence that one of Lu Xun's most celebrated works is the 1919 short story "Medicine," which traces a family's desperate attempt to cure a son of tuberculosis by feeding him a steamed bun soaked in human blood. In Lu Xun's story, the "medicine" not only fails to cure the boy—it kills him. A century later Han Song has constructed a world built around a new "Age of Medicine," where "treatment" has become not only a means and an end . . . but a purgatory-like state of being. As David Derwei Wang has observed in comparing Han Song's *Hospital* to Lu Xun:

> Han Song wrote *Hospital* to recapitulate and even deepen some of the themes inherent in modern Chinese literature: the illusory line between disease and medicine; the tension between claustrophobia and agoraphobia; the fear and temptation of cannibalism; and, above all, literature

---

1   Xu Mingwei, "Han Song: Women dou you bing, zai yuzhou zhege da yiyuan xunzhao jietuo" [Han Song: We are all sick, searching for release in this massive hospital called the universe], *The Paper*, September 7, 2016, http://culture.ifeng.com/a/20160907/49928076_0.shtml.

as both a symptom of and a cure for Chinese spiritual mal-
aise. More significantly, Han has echoed the master [Lu
Xun]'s twin engagement with both science and mythology,
or both enlightenment and "divine thought."[2]

Alternately dark and manic, strange and hilarious, disturbing and
absurd, and drawing on a set of disparate literary coordinates—from
Kafka to the Nirvana Sutra and from Lu Xun to Philip K. Dick—Han
Song has crafted a book unlike any other to emerge from contemporary
China.

Another unique facet of *Hospital* is the way the book mutates
language itself. Some of these mutations will be evident to all readers (e.g., replacing terminology like "military-industrial complex" with
"Clinical-Academic-Industrial Complex"); others are more subtle. One
dimension of the novel that may evade readers unfamiliar with the contemporary Chinese political and linguistic landscape is the myriad ways
in which Han Song employs Chinese "political speak" and politically
loaded keywords to create satire and black humor, including "prosper-
ous," "glorious," and "correct," which are often employed in glowing
propagandistic ways to describe the Chinese Communist Party and are
here used to depict the hospital. Curiously enough, *Hospital* almost
never employs the words "China" or "the People's Republic of China."
Han Song instead opts for lofty yet ambiguous phrases like "our nation"
and "the home country." Perhaps this is to emphasize that China has
already been subsumed by the hospital, to hint at the fact that the hospital is in fact a euphemism for the Chinese Communist Party itself, or
perhaps it is a metaphor for modern society, but whatever the case, this
creates a thin layer of fictional distance between Han Song's universe
and the reality of China today. Yet beyond the facade of *Hospital*'s surreal

---

2   David Der-wei Wang, Why Fiction Matters in Contemporary China
(Waltham, Massachusetts: Brandeis University Press, 2020), 177.

and nightmarish landscape are constant signposts that refer to still-recognizable remnants of China's political past and present, from the "Protect the Species Association" (Baozhonghui 保种会)—which refers to political reformer Kang Youwei's late-Qing "Protect the Emperor Association" (Baohuanghui 保皇会)—to the compulsory reading of *Medical News*, which seems to stand in for *People's Daily*, *Global Times*, or perhaps even *Xinhua News*, where Han Song still holds a day job as a journalist. The novel is riddled with references to contemporary China's "century of humiliation" at the hands of imperialist Western powers, which is nothing new for Han Song. One of his most famous works is the novel *Red Star over America* (*Hong xing zhaoyao Meiguo* 红星照耀美国), a dystopian masterpiece that takes its title from Edgar Snow's *Red Star over China*, a classic account of the Chinese Communist Party in Yan'an.

In *Hospital*, the United-States-as-enemy motif is handled with black humor—the Rockefeller Foundation emerges as a force of evil against "our nation"—and the denouement comes with the ultimate revelation that the United States is, in fact, nothing but a fabrication:

> A crucial question was posed for the first time: *Does the United States really exist?* Or had it been created just to scare us? This mirage-like country remained a real place in the eyes of many, but the details surrounding this fantasy nation seemed to grow richer and more elaborate by the day. This, too, must also have been some form of illness.

Another key example of the book's linguistic permutations can be seen in the names of the novel's characters, a detail that is unfortunately lost in translation. Character names often imply or refer to various ailments, often of a sexual nature. For instance, Ah Bi's name (阿泌) means "to seep, secrete, or leak," and Sister Jiang's name (浆姐) literally means "thick fluid"; taken together, the characters function as a couplet meaning "secreting thick fluid." Similarly, the name of the main female protagonist for much of the novel, Bai Dai (白黛), is actually a homophone for leukorrhea, or white-colored vaginal discharge (白带). And as David Der-wei Wang has observed, the name of the protagonist, Yang Wei (杨伟), is a homophone for the Chinese term for impotence (阳痿). Han Song's employment of medically inspired nomenclature for his characters also helps to set them up as a series of doubles (Ah Bi / Sister Jiang, Yang Wei / Bai Dai, etc.), which is further embellished through the plot.[3]

In the case of Yang Wei, the nomenclature is especially interesting in that it is at once a very typical Chinese name (think "John Smith"), which sets the protagonist up as an everyman-type character. But at the same time, Yang Wei has "impotence" branded onto his very identity, a detail that provides insight not only into the condition of the main character's psychology but also into the story as a whole. After undergoing gene therapy that renders the protagonist more or less impotent— there is no need for traditional intercourse when gene modification can produce much higher quality humans—Yang Wei's trash-room sex scenes prove to be more pathetic than erotic. But on a deeper level, all of Yang Wei's goals are, one after another, undermined, interrupted, supplanted, and derailed. Whether it be successfully writing the "corporate song" that first brought him to C City, getting a diagnosis, trying to escape from the hospital, discovering the truth about the death of doctors, or even figuring out how much of his nightmarish experience is real, Yang Wei is repeatedly revealed to be "impotent." He is an unreliable narrator (even *he* can't differentiate reality from his illusions), incapable of successfully guiding the reader through the nightmarish maze of the hospital. Eventually this "impotence" infects not only the protagonist but the novel itself: what began as a clear narrative, rooted

---

3   I am indebted to Professor Mingwei Song (Wellesley College) for sharing his insights about the character names in Hospital.

in Yang Wei's experience in C City, eventually devolves into an absurdist loop of narrative implosions, with each new character, subplot, and supposition supplanted by the next.

The fact that Yang Wei is quite literally a manifestation of "impotence" provides a potent clue that we are not dealing with a typical "hero" protagonist. In many ways, Yang Wei can be seen as a twisted reflection of Lu Xun's Ah Q, the most famous antihero in modern Chinese literature. A perennial loser, Ah Q transfers the exploitation he suffers onto others and eventually becomes a martyr for a revolution he doesn't even understand. By looking at Yang Wei through the lens of Ah Q, we realize that the entirety of *Hospital* is very much about subversion. To pull that off, Han Song takes his readers to a series of dark places, with depictions of not only violence and torture but also incest fantasies, the destruction of the family unit, and sex with a minor. These passages are among the most disturbing in the book, but they should in no way be read as an endorsement of said practices. Instead the novel should be read as a critical allegory about how the hospital destroys every conceivable convention of society, of the family, and even of morality itself. It is through these cycles of ethical subversion that the dark side of Han Song's literary project is revealed.

As Yang Wei's pain increases and his unspecified disease takes hold, some unknown force begins pushing the narrative itself into increasingly strange and uncanny realms of the imagination. After its Kafkaesque opening, *Hospital* eventually takes a philosophical turn, becoming more heavily dominated by dialogues, speeches, inner monologues, and even an extended mental tour of the cosmos led by a parasite-like entity that has taken over the protagonist. The collective effect of this philosophical turn is that, after Yang Wei is admitted to the hospital and explores the different wards and departments, his journey turns inward (literally underground), but as deep as he goes into this world, it remains dominated by the same dark absurdity, circular logic, and narrative impotence. There is no escape from the nightmare of the hospital.

The details surrounding the translation of *Hospital* were almost as strange as the factors that initially brought me to the book. Working from a digital file supplied to me directly by the author, I was more than halfway finished with the translation when I sat down one day with the print version of the book, intending to leaf through it and review what was coming up in the next chapter that I would work on the following day. What I read shocked me: passages didn't match up, plot details had been altered, character names had been changed (Dr. Bauchi was referred to as Dr. Hua Yue), and scenes that occurred in the middle of a chapter in my digital version opened the same chapter in the print version. Had I been working from an unedited version? An early draft? An unabridged version? An uncensored version? I was gripped with a sense of anxiety as I wrote frantically to Han Song. It took some time to sort through the textual variants, but we eventually figured out that Han Song had mistakenly sent me an alternate text, an early version that had later undergone significant revisions. It felt like a textual variant from the multiverse—a *Hospital* that Han Song had thought long deleted from his hard drive—had returned to supersede its later clone and take its rightful place as the canonical version of the text in English. My initial response was that, as painful as it might be, I would need to redo much of the translation, but after numerous texts back and forth with Han Song, we agreed on a middle ground approach, which would draw upon elements from both the early manuscript and the later published version. Han Song explained that much of the content he added later was at the behest of his Chinese editor, and that in many ways, the early draft was closer to his initial vision of the novel.

Thus the complex process of "surgery" began. I would send Han Song my English text, and he would insert long passages written in Chinese, which I would then translate and incorporate into the existing narrative. Other passages that I had already labored to render into English were simply removed. And in still other sections, Han Song would add brand-new English-language content not present in either the manuscript version or published edition. Over the course of this protracted surgery, I had a front-row seat to observe the creative genius of a great writer at work. During our revisions, Han Song attributed dialogue from one character in the published version to another character in this version. Superlatives were swapped out for denunciations. Passages brimming with his signature dark humor were simply deleted. New plot details were added. At one point he decided that he wanted to retitle the third act of the novel, "Surgery," as a "Postscript." When I explained that most postscripts are relatively short and that "Surgery" is actually the longest section of the book, Han Song was unfazed. He responded with his trademark wit: "I think it will be a most unusual postscript." At times I felt like Igor, helping to carry out the vision of the brilliant mad scientist.

Ultimately, after all this extensive surgery, Han Song came to prefer this version over all others. Through his process of sculpting the text, adding prose, deleting passages, and tweaking language, a new *Hospital* emerged, the result of an experiment in textual engineering in translation, a literary variant that, like Frankenstein's monster, would rise in a glorious display of terror and beauty.

M. B.

October 5, 2021; Los Angeles

ACKNOWLEDGMENTS

My deepest appreciation to Han Song for entrusting me with his work. Working with him so closely on this project has been one of the most collaborative and fulfilling experiences of my twenty-five years as a literary translator. Profound thanks to my friend and colleague Mingwei Song for introducing me to Han Song and being such a fervent supporter of this project. Thanks to Jennifer Lyons, who championed this book from the moment I first told her about it and has been there for every step of the journey. I would also like to acknowledge the support of David Der-wei Wang, Jing Tsu, John Nathan, Peter Sellars, and my family. Working with the Amazon Crossing team on this project has been a true blessing. Having an editor who is also a literary translator is a rare luxury, and I am lucky to have been able to work with Gabriella Page-Fort, who I think fell in love with the manuscript in the same way I first did. During the editing process, Jason Kirk brought a meticulous eye for details and a keen sense of literary style to the table and was able to extend the collaborative spirit behind this project in exciting new ways. Thanks also to Elyse Lyon for her editorial eye and wonderful suggestions, Stephanie Chou, Heather Buzila, Lauren Grange for production management, Jarrod Taylor for art direction, and Will Staehle for the beautiful cover. Finally, thanks to all the readers who join us on this strange and otherworldly trip through the hospital.

M. B.

ABOUT THE AUTHOR

Han Song is a journalist with Xinhua News Agency and one of China's leading science fiction writers. A native of Chongqing, Han earned an MA in journalism from Wuhan University; he began writing in 1982 and has published numerous volumes of fiction and essays. His novels include *The Red Sea*, *Red Star over America*, the Rails trilogy (*Subway*, *High-Speed Rail*, and *Orbits*), and the Hospital trilogy (*Hospital*, *Exorcism*, and *Dead Souls*), which has been described as a new landmark in dystopian fiction. Han is a six-time winner of the Chinese Galaxy Award for fiction and a repeat recipient of the Xingyun Award. His short fiction has appeared in the collections *Broken Stars* and *The Reincarnated Giant* and the anthology *Exploring Dark Short Fiction: A Primer to Han Song*. Han Song is also an avid reader and traveler, having traveled to the Antarctic and the Arctic. He's even searched for bigfoot in the forests of central China.

ABOUT THE TRANSLATOR

Photo © 2022 Eileen Chen

Michael Berry is a professor of contemporary Chinese cultural studies and director of the Center for Chinese Studies at UCLA. He is the author of several books on Chinese film and culture, including *Speaking in Images*, *A History of Pain*, and *Jia Zhangke on Jia Zhangke*. He has served as a film consultant and a juror for numerous film festivals, including the Golden Horse (Taiwan) and the Fresh Wave (Hong Kong). He is also the translator of several novels, including *To Live*, *The Song of Everlasting Sorrow* (with Susan Chan Egan), and *Remains of Life*.